A Handful of Secrets

A Hidden World Novel

Angel McGregor

Copyright © 2017 by Angel McGregor.
All rights reserved.

This book is a work of fiction; any references to historical events, real people or places are used in a fictitious manner. All other characters, places and events were created by the author and any resemblance to any person, alive or dead is purely coincidental.

No part of this publication may be reproduced or copied in any form without the prior written of the author.

Cover image belongs to the author.

ISBN 978 1 9995974 1 2

Published by Crooked Halo Books
www.crookedhalobooks.co.uk
www.angelmcgregor.co.uk

Acknowledgements

Thank you to Audrey, who brought Betsy to life for me. Since creating her character, she took on an integral role within the story and she has stolen the hearts of other characters along the way.
I hope she steals yours too - enjoy!

Also by Angel McGregor

Hidden World Novels

The Love That Binds Us

Part of the Pack

Inner Magick

Coming soon

The Cursed Novels

This one is for you, Grandma.
Though I know you'll never get to read it,
I know you would have been proud of me.

Prologue

Streaks of crimson and yellow shot through the sky and skimmed across the surface of the calm water where the ocean stretched out infinitely before me. The sand beneath me was cool to the touch as I sat on the beach in the little sandy cove that I liked to call home, but the light breeze that drifted lazily around me wasn't uncomfortable. I was in no hurry to move. I wondered idly what other people were doing right now; it was still early really, and I suddenly envied each and every one of them. They were all going about their lives without having to worry about running out of time; without having somewhere to be by nightfall.

I looked up then and sighed as I watched my time running out before me like seeing sand fall through an hourglass. Wriggling my toes in the sand beneath me and revelling in the feeling of it, I committed every detail of the grainy texture to memory. My sister told me that I should be thankful for the time I got, and that I should make the most of it during the sunlight hours. I tried, I really did. But I longed to be able to stroll down this beach after nightfall, to wake up the next morning in bed and start the day like everyone else did. One day was all I got; I'd had to learn to deal with that fact.

Whether it would ever be enough though, was another matter entirely.

As the sun sank low enough that it had almost disappeared completely behind the horizon, I let out another sigh and lifted myself from where I had been sitting for the last half an hour. I waded into the incoming tide filled with defeat. My long gypsy style skirt billowed out around me in the crystal blue water and I felt the shiver run up my spine. The water was still cold at this time of year and in my human body I felt the chill. I didn't worry about taking off my skirt; my Aunt Elsie would find it when the tide washed it up onto the shore. She would check the beach in the morning; there'd be more than just my skirt, though mine would probably be the only one if she had already done a sweep of the beach. I was the only one out this late; there'd only been four of us today anyway. Next time would be better.

I stood in the water, fending off the chill that crept across my skin, and thought of the others. They'd be long gone by now, back in the depths of the ocean where we belonged. A laugh escaped me; 'belonged', as if we were all the same and should just accept it. But none of them were drawn to the shore like I was; there were plenty of them that hadn't been ashore this month, the weather still too cold for them. But I always came; I spent every minute I could on my feet, on land.

The full moon had already appeared and hung heavy in the sky as the sun finally slipped behind the horizon and I felt the familiar tingling threading its way through my nerves. The white-hot prickle of the fire inside me tore away my human body and I pitched forward just before I would have fallen, splashing into the water and disappearing beneath the surface. The strong muscles of my tail propelled me through the water as I slipped free of my skirt and resurfaced, wanting one last look at the beach before I went back.

Ripples chased each other away from me as I broke the surface and I smiled to myself, safe in the knowledge that the beach would look just the same this time next month, but that it looked totally different with someone else's perspective.

To me, the sandy shore line, the huge rocks that lined the edges of the beach, the cliffs that stood protecting the cove from the world, and the rickety old pier with its peeling white paint and cute little railings were the gateway to freedom. The beginning of an adventure. But to a human who stood on that same beach, staring out across the ocean, they saw the edge of the world; a barrier between them and the deep blue sea.

If only they knew that there was a whole other world below the surface that they barely knew anything about. The sea didn't hold the freedom that they saw, it was as much of a cage as the shore line was, they just didn't realise it.

I ducked back under the water, having already broken the rules; I knew I shouldn't be surfacing once I'd transformed. It was too risky. So, with a final shake of my head and a strong push of my tail, I threw myself into the journey home. Dismissing the pain of leaving behind the beach, I concentrated on feeling my body cut elegantly through the water. A school of tiny yellow fish joined me for part of my journey and I smiled as they swam around me, flitting through the water with their own graceful glide.

When I finally reached the border to The Kingdom beneath the ocean I paused, as always, and took in the view. As much as I longed to be on land, I had to admit that it was pretty awesome down here. You only had to take one look at the magnificent city to know where Plato had gotten his inspiration from; although the Royals would still argue to this day that no human had ever even gotten close to The Kingdom, never mind seen enough of it to create their own world from it.

A mystery if ever there was one; though I just called it home.

Angel McGregor

May

I sat at the end of the bar, my favourite seat; with my back to the wall I had a perfect view of the entire area. There wasn't long till I had to return to the water, my time this month almost up, but the best thing about this time of year; the days were slowly growing longer. Today I was making the most of it in the beer garden of the seaside bar known to the locals as The Courtyard. The music from inside was playing through speakers out here too, making it hard to hold a conversation, though some people were still attempting it. I'd seen one couple gesturing to each other in what was clearly a heated argument before the man had left, and I had been watching a young couple that were obviously out on a date for the last hour. Most were just dancing, but it was the ones conversing that always held my attention. I loved to imagine what it would be like to have a life here, to know the people that surrounded me instead of being the outsider that just looked in on them from time to time.

The sea air and warm breeze made it cool enough that it was more comfortable to sit out here than it was to sit at the bar inside, and it was out here that most of the people were gathering. It was in the middle of daydreaming about what my life could be like if I could live with my Aunt Elsie, that the bar tender interrupted my thoughts.

'Excuse me, this is from the tall guy,' he said and gestured down the bar to where a guy around my age stood leant forwards on the bar to see around the small crowd of people that separated us.

I accepted the drink and thanked the bar tender, whose name badge identified him as Greg. When I looked back, sapphire blue eyes, the colour of the ocean on a hot summer day, met mine and I almost swooned. A warm smile had spread across his face now and when I smiled back and raised the glass in silent cheers the grin widened revealing a matching set of dimples.

I swirled the drink with my straw and disturbed the neatly prepared cocktail before taking a sip. The cold got to me first and I scrunched up my nose at the invading flavours; vodka, if I wasn't mistaken. I looked again at the glass and smiled to myself; Sex on the beach. Turning to look down the bar again, I had to look twice. He was gone. A strange rush of disappointment flooded me and I turned back to my drink. Had I read that wrong?

'That's not one of my better chat up lines,' a voice said behind me and I spun around to find a megawatt smile in front of me, 'Do you want to make out with me or punch me?'

His voice was smooth like caramel but with a raspy quality to it that made me smile despite myself, it wrapped around me and clung to me in all the right ways. The deep-set dimples on either side of his smile gave him a devilish grin and the light dusting of freckles across his tanned nose only made him more handsome. The close cropped-curls on his head were the colour of melting chocolate and I found myself longing to run my fingers through them, and the shadow of a beard across his cheeks gave him the look of a guy suited to his surroundings. His whole appearance screamed 'surfer'.

I realised then that he was waiting for a reply, and I had been sat here staring at him. Blundering for words that made sense, I blurted out the first thing that came into my head.

'At least it wasn't a Screaming Orgasm; that could have attracted a lot of unwanted attention.' I smiled as I spoke, but I heard the nerves in my voice.

'And she's funny as well as beautiful; some people get all the luck.'

The blush crept up my face before I could even acknowledge that I was self-conscious, and tall, dark and handsome in front of me just stood and waited me out. I genuinely couldn't decide whether I did want to punch him or not, but kissing him wasn't on the agenda either.

'Well, in answer to your question, I'm undecided. Your next move is critical,' I replied, trying to keep up the flirty conversation.

He laughed and moved to sit on the empty bar stool at the side of me. I swung mine around so that I was sat facing the bar again, and propped myself up on my elbows, watching him from the corner of my eye as he made himself comfortable, like he'd been there all along. There was a lot of self-confidence going on in that persona of his and I had to wonder whether it was all bravado for a slightly softer personality. My years of people watching gave me a good sense of character judgement, and I had to admit that he didn't seem like the douchebag he was acting as. He had the air of a bad boy from a novel, but the slight crinkle around his eyes and the way they seemed to see me rather than just eye me up, betrayed a softer side that he couldn't hide from me; I was far too observant.

Eventually he turned to me; his own drink left forgotten by his elbow. He looked me up and down with a critical eye, as if sizing me up and then grinned again, the dimples on either side so profound that I was sure he could hide secrets in there.

'How about we start over?' He held out his hand between us and looked at me pointedly.

I frowned as I put my hand into his, but couldn't help but smile again when he closed his fingers around mine and pulled it up to his mouth and pressed a kiss to the soft skin on the back of my hand. I'd expected a handshake; the kiss was like something out of a movie and I felt myself smiling like the typical damsel in distress would when her hero comes swooping in and takes her hand.

'I'm Aaron, and I was watching you from down the bar, you're by far the prettiest girl in the room tonight, and I'd love to buy you a drink.'

The smile widened. I dragged myself back into the here and now and left the fantasy that had suddenly developed in my head; how could a girl say no to a speech like that?

'How far does that line usually get you?' I asked with a giggle.

A giggle; since when did I giggle?

He let go of my hand and I let it fall into my lap, unsure as to whether I'd upset him or not. I was about to speak again but he finally replied.

'Ask me again in about ten minutes and I'll let you know.'

I frowned again.

'I'm serious, that one's a first for me.'

'Okay, I believe you,' I answered, taking another sip of my cocktail, 'I'm Luna, by the way.'

'Luna,' he said as if testing my name out, and I had to admit I liked the way it sounded on his lips, 'Like the moon, it suits you.'

I laughed at how ironic that statement was, if only he knew how close to the truth he had gotten in one little phrase. I'd always found it interesting that I was named after the moon, but my mother had died the day I was born, so I'd never been able to ask her why she'd chosen the name. Asking my older sister never really occurred to me, she didn't like to talk about our mother; too many painful memories, so I tended to avoid it and just stuck with the fantasy in my own head.

'Something like that,' I said in response to his moon comment, and smiled as he raised his glass again to take a drink.

He set the pint down and wiped the condensation off the side with his thumb. The thought crossed my mind as to what it would feel like to have him caress the side of my face like that, and I shook my head to clear the wandering thoughts. This wasn't like me; I blamed the paperback in my bag that I'd spent the last few hours reading by the beach. I had to stay impartial.

'So,' he began, breaking up my mental scolding, 'What scares you the most in the world?'

He gave me a pointed look as he asked the question, daring me to answer it. I shook my head. What a strange question to ask a girl you'd only just met.

'What kind of question is that?' I asked in lieu of an actual answer, I'd been expecting the usual; where are you from? What brings you here?

'Answer it first and then I'll tell you why I asked. I did ask first after all.'

He seemed genuinely serious, and I found myself answering before I'd even thought about the answer, my voice coming out in a whisper that I wasn't sure he'd even hear.

'To never feel the sand between my toes again and to never be able to walk on the beach at sunset. That's what scares me the most.'

I probably shouldn't have said that, after all, why would that scare someone? But I hadn't been able to help answering honestly; it was as if I was drawn to Aaron in a way that I'd never known before.

'Interesting,' he said and smiled as he thought about my answer.

'Your turn, why'd you ask?'

He seemed to consider my question, and I wondered whether he was going to fob me off with some vague non- answer. That disappointed me more than I cared to acknowledge when I realised that I had genuinely told him my biggest fear, even if he would never understand why I feared it.

'You can tell a lot about a person by their dreams and their fears, I always start with fears because they tend to run deeper than dreams. Yours is interesting, most people say things like heights or spiders; they are so superficial, I've never known anyone answer like you before,' he said with curiosity on his face.

'Well, I'm one of a kind,' I said with a shrug, hoping that he wouldn't push the conversation too far.

'Yes, you are,' he replied with a look that seemed to see straight through to my soul.

Of course, he couldn't know what I was, but he seemed to see me for more than I portrayed. I needed to move the conversation along, and fast.

'So, what is your greatest fear then?' I asked hoping to distract him from my answer.

'If you'd asked me that question this time yesterday, I would have answered the same way I have done for the last several years, but today I find myself with a different answer, and I promise you it's not a line.'

I laughed, sensing the direction this was about to take and already feeling uncomfortable.

'I'm afraid that when I walk away from you tonight, I won't see you again. You seem to have this air about you that says you have this great cloud of mystery surrounding you, and I feel like you're going to disappear when I turn my back,' he finished with a frown and sadness in his eyes, and then added with a chuckle, 'You don't turn into a pumpkin at night, do you?'

I didn't feel the wave of self-consciousness that I had expected, instead I felt a tidal wave of anguish that ran straight to my core. Without even knowing it he had me figured out; I would disappear, and soon. I looked out to the horizon that was just visible over the back fence of the bar and saw the sun sinking low in the sky. Elsie would be wondering where I was, I needed to get going. My time was nearly up.

'I have to go,' I said in a voice low enough that I barely even heard myself, but he leant in and brushed a stray lock of hair out of the way so that he could look into my eyes.

'I'm right aren't I? You're going to disappear on me, like something out of a fairy tale?'

I laughed, I couldn't help it. If only this was just a fairy tale.

'I'm not from around here,' I answered with as much vagueness as possible; I didn't want to hurt Aaron, but I had to get back to the beach.

'Do I at least get to go home with your number?'

Now there was the million-dollar question.

'I'm only in town today; I'm just visiting my Aunt,' I tried again.

How many times had I had to spout this excuse, the odd friend I had made in my time had found this very confusing.

'Okay, well I'm assuming that you'll be back to visit her again some time,' he asked, raising his eyebrows for an answer.

'Yeah, next month,' I replied quietly, making sure to use the right words like Elsie had kept reminding me.

Suddenly hopeful, I smiled. I kind of liked Aaron, there was something different about him compared to the other guys I had met on my odd venture into town, and he seemed genuinely interested in me - despite my odd behaviour.

'Well, I'd really like to see you again,' he pressed on.

'Okay,' I paused considering my next words, 'I don't have a phone. How about you give me your number and I'll ring you the next time I'm here?'

It sounded so much like a brush off, I knew it did, I used it all the time hoping that would be how the other person took it. This time however, I held my breath in the hope that Aaron didn't see it like that.

'You don't have a phone?' he clarified with a bemused look on his face.

I shook my head with a shy smile.

'Okay. I can work with this, it just adds to the mystery about you. I think I like that.'

His words wrapped around me and filled me with a sense of confidence that I'd never felt around a human before. Well, none other than my Aunt Elsie of course, but she was different; she knew the real me. Was there a chance that I could really see him again? Would he question my absence all month, or could he really live with the mystery that surrounded me like a toxic cloud of smoke?

He wrote his number on the back of a cocktail napkin from the bar, his writing looked like a spider had crawled across the white tissue paper, and I smiled, feeling like I'd learned something about him. I tucked it safely into the back of my purse with a smile, he'd even written his name on it, as if I was ever going to forget it, and drawn a little smiley face underneath. He was too cute; gone was the bad boy image he'd shown me to begin with.

He walked me to the road in front of the bar and then he leant against the low wall that ran along the edge of the drive way down to the beach.

'Luna,' he started when I went to keep walking.

I looked out to the horizon and balled my hands up into fists; I was pushing my luck with time. Turning back, I wiped the look of worry from my face and stood in front of him. Without speaking, he reached out and hooked a finger through the belt buckle of my cropped jeans and tugged gently as if testing my resolve. I let him pull me towards him, and put out my hands to stop myself from falling. My hands met his chest and I felt the wall of muscle that was hidden underneath his shirt. A smile pulled at the edge of my mouth as I looked up and met his eyes. They sparkled in the dying light as they searched my face for something. I knew what was coming next, and I wanted him to, he must have seen that eventually, because he leant down and pressed his lips gently to mine. He tasted like oranges as I opened my mouth up to him and kissed him back. A hand slid up my back and tangled in my hair as he kissed me harder, the gentleness wearing off and making way for the desire that had obviously built up. When I let out a tiny moan, he pulled back and smiled.

'I should probably let you walk away now,' he said, his voice husky from the kiss.

I nodded, not quite trusting my voice, and pulled back from him to stand up unaided. After taking a deep breath and running my hands through my long wavy hair to right myself, I looked up and met his eyes again with a bright smile.

'I'll call you next time I visit,' I said as I turned to walk away, 'I promise.'

He didn't reply, he merely held up a hand and waved as I started to walk away. I couldn't help but look back over my shoulder before I turned the corner, and I found him still watching me go. Waving back, I turned the corner and disappeared. Then I ran.

'Aunt Elsie!'

I rushed into the house yelling her name. I was cutting it close now, I had never left it this late to return to the beach; to the water, yes, I left it till the last possible second, but I was always on the beach before the sun began to sink behind the horizon.

'Luna?'

Elsie appeared at the top of the stairs, her hair wet from a recent shower.

'I assumed you had headed straight back to the water tonight, what are you still doing here?'

'I know, I'm late, but Aunt Elsie I met a guy, a really nice guy, and he wants to see me again on the next full moon,' I rushed my words as I flew up the stairs to put my bag in my room and swap my shorts for a skirt.

'Luna, you didn't?' Elsie asked sharply from the doorway.

'What? No! I just told him that I was visiting you. I don't have time to explain properly, I'll tell you everything next time.'

'Darling, I'll come down to the water with you.'

She followed me from the house as I headed for the cliffs that led down to the beach. The sun was almost gone; I had only minutes left before nature took my legs from me. I had to be back in the water when that happened. The consequences of not being there scared me more than the thought of not being able to walk on the sand again. What happened to a mermaid out of water?

Once on the beach, and we had scanned the area to make sure we were alone, I turned to Elsie and poured my heart out to her. I told her everything that had happened in the last couple of hours; about the drink he had bought me, the conversation we had had about fears, and about how he had been so persistent about seeing me again next time.

'He said I was mysterious, like something out of a fairy tale, and that he liked that about me. I know that I must be careful, but I really want to see him again next time. Aunt Elsie, is it possible? Can I see him again?' I asked, knowing that her answer would be the right one.

She would consider all the risks, and what was best for me and I knew that, even if I didn't like the next words that came out of her mouth, I would follow her advice despite my own feelings. It was her job to look out for us, to care about us and to protect us. She would know the right path for me to take.

'Luna, your mother would have wanted you to be happy. And if this boy makes you happy, then I think you should call him next month. Just promise me that you'll be careful.'

I threw my arms around her as I rushed out my promise; the rules were clear. Tell no one what we were. The humans couldn't be trusted. A familiar tingle spread through my body and I pulled back from Elsie ripping off my skirt and turned to the horizon. No. I needed more time. I still had things I wanted to ask her, specifically about my mother. That was the first time anyone had mentioned her in years, but I knew my limits. I couldn't fight this. A pained look crossed my face as I threw a look to the cliff tops to make sure we were still alone, before I turned to run down to the water and dove under the surface. There were only a few seconds left. I surfaced to find her stood in the wet sand where the waves lapped at her ankles, a strangely peaceful look on her face.

'See you next time Luna,' she said blowing me a kiss.

I nodded, but couldn't get the words out as I felt my legs kick for the last time and my tail trap them till the next full moon. The water flowed over me as I let myself sink below the surface and I watched as the blurry image of Elsie turned and headed back up the beach. How I longed to go with her, to be able to go back to the house and sleep in the little bed that was made up in my bedroom. I'd never slept in it, I never would, but it was always neatly made when I came ashore, always there waiting for me. It was almost cruel. The other bedrooms in the house just had sets of drawers in them, each labelled for the girls; the basics, that's all they needed. But I knew that Elsie was just trying to give me a little piece of what I desired the most, a home, a family, a life on land.

I turned and pushed gracefully through the water. Four weeks was such a long time for only one day, it was so unfair. I closed my eyes and pushed harder trying not to think about what Aaron would be doing now. Would he still want to see me by the time the next cycle came around? Or would he have found someone else, someone who wasn't so mysterious? Someone who wasn't just some fairy story?

Angel McGregor

June

The newly awakened morning seemed even brighter this month as I waited in the shallow water by the edge of the cove. A runner was energetically making their way down the shore line, cruelly trapping me in the water; as if the last twenty-nine days hadn't been torture enough. I couldn't wait to phone Aaron and see him again. I felt like there was just a little bit of normal making its way into my mixed-up life; would it be possible to have any sort of relationship with him? Or was I setting myself up for a heart ache? I didn't care. As soon as the runner was far enough back up the steps that I dared leave the water, I made a break for the rocks that littered the bottom of the cliff. Elsie would have hidden our bags there, she always did. It was far enough away from the ocean that the water only ever made it that far up the beach in high tide. I found mine easily, it was the one on top; I was always the first out in a morning. The weather was warm enough that I didn't need clothes on just yet, so I pulled the towel around my waist and a dry top on before heading across the sand towards the steps. The runner was already at the top of the steps and disappearing over the top of the cliff, so he wouldn't notice me now.

The opposite side of the cove had been fashioned into an escape route from the cosy little private beach. Steps had been landscaped into the bottom of the cliff where the earth was more secure, and then wooden steps had been built into the cliff wall, its structure seeming to add to the beauty of the whole place rather than ruin it. When the sun was round in the afternoon the cove was a natural sun trap, the cliffs providing shelter from the coastal winds, and the pier providing what little shade could be found. It was a little piece of heaven for those who could access it. As I made my way up the steps, I stopped to look back out towards the ocean. There'd be more of us today than there had been last month;

summer was on its way after all. A smile stayed on my face all the way back to the house; a white two storey building with a balcony on the second level and a wraparound porch on the ground floor. Elsie had already been busy, the planters on the porch were bursting with colour and the hanging basket by the front door was teaming with life.

I looked up to my bedroom as I made my way down the gravel path that led to the back garden and smiled to myself. Elsie had opened the balcony door and the white organza curtains were billowing out into the light breeze. It looked like something from a dream; maybe Aaron had been right about the whole fairy tale analogy. I rounded the side of the house and swung through the front door to the smell of waffles and bacon; Elsie really had been busy.

'What's got you so happy this early in the morning?' I asked, confirming the time on the grandfather clock that sat in the hallway.

It wasn't even five a.m. yet.

Elsie turned as I walked into the kitchen and smiled as she took me in. She'd always done it, for as long as I could remember, checked me over to see how much I had changed since the last time she had seen me. When I was a child, there had been significant differences in both my appearance and my learning, but now that I was older there was very little changing. Apparently, that wasn't going to be enough to break the old habit, because I found myself under scrutiny as usual, and even turned in a little flourish to show her that I was still me.

'Do I have time for a shower?' I asked as Elsie finished up her inspection and smiled at me with that same warm smile I'd known all my life.

'Breakfast will be ready in about ten minutes,' she said in place of an answer.

'I have time.'

With that I scooted back out of the kitchen and took the stairs two at a time. I dropped my bag on the bed and stripped out of my now damp top, leaving a trail of items as I made my way across the landing to the bathroom. The shower was like heaven. I let the water beat down on me for a few minutes before soaping up and rinsing the salt water off my skin, as much as I knew the salt was good for me, even when I was in human form, the feeling of refreshment after I'd had a good shower still couldn't be beaten. I stepped out and wrapped myself into one of the fluffy towels from the heated towel rail and followed my clothing trail back to my bedroom. After towel drying my hair and pulling on clean clothes, I headed back down the stairs to be greeted with the not so inviting smell of burning.

'Aunt Elsie, what happened?' I asked as I turned off the grill and wafted the smoke towards the back door.

She was stood in the open doorway with a look of pure confusion on her face.

'I don't know,' she admitted, then suddenly seemed to snap back to life.

She came and opened the oven door, pulled out the tray of burnt bacon and took it outside where it continued to smoulder for a few more minutes before revealing itself for the inedible charcoal it now was. Not quite what either of us had had in mind.

'I only popped outside for a few seconds to put some bread on the bird table; I must have gotten distracted. I'm sorry Luna dear,' she said when she came back inside.

After reassuring her that it was okay, and ensuring that she was okay, we settled for putting maple syrup on the waffles, and sat down for breakfast at the large dining table in front of the glass doors that led to the back garden. The table always seemed massive when Elsie and I sat at it alone, but on the odd occasion that all the girls came out during one of the summer months, it got extremely crowded in here. We had even been known to open the double doors and use the patio furniture.

When it was just the two of us like this, we sat side by side at one corner, cosy in its own little way.

During breakfast Elsie peppered me with questions about what I had been up to during the cycle, how the other girls were, what she'd missed. It was the same conversation, our own little routine, but I loved that she was interested. As we finished up though, she fell silent and I watched her with curiosity, as a slightly glazed look clouded over in her eyes. My worry had been quite fleeting when I had found the smoking bacon, but now that I searched her face, I saw that she was still removed from the situation. Was I reading too much into it? We all had accidents from time to time. Elsie was no exception, surely. It still unsettled me that it was so out of character for her though.

Stashing the information at the back of my mind ready to tackle at a more convenient time, I shuffled in my seat which gained her attention.

'Is it too early to call Aaron yet?' I asked, getting up to help clear the table.

The clock chose that moment to start chiming, informing me that it was now six, and I pulled out the number from my pocket where I had stashed it after my shower.

'You could try him, he may still be asleep though, it's Monday morning, he probably has a job to go to at some point today,' she answered with honesty.

I managed to control myself for an hour by helping clean the kitchen and by rearranging the books on the bottom shelf of the book case in the living room. But by seven I couldn't wait any longer.

The phone rang, and I found myself dreading the thought of him not answering. At that moment I just wanted to hear his voice, to reassure myself that it hadn't just all been some elaborate dream. So, when he answered the call with a groggy hello, I nearly jumped for joy.

'Aaron? It's Luna,' I started not really sure what to say, 'I'm sorry it's still so early.'

'Luna?' he asked, and I heard him moving in the background of the call, the springs of his bed groaning under the pressure; I'd woken him up.

For a split second I thought he didn't remember me, and the tidal wave of pain that threatened to crash over me was right on the precipice when he spoke again.

'I didn't think you were going to call, it's been weeks.'

He did remember me. The warmth that spread through me had me giddy all over again as I tried to put together an explanation that didn't sound too far-fetched.

'I'm sorry, I said it would be a month though,' I started, hoping that he would understand.

Had I said a month? Or had I told him that it would be this month. It was very late in the month, maybe he'd given up on me. After all, it had sounded so much like a brush off, even to me.

'Yeah, I guess,' he said with a sigh.

What was he thinking? This was torture, I hated phone calls, you couldn't see what the other person was thinking or feeling. I liked to be able to see a person's reactions, watch their facial expressions; it helped me to understand situations better as I often got confused with human emotions and reactions to things that I didn't necessarily understand properly.

'Aaron, is everything okay?' I asked quietly into the phone, one hand nervously twisting the wire on the phone while I held it in a death grip with the other.

'I just wasn't expecting you to call.' My heart dropped. 'Don't get me wrong, I'm glad you have, it's just been so long.'

A flicker of hope pulled a small smile to my lips, but I felt the need to explain myself. I didn't know where to start without lying to him; a downside to attempting to hold a relationship with a human.

'Aaron,' I started again, liking the way his name rolled off my tongue, 'I'm here just for today, and I'd really like to see you again.'

I left my comment open, hoping and praying that he wanted the same thing. Several second passed in silence and I began to wonder whether he doubted his 'your mysterious side is attractive' attitude. When he finally spoke, I released the breath that I hadn't realised I was holding.

'Of course, I want to see you again, let me take you to lunch.'

After making plans with Aaron for midday, I spent a couple of hours out in the garden at the back of the house, trying to keep myself busy so that the time would pass quicker. Every time I checked the clock on the wall by the back door though, barely any time had passed at all. I pruned the little shrubs that were making themselves known down in the rockery, and I moved a few things for Elsie that she said she had been wanting moved for ages, but didn't have the strength to sort herself. All the hard work made me hungry and I ate again before taking another shower and getting ready for my lunch date.

'What do I wear?' I shouted down to Elsie as I rummaged through my wardrobe, pulling random items of clothing out as I went.

Now that I was getting ready the time seemed to have sped up and I was running out of it. I heard her footsteps on the stairs as she made her way up to me and smelt the coffee that came with her. She came into the room and sat on the edge of my bed, moving the untidy pile of options out of her way.

'Where is he taking you, did he say?' she asked, taking a sip from her mug.

'The Hut,' I answered.

The Hut was one of the local restaurant-cum-bars that lay along the cliff top. It was relaxed but sophisticated, and had a stunning sea view; something that the residents of this sleepy little sea side town deemed necessary for every establishment within a hundred-foot radius of the beach.

'Okay, then you want something casual and comfortable, but maybe with a little sparkle so that you look like you have made an effort.'

She paused and seemed to think for a few seconds as I straightened up from my position with my head in the wardrobe. I had a long turquoise skirt in my hand that had sequins and beads around the bottom hem and matched Elsie's description perfectly. I held it up against me and swished it so that the sequins caught the light.

'Perfect,' Elsie exclaimed with a smile, 'What about that lacy black top over a turquoise crop top to go with it?'

'That isn't mine Aunt Elsie,' I said with a frown.

The black lace top she was talking about belonged to my sister. Elsie had never gotten Marina and I mixed up, in fact she never mixed up any of us, or our belongings. I often wondered how in the ocean she managed it. She looked at me for several long seconds with a confused look on her face, before blinking it away and smiling.

'I'm sure she won't mind if you borrowed it. Did you tell her about the boy you met?'

I shook my head. I'd chosen not to mention Aaron to anyone back home; I didn't think my plans to see him again would have gone down well.

'It's not that I meant to keep him a secret,' I justified to Elsie, 'I just didn't want them to worry.'

She smiled again and then made her way over to the chest of drawers in the corner of my room. That was the only thing in this room that didn't belong to me, both the chest and its contents belonged to Marina, her clothes and other bits and bobs were inside it. Elsie rummaged through two of the drawers before straightening with the black top in her hands.

'You're sure she won't mind?' I asked as she handed it to me.

'I'm sure she'd want you to wear it if she knew the reasons behind it. She may even be out later for you to tell her yourself.'

'Maybe,' I reasoned as I held it up.

An hour later I was ready. My hair fell down my back in its natural beach waves, I had a neutral layer of makeup on, just to give some definition to my eyes and lips, and I had on the outfit Elsie and I had put together. I had to admit, I felt pretty good. The excitement that I was harbouring for seeing Aaron again was slowly turning into nerves. What happened if I wasn't like he remembered and changed his mind about wanting to see me when I was here?

I shook my head to clear my thoughts as I grabbed my bag and slipped on my black canvas shoes, promising Elsie that I would be home for dinner. There was half an hour before I was due to meet Aaron, but I had a twenty-minute walk ahead of me in the midday sun. I decided to set off and take it slow. The sun was warm on my skin and the shadows were short as I made my way down the path that wound its way around the cliff top. The water was choppy today and I could hear the waves as they crashed against the shore down below me in the coves. Making my way around the cove that we used as our exit and entry point I followed the windy path through the long grasses before it opened out into the flat space that held some of the most popular hangouts for the town. I kept to the path and made my way past, glancing down over the edge of the cliffs to see the other little coves that they protected. There was no way down to them, though I longed to explore them.

As the ground began to slope, I concentrated on my footing and followed the path to the bottom, where it opened up onto the sandy beach that stretched along the rest of the coastline. Checking my watch to check how long I had left, I removed my shoes and continued down onto the sand. The Hut was about half a mile down, their outside eating area opening out onto the beach. I made my way slowly across the sand, curling my toes into its soft warmth as I went. When I made it to the back entrance of The Hut, I sat down on the little grassy verge and slipped my shoes back on. I still had ten minutes before midday, so I sauntered around the side of the building and perched myself in a spot of sunshine on the low wall that ran around the front, separating the lawn from the car park.

I watched the vehicles pulling in and out of the car park with interest, making up stories in my mind about where they came from and what their purpose was here today. When a small, red, open backed Jeep pulled into the car park, I recognised Aaron behind the wheel instantly. He wore a black vest that showed off strong muscles at the top of his arms, which flexed as he manoeuvred the car into a space at the other side of the car park to where I sat. A black tribal tattoo crawled around one shoulder and disappeared under his top; my mind raced at the images of what it looked like on his back. He had been wearing a sleeved shirt last time I had seen him and the ink had been completely covered. Now, he was beginning to look more like the rogues out of a dirty novel than the cheeky boy next door I remembered.

He looked cool and casual as he made his way over to me, as if he knew that he belonged here. His confidence levels were sky high and he exuded an air of self-assurance that I'm sure would have had any girl on their knees. As he approached me, he pulled the pair of dark shades from his eyes and smiled, the dark blue sparkle seeming to pull at something deep within me.

'Hey gorgeous,' he said as I stood up; he towered over me, but not in an intimidating way, I felt safe with him by my side.

'Hi,' I said, suddenly feeling ridiculously nervous.

As I searched for something else to say, Aaron leant down, sliding one hand around my waist and the other into my hair, before pulling me in and pressing his lips against mine. The kiss was slow and testing, as if he was expecting me to push him away, but my body reacted instinctively, pressing myself to him and kissing him back. When he pulled away, he smiled and ran one hand through his hair, the other staying on my waist.

'I've been waiting to do that again for weeks,' he stated without apology, 'You hungry?'

I nodded not trusting my voice not to betray me. My knees suddenly felt weak as I let him guide me inside, his warm hand never leaving my waist. He spoke to the waitress just inside the door and she led us to our table; a corner booth by the open doors that led out to the beach. I smiled as he followed me into the booth, choosing to sit by my side rather than across the table from me.

'Did you miss me?' I asked nervously, wondering if he had even spared me a second thought after we had parted ways on the last full moon.

'Of course I did, I've been waiting for you to call for weeks,' he answered, looking over the top of his menu at me where he sat sideways on the cracked leather seat.

A smile spread across his face with his words and I felt mine answer his in return. There was something intoxicating about Aaron, and I felt the pull towards him. I was going to have to tread carefully if neither of us were going to get hurt from all of this. What was I thinking could happen?

The waitress arrived then in her sunshine yellow dress and white apron, distracting me from my train of thought and asking for our order. Aaron looked to me and nodded, playing the perfect gentleman and letting me order first. I glanced down the menu again and told the waitress my order; there was no way I was going to be one of those girls that ordered a salad, and Aaron didn't strike me as the kind of guy who went for girls that were always watching their figure. It wasn't like I needed to watch mine anyway; have you ever seen a fat mermaid? The answer is no, our metabolisms and the amount of energy we expend just moving around in the water keeps us in form.

When I finished my order of a burger and fries with a banana milkshake, Aaron looked at me with a satisfying smile and I felt like I had just passed an unspoken test. He glanced up at the waitress and held up two fingers.

'Make that two, but make mine a chocolate milkshake.'

The waitress nodded, her curly brown hair bobbing around her defined cheekbones as she smiled and turned away, tucking her notebook back into her apron pocket.

'Nice choice,' Aaron said with a smile when I turned back to him.

He had been watching me, and I felt myself blush at the attention. I was so used to trying to go unnoticed in places that having him watch my every move kind of made me nervous. What if he noticed something that I did that wasn't exactly human? Elsie had been right when she'd told me that I needed to be careful.

'I'm not a salad kinda girl,' I answered with a broad smile that completely contradicted how confident I actually felt.

'Good to know, makes taking you out places much easier.'

The conversation continued easily, Aaron firing questions at me that were just as bizarre as his deepest fears question that he had caught me off guard with at the bar. I was more careful with my answers this time and made sure to ask him for his answers when I was finished, though I never asked a new question. Mermaids were non- inquisitive by nature, having grown up being told information when we needed to know it. The Royals controlled everything under the ocean, including who knew what and when; it never occurred to anyone that it should be any different to that. So, when Aaron fell quiet half way through the meal, it stayed a comfortable silence as I didn't feel the need to fill it with mindless chat.

When dinner was over, Aaron paid for the meal despite my best efforts to go halves with him. He literally took my purse off me while he paid the waitress so that I couldn't give her any money. It was chivalrous of him, I'd read it in books, but I'd never come across it in my life time before and it felt odd.

'I asked you out, I brought you for lunch, it was my treat,' he argued again as we left the restaurant by the back doors and wandered down onto the beach.

'I'm just saying that you didn't have to,' I replied, 'Thank you though,' I added afterwards, not wanting to sound ungrateful.

His kind act had made me smile and his warm hand against my lower back where he walked beside me was making a strange bubbly feeling build low in my stomach. When we made it to a spot where there weren't too many other people, he stopped and gestured to the sand. I smiled then, and I mean really smiled, when I realised he intended us to stay at the beach. The sand was one of my favourite things on land, and I loved to spend time on it barefoot. I immediately toed off my shoes, dropped my bag by them and plonked myself down on the warm sand, my skirt fanning out around me. Aaron chuckled to himself before sitting down beside me and putting his arms out behind him.

As he leant back and closed his eyes at the sun shining on his face, I turned to study his features. His dark hair was thick with close cropped curls that reminded me of chocolate melting in the warmth and his eyelashes matched; almost black but tipped in brown, sat against cheeks which were dotted with freckles. His arms were strong and muscled and tensed as he manoeuvred in the sand to get comfortable, making me want to be in them again. The way he had taken charge when he had first come to me in the car park made my knees weak and had desire pooling between my thighs; there was no doubt that I wanted him to do it again.

I reached out tentatively and stroked my fingertips up the inside of his wrist and then traced up the black ink that coloured his bicep.

'You like it?' he asked without opening his eyes.

Clearly, he'd had it a long time if he knew exactly where it was without him looking at it. I continued to drag my fingers up his arm, gently pushing his top out of the way to get a sneak peek at where it went.

'I do,' I said with a smile, 'Did it hurt?'

I didn't know much about tattoos, other than what I had seen on TV, and even that wasn't much. There wasn't much time for TV when you only had one day to explore on land every month, I only watched it when the weather was really bad in the winter months and I couldn't get outside much, but generally I preferred a good book. He shook his head in response to my question, peeking at me through hooded eyes.

'Where does it go?' I asked, curious as to what the rest of it looked like.

I wasn't used to the feeling of curiosity and it bemused me that I was so interested. It was like I had to know.

In lieu of an answer, he sat up and pulled off his top in one swift movement, startling me at first. His arms, shoulders, chest and stomach all rolled with muscles; he had to work out for that body, but the main thing that stood out to me was the ink. The design, tribal in nature if I wasn't mistaken, crawled up his arm, over his shoulder and down on to his chest in a series of swirls, dots and points, like the vines of a thorn bush weaving their way across his skin.

I gazed in awe and held out my hand again to brush my fingertips across the intricate design and he smiled. After I had looked at the design, he gently moved my hand before turning his back on me, and I was surprised all over again when I saw the tattoo crawl across his shoulder and down his back and side too.

There was an inordinate amount of time and money on his body and every inch of it looked stunning. There had to be a story behind it, and I couldn't wait to find out what it was. As I let my gaze wander, I noticed the little red rose that was tucked under his arm, peeking through to his front and I wondered how I had missed it there. He let me lift his arm and I traced the image of the rose gently, completely in awe of the stunning artwork.

'You wanna know about it?' he asked with a gentle smile.

I nodded eagerly, letting him sit back again, though he made no move to put his top back on. The sun was warm now that summer was on its way, and I guess living around here all the time you'd get used to it.

'It wasn't all done at once,' he explained meeting my gaze as he spoke.

I was riveted as he explained how it had started as just an arm piece, a random tattoo that he had no plans for. Then he called it 'the itch', when he had started wanting another one, and instead of having separate ones, had decided to incorporate it all into one.

'I have a few hours at a time done, and it always looks finished when they're done so that I can decide when I want to go back.'

I marvelled at the time he had put into it when he told me that there were at least six different sessions there and that each session had lasted a few hours.

'What about the rose?' I asked with a nod towards his side.

'The rose is for my mom,' he said breaking the look between us to stare out to sea, 'She died a couple of years back, so it's just me and my dad now. Her name was Rose.'

There was a slight smile on his lips as he remembered, and I kept quiet while he reminisced. An inordinate amount of questions ran through my head now, and I had to concentrate to make sense of them. Was this what it was like all the time for humans? I was beginning to wonder how in the ocean they got anything done for all the confusion. There was so much that I wanted to know about Aaron, that suddenly, a day just didn't seem long enough.

I waited patiently for Aaron to turn back to me before speaking again, but he beat me to it.

'She loved the ocean, was out here every morning swimming before getting ready for work.'

Again, he drifted off into silence and I had to wonder what had happened to her. I refrained from asking; knowing that it was personal and that he would tell me in his own time if he wanted to. But it didn't change the longing I had to want to know everything about him. So instead of asking about his mother, I changed the conversation for a while.

'What is your dad like?'

I didn't know much about male role models and family members, mermaids were all female by nature; we didn't need a male version of the species. We survived just fine without them. But I had read about fathers, brothers, grandfathers and husbands etc. in books. They sounded fascinating, if not a little gross at times. Women were much more delicate and clean.

'Dad is,' Aaron seemed to struggle for words, but I let him find the right ones, 'Let's say he's distant. We don't talk much since Mom died. I still live at home, but I'm barely there, and he spends his time in front of the TV with a drink in his hand. I've tried to talk him round but he doesn't see a problem.'

I didn't know what to say, so instead I put out my hand and rested it on Aaron's knee on the material of his shorts. Rather than continuing, he looked down at my hand and then up into my eyes which I'm sure were sparkly from the unshed tears I was holding back. He smiled and reached out towards me, putting his hand in my hair and pulling me closer.

'Bit of a lousy topic of conversation for a first date?' he asked before pressing his forehead to mine.

I shook my head in the limited wiggle room I had from his hold and smiled; I wanted to know about him, about his life on land. It didn't bother me that it wasn't all sunshine and roses.

'How about a swim?' he asked, releasing me and nodding to the water.

My eyes widened and I pulled back, scrambling for an excuse. I didn't go in the water on the day of the full moon, I was on land with my feet. It wasn't worth the risk.

'I don't have a change of clothes with me,' I said hoping that it was enough.

'Neither do I, we'll dry out though.'

I shook my head, lost for words.

'I can lend you a spare shirt, there'll be one in the truck,' he said with a grin.

As much as I liked the idea of wearing his top, I still wouldn't be getting in the water. Aaron seemed to sense my apprehension and took it as a lack of interest.

'Don't tell me you don't like the water?' he laughed, 'You live in a seaside town.'

I laughed then, that was an easy response.

'I don't live in the seaside town though, do I? I'm just visiting.'

He laughed and fidgeted on the sand a little.

'Okay, fair play, but you like the water?'

Remembering what he'd said about his mother loving the ocean, I realised that it was important to him, so I gave him a truth that he wouldn't realise was so honest.

'I spend near enough all of my time in the water; it's safe to say I like it there. But it's nice to stay dry occasionally.'

'Okay, next time then.'

A genuine grin spread across his face and he reached over to me and pressed his lips to mine. A couple of seconds passed before I kissed him back as he took me by surprise, but then I melted into him and let him take control. His tongue gently touched my bottom lip, tracing the edge and seeking out mine. I opened up to him and let the tip of my tongue touch his. A fire ignited in my tummy and I pressed myself against him to get closer. He didn't object, wrapping his arm around me and slipping it up the back of my top, pressing his hand flat to the bare skin there.

His skin was hot against me, and the wall of muscle was hard but inviting; I wanted to stretch out on top of him and curl up like a cat. Everything about him was inviting, right down to the way he smelled; that pure masculine scent mixed with what I thought was sun tan oil, which also explained the slight sheen on his skin. He was a beautiful honey colour where the spring/summer sun was marking his skin and the ink shone dark against it. Where he kissed me, I could taste the lingering chocolate from his milkshake and I moaned a little into his mouth.

He pulled back then with a wicked glint in his eyes.

'I think we should stop before I make a public indecency out of the pair of us; I can't keep my hands off you.'

The truth was that I didn't want him to, but I glanced around to see small children playing and splashing in the tide. This wasn't the time or the place, plus I wasn't that type of girl.

I smiled back and made to stand up, pulling him up with me.

'Want to go for a walk?'

He nodded enthusiastically and pulled on his top, much to my disgust.

We meandered around the cliff tops, peering down into the coves that were trapped down there. I explained to Aaron how I'd always wanted to explore them; they were like this big mystery to me that I felt I needed to answer. Maybe I was more human than I knew, the pull towards the unknown was something that none of the other girls understood. They followed their orders from the Royals, did as they were told, and even on land they just got on with things. They didn't ask questions, didn't hunt for information. I had always been the odd one out in that way.

When we reached the cove that lay next to the one that was accessible, the one I'd used just this morning to get out of the ocean, we sat down on the grass with our legs over the edge. The incline wasn't too steep at the top so there was no big drop to scare me, and we sat side by side staring out at the ocean which was rather calm and quiet now as the waves rolled in towards the beaches.

From this point, I couldn't see the cove we came out of the water from, but I hoped that some of the other girls were out by now, that they'd come to see Elsie. I knew that she missed them over the winter months, and it was warm enough now that they had no excuses. Aaron's hand was next to mine, our little fingers touching in the grass and I couldn't help but smile. It felt so right being here with him.

'Let's go down there,' I said, suddenly wanting to explore.

'Down there?' Aaron questioned, his eyebrows shooting up so quickly that they made me laugh.

'Yeah, it'll be fine, and we can look out for each other. I've never gone down there before because I was worried that I'd hurt myself and no one would even know where I was,' I trailed off into silence, hoping that he was up for the adventure.

He stayed quiet for a few minutes, leaning forward to inspect what we could see of the cove from here.

'Okay, let's do it,' he said finally and pushed up to his feet.

He held out his hand to me and I let him pull me up from the floor. I brushed off the dust from the back of my skirt and then looked up to find him smiling.

'You going down there in that?' he gestured at my attire and I nodded, swishing my skirt for effect.

Nothing had ever stopped me from exploring before, most definitely not my clothes. When he nodded his approval, we made our way over to the corner of the bend and stared down the easy incline. I knew that after the grass banking the cliff became more inaccessible and we were going to have to manoeuvre across the rocks and climb down. It didn't worry me; I'd done other stuff like this and never had a problem. It made me happy that Aaron was up for the adventure too and I started imagining all the places we could go and explore together. He followed me closely, watching me all the time as if keeping an eye on me and making sure I was safe. It made me smile and I stopped where I was with my feet on a little ledge so that I could wait for him to catch up.

'You okay?' he asked when he put both feet on the ledge at the side of me.

He reached out and put his hand in my hair, pulling me in to press his lips to mine. I opened to him immediately and let my tongue touch his, stroking gently as he explored my mouth. When he pulled back I let out a tiny whimper, but managed not to pout.

'Come on, or we'll never reach the bottom,' he said with a chuckle.

I took the risk, seeing the sand only a couple of feet below me, I arranged myself against the wall and pushed away from it and jumped to the floor. Landing with a soft thump in the warm sand, I looked up to see a look of pure horror on Aaron's face and he began to scramble down the last few feet to join me.

'My god, are you okay?' he asked, running his hands up and down my arms.

I nodded, watching his facial features to try and understand what had just happened.

'You're not hurt?' Aaron said when I stayed silent.

Got it.

'You thought I fell?' I asked, everything suddenly falling into place.

He raised his eyebrows at me and then frowned.

'You didn't?'

I shook my head and smiled, putting my hands into his and pulling him down the beach. The afternoon sun was high in the sky now and the cove was acting like a sun trap just like its partner next door. The air was still and muggy, the sand hot beneath my feet as I pulled off my shoes so that I was barefoot.

Before I could say anything else Aaron pulled me back to him, my back against his hard chest, and kissed the side of my neck. His hands on my waist were firm and I got the same sense of him taking over as I had done in the car park that morning. I relaxed into his hold and when I softened, I felt his kisses increase in pressure and his fingers splay under the edges of my top so that his hands sat against my bare skin. There was no one here now to stop us, no reason that made this inappropriate and I let it happen, loving how it felt to have his hands on me.

When he finally released me, I turned in his embrace and pressed a kiss to his lips before bouncing backwards out of his grasp. I dropped my bag by my shoes and turned to the cove. For years I'd wanted to get down here; I hadn't been able to convince my sister to come with me, and what I'd said to Aaron was true. It would have been irresponsible to come down on my own.

The walls were similar to the cove I used, eroded and jagged, making them climbable, and the bottom of the cliffs were scattered with fallen debris from where the rocks were sliding. The beach itself though was beautiful, a line of seaweed at the back showed me that the water level washed the entire beach away when it came in and the sand turning to shingle near the cliffs was lying in lines where the tide had washed it into patterns. From where I stood now, with my back to the water, I could see the undisturbed sand and the layers of sediment that detailed the water's movement. Turning to find Aaron with his shoes off and his feet in the water, I smiled at the sight and dug out my camera from the pocket inside my bag. It made a beautiful shot. Lining it up so that I couldn't see the cliffs, I positioned him to one side of the image and captured the moment with a loud click that caught his attention.

I smiled as he did and caught the Polaroid photograph as it slid out of the camera, shaking it a little so that it developed quicker. Aaron splashed back out of the water and made his way up to the beach to where I stood and peered over my shoulder at the photograph in my hand.

'So, you're a photographer too?' he said quietly.

I shook my head, I'd hardly class myself as a photographer. I just liked documenting my time on land. He laughed at my denial and took the camera from me.

'I haven't seen one of these in years,' he said, studying it.

I smiled then, I loved this camera.

'I don't like those ones with the screens on; it takes away all of the magic.'

He grinned at me as if he understood what I meant and then turned the camera around in his hand and pointed it at us. I turned to give him a questioning look as he clicked the button and laughed when I heard the shutter sound. As the whirring sound finished, signalling the camera reloading, he turned and kissed me, pressing the button again. He pulled away in time to catch the first photograph, and I smiled as it cleared and revealed me laughing whilst looking at him like I'd found the world in one guy. We weren't quite in the middle of the picture, but I loved it all the same. When the second one came out and cleared, it made my smile even wider and I turned to kiss Aaron again. Was it possible that I could be this happy? I couldn't get enough of him, and I was dreading dusk when I would have to make my excuses and disappear again.

The afternoon drifted past lazily as we explored the little caves in the back of the cove. Having been so undisturbed by human exploration this far, there was no evidence of anyone having tried to alter the natural state of the place. Evidence of the water was everywhere; it had cut holes in the rocks and smoothed over the pebbles that lined the back of the cave that opened up in the bottom of the cliff face. We had poked around inside it, using the tiny light on Aaron's mobile phone as a torch and found some pretty pebbles that I had put in my bag to add to my collection back at the house. I had a few from each of the coves sat on the top of the dresser with a tiny candle in the centre, a little reminder of all the places I had been while on land.

We sat down on the sand for a rest after our explorations and talked about Aaron's life in the sleepy little seaside town. He peppered me with more questions about my life, which I tried to answer as truthfully as I could, without giving away any of my secrets. I didn't want to start lying to him, apart from the fact that it would be too hard to keep up with what I had told him, I wanted him to know me. I wanted to tell him about myself, the way he was revealing himself to me. He didn't have to think about what information he gave me, he handed it out freely, explaining things where I didn't quite understand them. He never once questioned my lack of understanding about anything; things that were probably ridiculously simple to a girl that lived a normal life here on land. The only clue that I saw that told me it was something I should know, was the tiny raise of his eyebrows and the twitch of his lips into a small smile when he explained them to me. So many times, I wondered what he thought, whether he realised just how naive I really was to this way of life, or whether he just explained it away with the idea of me being a little eccentric.

When the sun began to move over the horizon, showing me that it was nearly dinner time, Aaron and I made a move to start our way back up the cliffs. It took much longer to climb back up than it had to make our way down, but we talked and laughed all the way; being around Aaron was so easy that I couldn't help but imagine what a life with him would be like.

At the top he held out his hand and pulled me up the grass banking and straight into his arms where he pressed his lips to mine in a heated kiss. Taking a deep breath as he released me, I smiled up at him and giggled

'What was that for?'

'That was because I had an awesome time today, and I'm really glad you called,' he responded with a smile of his own.

My answering smile was even brighter and I threw myself back into his arms and kissed him again. I wanted so much for this to be the start of something, but the heavy feeling in my heart kept me from doing or saying anything silly. I knew the boundaries. I knew that my time was coming to an end this cycle. If I wanted to see him again then I would have to wait till the next full moon and just hope, with everything that I had, that he would want to see me again then.

Aaron's phone chose that minute to start making a noise, and he pulled back with a disgruntled sound and pulled it from his pocket. Glancing at the screen he smiled and gestured for us to start walking back towards the car.

He pressed a button on the phone and then answered it whilst linking his fingers with mine.

'K, what's up?'

We headed back up the winding path that would take us back to where his Jeep was still parked by The Hut, and I smiled to myself at how easily we had slid into being around each other. A few girls turned to watch us pass, and I saw them look Aaron up and down and then watched as their eyes fell to where our hands were joined together. I wondered what they thought; none of them knew who I was, and I began to wonder how many of them did know Aaron. Everyone seemed to know everyone in this little town, and I always gained attention for being the newcomer. The odd one or two people knew that I was here for Elsie, they thought me her niece as we had agreed to portray, but none of them ever asked many questions. Elsie must have given them enough that they didn't feel the need to pry any further.

I tuned back in to Aaron's phone conversation as he agreed to meet whoever had called him in an hour. Letting out a sigh at the fact that I was going to have to say goodbye soon, I tightened my grip on his hand as if I could hold on to him if I just didn't let go. He responded by lifting our hands to his mouth and pressing a kiss to my knuckles as he pushed the phone back in his pocket.

'Want to come to the pub for a drink, or do you need to be getting back?' he asked as we made our way over to the Jeep.

'I promised I'd be home for dinner,' I answered quietly.

'No problem, I can drop you off if you like.'

I smiled, nodding as he opened the door to the Jeep and helped me in. Rearranging my skirt, I pulled on the belt and turned to watch Aaron jump in beside me. He drove with ease, sliding his hand onto my leg and seeking out my hand as if it was something we did every day. It was driving me mad not knowing what he was thinking.

'Are you around tomorrow?' he asked as we drove back towards the house.

'I go home tonight,' I answered, shaking my head.

Aaron didn't answer for a few seconds and I wondered again what he was thinking. I couldn't see his face from this position either which made it even harder.

'When do you visit again?' he asked eventually.

'A few weeks.'

'Can I see you again then?'

I smiled and nodded.

'I'd like that.'

'I don't want to keep you from visiting your Aunt, we can just go for lunch or something if you want to,' he said as if hedging his bets.

'I'd like to see more of you than that, Elsie doesn't mind,' I answered quietly, 'But if you don't want to it's okay.'

I had to wonder why he would want to spend too much time with me when I was so elusive. He had to have plenty of friends, and I'd seen the way girls looked at him; he could probably have any girl he wanted. I didn't doubt that he probably had been with plenty of them already; I hadn't forgotten the way he'd hit on me in the bar last time.

He pulled the car to a stop on the front of the house when I pointed it out and then turned to me, pulling my hands into his lap.

'Luna, I've loved today, and would love to spend the day with you every day, I'll take as much time as you'll give me.'

His honesty caught me off guard and I smiled, staying silent for a few minutes. The tough guy act that I'd seen in the bar was nothing like the guy I had seen today. He seemed to be wearing his heart on his sleeve and I appreciated it more than he would ever understand. It made him a little easier to read if nothing else.

'I'll call you the next time I'm here?' I asked, hoping that it would be that simple.

'You not know the date now? Then I can make sure I'm free,' he asked in place of an answer.

I panicked for a second before calming myself down with a mental shake. No, I didn't know the date; I hadn't even known what day it was today until Elsie had mentioned it this morning. Days and dates didn't mean anything to me; my life revolved around the phases of the moon. Could I get away with mentioning the full moon or was I asking for trouble? I knew the answer; Elsie would know the date. She had a calendar on the wall in the kitchen that had the phases of the moon on it.

'I can check the date when I get home and call you back,' I said, hoping that sounded like a reasonable thing to say.

'That sounds great,' he replied with a smile before releasing my hand and jumping out of the Jeep.

He came around to my door and helped me out. I landed on the floor in a little cloud of dust and he pulled me in for a hug. Rearranging my feet on the floor so that I had some stability, I pushed up onto my toes and pressed a kiss to his jaw. He got the message and tilted his head down to kiss me.

When I pulled away to head back to the house I felt instantly bereft without him, but held my head high as I made my way down the path and turned to wave as he got back in the Jeep. I watched as he pulled away from the front and waved again, then opened the door and went inside, making my way straight to the calendar to check out the date of the next full moon.

As I rounded the corner into the living room I came face to face with Mia who was clearly heading upstairs, her bare feet stepping on my toes before stepping back with a mumbled apology. I fumbled with my bag, nearly dropping it, and stared blankly at her, her silvery grey eyes shining in the low light. Mia regularly came out to see Elsie but never usually stopped this late.

'What are you still doing here?' I asked rather bluntly; but in my defence, she had taken me by surprise.

'Mia decided to stay for dinner,' Elsie said, coming up behind her and putting her hands on Mia's shoulders, 'Did you have a nice day?'

Looking back to Mia, I smiled when I saw her smile and relaxed a little. For a split second I think I had panicked that Elsie had sold me out and Mia was here to berate me for being too risky by spending time with Aaron. She slid past me to head upstairs and Elsie gave me a knowing look as if she knew exactly what I was thinking. She always did say that I wore my emotions on my sleeve; even thought that didn't make any sense to me at the time, but she'd explained that it was easy to read my facial expressions and work out what I was thinking.

'Sorry,' I mumbled as I put my bag down at the foot of the stairs.

'Did you have fun at lunch?' Elsie asked again after nodding to accept my apology for doubting her.

I nodded then, my words spilling out excitedly as I told her about lunch and our adventure down into the cove in a hurried whisper so that Mia wouldn't over hear. Elsie smiled and nodded along to my story as she ushered me into the kitchen where the smell of a home cooked roast dinner was steaming up the windows and making the temperature unbearably stuffy. She opened the back door and laughed as she apologised for the bad decision.

'When Mia said she was going to stay too, I figured we could have a proper meal, but it wasn't till after I started cooking that I figured it was probably bad planning to cook a roast on one of the warmest days of the year so far.'

She finished with a shrug and we laughed as Mia re-entered the room.

'What's so funny?' she asked, coming to a halt in the doorway.

'Nothing dear, do you want to set the table?' Elsie said, opening the draw and pulling out a handful of cutlery.

Mia and I set about sorting the table while Elsie checked on the food. Once done, I slipped over to the calendar on the wall and checked out the page for next month. Elsie had marked several dates off and put some little notes by the side of some, but the full moon was highlighted in neon blue pen. It was a Tuesday by the time the cycle came around again and I wrote the date on my hand before excusing myself from the room to go and call Aaron.

As I hung up the phone with a smile, Mia popped her head around the doorway where I was sat on the bottom step of the stair case to tell me that dinner was nearly ready. I got up and settled the phone back onto the cradle and skipped through the house after her.
'What's got you so happy?' Mia said as we reached the kitchen.
'Oh, you know,' I started, not really having to lie as it was true enough, 'Having you out for dinner, I know it makes Aunt Elsie happy, and that makes me happy.'
I shrugged and Mia's smile fell a little.
'Are you staying out till sunset with me?' I asked, already knowing the answer.
'Not this time, I'm going to head back after dinner. I'll see you back at The Kingdom though. Marina missed you she popped out at lunch time for an hour, but Elsie said you'd gone out for lunch.'
My heart sank a little when she said that my sister had been out; Marina didn't come ashore much these days. Things had been different when I was younger, she'd come ashore for hours each full moon to be with me and Elsie, but as I'd grown more independent, she'd stayed in the water more. When I'd spoken to her last night, she'd made no comment about coming ashore.

Dinner went smoothly, we talked about times gone by; Elsie bringing up childhood memories about the pair of us. Mia was technically the generation above me; she was only a few years younger than my mother would have been had she not died when I was a baby, but time passed differently under the ocean, and she didn't look old enough to be my mother. She only appeared a few years my senior, and the way Elsie talked about us, anyone would have assumed us a similar age; though in reality the memories were decades apart.

A few hours before sunset, I walked back down to the beach with Mia and we talked about meaningless waffle on the way down there. She made quick work of getting back in the water once we had checked for privacy and I waved before heading back up to the house to spend a couple of hours with Elsie before I had to return too. Today was the longest day of the year according to Elsie's calendar, meaning that next time I'd have to be returning to the water sooner. It wasn't fair. I should get more time on land than I did, we should get more of a choice.

By the time I had made it back up to the house, Elsie had cleaned up the dishes from dinner and was drying the last few plates. I helped her put them away before telling her more about my afternoon down in the cove. She accompanied me upstairs where I showed her the photographs that we had taken, and I pinned them to the big cork notice board that I had on the wall above my bed. I scanned some of the other photos that were still there. Ones of me and Marina through the years; you could literally watch us grow up in photographs if you looked through the dozens I had stashed under the bed in a box. The ones on the board were some of my favourites. One of Marina, Shae and me down on the beach, some of Elsie and me on some of our adventures, several of us as a group where Elsie had persuaded strangers to take a photo of us all together, and one in the middle of Elsie and my mum from just before I was born. Elsie was standing with her arm around her, smiling at the camera, and my mother was smiling at whoever was behind the camera, her baby bump not hidden at all under a floaty white top that was blowing in an unseen breeze and her hair caught by the same wind while Elsie was laughing. They looked so carefree and happy that I wished that I could have been a part of her life as more than that bump.

Angel McGregor

I didn't know many details about my mother, no one liked to talk about her much, but I knew that she had died the day she gave birth to me. Marina had told me that she had loved me very much, and had named me herself, but didn't like to talk about her and tell me her own memories of her. Instead I just had the photographs that Elsie had all over the house, and the odd few bits of information that people let slip in conversations.

I returned to the beach as the light began to fade, I was still thinking about my mother and wondering how different my life would have been if things had worked out differently. I longed to know all about her, to have known her like Elsie had. She'd never said it as such, but I often wondered whether she had been Elsie's favourite; there weren't many photos of Elsie, she'd told me that she preferred to take them. It was from her that I had gained my love of photography, and the camera had been a gift from her to fuel my passion for taking photographs. The ones I had seen around the house, other than group photographs, she was always with my mother and the smile on her face was always real. I'd learned to tell the difference long ago between real and fake smiles, and Elsie's was always genuine. She'd said it wasn't worth smiling if you didn't really mean it.

I smiled at the words in my head, hearing her voice as I remembered them. The sun was slipping silently behind the horizon and I shook off my skirt and left it on the rock for Elsie to grab in the morning. I'd changed out of Marina's top and put on a loose T-shirt with an image of a hermit crab shell on the front. It would do for the swim back. I tried to keep my body covered as it drew less attention to me as I swam in and out of The Kingdom. The last thing I needed was for the Royals to take too much of an interest in my comings and goings; I didn't want them sticking their fins into my life on land. I knew that my interest in being ashore had been noted long ago, and I was probably monitored, I couldn't afford for them to learn about Aaron.

Watching the sun disappear, I drew my last breath of air for the day and plunged back into the warm salt water, concentrating on the beat of my tail in the water as I sliced through the incoming tide and made my way deeper into the ocean. The cycle couldn't go fast enough; I was already checking off the phases until the next full moon; until the next day I got to spend with Aaron.

Angel McGregor

July

I waited just under the water, waiting for the first tendrils of sunlight to begin creeping from behind the horizon. I pushed hard with my fins one last time and broke the surface of the water, watching the ripples dance away from me as I disturbed the early morning serenity. I concentrated hard on kicking, separating my legs as I breathed my first breath of fresh air this month. I would be the first; I always was - so there was no point looking for the others. I'd been waiting for this moment since the last time I'd set foot on the sand.

Now I swam to the shore, kicking and splashing all the way. Elsie would have left our clothes out by now, although the others wouldn't be out for hours yet and some of them not at all. But Elsie knew me; she knew I'd be out before the sun was all the way up. As I got to the shallow water I stood up, pushing my feet into the sand and feeling the smile spread across my face. I found my bag hidden behind the rocks by the foot of the cliffs and pulled on the sarong skirt before gently squeezing some of the water from my long curls. Wrapping a towel around my shoulders, I started up towards the house. I padded up the sand, curling my toes into it with each step, and headed for the steps up to the pier. The house was only just over the hill, the stunning sea view making it a perfect home for the day we spent on land.

Aunt Elsie had lived there for as long as some of us could remember, and I'd never thought to ask what it had been like before then. We learned from a young age that we were told the things we needed to know in life, anything else was just pure curiosity; and we all know what that did to the catfish. It was Aunt Elsie's job to protect us, to look out for us and to provide for us. I knew little about what she did for the rest of the month when we were back home, but I knew that she loved us all more than she could ever say. She spoiled me;

sometimes I wondered if she was just indulging my fantasies of being on land more, but I got the feeling that it ran deeper than that, though I'd never asked why. Maybe I should. Maybe it was time I started asking more, and finding out the answers to some of these questions I'd had for so long. It just wasn't in our nature to ask lots of questions, the Royals gave us what we needed in life and we trusted that they knew what was best for us. But now that I was thinking about it, I wondered why we just assumed that what they said went; it was something that I had never thought to question before. Maybe Aaron was rubbing off on me, his questions always puzzled me a little, but maybe he was right to question life. After all, that was what made him so adventurous.

When I reached the house, I made my way straight up the stairs, Elsie was most likely still in bed; it was still mega early after all. I crept down the landing and into my room, dumping my stuff on my bed and pulling another towel from the drawer. The creak outside my bedroom door made me jump and I laughed as Elsie stuck her head around the door and whispered good morning. She always whispered at this time in the morning, as if we were going to wake someone else up. The house was empty.

'Morning Aunt Elsie, what are you doing up so early?' I asked.

'I was awake reading when you came in,' she said again in a whisper before smiling and retreating.

I heard the bathroom door close and then returned to towel drying my hair, though now I knew she was awake, I could have my shower.

After towelling dry my curly hair and getting dressed in a pale-yellow sun dress, I went back down stairs to call Aaron. I'd been waiting for this since I'd returned to the water last time, and had been lost in dreamy thoughts of him throughout the whole cycle. I picked up the phone and started to dial the number from memory when Elsie's voice shouted down the stairs.

'It's too early Luna, he'll still be in bed.'

I glanced up at the large clock on the wall above the fireplace and let out a small huff of air. She was right, the clock only read just after six, far too early to be making social calls. What was I going to do now?

I rested the phone back on the receiver and made my way slowly back up the stairs. Elsie came out of her bedroom fully dressed as I reached the top and gave me a knowing smile.

'Fancy a walk?' she asked as she pulled the door to and headed towards where I was lingering, 'I thought maybe we could have breakfast at that little café on the corner of Main Street.'

I smiled then, and nodded, then rushed to grab my bag and a pair of shoes. She always seemed to know what to say to make a situation better; she'd had years of practice, especially with me.

We left the house and walked quietly to the end of the driveway before turning our backs on the sea view and heading for the café she'd mentioned. This whole town was small enough to walk around in a day, so there was little need to be taking the car now. When I was younger, Elsie had driven me around so that my legs didn't get too tired, but I enjoyed being out in the fresh air, being able to smell the salt on the wind and hear the seagulls calling where they circled above us. I knew that Elsie was the same, she loved to be outside, the garden of the house was her little piece of Heaven, and she looked after it with the same care and devotion that she showed us. It was always bursting with colour as soon as the weather would allow it, and through the winter it was decorated with pretty windmills and ornaments so that there was still something for her to look at out of the glass doors on the back of the house. She also had a tiny herb garden on the windowsill of the kitchen that was always teeming with life, no matter the weather outside.

The café offered a cutesie environment that reminded me of something out of a story about a doll's tea party. The walls were decorated in pale pink and chocolate brown giving it a shabby chic look and the china was all white with lacey decorative patterns on. Elsie loved it here, and often suggested it for breakfast; their selection of pastries was second to none, their signature home baking the reason they had survived the bakery chain that had moved in on the next street over a few years back. Most of the townspeople still came here; the family that ran it had lived here for generations and knew just about everyone who walked through their door and made the little bell above it tinkle.

Elsie asked about the girls and what I had been up to since the last full moon. I gave her the play by play and she hung on every word I said, though I never felt like it was very interesting. My one day on land held much more excitement than the rest of the days all put together. They seemed monotonous to me, boring in their simplicity and routine. The day I spent ashore was full of adventure and held new and interesting things for me to see and learn about. My life under the ocean was like a movie playing in black and white, yet the colours here made me smile and want to burst into song like they do in the musicals.

When breakfast was over, Elsie held out the little phone from her bag in the palm of her hand and smiled.

'It's a reasonable time to phone him now.'

I smiled; she'd succeeded in taking my mind off the slow-moving time between coming ashore and being able to call, and it made my heart warm and tingly to know that she supported my decision to keep seeing Aaron.

I dialled the number and held the tiny phone to my ear and waited out the four rings before he answered with a weary hello.

'Aaron, it's Luna.'

'Luna, I was just wondering what time you'd be here,' he said and I could hear the smile in his voice.

'I'm here now,' I replied, feeling my answering smile, 'You free to do something?'

He'd said he would make sure he was free, but there was a little tiny seed of doubt in my mind that kept telling me that he would be busy.

'I am, want me to come get you? I can be at the house in about half an hour.'

I mouthed the timing to Elsie and she nodded; a genuinely happy smile on her face. I'd worried about leaving her when I was supposed to be ashore with her, but I'd always gone out exploring on my own, and she was encouraging my relationship with Aaron at every step so far.

'That sounds great,' I answered before we said our goodbyes and Elsie and I headed out of the café.

Aaron arrived exactly on time and I was out of the door and half way down the path to the car before he had even gotten out.

'Hey you,' he said as I bounced towards the car and held out his arms for me to walk into them.

'Hey yourself, did you miss me?' I asked as I wrapped my arms around him.

Being around him felt so easy, there had been no awkwardness, no feeling uncomfortable. I wondered whether it was the same for him. He never appeared to feel awkward, he'd kissed me last time like he had been doing it forever and now, he held me so tightly, like he was afraid I'd disappear again as soon as he let go.

'Like you wouldn't believe,' he replied when he finally released me from the hug.

I smiled and pushed up onto my toes to press a kiss to the underside of his jaw, but he turned at the last second and pressed his lips to mine. A tiny sound of pleasure escaped me at the touch, and he pushed one hand into the back of my now dry hair to hold me to him. Did it always feel this right?

He bundled me into the Jeep after releasing me from the kiss, sounding almost as breathless as I did, and hopped in at his side.

'Where are we going?' I asked

'The pool hall,' he answered, referring to what I assumed was the little bar across the road from the pub. It had been nicknamed the pool hall years ago when the owner had agreed to open it up in the afternoons for the kids of the town, in an attempt to keep them out of trouble. It had quickly become one of their favourite hangouts, and had succeeded in its agenda. The town barely had any trouble from the youngsters, and the guy who ran it, and his wife, had set up all sorts of projects over the years to keep them busy outside of the pool hall too. It was a win:win situation really.

'You have to line up the shot,' he joked as I pushed the cue into the white ball, 'Have you never played pool before?'

I watched the white ball roll clumsily towards the red and yellow ones at the other end of the table and laughed as it missed the three red ones I'd been aiming for. Turning to face Aaron, I shook my head. I was quickly proving that pool needed skill, or at least some practice; I'd never even picked up a cue before today.

'No, I never learned how to play,' I answered honestly.

Of course, I'd never learned to play, I'd never needed to. There wasn't long enough on land for me to dedicate too much time to one thing. I preferred to be out and about rather than stuck inside anyway. This was fine though; I got to watch Aaron show off another one of his skills.

He was wearing a tight black top with a band name on it that I didn't recognise and that showed off his sculpted body beneath it. His jeans were low slung and revealed a thin band of his black boxers at the waistband. His tattoo peaked out from under the sleeve when he bent over and leaned across the pool table to line up his next shot. I watched as he positioned himself against the table, leaning over the edge, but not actually on the table. He looked down the length of the cue and pushed it between his fingers a couple of times while he judged the right distance and power he needed to execute a perfect shot. When the cue finally made contact with the white ball, it slid silently across the green felt, knocked the yellow ball with a soft click and the yellow one rolled perfectly into the corner pocket.

I smiled when he stood up and grinned at me. He was clearly good at this, and I was lousy, but I was still enjoying watching him play. When he missed the next shot, he rounded the table as I stood up and put down my glass.

'Here,' he gestured to the edge of the table and I walked up and stood where he pointed.

He immediately moved behind me and put his arms around me, guiding me down to lean over the table. His hands were warm on mine and his stomach lay flush to my back, his skin warm even through the layers of our clothing. He whispered gentle instructions in my ear, but I didn't hear the words, instead all I heard was the warm caramel tone of his voice sliding over me and making me feel all gooey inside. He surrounded me completely, his smell, his warmth, his body; how was I supposed to concentrate?

'Look down the cue,' he whispered as I tried to focus on his words and do as he had said.

The cue was lined up so that the white ball was sat directly in front of one of my red balls further down the table, and the pocket sat just beyond that. Surely it couldn't go in from that far away. He pulled the cue back a little and then took his hand away from it and placed it on my waist. His breath was hot against my neck and I struggled to concentrate on anything other than his presence so close to me, possessing my senses. I could hear his breathing, low and throaty by my ear, smell the delicious scent of his skin mixed with the stale smell of beer that the pool hall held, feel his skin against mine when his fingers splayed out on my bare hip.

'Now take the shot.'

He made it sound so simple, yet even without him distracting me by being in such close proximity with me, I'm still not sure it would have worked. I concentrated on the shot, pulled the cue back gently and hit the ball. The white one rolled and hit the red one, but then the red on bounced off the corner and came back to near enough where it had started.

'Not bad, at least you hit the red one this time,' he teased.

I smiled back, his grin infectious, and took a step back from the table so that he could take his turn.

'I think it's safe to say that you won,' I said as he took shots to clear the table of the six red balls left.

'You got one in,' he said glancing up from his position at the opposite end of the table, 'That's not bad for a first game.'

He smiled, a wicked glint in his eyes as he looked me up and down, his gaze settling on my bare legs again for a few seconds longer than necessary. I stood still, not ashamed of my body in any way that made me feel I had to cover up, if I was honest; I liked the way he looked at me. It made my blood run hotter and my cheeks flush, but it made me feel good. He wanted me, despite my odd behaviour and lack of contact; I could see it in the look he gave me every time our eyes met, and the hungry way in which he eyed up my body.

'Want another drink?' he asked when he slid the pool cue back into the wall holder.

His glass was empty, and mine just had the ice slush left in the bottom. I nodded and smiled as he headed back over to the bar, throwing a look over his shoulder that had me crinkling up my nose in a way he called cute.

I studied him from behind, realising that he looked just as handsome and roguish from this angle as he did head on. His jeans hugged his hips snugly, showing off his size, and his top showed off the definition in his shoulders as he leant on the edge of the bar. My ears pricked when I heard my name and I strained to hear what he was saying.

'She's in town visiting her Aunt, and you can keep your eyes off her,' he joked with the older gentleman sat on the bar stool next to where he stood.

'She's a stunner, I'll give you that. You need to watch these out of towners though; never know when they're gonna disappear again,' the old guy said with a waggle of his index finger.

'Leave it out Fred,' Aaron said with a mock tap to his shoulder, and then picked up the glasses the bar tender slid in front of him.

He nodded to the bar tender and smiled at the other guy before making his way back to me, giving me a moment to appreciate him from the front again. The glass was cold when he pressed it into my hand and I squeaked a little before putting it down on the table.

'Who's that?' I asked, gesturing to the old guy he'd called Fred.

Aaron turned to see who I was looking at then turned back to me, taking a drink of his pint before answering.

'That's just Frederick; he lives over the road in the house next to the pub. He was asking about you, said he'd never seen you before.'

I didn't think I liked anyone asking about me, I didn't like to be noticed; it drew too much attention to the fact that I wasn't around much. Instead of making a big deal out of it though, I changed the topic of conversation.

'So, what do you want to do now?' I asked, not wanting to waste any of my time with him.

At some point, I wanted to nip back to the house to see if my sister or any of the other girls had come ashore this month. If they were going to, just after lunch was the most likely time to catch them.

'I don't mind,' Aaron answered, 'We can go for some lunch if you like.'

I nodded, and now that I thought about it, I was getting hungry.

'I have to nip back to see Aunt Elsie after lunch,' I slid into the conversation, 'If you're free later though I can come back for a bit before I have to leave.'

Lunch proved a little harder than the last time as Aaron's questions, though seemingly innocent, were proving more and more difficult to answer. He was peppering me with trivial questions like what my favourite movie was, who my favourite band was and what my earliest childhood memories were. They seemed like such obvious small talk when getting to know someone new, but the truth was, I didn't watch a lot of movies, or listen to much music, and my childhood memories included a lot of water.

I managed to use enough truth that I wasn't lying when I answered them, but also had to make jokes to cover up the oddities of some of the answers. I genuinely couldn't answer the music question, as even though I heard songs on the radio, I had no idea who the bands were that sang them. After trying to explain a song that I liked and us both ending up in a fit of giggles, I gave up on that one and moved on. My favourite movie had been hard to answer because as soon as I had been old enough to leave the house without supervision, I spent my time out exploring the town rather than being cooped up in front of the TV. The last film I remembered watching had been an old musical that Elsie and I had watched one miserable winter's day last year. I had to give him the name of that, which he had chuckled at and called me old fashioned. Questions like what my favourite colour was and what I liked to eat were much easier.

'My favourite colour has always been blue,' I answered, 'not like a bright blue though, the clear turquoise blue of the ocean,' I explained.

He smiled at me and nodded as he took a bite of his burger. We'd agreed on the burger bar on the corner of the street rather than heading all the way back down to the beach. We could go down there later, after I'd been back to the house to check on Elsie and see if my sister was out yet.

'Why the sea?' he asked.

I smiled, meeting his eyes and seeing the colour that I was describing.

'Because it's such a magical colour, so pretty and powerful all at the same time; think about what the water is, how demanding it can be one minute, then how calm and serene it can be the next.'

I fell silent, wondering whether I was revealing too much, but when he looked up again he was smiling.

'You really do love the water, don't you?' he asked, and I knew that he was thinking about his mother, not about how odd my answer sounded.

He understood. She'd understood. It crossed my mind that I would have loved to have met her, this woman that he held so highly in his heart. He talked about her as if she'd been everything to him, and I guess that was what a mother should be, someone who loved you unconditionally and made you happy with every breath they took. Her love for the water sounded like a massive part of who she was, and I was sure that had we met, we'd have bonded over that even though she would have never understood why.

I nodded in answer to his question, realising that I had been quiet a little too long, but he just smiled again as if he saw my thought patterns and understood my train of thought.

After we had finished, he drove me back to the house and promised to come back around five to pick me up and take me out for dinner somewhere near the beach. It was as if he had to spend time near the water every day, and it made me smile to think that he was so drawn to the ocean, that he was in the water regularly. It made the distance between us all month long a little less unbearable.

I wandered around the outside of the house, noting how quiet it was, and found Elsie in the back yard, sitting at the patio table with the parasol open to cast a shadow across the book she held in her hands.

'No one else come ashore?' I asked, sitting down on the little swing so that I could soak up some of the sun.

Having spent most of the morning inside with Aaron, I was missing my vitamin D. Elsie looked up from her book and set it on the table face down so that the spine creased under the pressure.

'Marina is out, she nipped into town to run a few errands, and Janine is upstairs sorting out a few things. I haven't seen any of the others yet, though your sister claimed there would be a couple of others.' She laughed. 'I just expect them when I see them these days.'

She joked about it most of the time, but I knew she hated that she didn't see as much of them anymore. I still didn't understand what had changed. When I was younger the girls were out all the time. We came out together in a morning to have breakfast, and then split up to do different things during the day time. Some of them returned to the water through the day, the rest of us stayed for dinner in the evening before heading back. When I got old enough, I talked Elsie into letting me stay till nightfall and she made sure that I returned in time. So much had changed since then; the girls didn't come ashore much through the winter at all now, and even when the weather improved, they weren't around much. I didn't understand it, but I held no power to change it, and now even when I was ashore, I was spending my time with Aaron. Was that selfish of me? Should I be spending my time with Elsie; why couldn't I have more time on land, then I wouldn't have this dilemma?

Before I could dwell too much on the idea, Janine came through the dining room with a small bag in her hand that she left on the table before stepping outside onto the patio. I smiled, but stayed quiet. We had never quite seen eye to eye in life, Janine was a couple of generations older than I was; I worked it out at around seventy if she'd been human, but she didn't look as old as the pensioners around town. She didn't agree with the amount of time I spent on land, she thought it reckless and odd, as mermaids we belonged in the water. I'd tried until I was blue in the face to explain to her that I felt like I belonged on land, but she wouldn't hear it, so we'd drifted into a silence that wasn't exactly uncomfortable, it just existed. We were taught to respect our elders, and I did, I had every respect for her, she was a powerful mermaid and a force to be reckoned with back in the ocean, but out here she was a literal fish out of water. I had to wonder what was so important for her to be on land; she didn't come ashore often.

She sat down in a chair next to Elsie, her back not quite to me, but not facing me either. I leant back on the swinging sofa and closed my eyes to soak up some of the sun whilst they talked. It wasn't quite loud enough for me to hear, but I caught snippets of the conversation. Janine mentioned a guy, though I didn't quite catch his name; Emmet maybe? And Elsie seemed somewhat distressed at whatever Janine was suggesting. In an attempt to stop whatever was going on, I stood up and headed for the kitchen, they clearly didn't want me to overhear if their hushed voices were anything to go by, so by stopping by them and asking if they wanted a drink I put a stop to the conversation. Elsie stood up to follow me, offering her help, and I heard her state, in no uncertain terms, that the 'conversation was over'.

Janine didn't follow us inside, but she didn't make any move to leave either and I hoped that she didn't intend on upsetting Elsie any further.

'I'm going back out for dinner Aunt Elsie,' I started quietly once we were in the kitchen, 'Do you think Marina will be back before then?'

She busied herself with the glasses as I pulled a glass jug of orange juice from the fridge, and turned to look at me once she had composed herself.

'She should be dear, she said she wouldn't be long,' she answered glancing at the clock on the wall, 'In fact I bet she's not long at all now.'

'Do you think Janine is waiting for her to go back with, or will she leave soon?'

My poor relationship with Janine was no secret to anyone, but Elsie understood more than anything. She knew just about everything there was to know about me, she knew more than even my sister did these days because she seemed to recognize my desire to be ashore, she listened when I spoke rather than telling me how I should be feeling. Plus, she'd known Janine a long time, so she also understood her beliefs about the water, therefore understanding our differences.

She laughed quietly as I poured the juice into the three glasses and then returned the jug to the fridge.

'I'm sure she won't be long Luna, you know how she is. She just needed to get something for the Royals.'

Before I had time to process what she had said and comment on it, she had passed me with two of the glasses and taken them back outside. I picked up mine from the side and followed her out, my mind buzzing with possibilities. Why would there be something out here that the Royals needed?

Returning to my seat on the sofa, I laid out on it to sunbathe while Janine finished up talking to Elsie. I kept glancing sideways at them, judging the look on Elsie's face, but she seemed more in control of the situation and Janine stood up not long after and said her goodbyes. I waved when she said bye to me, and she headed back inside, grabbing the bag she'd left and headed straight out of the front door.

Elsie looked at me over the top of her glass and her eyes dared me to ask what had just happened.

'Do I even want to know?' I asked with a soft chuckle.

'Probably not to be fair, she's been hot headed like that for as long as I've known her. Never gets any better for keeping.'

'What did the Royals want?' I asked, wondering whether I'd get a straight answer after the hushed conversation.

'Nothing important, they contact me from time to time that's all. Now tell me about your day, you said you were going back out again, where is he taking you?'

Her questions dismissed the last conversation and I knew better than to push the matter further. Instead I sat up to face her and answered her questions, excitement creeping back into my system at the thought of Aaron.

'He took me to the Pool Hall and tried to teach me how to play pool,' I said with a laugh and I saw it in her eyes that she knew I'd have been terrible, 'And I don't know where we're going tonight, we didn't decide.'

I fell silent, a plan falling together in my mind.

'Would you like to come with us Aunt Elsie? I'd like to know what you think of him.'

Her smile brightened at my question and she got up and came over to sit by my side as I rocked gently.

'I'd love to meet the boy who is putting that beautiful smile on your face, as long as you're sure I won't get in the way. I know you don't get to see as much of him as you'd like to,' she said in response and I felt the tears well in my eyes before I could stop them.

She put her hands over the top of mine and I looked down at her pale skin, the dark blue of her veins visible along the backs of them. When had she gotten so old? It was as if it had happened over night, her age was creeping up and I was beginning to worry about her spending so much time in this house on her own.

I didn't get a chance to answer her again before we heard the front door bang in the distance. Elsie looked up, the smile still on her face as she turned back to the house. Marina. It had to be. I stood up, helping Elsie up, and headed for the house. Marina came into view and I flung my arms around her neck, taking her by surprise enough that she let out a tiny squeal.

'Hey little sister,' she said as she put her arms around me to return the hug.

I don't know why it meant so much to me that she was here, I'd only seen her late last night before getting some sleep, but it felt like forever.

'How long you staying for?' I asked when I released her and she took a step back, smiling over my shoulder at Elsie.

I saw her nod, and turned to look at Elsie, but I was too late to catch whatever had just passed between them. Turning back to Marina, I saw the answer in her eyes. She wasn't staying much longer.

'I told the twins I'd take them for a swim before bed time, so I have to get going soon otherwise I won't be back in time. I'll come ashore next time though and we can go out for a bit if you like.'

'I'd like that a lot,' I answered with a smile.

After saying goodbye to Marina and agreeing to meet her by the border to The Kingdom after sunset, I returned my attention to Elsie.

'Want me to ask Aaron if he'd be okay with you coming?' I asked, picking up the conversation where we had left off.

'Coming where sweetheart?' Elsie asked, looking up from whatever she was doing on the sofa.

I left the pile of papers I was shuffling through on the side and went to stand in the doorway so that she could see me.

'Out for dinner with Aaron and me?' I reminded her.

'Oh, yes, I'd love to, go call him,' she answered enthusiastically.

The phone only rang a couple of times before Aaron answered and I smiled as soon as I heard his voice.

'Hey you, everything okay?' he asked.

'Everything is fine, I just have a question to ask you.'

'Go on,' he said, his voice full of interest.

'Would you be okay if my Aunt Elsie came with us for something to eat? I'd quite like for you to meet her, and obviously she's heard me talk about you, so,' I drifted off suddenly thinking that I was rushing him.

'I'd love to meet her,' he said before I could take any of it back.

'Yeah?' I asked, smiling again at the way he hadn't even had to think about it.

'Yeah, still okay for five?' he asked and I heard a car door slam in the back ground.

I looked over at the clock it gave us over an hour.

'Make it half past, I don't know whether she will want to get changed or not.'

After saying our goodbyes, I went to tell Elsie, and found her sat on the edge of the sofa waiting for the answer.

'He says he'd love to meet you,' I said and watched her smile widen like a child.

'I guess I'd better go get a shower then,' she said, standing up.

'He's coming to pick us up at half five,' I said as she rubbed my shoulders on her way past.

'That's fine,' she said and disappeared up the stairs.

I followed her up to change, smiling to myself all the way at how easy everything felt, and how the little pieces of my life were slipping together so seamlessly. If only it could be like this every day.

I was sat at the bottom of the stairs fastening the buckle on my sandals when Aaron knocked on the door.

The clock read twenty-five past; he was early and Elsie wasn't ready.

'Aunt Elsie, he's here,' I yelled up the stairs before opening the front door.

'I won't be a minute,' she replied, shuffling along the landing back to her bedroom.

She'd taken a shower and then dressed in a long purple dress with sequins around the bottom hem line. It looked lovely, and kept catching the light when she walked. She'd already admitted that she hadn't been out for a while, and was excited to meet Aaron.

'Hey you,' I said as Aaron turned my way when I opened the door.

He was wearing black jeans and an emerald green button-down shirt. It would seem Elsie wasn't the only one who had made an effort. I looked down at my little blue dress and suddenly felt extremely underdressed.

'You look beautiful,' Aaron whispered as he stepped over the threshold and put his hand on my waist to pull me in.

He really did say the right things at the right times. I smiled and pushed up on to my toes to meet him half way, his warm lips pressing against mine in a soft kiss before he pulled away and straightened up again.

Elsie came down the stairs then, bag in hand ready to go. When she got to the bottom, I felt the nerves running through my body.

'Aunt Elsie, this is Aaron,' I said without stepping away from where he still had his hand on my waist, 'Aaron, this is Elsie.'

Elsie smiled as Aaron held out his hand as if to shake hers, but when she put her hand in his, he did the same as he'd done when he had met me; he turned it over in his hand and pressed a kiss to the back of her hand. Such a charmer. Elsie was won over though. The smile that spread across her face reached her blue eyes making them sparkle and a faint blush appeared in her cheeks.

They hit it off straight away and the car journey was filled with conversation and laughter. I kept quiet for a little while, revelling in the happiness of two of the people I cared about getting along. How I hoped that it would be like this if I introduced Marina to him too, I wanted her to approve of him the way Elsie did. It was important to me that she liked him. But I'd deal with that one later down the line. For now, I liked that my life with Aaron was separate to the life I lived in the water.

Aaron took us back to the beach where he had made a table reservation at The Hut. Elsie smiled and linked her arm with mine as we made our way to our table in the little outside area. The sun was still warm on our skin and the light sea breeze that carried the salty air was refreshing, though it was a constant reminder that I had to go home again soon. I glanced up at the sky, noting the position of the sun; I still had a few hours yet.

Dinner passed in the same comfortable conversation filled way that the car journey had. Aaron asked Elsie a lot of questions like he had me, and she asked some of her own, clearly trying to figure him out. It made me realise that I had barely found out anything about him so far, so I listened eagerly, taking in every little detail so that I could sift through them later and work out which bits were important and which bits I didn't really need to remember. I found out that he worked several jobs. He'd told Elsie that one of his hopes was to run his own garage one day, so he was working for the garage in town three days a week. He also helped out Old Man Jones at the fruit and veg shop on the market. The way his eyes lit up when he spoke about that one told me he loved what he did, though I couldn't work out why. He also worked evenings and weekends at the rent-a-board surf shack on the beach. It was a wonder he ever had any time to himself, never mind time to spend seeing me.

I realised that I had zoned out of the conversation when Elsie nudged my leg under the table and looked at me expectantly.

'Sorry?' I said, not having heard whatever it was I was expected to answer.

'I said, you're coming back to see me again on the eighteenth of August, aren't you? Aaron here has made sure he wasn't working today so that he could spend time with you, he is going to do the same next month.'

I turned to Aaron who was sitting at the side of me and I smiled. He was taking time off work so that he could see me. As if he could get more perfect. I trusted Elsie knew what she was talking about and I nodded.

'Yeah, I'm back again next month,' I said, using her words so that I knew they fit right.

The rest of the evening slid by in a daze, I couldn't believe that Aaron fit so easily into my life despite the massive barrier between us. Elsie had smiled all night, and kept winking at me when Aaron wasn't looking. It was clear that she liked him, and that gave me a little hope that maybe, just maybe, this could all work out okay. When the sun started to fall towards the horizon, Elsie made the perfect excuse for it to be time to head home, meaning I didn't have to sound like the crazy person this time.

'Well, I think it must be nearly home time, and you have to be going soon too Luna,' she said checking her watch.

I nodded, linking my fingers with Aaron's where his hand lay on my leg under the edge of the table.

'I'll drive you home,' he said, reaching for his wallet to settle the bill.

'That would be lovely, though you can put that away, this is on me,' she said gesturing to his wallet and pulling out her own purse.

'You don't have to do that,' Aaron and I said almost in unison.

'I know I don't have to, but I want to,' she said with that, 'don't argue with me' tone.

I went quiet, knowing better than to argue, and Aaron conceded quickly too, obviously recognising the tone.

'It has been lovely to get out of the house, and it's been nice to meet the person responsible for the smile on Luna's face. I'm glad you found each other.'

I smiled and Aaron squeezed my hand, his smile the same. He'd never understand what it meant to me to have Elsie's approval, but it clearly meant something to him too, if his smile was anything to go by. He looked like the clam that kept the pearl.

The drive home was quieter, but no less comfortable. I'd let Elsie sit in the front, and I was knelt on the back seat behind Aaron, my hands draped over his shoulders, one hand linked with his while he used the other to control the car. The breeze blew through my hair, and the soft evening light cast shadows on the ground that crept up the walls they were so long. Everything seemed so perfect, until I remembered that I had to go back to the water soon. Less than an hour if the sun had its say, and it always had the last word.

Elsie went straight inside after thanking Aaron for a lovely evening, leaving me to say goodbye. The next full moon seemed to be so far away, the pain in my chest a physical representation of the loss it would be when I let him walk away again.

'Tonight was fun, your Aunt is great,' Aaron said quietly as he stood back against the Jeep.

I nodded, leaning into him and wrapping my arms around his waist. His arms slid around my shoulders and held me tight, like he was hoping that by holding on to me that I wouldn't disappear this time. It hurt knowing that I couldn't contact him, what must he think? I knew that it wasn't normal; everyone had a phone in the house, even if they don't have a mobile one. But he hadn't asked, hadn't pushed. He just held on like his life depended on it.

When I felt his lips against the top of my head, I turned to look up at him. His eyes shone in the dying light, that beautiful aquamarine colour that I loved so much. It had always been a favourite of mine, but now it held even more significance to me. He leant down to seal a kiss against my lips and I opened up to him, his hands sliding into my hair to hold me still. When he broke the kiss, he pulled his eyes from mine and looked out towards the sea as if he knew. I turned to look too, the sun setting quickly now, I had to get going.

As if he sensed the change in me, he released me and let me step backwards.

'Till next time?' he said, shoving his hands into his pockets.

'Next time,' I breathed quietly.

He didn't move as I made my way back down the path and to the door, and only turned to get back in the car after I had opened it and stepped inside. I watched him pull away from there, waving as he smiled back at me. Then I closed the door on that part of my life and headed up the stairs to where I could hear Elsie.

'I have to get back to the water,' I said, letting the defeat in my voice hang in the air.

'I know sweetheart, I'm coming with you.'

She stuck her head around the door and smiled, that little knowing smile that told me she knew how I was feeling without me having to say anything.

Back on the beach with the sand between my toes and the water lapping around my knees, I turned back to watch Elsie with her toes in the surf. The sun had almost disappeared now, and I felt a calmness come over me that I couldn't explain. Elsie liked Aaron; she'd spoken about him all the way down here, and said that she thought he was good for me. He was pushing my boundaries and showing me how to question my life on land. And most of all, he was putting a smile on my face that she said she hadn't seen since I was a child. I smiled in the security that she would always have my back, and that she saw the potential in Aaron and me, despite knowing the problems we were facing. She hadn't told me that it was a waste of time. She hadn't told me that I was being silly, fantasising about something that could never happen. She'd just smiled and told me that she approved.

She glanced up from the water to meet my eyes then, and nodded gently as a fair well. I turned back to the horizon and watched the sun disappear, throwing myself forwards into the tide and disappearing below the surface too. I pushed out of the skirt I was still wearing, and let it float back to the surface, my tail already trapping my legs until the next full moon. I pushed hard to go deeper into the ocean and let the salt water refresh my skin.

Till next time; his words still echoed in my head, and I held on to them with every fibre of my being.

Till next time; it couldn't come fast enough.

Angel McGregor

August

I loved summer; the sun came up so early and didn't set till late. There were far more hours in a day in summer, I always dreaded the winter months, so few hours out of the water. I watched from the depths as the nights quickly drew in, the daylight hours getting less and less every day; less time for me. It always shocked me, the difference only a month could make...

I saw him before he saw me this time; he stood with his back to the railings, casting a shadow down the steps to the beach. His jacket moved in the breeze as he stood motionless, just gazing out at the ocean. I wondered what he saw when he looked out there and I wondered what it must be like to live in a seaside town. The ocean held endless possibilities for those that stood on the beach and looked out across it, the horizon beyond their reach; the idea of freedom pulling them towards the unknown. Tearing my gaze away from him and out to the view that had him captured I sighed quietly to myself; I saw a watery prison that held me captive from the life I longed to be a part of. For a moment I wondered how he would react if I told him the truth, he seemed to love the ocean so much, but I dismissed the idea almost as quickly as I had thought about it. It was ridiculous. How many times had we had it drilled into us as merbabies that it was too dangerous to reveal ourselves to humans?

Shaking off the idea, I stuck close to the railings and crept up behind him to wrap my arms around his waist from behind.

'Miss me?' I asked when he turned around to wrap his arms around my shoulders in return.

'Always,' he replied.

I loved that response. I wondered what he thought about my lack of communication through the month, I knew that it wasn't normal for a girl my age not to have a mobile phone or social media accounts. I had seen the way they behaved while I was on dry land; he must think me very strange, but he had never brought it up since that first meeting. I'd considered setting something up a few months before I'd met Aaron, but decided that it would just highlight the fact that I wasn't around all month; something that wouldn't go down well as far as keeping our identities a secret. Instead, I stuck to the old-fashioned ways, a telephone and a pen and paper. I had a friend that I'd made when I was younger, who had moved further up the country when she was eleven. Now we wrote to each other. The time spans weren't a problem as it often took the letters a while to reach each other anyway. Elsie encouraged my friendship with Naiya as she and her mother knew who we were; they'd known Elsie a long time and Elsie had told me that they had their own secrets, so ours were always safe with them.

I stood almost eye to eye with Aaron due to the way the beach fell away from the ground, and he stood on the sand. The cut off denim shorts he was wearing looked damp and when I looked him over, his hair was wet.

'Been in the water?' I asked casually, whilst daydreaming of swimming with him, of splashing around in the shallow water and having his strong arms encircle me.

'I've been surfing this morning yeah, the guys just left,' he answered.

His bad boy image seemed to up its game every time I saw him.

'I didn't know you surfed,' I said with a mock pout.

He asked so many questions that he already seemed to know me inside out, despite how much vital information I had to leave out of my answers, yet I hardly knew anything about him due to not always asking questions back.

'You never asked,' he said as if to highlight my thoughts, 'But I think pretty much every guy, and many of the girls, in this town can surf. Can you?'

I shook my head.

'Nope, never learned.'

He tutted dramatically as he pulled me in to kiss me.

'We can't be having that, maybe I'll have to teach you.'

My skin warmed at the idea of him trying to teach me, about how much time it would take and how long we would have to spend together while I mastered it. But the smile never reached my face as I knew it was impossible. I couldn't go in the water too much or my nature would take over; assuming that I was returning to the sea.

'Yeah maybe,' I answered eventually, a very non-committal answer if ever there was one.

Instead of staying on the beach, we headed to the arcade on the strip of promenade that overlooked the beach. There were only three arcades in the town, it wasn't exactly a huge tourist attraction, but it got a few every now and again, and apparently part of the attraction of the sea side was gambling away your money. I laughed when we entered the little arcade, the coloured lighting giving off an ethereal effect that was a little disorientating to begin with. There was so much noise and so many lights that I stopped to blink hard and regain my stability. I was so used to the calm serenity of the water that the violation of my senses was almost too much to handle.

Aaron seemed to sense my resistance and backed up to where I had stopped just inside the doorway.

'You okay?' he asked, leaning in so that I could hear him without him having to shout.

'It's very loud in here,' I said in response, trying hard not to grimace at the invasion to my ear drums.

He laughed and slipped his hand into mine.

'Yeah, it can be a little overwhelming.'

We wasted a little money in the machines, played a game of air hockey, which I lost miserably at, and spent a fortune trying to get a dinosaur toy out of a claw machine. Aaron seemed to enjoy every minute of it, but after an hour I had to call it and asked if we could go back out into the sunshine.

One, I was missing the sun, I didn't understand why anyone would want to stay cooped up inside when the sun was shining so bright and warm outside; and two, the loud intermingling noises and the bright lights and flashing coloured bulbs on the machines were starting to get to me.

He didn't argue, just slid his hand into mine and led me back out towards the beach. We sat on a low wall that ran near the sand and he put his arm around my shoulder, pulling me close and pressing a kiss to my temple.

'Is it me, or does it feel like we've known each other forever?' he asked quietly, as if he didn't really expect an answer.

I smiled to myself, hadn't I just been thinking that earlier? Snuggling closer, I felt him tighten his grip around me and I revelled in the feeling of being wanted. Was this what love felt like? I'd read about it in fairy tales and romance novels, and I'd seen it on TV. I wondered whether this was what it felt like, this warmth inside me that always seemed to blossom when Aaron was around. The way my heart fluttered a little when he kissed me; how my skin tingled when he touched me and how it felt so right when he held me close like he was doing now.

Could it be, that a mermaid could fall in love with a human? And what of it? Could I really be happy like this, could I expect Aaron to be happy with this? Only getting to see me once every cycle, having to go weeks without hearing from me. Surely, he was going to start asking questions eventually, start wondering why I just disappeared when I left at night. Surely, he wouldn't go forever being content with this arrangement? But I'd be damned if I was ready to give it up yet. There had to be a way that I could make this work, I had to find a way that I could help him to understand.

When the sun reached its highest point, I told Aaron that I had to head back to the house for lunch. I wanted to see Elsie for a while, and I knew that Marina would be out this month. She always came ashore in August, I wasn't totally sure what the significance was, maybe because it was always reasonably warm by this time of year, but she was always out for a while this cycle and I wanted to spend some of it with her.

'I can come back out after, there'll be a few hours before I have to head home,' I said, hoping that I could see him again before I left.

'I'll be on the beach if you want to come back down there; I said I'd meet the guys for a surf. We can head back to mine for a bit if you like?'

He said it nonchalantly, but I saw the quick sideways glance he shot me and my heart beat increased a little. Was he suggesting what I thought he was? My pulse quickened now, and I felt the colour rising in my cheeks. I looked away, biting my bottom lip as the excitement at the possibility of seeing the rest of Aaron's body filled my mind with images.

I nodded, looking back to him and smiling, hoping that my face didn't give away what I was thinking.

'We don't have to do anything, we can just watch a film or something,' he said, apparently reading the expression on my face easier than I read the words on a page.

After arranging a rough time and stealing one or two more kisses, I headed back up the path towards the cliffs. The light breeze coming off the water was stronger up here and I pulled my hair over my shoulder and twisted it to stop it from flying around too much. I never tied it back, I loved my hair, and didn't like damaging it with the hair ties that girls used to style their hair. None of the girls in the water ever restrained their hair like the girls on land did, though some of them did cut it shorter, making it easier to manage, and we had our ways of styling the hair of the younger ones so that they didn't damage it; the whole starfish in the hair idea had to come from somewhere right? Elsie sometimes twisted her hair up into a bun, I liked that look on her, but her long grey hair was thinner than mine was, and when she left it down it seemed to be almost transparent, the light filtering through it making her look older than she was. The bun made her look younger somehow.

By the time I reached the house, I could hear the laughter and chatter coming from the open windows. I went in through the front door and ditched my shoes and bag under the little table so that they weren't in the way. I heard Mia first, and smiled as she came into view in the living room. Then I heard Betsy. I laughed and Mia gave me one of those knowing looks. Everyone heard Betsy. She couldn't creep up on a deaf man she was so loud sometimes.

'I can hear you Betsy,' I said as I walked through to the kitchen where she was hiding.

My sister was stood with the fridge door open and smiled to me as I passed her and stood in the gap with my hands on my hips. Betsy was exactly where I thought she was; crouched down next to the cabinet with her head tucked between her knees. Her turquoise hair caught the light and made me smile, no one could ever mistake her for anyone else with hair like that. No one was sure where it had come from, or why it was that colour, but it was all natural; her tail was the same colour when we were in the water. Now though, she wore a pale lavender long sleeved jersey top and jeans.

'Cold Betsy?' I asked with a smirk.

A Handful of Secrets

I was walking around in shorts and a strappy top; it was beautiful outside, a light breeze making the afternoon sunshine bearable.

'It's cold in here,' she replied, finally standing up from her hiding crouch.

Betsy was one of those girls that everyone loved, and as I stood here looking at her, wondering what Aaron would make of her, I realised why. She was so full of life, always happy and exploding with energy. It was the same as being around the merbabies; all that excess energy that they didn't know what to do with. That just about summed up Betsy. That and the clumsiness of course, and as if to prove my point, as she stood up she knocked the side with her elbow with a loud bang. Marina turned from her investigation into the contents of the fridge in time to see Betsy pull away from the side to protect her elbow, and knock straight into the bowl of salad at the other side of her and sent it tumbling to the ground.

'Betsy, be careful,' Elsie said sternly as she came to investigate the commotion.

How many times had I heard that in my lifetime? Betsy was a whole calendar year of moons older than I was, so I'd grown up hearing those words, 'Be more careful Betsy.' She could be such a klutz. Her heart was in the right place, but chaos seemed to follow her everywhere she went, causing more hindrance than help.

I moved to help Betsy clear up the mess she'd made and bumped up against her shoulder lightly. She turned to look at me with her 'oops face' as we called it, the 'I'm sorry, I didn't mean to' look that made her look so innocent. I smiled in response, knowing she hadn't meant to, and finished up with the salad leaves on the floor. We put them in the bin and I offered to help wash and prepare some more ready for lunch.

Without showing my distress at the hold up, I smiled through the chaos and helped until everything was back on track again. I was dying to get back to Aaron, but I had wanted to come back for lunch, knowing that there would have been more of the girls out this month. There were only three of them, which made my heart bleed for Elsie, I knew that she missed them terribly; she was always talking about them when she had the chance, always asking about them and how they were doing. I hated that they wouldn't come out more, even if it was only for Elsie. Personally, I couldn't see why they didn't want to be out every full moon like I was; why they didn't want to spend as much time as they could with their feet. But I also knew that I was the abnormality there. No one could understand my love of the land, no one, not even my sister understood my longing for more time without my tail. What I wouldn't give for the fairy tale ending like the mermaid in the movie had gotten; I think I'd have even given up my voice for it.

'Are you going back to the water now, or are you staying here with Elsie?' I asked Marina as I gathered my bag ready to head back to the beach where I'd left Aaron.

'I was going to stick around for a little while yet, at least until the temperature starts to drop, but I doubt I'll still be here when you get back,' she said as if she was afraid to upset me.

'That's fine,' I lied, I'd have loved her to wait till dark with me, I wanted her to watch the sunset with me, even if it was just once.

'I'll head back for you at sunset and swim back to The Kingdom with you if you like?' she asked instead.

I smiled then, she hadn't done that in years. She used to come and get me like that when I was younger, meet me just below the surface where Elsie could see that we were back together, and then swim back with me, racing and chasing me all the way. She'd ask about what I had done on land, what I had learned, and I'd talk all the way, chattering excitely about all the new things I'd seen. Even then she hadn't understood what had drawn me to the shore, she rarely came with me, and even then, it was only for a few hours. Now though, the journey seemed so far that it wasn't worth travelling more than necessary.

'I'd like that,' I said, genuinely happy that she would put in the effort to swim the distance twice in one day.

We agreed to meet just around the corner from the bay, a little after dark, and then I made my way back down to speak to Elsie. As I made my way through the living room towards the back of the house, I stopped to speak to Betsy who was perched on the arm of the sofa, her socked feet pushed behind the pillow where Mia sat looking at a magazine. I couldn't believe they were going to spend their few hours on land here in the house.

'Why aren't you at least out in the garden where the sun is shining?' I asked, genuinely confused.

She shook her head and Mia looked up from her magazine.

'It is one of the warmest months we'll get; enjoy it while you're ashore.'

'Can I come with you?' Betsy asked, suddenly sitting straighter, a look of excitement crossing her pretty face.

'That wasn't quite what I meant,' I said, not sure I wanted her to meet Aaron.

'Where are you going anyway?' my sister's voice drifted down the stairs ahead of her.

I frowned. This wasn't how I'd planned on telling her. It was on my 'to do' list, but I'd wanted to speak to Marina alone, and in the water where she was more comfortable.

'To meet a friend,' I offered, hoping she wouldn't probe too much.

'Yeah? Where are you going?' she asked, giving Betsy a nudge as she drew level with the back of the sofa.

Betsy wobbled and slid down the chair arm, landing in a heap on top of a rather disgruntled Mia. I laughed as she shoved her off and Betsy ended up sprawled across the rug.

'You're so un-elegant it really is a wonder you've survived this long,' Mia snapped as Betsy sat up and huffed.

Marina turned back to me and then looked down to Betsy who was looking hopeful.

'We're going to the beach,' I said, purposefully being obtuse and offering as little information as possible.

'Can I come?' Betsy asked again when I didn't answer her from before.

'We could all go,' Marina said suddenly, 'I'd like to see who you're hanging out with these days.'

She smiled, and I wished that life was simpler. A part of me swelled with happiness at the idea of Marina wanting to look out for me and get to know Aaron, but the other part of me knew that she wasn't going to approve of the relationship that I was attempting with him, even if he did have rather a lot of gaps in his understanding about my life.

'I think you'd change your mind pretty quickly when I tell you who he is,' I said with a sigh.

'He?' Mia questioned, suddenly interested enough to close her magazine and put it on the floor.

'He,' I confirmed, 'His name is Aaron, and I really like him, and for some ridiculous reason he likes me too.'

I saw the look on Marina's face and knew that she was about to lose it when Elsie walked into the room and put a hand on her shoulder, looking to Mia and then to Betsy before speaking.

'Aaron is a lovely boy, Luna is being very careful, and I am aware and watching the situation,' she said calmly.

She looked at me as she spoke the next bit, confirming that I understood the risk I was taking by spending so much time with him.

'Luna is a smart girl and she understands that the secrets are secrets for a reason. Aaron seems to have accepted her distance during the month, he pops over occasionally and asks about her, and I tell him the same thing every time; that I haven't heard from her either. I don't know why he takes that answer without question, or why he hasn't asked more questions. He trusts Luna, and I trust her too. Don't assume you know what is best for her when you don't spend your time with her ashore. She knows what she is doing.'

Elsie went quiet and the others remained silent. No one argued with Elsie, and I couldn't explain in words how much it meant to me that she was on my side. I smiled at her and she nodded, leaving as quietly as she'd entered. Following her from the room with none of the girls stopping me, I promised her I'd be back before dark so that I could see her before I returned to the water, then I headed back to the girls.

'Still want to come with me?' I asked, hoping that they'd changed their minds.

'Maybe next time,' Betsy said from where she now sat cross-legged in the middle of the rug.

Marina gave me a hug but didn't say anything as I left and I had to wonder now whether she'd be waiting for me like she'd promised, or whether she would just see me back at The Kingdom.

I headed back out and skipped down to the path that led along the cliff tops. Aaron had said he'd be on the beach, or in the water. I headed that way, a spring in my step now that Marina knew about him, even if she wasn't sure about him, I could work my way up to that. It wasn't quite how I'd planned on her finding out, but at least now she knew, and I could work on getting her to meet Aaron one day. I think if she gave him a chance, she'd like him too. He would make her laugh just like he did me, and she'd understand what I saw in him despite her reservations to being on land so much during the full moon. Maybe this would help her understand what drew me to the shores; Aaron was giving me purpose, perhaps that would be enough to help her see why I loved the land.

The sun was starting to sink slowly when I made it back to the beach, I still had a good few hours before I had to be back in the water. Aaron had said we could go back to his for a couple of hours if I wanted to, and now that I was stood on the sand watching him surf, I could feel the nerves building inside me alongside the excitement. I knew what could happen if I agreed to go back to his place, in theory we had known each other months now, even if in reality we had only seen each other for a few days. It didn't feel like just a few days when I was with him, I felt like he knew me, the real me, just without all the baggage of being a mermaid. But aside from that, he knew more about me than anyone, apart from maybe Elsie.

He saw me standing on the beach and waved from his position on his board. Him and two other guys were sat straddling their boards just behind where the waves were breaking. The tide wasn't very strong, so the few attempts I'd seen of them actually surfing weren't great; they only really glided for a few seconds before turning and paddling back again. It was just another place for them to hang out, and the sun was still shining, the temperature still hot enough for them not to need shirts on, so why end up indoors? I couldn't blame them, but I daren't join them either; it was too unpredictable what might happen.

I made myself comfortable on the sand while I waited for Aaron to join me. When he did, the other two stayed in the water. Aaron came up to me, blocking the sun with his body and I couldn't help but stare. The water ran from his oil-slicked tanned skin like something from a magazine advert, and when he ran his hand through his hair, the curls wrapping around his fingers, he shook water on to the sand by my feet making me squeal. I smiled up at him and he knelt down in front of me, leaning in to kiss me. Water dripped from him onto my dress, but I didn't care, I slid my hand into his hair and pulled him closer as he sealed his lips over mine. I could taste the salt water on his lips and revelled in the familiarity of it, licking the residue from my bottom lip as he pulled away.

'Sorry,' he said as he pulled back and laughed, gesturing to the water droplets all over the dress I'd changed into.

'I'll live, I'm sure, you have fun?' I asked nodding back to where his friends were still messing around in the water.

'Yeah, I'm going to have to teach you one day,' he said as he stood back up and reached for the surf board.

We headed back to the Jeep, where he loaded the board and pulled a towel from the back seat to dry his hair and shoulders. He pulled on a dry shirt then simply put the towel on the seat and hopped in.

'I'll dry off and change back at home, you still okay going there?' he asked before putting the car into drive.

I nodded; the excitement and nervousness battling for top spot inside me. The journey was quiet for us, no questions or silly conversation, but it wasn't awkward either; it never was. When he pulled up in front of a little house in the middle of several others, I smiled at the ordinary look of it. I was so used to Elsie's big white house sat on the cliff top that I sometimes forgot that most houses were these cute little red bricks that stood in a line in town. Aaron had parked at the back of the house and he led me up the garden path and in through the little brown back door.

The sound of cheering floated down the hallway from what I presumed was some sort of sport playing on the TV and there was a faint smell of stale beer, but the house was cheery in its own way.

'Remember I have to be home before dark, I have to go home at nightfall,' I said using as much truth as I dared, though not knowing how to word it to make it sound more normal.

He nodded, as he pushed open the door to his bedroom. The rest of the house fell away as we stepped over the threshold; I could tell that Aaron had put a lot of effort into making this space his own. Three walls were a beautiful lagoon blue with shells stencilled across the bottom and the wall behind me was the colour of the sand on the beach where I first set foot each full moon. There was no way that I couldn't imagine his mom when I stood looking at the way it was decorated. He propped his surf board up by the door and then closed it with a gentle click.

'We don't have to do anything,' he reminded me again, though the warm fuzzy feeling deep in my stomach had different ideas.

I had no idea whether mermaids were supposed to have sex with humans, but it wasn't going to stop me trying. Biologically we were human when we transformed, so surely it could all work like normal.

Instead of a reply, I pulled him towards me and took a step back up against the wall so that he pressed against me, trapping me against the cool paint with his hot hard body. His shorts were still wet and the water quickly started seeping into the material of my dress. He put his hands on either side of my shoulders, pressing them flat to the wall and then leant in to kiss me. He didn't kiss me as I expected though, at the last second, he missed and pressed his lips to my throat, gently nipping with his teeth before moving a fraction lower towards my collar bone and doing the same. I melted. My hands moved of their own accord and slid up the edge of his top and pressed against the hard muscle of his abdomen, still damp from his swim. He responded to my movements by slipping one hand from the wall and letting it drag over my shoulder, disturbing the strap of my summer dress so that it slipped down my arm and he continued down to my waist where he gripped my hip and pulled me against him.

A gasp left my lips as I felt his erection press against my belly; for some reason I hadn't expected that, though with some thought I knew the ropes. I'd read enough books to know how this worked, Elsie's shelf was full of romance novels and the odd erotica novel; it was amazing what a girl could learn from them.

Aaron covered my mouth with his, breathing heavy as his tongue sought out mine. Kissing him was becoming second nature now, and I melted into him, exploring his mouth with mine. I let my hands wander up towards his chest, my nails scratching lightly against his sweat damp skin. The weather was still warm and humid, making everything sticky, and damn it was hot.

It felt like someone had suddenly turned up the heating, and my pulse skyrocketed. Aaron's body against mine was like fire on my skin, but in a good way, and I pushed forwards so that my body was flat to his. In response he pushed back, making sure that I was firmly pinned to the wall and he slid the hand still by my head into my hair at the nape of my neck and pulled gently. My head fell back as he took charge, exposing my neck to his kisses once more and making my knees go weak.

Slowly, he pulled away, stepping backwards towards the bed and pulling me with him. He turned me at the last second and I fell backwards, giggling as I hit the mattress with a soft thump. I rearranged the skirt of my dress to cover up my modesty as he put one knee on the bed by my legs.

'I've never done this before,' I whispered as he moved over the top of me, the nerves suddenly taking pride of place.

He froze then, pulling back and meeting my timid gaze. I knew what was coming, and I wanted it to happen, but now that we were considering it, I realised that all the books in the world couldn't prepare me for what happened next. I didn't have a clue what I was doing; I barely knew this body, never mind what to do with it.

'Never done what?' he asked, although I was positive he knew what I meant.

'This, any of it,' I said hoping that he didn't make me explain in too much detail.

He sat up then, straddling my thighs where my dress was bunched up a little from his previously wandering hands. His gaze drifted hungrily down to where my skin was exposed but he let out a deep sigh and looked back up to meet my eyes.

'We don't have to do anything Luna, I can put on a film and we can just lie and talk.'

I frowned, a little disappointed. Did he not want me like that? Had I read this all wrong? Not finding any words to respond with, I lay quietly beneath him, watching his chest rise and fall as his breathing slowly returned to normal. I linked my fingers on my stomach and tried not to fidget

'Luna?' he asked, searching my face for something.

I looked up, trying hard not to fist my hands in my dress and show my nerves.

'I didn't say I didn't want to,' I whispered, 'I just thought you should know that I didn't know what I was doing.'

Admitting my lack of knowledge suddenly seemed more revealing than some of the other situations we'd found ourselves in recently. How could I explain how I was still so inexperienced at my age without it sounding silly?

'Do you want to carry on?' he asked.

I nodded, pushing myself up into a sitting position so that I was facing him. Nervously, I pushed my hands into his hair and pulled him to me so that I could kiss him again. I hoped that it was enough of an answer, and was rewarded when his hands returned to my waist and he pushed me back down onto the bed.

His hands held me firmly as he pressed a hot kiss to my lips, gently searching for more. I gave him everything I had in the kiss, hoping that it proved that I was up for this; my nerves were totally due to my lack of experience, nothing else.

After a few minutes making out, he rolled off me and propped himself up on his elbow at the side of me, his free hand resting gently on my stomach.

'So, you've never done anything with a guy?' he asked from beside me.

I shook my head; this wasn't really something I wanted to discuss.

'Luna, how? I bet you had guys all over you at school,' he said with a genuine look of confusion on his face.

I shook my head again, figuring it was better to stay quiet than start coming up with lies to cover for my inexperience.

'Okay,' he said, obviously realising that I wasn't going to get into any details, 'We'll take this slow.'

He slipped my lacy white underwear down my legs and dropped them on the floor then positioned himself on his elbows over me. A smile turned up the corners of his mouth giving him a devilish look about him as he slowly pushed my legs open and settled between them. My dress was still covering me up for now, but my blood began to pump faster at just the thought of him down there.

Slow, I reminded myself. He'd promised we'd take it slow.

As I relaxed and let him ease open my legs, he ran his hands up the inside of them making me squirm. He stopped as he reached the tops and then moved back down, gently massaging my inner thighs, his touch getting firmer with each stroke, and not to mention higher.

I felt the tingle run through me when his fingers grazed the sensitive parts of me and a shudder escaped me along with a little moan.

'Relax, Luna,' Aaron said quietly as he moved my dress up out of his way.

I tried, I really did. I relaxed my legs a little and let him keep massaging them, his touch a lot firmer now, and his fingers rubbing gently down the most sensitive part of me. My breathing had become quick and shallow and my heart felt like it was trying to batter its way out from behind my ribs, but damn it felt so good.

When I felt his breath at the apex of my thighs I felt myself tense up again. I closed my eyes and tried to concentrate on relaxing. It made it worse. Taking a deep breath, I let my legs fall open again and I felt the soft laugh escape Aaron in the evidence of his warm breath. But when the tip of his tongue traced my wet opening, there was no way I could concentrate. My body took over and the shudder that ran through me was too powerful to control.

'Damn you're sensitive,' Aaron said looking up at me, 'You okay?'

'Mmhmm,' I managed before letting my head fall back to the pillow.

When he pushed his finger inside me I thought I was going to explode, the sensation that rocked my body was exhausting and I wondered how on land or water I was going to survive it. My breathing was laboured and Aaron kept eye contact with me the entire time. He was still inside me as I breathed through it, gulping in air to keep me awake.

After a few minutes of moving gently inside me, he pulled away and I let out a sigh of disappointment which he heard and flashed me a cocky smile. He crawled back up the bed, his wet shorts drying out now, and sat straddling me.

He slid my dress straps down my arms gently and I sat up from the bed to let him pull it up and over my head. A tiny gasp escaped him and I saw his eyes roam over my upper body. I wasn't wearing a bra, I never did. That was one of those things that I didn't quite understand, and wanting to be human or not wasn't going to make me wear something that was so unnecessary, and so damn uncomfortable. Swimming didn't cause me a problem, so walking sure wasn't an issue.

When his eyes met mine again they were alight with passion and as my dress hit the floor, I found myself flat on my back again with his body pressed to mine. He was naked from the waist up, and his skin was hot against mine.

His hands were on me, and his mouth sealed back over mine. There was a new hunger in his actions now, as if seeing my body had fuelled his. My hands roamed his back and sides, my nails scratching lightly and my fingertips digging in when his hands began moulding my breasts.

He worked my body into a frenzy; his hands everywhere, his lips and tongue close behind. I was laid flat on my back, my arms by my sides and my hands balled into the sheets as he pushed two fingers inside me again. A moan slipped past my lips and he looked up, checking that it was a good noise. I saw the corners of his mouth tip up in a tiny smile as his gaze met mine and I drew in a sharp breath when he pushed a little harder inside me.

When he pulled away from me again and stood up, he pushed down his shorts and ran his hand up and down himself. I felt my eyes widen, the sight sending pure need zapping straight through me. He smiled when he saw me looking, and returned to the bed, climbing on top of me and leaning in to kiss me again. I could feel his erection laying hot and hard on my belly as he pressed against me now, no barriers between us. It felt right, despite the nerves that were rattling around inside me, the contact between his skin and mine felt right.

One hand roamed my body again, slipping down to my hip and then back up, tracing a line up my chest and between my breasts. I wasn't very big on the chest, I'd seen the way some of the girls had developed, but I wasn't exactly self-conscious about my body. We were who we were and I didn't need a massive chest to make me attractive. Aaron didn't seem to mind either, his hands cupping me and massaging gently as if I'd been made to fit him.

When his hand returned to the bed by my head, he leant down to press a kiss to my forehead, his hips gently pushing against mine.

'This is gonna hurt Luna, I'm not gonna pretty it up for you,' he said as he held himself steadily over me.

'Really?' I asked with a grimace.

He'd said I was tight inside, which I guessed was because nothing else had ever gone in there, but surely it shouldn't hurt. As he reached for the draw beside the bed and retrieved a small shiny packet from a box just inside it, he just nodded.

He tore open the packet with his mouth and offered the contents to me. I frowned. I was pretty sure that this part wasn't in the books.

'Want the honours?' he asked gesturing to the packet with his chin.

I pressed my lips together so that I didn't say anything stupid right about now and gave him a shy smile.

'I get it,' he said, though I was pretty sure he didn't, 'Just take the condom, I'll do it.'

Carefully, I took the little cream disc from the packet and tried not to drop it. Slippery little thing. Aaron discarded the shiny wrapper and took the disc from me then manoeuvred himself so that he could put his hand between us. I let out a little gasp when he slid the disc over his erection, smoothing it down to cover himself. Yep, that was definitely not in the books, and I had to admit that it was a little hot watching him stroke himself like that.

He held himself in his hand and nudged my legs apart with his knees, then positioned himself at the entrance to my body. I was still wet from all the foreplay, and he slipped pleasurably against me.

It didn't take long before I was writhing beneath him, especially when he rubbed all the way up and over my clit. I bucked against him, not sure whether I wanted more pressure or less and then he slid the end of himself into me. I gasped, the pressure strange yet immensely satisfying.

'You ready?' he asked, waiting for me to look up from where our bodies were now joined.

I nodded with a smile and felt my teeth in my bottom lip. He leant down and kissed me, releasing my lip with a little growl.

'You want me to go slow, or all at once?' he said, and I had to wonder how much effort it was to keep so still inside me.

I wriggled slightly, feeling him move a little and inhaled at the slight tingle of pain that ran through me. Shrugging my shoulders, I frowned again. How could I answer that when I had no idea what was coming next?

'Okay, all at once, then you can relax a bit, breath in,' he said as he pushed a little more into me, 'And breath out fast.'

I breathed out quickly just like he said and as I released the breath he pushed into me all the way, his hips meeting mine with the sound of skin on skin. The tears slid down my cheeks before I could stop them and my breath came in short, sharp bursts.

'Deep breaths Luna, once it passes it'll feel much better. I promise.'

I could hear in his voice how much he didn't like hurting me, but I realised that it was a necessary evil. He adjusted his position over me so that he could wipe away my tears with gentle hands, his erection now pulsing inside me. I felt stretched, he shouldn't have fit and I could feel it where he had forced his way through. As he kissed my cheeks and mouth, he kept still while my breathing slowly returned to normal.

When the pain started to subside a little, I began to wriggle beneath him. The fullness of having him inside me was sort of exciting, and the pressure that it was forming in my stomach was sending a fluttering through me that was making me clammy.

He put a hand behind my knee and lifted my leg up towards my chest when he began to move and I felt the pressure build quickly, and the friction inside me set off a series of events that I could barely describe in words. The fire in my tummy increased to the point where I couldn't lay still, and Aaron kept laughing at me when I voiced it. He pressed a kiss to the hollow at the base of my throat while he was still sliding in and out of me and my skin went tingly all over. My breathing became laboured once more and I began to feel faint from the lack of oxygen entering my body. I felt my body clench around him, and the sensitive nerve endings inside me exploded, sending a tidal wave of pleasure through me.

'Aaron?' I said, not really sure what I was asking for.

'Let go Luna,' he replied, his voice deep and husky with want.

Let go of what? I released his arm where I had a death grip on it and felt the build-up low in my tummy that was threatening to burst. It felt like needing the toilet, but tingly in a different way.

I let out a series of tiny moans and felt my body rising off the bed. Aaron pushed me back down and gripped my hip to hold me in place. He pressed his body over mine, his skin slick with sweat from the exertion, and whispered in my ear, his breath hot against my already flushed skin.

'That feeling in your tummy, push against it.'

I didn't quite understand what he was talking about, but I tried to follow his instructions. Instead of tensing and tightening against the pressure that was built up inside me, I relaxed and pushed against Aaron, meeting his thrust with a little more force than he'd accomplished on his own.

Whatever I did was what he'd intended, I was sure of it. A series of reactions ricocheted around my body. The pressure in my lower abdomen exploded with force and sent shivers racing across my skin, I grabbed Aaron's arms where they were holding him up over me and dug my nails into his skin. The moan that escaped me was more animal than human and I heard his responding growl deep in his chest. White spots appeared in front of my vision and I realised a second too late that I had forgotten to breathe. Darkness filled my vision before there was nothing.

'Luna?' I heard Aaron's voice as if he was stood with his head in a metal bucket.
'What happened?' I asked when I opened my eyes and found him looking down at me with concern clear in his.
'I think you passed out,' he said with a chuckle, 'I can honestly say that I have never had that happen to me before.'
When I made a move to sit up I felt dizzy, and he pushed me back to the bed. I realised then that he was still naked, and when I glanced down at my own body, so was I, though he had thrown a blanket over me. I felt like I should be concerned that I had no clothes on, or that I had lost consciousness, but my body was too exhausted for me to expend too much energy caring. A smile crept across his features as he watched me with eyes full of desire.
'You okay?' he asked, leaning in and pressing a kiss to my forehead.
I nodded, licking my lips and realising that I was ridiculously thirsty. How did anyone do this regularly? I was knackered, and I had to swim home yet. Sleep had to be on my agenda soon, I was already planning the possibility of sleeping for the next few stages of the moon in my head when Aaron's low husky laugh interrupted my thoughts.
'What are you thinking?' he asked.
I laughed in response.

'I was considering how long I was going to have to sleep to recover from this,' I said, not feeling as shy as I expected to.

When I looked at him, his eyes were still foggy with desire and the crinkles around his eyes from his smile made me smile too. There were little crescent marks in the tops of his arms from where I had dug my nails in too hard, and his skin was damp with a shiny layer of sweat. I dreaded to think what I looked like, and made no effort to do anything about it. Aaron didn't seem to care; he was looking at me like he had uncovered the secrets of the world. I still couldn't believe that he seemed to care so deeply for me when he only got to see me once every thirty days.

We knew so much about each other, and he seemed to understand me so well, yet we had only actually seen each other a handful of times. He was bound to lose interest soon. He could have any girl he wanted; I knew that as much as I knew that the sun would set tonight. Eventually he would get bored of waiting around to see me; I had to make the most of this while I could.

'How dark is it?' I asked suddenly, aware that for the first time ever on land, I had lost track of the sun.

'It's a little after seven,' Aaron answered.

'But where is the sun?' I asked again, sitting up and looking out of the window.

He frowned, and I realised too late that my question seemed odd, he'd given me the time, that should be a normal answer. But I didn't know what time the sun would set, I never checked because I knew how long I had from the position of the sun in the sky.

Aaron got up and went to the window. He was clearly confused by our conversation, but he answered me none the less.

'Sun is setting, why?'

'I have to go; I have to be back at the house before dark. I have to go home.'

My dress was on the floor and I slid it back over my head while I searched for my underwear. I didn't want to leave, but there would be serious consequences if I wasn't back in the water. I would change back despite my location; I couldn't do that in front of Aaron. I couldn't do that in front of anyone. The water was our only safety.

'I'll take you home,' he said, sounding reserved to the fact that I was going to disappear again.

When I looked up at him he had my lacy boy shorts hanging from his first finger of his left hand and he crooked the one on his right at me, beckoning me towards him. I obliged, with a grin on my face.

When I reached him, I put my hand out to take them from him, but he pulled them away from me.

'When are you back again?' he asked, sliding both hands around my waist.

'Next month,' I replied, kissing him.

He mumbled something against my lips that I couldn't quite work out, but when I pulled away he repeated it.

'Can I convince you to make it sooner?'

The look on his face shot straight to my heart, how I wished I could. How I wished it was that simple.

'I can't,' I said, dipping my head and dropping my gaze.

In lieu of an answer, he tipped my head back up with a gentle press of his finger and sealed his mouth over mine again.

'It's okay.'

He dropped me off at the front door and we made the arrangements for next time; I'd checked the full moon using the calendar on his phone so that I could give him the date, and he promised to pick me up at ten that day. I made my way back into the house slowly, I still had about an hour before the sun was gone, so I wasn't too worried about time, but I wished that I'd been able to give him a different answer when he'd asked if I could come back sooner. Aaron waved from the Jeep as I shut the door and the last thing I saw was his smile.

The soft click echoed through the house, and I heard Elsie speak upstairs. Who was she talking to? And at this time of night? Surely the girls were all back in the water by now. I tiptoed up the stairs and put my bag on the bed, slipping out of my shoes and kicking them into the shoe bin by the door.

'Don't worry about it, there is no risk. She knows what she's doing, and I'm keeping an eye on the situation.' A pause. 'I know that too, but like I said, she's a smart girl. I know the plan, but today is not that day.'

Was she talking about me? Or was I just reading too much into the call because it was unexpected. I suppose she could be talking about anyone, I had no idea how many people she socialised with during the month.

'I will do that in the next couple of days, and I will try and get up there soon. If not though, I will see you at the next council meeting.' A shuffle as if she had gotten up from her seat. 'Talk to you soon.'

I heard the click as she returned the phone to the cradle and then her footsteps as she came down the hall. She poked her head around the door with a warm smile.

'I thought I'd heard you get back, you want me to come down to the beach with you?'

I smiled. It was silly, she didn't have to, but I loved it when she took me back to the beach; it brought back so many happy memories from when I was a child. She'd always walked back with me then, though there was usually someone else around too. She never took me into the water, but she had always watched, standing just where the water rushed around her ankles as we left.

'Who were you talking to on the phone just now?' I asked, curious as we headed out for the path that wound down to the cove.

'An old friend,' she answered without missing a beat.

I was almost positive that she had been talking about me and my relationship with Aaron, but I couldn't figure out who would have a vested interest in me or my comings and goings. Staying quiet for a few hundred yards, I mulled over the possibilities, Elsie stayed quiet beside me, and I had to wonder whether she was trying to work out her own next move.

'Anyone I know?' I asked, already knowing the answer would be no.

'He is a friend that lives in the city, maybe one day I will introduce you. I think you'd get on with his daughter, she's about your age if I remember rightly.'

Elsie drifted into silence and I jogged a few steps ahead so that I could turn to face her. She looked confused, as if the information that she had just shared with me had crept up on her in some way. I wondered whether to push her, but she seemed to be fighting her own demons, so I left her to think. For now.

When we made it to the steps that hugged the side of the cliff wall, I took the lead; a pattern that I followed without really thinking about it. It made sense to me to go first, the same way that Elsie had always looked after me as a child. Even though I didn't understand what was going on with Elsie, I knew that she wasn't well. I knew there was something going off, and it was my job to look after her. Role reversal much?

When I reached the beach, my toes curled into the sand immediately as it rushed up and over the edges of my pretty white sandals, I held out my hand to help Elsie down the last step. It was a killer if you lost your balance, I'd hit the sand on all fours too many times. She stepped down with elegance and grace, as usual, and I released her hand so that she could lift her skirt.

'Did my mother know this friend of yours?' I asked almost nonchalantly, trying not to show just how interested I was in the information.

She turned to me with a warm smile on her face, the frills of her skirt flowing beautifully in the light summer breeze that filtered through the little cove. Even though the weather was still warm, the beach down here was deserted, it was a little too far off the beaten track to have anyone down here in the evenings.

'She met him once or twice. I took her with me to the city every now and again. She loved to get out of this little town.'

I smiled at the titbits of knowledge that Elsie threw my way; she would never understand how much they meant to me.

'You're a lot like her you know,' she said quietly, which halted me in my tracks, 'The restlessness I see in you, your need for freedom; she was the same.'

The twinkle in her eyes betrayed the feeling she had for my mother, and I wondered again at what their relationship had been like.

'Did she like him?' I asked with a smile.

Her answering smile told me everything I needed to know without her words, but she answered me anyway.

'She did, she used to drive him round the bend though; he called her tenacious,' she finished with a chuckle.

I laughed at the thought. I knew so little about my mother that these snippets of information helped me to build up a clearer image of her in my head. Her physical appearance wasn't an issue for me. Apart from the fact that Elsie had photos of all of us around the house, including several of my mother; I got to see her every time I looked in a mirror. Even though Marina didn't like to talk about her, she had told me that I was her double as I'd grown. We both had her eyes, the aquamarine green that imitated the water that we called home. I looked into my sister's eyes and I saw the little piece of my mother that she gave to her. I looked in a mirror and I saw her looking back at me. Her eyes, her smile, her wavy blonde hair. I'd refused to have mine cut because in the photo that Elsie had put in my bedroom, my mother's hair had fallen down past her waist. Mine was almost there; it fell down my back in a cascade of silvery blonde waves that curled at the bottom, just about level with my waist. A few more inches was all I needed to beat her in length.

'Do you think he will like me?' I asked hopeful that I would one day get to meet this friend of Elsie's.

'I think you'd drive him round the bend with all these questions,' she chuckled, 'But I think that he would love to meet you, and that you could probably learn a thing or two from him one day.'

She looked thoughtful as she fell silent and I moved a few feet away from her so that the tide caught my toes as it rushed in to caress the beach. The water soothed me in a way that I couldn't explain. Even though I wanted to be on land more than anything, the water was my home, and to feel it rushing around me always brought me a sense of peace.

Elsie followed me to the water's edge and let the tide pool around her ankles like always. The same sense of serenity came over her face and I longed to know what she was thinking. I wondered how she had gotten involved with us all in the first place, and how she had come to end up looking after us the way she did. Had she come across one of us by accident? Had she found out our secret and pledged her allegiance to whoever had been around at the time. How much did the Royals know about her?

As far as I was aware, the Royals didn't come ashore. They never left The Kingdom, personally I'd never even seen them, but surely they knew Elsie. Surely, they had made an exception so that they could meet the extraordinary woman that had promised to look after us and our secrets. I owed Elsie everything that I was, and I knew that my mother would probably have been able to say the same. She loved us, we weren't just some promise to her; we were family. I knew that with the look she gave me every time that she saw me on the morning of the full moon.

I believed that it was the way that a mother would look at their daughter.

September

I splashed through the shallow water safe in the knowledge that Aaron would be here to pick me up soon. I had no idea what time it was yet, not until I got to the house and looked at the clock in the hallway. It was weird how the time had suddenly become so important to me; I could honestly say that for as long as I could remember, the date and time had never been an issue. Elsie had taught me how to tell the time, and I knew how may days were in each month and all that, but I only really needed to know how to read the sun; I knew how long I had by watching the shadows and how they formed and by looking at the position of the sun in the sky. The actual time had never been important to me, but now, with Aaron giving me times, it was suddenly significant to my life; I'd have to put a clock in my bag so that I knew the time as soon as I got out of the water. As it was there was just a skirt and a towel in the bag that Elsie had stashed by the rocks. Maybe I would have to start and pack it before I left so that all she had to do was put in clothing appropriate to the weather.

I pondered the idea of time all the way back to the house, and ran the last of the distance up the garden path, swinging through the front door and coming up in front of the clock. It wasn't even seven yet, I had hours. That slowed me down. I made my way up the stairs to hear Elsie already in the shower, so I laid out my towel on the little bay window seat and plonked myself down to look out over the water.

It was late summer now; the temperatures would still be warm; I hoped that meant there would be a few of us out today. Elsie would love to see some of the other faces before the winter drew in.

When I heard the water turn off and Elsie moving around in the bathroom, I unfolded myself from my position by the window and started to rummage through my drawers in search of an outfit to wear for the day.

'Morning Luna dear,' Elsie said when she stuck her head around the door and smiled.

'Morning Aunt Elsie,' I answered, throwing a lightweight skirt on the bed then standing up to face her, 'Do we have a small clock?'

I asked thinking I already knew the answer; if we had one it would be out somewhere, but I had to ask now that I had thought of the idea.

'A clock?' she asked, opening the door a little and straightening in the doorway.

'Yeah, just a little one that I could keep in my bag for when I surface, so that I know the time,' I clarified.

She smiled and began to turn, signalling for me to follow her.

'I have just the thing.'

I followed her back to her room, where she headed straight for a chest of drawers in the corner that I knew held some of the other girls' belongings. She knelt down, holding on to her towel, and routed through the bottom drawer and pulled out a small box. I didn't see the contents as she only tipped the lid enough to pull out whatever she was searching for, before she put back the box and stood up again. She turned and held something out to me on the palm of her hand.

'Will this do?' she asked as I took a step towards her.

On her hand lay a small watch, a little like the one she wore sometimes. It had a black leather strap with white stitching, and the face was black with white hands. It looked very elegant and pretty, but would be perfect for what I wanted it for. I took it from her and held it up to the light in one hand. Smiling, I turned back to her.

'It's perfect,' I said, turning it over in my hand.

'It was Marina's once, but she never wore it, told me to look after it until someone else wanted it.'

I smiled, wondering why Marina had ever wanted a small clock, she spent very little time on the shores, even back when I was younger, her time was limited, and I never remembered this on her wrist then. Maybe she had worn it so that she could keep track of the time with me and I'd just never noticed before.

After thanking Elsie again, I headed for my shower and then got dressed, putting on the watch and securing it around my wrist. It was perfect. It told me that I had just less than two hours before Aaron was coming for me. The first thing I needed to sort was breakfast.

While I sat eating my breakfast, I kept turning my wrist so that I could read the time on the watch face, and I made the discovery that time moved incredibly slowly when it was being watched. I could look at it and then speak to Elsie, and when I looked back what I thought was at least a few minutes later, it had barely moved.

'Are you sure this is working properly?' I asked Elsie eventually.

She glanced backwards as she made her way into the kitchen and saw me waving my arm at her. I heard her soft laugh and turned to see her smiling.

'Is it ticking?' she asked, leaning back against the sink with her glass of orange juice in her hand.

I looked at her blankly for a second and then brought the watch to my ear. It was ticking; a soft gentle tick that held a rhythm.

'Yes,' I answered, fearing that I was missing something vital.

'Then it is working,' she said simply.

'Well how do you know that?' I asked again, now watching the face of the clock.

'Because the ticking is the seconds passing, like the fast hand on the grandfather clock in the hallway, the ticking sound represents the same thing. So, if it is still ticking then time is still passing.'

I mulled over what she was saying. I had sat watching the second hand on the clock in the hallway before, counting down the time until I could do something. The most recent had been the first time I had phoned Aaron. I'd counted down the time until Elsie had said it was a reasonable time to call. Now, I sat listening to the ticking, seeing nothing happening.

'Maybe we ought to buy you a new watch, one with a second hand,' Elsie mused from the kitchen.

Now there was an idea. Then I could watch the time move. I glanced back at my wrist; I did like that this was Marina's though; it had meant something to her at some point in her life.

'Maybe Marina could go with you into town and choose a new one,' Elsie said as she came to sit back down with me at the table.

I smiled and looked up to find her looking at me with that knowing look of hers. She knew what I was thinking. She knew me better than I knew myself some days; that was why she'd given me this watch in the first place. She knew I'd love that it had been my sisters.

'That could be good,' I answered half-heartedly.

Marina had said she wouldn't be out this month, she had no reason to, but she had promised to come ashore next month before the weather dropped and it would get too cold. She was always cold when she came ashore, I blamed it on spending too much time in the water; it was always lovely and warm in there, even in the winter it was warm, especially when you went as deep as we did. But that didn't matter much, when in mermaid form we barely felt the temperature, it was part of our makeup, can't be having mermaids with goose bumps all the time, it would mess with the idea of us looking so attractive to the humans. Maybe Marina would take me shopping then, I could wear this one for today.

Elsie stayed quiet, letting me think it over, and when I looked up I saw her watching me with a smile.

'How do you always do that?' I asked, 'How do you always know what I'm thinking?'

'You're like an open book most of the time, your emotions play out on your face making it easy to work out what you're thinking,' Elsie explained.

At precisely ten, according to my watch, Aaron pulled up on the front, I was watching from the front window so that I saw him coming, and had my shoes on and was half way out of the door by the time he made it part way down the path.

I threw myself into his arms when he stopped and opened them to me, pressing my nose into the crook of his neck and inhaling. He always smelled of the ocean and some darker scent that I had decided was just him, and I missed it while we were separated. His arms snaked around my middle and held me tight as we just stood there with the weak morning sun shining down on us.

'Miss me?' I asked when I finally pulled back a little.

'Always,' he answered, making me smile, before leaning down to kiss me.

His lips were soft and he tasted like salt water. He'd clearly already been surfing this morning, and I smiled again as I remembered watching him last time. He looked so at home in the water that it was hard to think that humans were so different to mermaids. The way his body handled itself when he was surrounded by the power of the ocean, and the way he cut through the water when he was swimming showed me another side of him. He was strong and dependable on land, but what I'd seen of him in the water amplified all of that; he was sure of himself, and he'd looked just as comfortable in the water as he did on the shore.

'So, what would you like to do today?' he asked as he turned and led me back to the Jeep.

I turned to look up at him, squinting a little due to the brightness of the sun. He normally had our day all planned out, what had changed? He glanced down at me and let out a soft laugh as he opened the door and helped me in. After closing the door, he leant on it where the window was wound all the way down and continued to speak, answering my unspoken question as if I'd spoken it out loud.

'I figured that I was always making the decisions, so we were always doing what I liked. I thought it would be nice for you to choose, that way I get to see what you like doing.'

He made his way back around the car and hopped in behind the wheel, turning in his seat to look at me. I had stayed silent after his declaration. I liked that he made the decision, I wasn't used to being in control of things, it made me nervous now that I had been given the reigns, so to speak.

'I kinda like it that you plan our day together,' I said quietly.

He reached over and tipped my chin up so that I had to meet his eyes and he smiled, leaning in to press another kiss to my lips.

'I just thought it would be nice to do what you wanted for a change.'

'We did what I wanted when we went into the cove,' I said, remembering my decision the first day.

'True, and you loved exploring it down there, is there somewhere else you'd like to explore? Maybe we could do that today.'

He fell silent and let me think for a few minutes.

'What about going to the aquarium?' I asked, though I had little enthusiasm behind my words.

Elsie had taken me to the aquarium one day, trying to teach me about some of the animals there that I didn't necessarily see in the ocean around this area. I had loved seeing them and learning about the different types of creatures from the ones I saw every day, but I hated that they were all locked up in little tanks. It made me feel sorry for them, and I think that had played a part in how I felt about the water. To me, the ocean was a cage; the same way that their little tanks held them captive, the ocean held me captive from the shores. I'd never been back; maybe now I was older I could appreciate it more.

'You don't sound convinced,' Aaron said, clearly reading my emotions like Elsie had.

'I'm not a fan of them being kept in tanks,' I admitted and he nodded.

'Yeah, I know what you mean, seems a bit harsh when they could be swimming out there in the big blue sea.'

Eventually we decided on going for a walk down the beach until we could come up with another plan, rather than sitting on the front in the car all morning. The sand was soft and warm between my toes, and my dress blew lazily around my legs in the breeze that was coming off the water. We had walked for miles, following the curve of the beach around the shore and heading towards where it disappeared around the headland. There wasn't much down here, only the odd family that had little children digging holes and splashing in the edge of the water where it was casually drifting in and out as the tide ebbed away from the beach.

The road was lined with cars where they had chosen to come down here where it was quiet, and I found myself people watching like I used to before I'd met Aaron. I realised that now I spent my time with him, I'd stopped watching others and thinking about their lives. I had a life now, I had something of my own that others might be watching. Stopping in my tracks, I pulled gently on Aaron's hand where we had been walking hand in hand, and he turned back to face me. I smiled and reached up onto my toes, sliding my other hand into his hair to pull him down to where I could kiss him. It wasn't like me to instigate this, and I felt Aaron's surprise in his kiss, before he took back the control that I gave to him, and he wrapped his free arm around my waist.

When he pulled back from me, he picked me up effortlessly and spun me around, kicking up sand as he twirled around on the spot. I heard my laugh and felt the happiness inside me swelling. I really was happy. For as long as I could remember the shores had made me happy, but now that Aaron was a part of that life, I realised that it had never been happiness I was feeling, I had been surviving. Now I was truly happy, and I hoped that one day each cycle was enough for him to be happy too.

He finally put me down and I felt my smile drop a tiny bit.

'Are you happy?' I asked, a tiny part of me dreading his answer.

'Are you kidding?' he said, putting his hand back into mine and turning back the way we had come, 'I have the prettiest girl around holding my hand, and wanting to spend her time with me, I am the happiest guy in town.'

'But it's only one day a month,' I said, choosing the right words.

'It's the best day of the month,' he answered without hesitation.

We made it back down to the more populated area of the beach where we could see the square with all its mismatched little buildings, and we sat down in the sand near the dunes, out of the way of the families playing by the water. I sat between Aaron's legs as he propped himself up on his arms. Leaning back, I revelled in the warmth of him at my back and the sun's rays on my face. Tilting my head backwards a little, I tipped my head towards the warmth and closed my eyes. This really was perfect.

'When are you next back?' Aaron asked after a couple of minutes.

I stayed silent for a few seconds longer than was normal, and he moved behind me trying to see my face.

'Luna?'

I had forgotten to check the date on the calendar before coming out.

'Erm, I'm not sure what the date is,' I said carefully.

'Okay, but you are coming again?' he asked gently.

I turned slightly so that I could see his face too; he looked worried.

'Of course I'm coming back, I just don't know the date, I will check it when I go back for dinner.'

He fell silent again and I began to worry. I sat up and turned to face him, rearranging my dress on the sand to protect my modesty.

'Aaron, what's wrong?'

He looked up and smiled; a gentle smile that didn't quite reach his eyes.

'I guess I just miss you when you're gone that's all, it's a long time, and you never seem sure about when you're coming back. You sure I can't convince you to come in between your visits?'

I sighed gently and turned back around, pulling his arms around me to hold me against him.

'It's not that simple,' I said quietly.

'You know you could tell me, it'd be okay. I promise.'

He sounded so sincere that he made it easy to believe him, but I'd been brought up not to trust those words. Even with my building trust in Aaron, it was hard to shake the habit of a lifetime. I was over three hundred and twelve moons old, Elsie said that it was twenty-six human years since I was born, she had a little party for me with each human year that passed, always bought me a present, but I knew that I didn't look like every other twenty-six-year-old human girl. Time moved differently under the ocean, and I only looked twenty-ish when I compared myself to the other girls that I came in to contact with on land, but it was a long time of being told not to trust humans. But truthfully, how many months could I expect him to wait for me? How long before he got bored, or met someone else; someone that he could spend every day and every night with, not just one day during the daylight hours?

'You wouldn't believe me even if I did tell you,' I replied without turning to look at him.

In honesty, I wanted to tell him. I hoped that Aaron would be different, I longed for him to understand. I wanted him to know me like Elsie did, but it wasn't safe. The Royals said that there were disastrous consequences when mermaids revealed themselves to the humans. She'd mentioned being subjected to examinations and kept out of the water after we had transformed, and I knew that to go dry was a death sentence for any one of us.

'Try me, Luna.'

I turned in his embrace shaking the morbid thoughts from my head and looking away from the ocean and into his eyes; a perfect replica. The clear crystal blue that I saw when I looked deep into his eyes reminded me of home; I saw home, and it was with that realisation that I made my decision. It wasn't made lightly, although that was all the Royals would see; after all, I'd only known Aaron for a few moons, but I couldn't believe I hadn't seen it before; he really was perfect. It was like it was meant to be. I also thought about the things Elsie had said; she'd defended me to the girls, told them that I was smart enough to know and obey the rules. The phone call I'd overheard on the last full moon, I was positive that it was about me; she'd defended my relationship with Aaron then too, telling her friend that I was a smart girl. Would she be angry if I defied the rules and told him? Would she understand why I could trust him?

I glanced around us, checking out the slowly emptying beach as people made their way home for dinner and made my decision. This was my life, I knew the risks, but I trusted Aaron; with my life and my secrets and my days were getting shorter again. I only had a few hours left this month, and there would be even fewer by the next full moon.

'Okay,' I said taking a deep breath and then blurting it out, 'I'm a mermaid.'

He blinked slowly, just staring at me, and then he began to smile; surely it wasn't that simple. A look passed across his eyes, but it wasn't one I could identify and it was gone almost as soon as it had appeared. An errant thought that had betrayed itself in his eyes.

'A mermaid?' he questioned, 'Like with fins and a tail? That kind of mermaid?' he asked, his gaze flickering briefly to my legs before returning to meet my eyes.

'Yes, exactly like that,' I answered, suddenly fidgety.

I pulled away from his embrace so that I could sit up unaided and shuffled in the sand so that I was more comfortable. He looked confused, his eyes continually glancing down at my legs though he tried hard to keep eye contact with me.

'You do realise how ridiculous that sounds don't you Luna?'

'Yes, I do, but you asked me to tell you the truth, and that is the truth. At sunset I can show you.'

'You can show me? As in you can just change; just like that?'

'Pretty much yeah. The full moon allows us to walk on land, by sunset I have to return to the water. It's a little bit more complicated than that obviously, but that's the general gist. It's why I have to leave before it gets dark every month. I have to be back in the water.'

He stayed quiet for a few minutes and I kept my silence, letting him mull over my revelation.

'So, it's a bit like a reverse werewolf?' he asked with a chuckle.

I laughed; I had to.

'No, it's nothing like being a werewolf. Firstly, I'm real. Secondly, it's a choice; we don't have to leave the water if we choose not to, and we can return at any point in the day; I just choose to stay on land for as long as possible.' I looked up at him again suddenly nervous. 'I like being on land. I want a life.'

The look in his eyes began to change and I saw him beginning to accept the crazy that I was offering as a reality, he slowly began to understand, even if it was only a little.

'I want a life with you,' I admitted quietly, averting my eyes down a little and concentrating on the ink on his arm that I could see peeking out from underneath the edge of his top.

'You're for real, aren't you?' he stated rather blankly, 'You're really a mermaid?'

I nodded, 'There is a whole other world at the bottom of the ocean, one so deep that no human could reach it before their bodies gave out, but it doesn't make us any less real.'

'You realise that you're asking me to believe in a fairy tale,' he said with a little uncertainty, 'Like *The Little Mermaid* on TV, she wanted to be on land too, gave away her voice in exchange for feet so that she could marry the Prince.'

I knew the story; I'd seen the movie as a kid. It had given Elsie and me a good laugh as it was so far from the truth that it was still fiction, but it hadn't stopped me wishing that I could get a happily ever after ending just like she had.

'Yeah, I know the one,' I said with a smile, 'Trust me when I say that it is nothing like that, fish most definitely can't talk and neither can the birds; though I guess I've never spoken to one of them to know if it would speak back,' I said with an amused glint in my eye, 'Their depiction of The Kingdom is really good though, very shiny.'

I finished my little speech and fell silent; Aaron's face looked like he was trying too hard to focus. His nose was all scrunched up and there were little lines forming on his forehead.

'It's not that hard Aaron, stop over thinking it. I'll show you, but for now, let's eat.'

Explaining had somehow brought on my appetite and I was suddenly starving. The thought of showing Aaron what I really was, was both frightening and exhilarating all at the same time. I somehow knew deep down that I could trust him with the secret, but would he still be waiting for me next month after he knew that I wasn't real. I was just a part time human who didn't have a life to call her own. My life under the ocean was dull and monotonous compared to the fun I had on land. I knew that I could form a life up here, if I was given half a chance. Maybe I should seek out an octopus, maybe there is some truth hidden in the story of *The Little Mermaid* after all.

He was quiet on the walk back up the beach to The Hut where we headed for some food. It was a little busy due to it being the lead up to dinner time, but we only had to wait for a few minutes before a booth opened up. I left him to think about everything that I had said while we navigated our way through the restaurant to our seats, the waitress gave us our menus then disappeared with a promise to be back with our drinks when we were ready to order.

'What are you thinking?' I asked quietly.

He looked up from his menu and smiled when he met my eyes, the little sparkle I was used to seeing there still present. At least I hadn't completely put him off by revealing my truths to him.

'I was just trying to imagine you in place of the red head in the story,' he said in return, his voice low where he understood that it was a secret.

Though he obviously understood, I had to be sure that he wasn't going to betray my secret as soon as I was back in the water, even if only by accident.

'You know that you can't tell anyone don't you? We're not supposed to reveal ourselves to anyone, it can be dangerous. You have to keep it a secret.'

I pleaded with him with my eyes as I spoke, I needed him to protect my secret the way Elsie did; with his life. I needed to know that I hadn't put us in any danger.

'Your secret, and you, are completely safe with me, you always will be,' he said with sincerity, and I believed him.

He wouldn't put me in any danger; I knew that in my heart and soul. I would hold my judgement as to whether he would ever want to see me again after he knew, or whether he would at least want to keep seeing me, knowing that it wasn't going anywhere, or that he would never see me more than once a month, apart from the rare blue moon where I could see him twice. It made my heart bleed to think that he would move on with someone else, lead a life like the one that I so desperately wanted with some other girl. It would break my heart to see him put his arms around some other girl's waist and kiss her like he kissed me.

Aaron cleared his throat, gaining my attention and when I looked up he seemed to understand a little about what I was thinking. He slid out of the booth and into the seat at the side of me. I loved it when we sat like this; it made me feel safer somehow, like he didn't want any distance between us. And when for an average of thirty days every calendar month we were so far apart that I couldn't even work it out, knowing that he wanted me close while I was here made my heart swell with my love for him.

Lunch was quiet, but not awkward. I didn't try to fill the silence with pointless conversation; I left Aaron to think about what I'd told him. I wasn't quite sure he believed me, but at the same time, he didn't think I was crazy, so that had to be a good sign. He got a little chattier while he drove me back to the house so that I could see Elsie and the girls but barely made any reference to me telling him about being a mermaid. We talked about his friend who played in a band, he said he thought I'd like him, and that maybe one day I might like to meet him, and he spoke about his mother a little more, telling me that she would have loved to have met a mermaid. That was the only time he said anything that made me understand that he had actually taken in what I'd said.

I left him at the car, and made him promise to come back at around six and we would go down to the beach where I planned to change in front of him and show him. It felt like I had something to prove to him, though I knew that he would never have asked me to do so. I wanted him to understand though; I wanted him to know the real me. He kissed me goodbye like always, the kiss didn't seem any different, it must have been my own thoughts and feelings that were affecting the way I was seeing the situation. In all honesty, I was afraid. I was afraid that this would be too much, that it would scare him away, and the thought of going back to the life I'd led before I met him was one that made me feel rather empty inside.

'Elsie?' I called as I pushed the front door closed behind me.

The house seemed still and quiet, something I wasn't really used to with this place; there was always someone coming and going. But as I made my way from room to room, I decided there was definitely no one home. Maybe she'd popped to the shops for something for dinner. I headed upstairs and put my bag on my bed, looking around to see Marina's drawers open and an array of clothes exploding from them. She was here obviously.

As I was half way back down the stairs, the front door burst open and Elsie, my sister and Shelley came tumbling through it in a crack of laughter and chattering. I smiled, this was what Elsie lived for; the days when we were around, the smiles, the laughter. We were her family.

Shelley had two bags in her hand from the shop around the corner and smiled when she saw me standing at the foot of the staircase.

'You in for dinner? I'm cooking fajitas,' she asked as they all bustled in and started to shed their lightweight coats.

I nodded whilst secretly wondering why they needed coats, the temperature outside was still lovely. Elsie was the only one without one; the girls were clearly too used to the water.

I followed Shelley through to the kitchen where she began to empty the contents of the bags onto the worktop. She continued talking and Marina followed us through and joined in. They had been for a walk-in town by the sounds of things, and decided on grabbing the things for dinner on the way back. Whilst they were still chatting, I excused myself and went in search of Elsie. I found her out on the back garden on the little swinging sofa.

'Hey Aunt Elsie, you feeling okay?' I asked as I sat down carefully beside her.

'Of course darling, just a little tired. I'm getting old now you know, all this gallivanting takes it out of me,' she answered with a genuinely happy smile.

We sat in comfortable silence for a few seconds and she leaned her head back and closed her eyes. I mulled over how to tell her that I had told Aaron, and decided that I should just come out with it.

'Aunt Elsie I told Aaron that I was a mermaid.'

She didn't respond straight away and I wondered whether she had heard me because I was whispering. I didn't want my sister to hear, she wouldn't understand but I needed Elsie to. Slowly she lifted her head and opened her eyes to look at me, they were soft and she smiled; not what I had expected. I'd expected her to be angry, or at least upset with me.

'I knew you would at some point,' she said and leaned over to hug me, 'Does he love you?'

I pulled back at her words and thought about them for a minute.

'I love him,' I answered eventually, and I did.

Would it be enough? Did he love me too?

'As long as you're safe, and you're happy Luna, then I am happy for you,' Elsie started and then sat up and turned towards me, 'There will come a day when I can't look out for you, and it makes me feel better knowing that you'll always have someone to do that for you, someone who understands who you are, and will protect you with their life. I think Aaron could be that person for you, if you let him.'

Her words brought tears to my eyes and one leaked from the corner and ran silently down my cheek. She reached up and brushed it away before speaking again.

'Just be careful, the others won't understand until you make them, they need to see that it will work if they are going to support you.'

I nodded my understanding, not being able to form any words around the lump that had formed in my throat. The feelings inside me were warring for top spot; on the one hand I was happy that she understood, but on the other I was afraid of what she meant by not always being here. She had always been here. I knew that she was getting older, but there were plenty of women around the town much older than she was. Surely, she wasn't going anywhere just yet.

Dinner passed in a blur around me as I tried to concentrate on the conversations going on, but my mind was elsewhere. Somewhere between the conversation I had just had with Elsie, and the one I was going to have with Aaron. My sister and Shelley left straight after dinner to get back to the water, leaving me with a few more minutes to speak to Elsie before Aaron got here. Secretly, I was glad they had left today, as I planned to take Aaron down to the same cove they had just departed from, and it probably wouldn't have gone down well for us all to have ended up there together. One beat of the fins at a time and all that. Elsie never swayed in her opinion of what I'd told Aaron, nor was she surprised when I said I was going to show him either. Again, she told me to be careful, and made me promise to ask him to come up and see her at some point through the month so that she could speak to him. She said it didn't have to be straight away, that he could have some time to digest everything he had learned today, but she'd like to speak to him before the next full moon. I didn't see Aaron having a problem with that, he liked Elsie, but if he decided that this was all too much to handle, would he want to go back to the house?

At the stroke of six, I was stood on the front garden waiting for Aaron. He was late, and the rising panic inside me that told me he had changed his mind, that he didn't want to know, was getting beyond my control. Just as I was about to go back inside the house to ask Elsie if I could ring him, the Jeep pulled around the corner and he came to a stop by the front gate.

'Sorry I'm late babe, my dad decided he needed a father and son talk before I could leave the house.'

He sighed as he spoke and I could see the effect it had had on him. I hated that his father could make him feel like that. I stepped into his open arms as I reached the Jeep where he had climbed out and pressed my face against his chest, listening to the steady thump of his heart beating there. When I finally let go, he held me away from him and looked deep into my eyes with a quizzical look.

'I thought you weren't coming,' I said in a little voice, fighting the wave of emotion that had tormented me for the few minutes I had waited for him.

'Luna, I'm sorry, I would have never just disappeared like that; I promised you I would be here.'

I nodded, I was starting to feel a little foolish, but I was vulnerable now, he knew me, he knew the darkest of my secrets, of course I was going to feel a little insecure right now.

Instead of keeping talking, he slipped his hand into mine and started towards the cove. His hand was warm and I shuffled closer so that our shoulders kept bumping together as we walked. I felt the smile creeping back across my face as we walked in easy silence. As we reached the top of the cliffs and began our way towards the cove however, the nerves began creeping back in.

'You sure you want to see this?' I asked as I led him towards the path that took me back down to the ocean.

Elsie was on board with what I was doing, despite her reservations for my safety, so I was a little more confident than I had been earlier. The sun had begun its final descent towards the water so I had around an hour left with Aaron before I had to return to the water. I knew he had questions, but I'd made him wait till we were in the privacy of the little cove before I would answer them. I couldn't risk us being overheard.

He nodded as we headed down the unlevel steps and he pulled back slightly on my hand, stopping me in my tracks. I took a couple of steps back to where he had stopped and looked up into his eyes. He pulled me close and sealed his lips over mine before I had a chance to ask why we had stopped.

When he pulled back with a smile that I recognised now as his love for me, I smiled back.

'I want you to know that whatever happens down there,' he nodded with his head to the steps before carrying on, 'isn't going to change the way I feel about you.'

'Save that declaration for after you know all the facts and have actually seen me,' I said, desperate for those words to be true, but not wanting to get my hopes up.

If he chose to walk away after this, I wouldn't stand in his way. I wasn't selfish enough to hold Aaron back from a life he was entitled to; mine was only a dream. I made to carry on but his arms around my waist held me still.

'We're not moving until you accept that as a fact Luna. I won't have you doubting us just because you don't think that you deserve what we have.'

He spoke as if he could read my mind; he made a habit of it, and I wondered if what Elsie had always said about wearing my emotions like a play script were truer than I had always given her credit for.

I agreed, and he pulled me in to kiss me, reassuring my belief in the fact that he might still be here next time.

Colour skipped playfully across the surface of the ocean as the sun began to disappear behind the horizon. It looked so beautiful and appealing I wondered how I would ever make Aaron fully understand how I felt. We found a spot, just out of the reach of the tide and sat down on the warm sand.

'Okay, ask me anything,' I said, wondering what he might have come up with since this afternoon.

For a few minutes he stayed silent, letting me get comfortable and lean against him where we sat watching the sunset paint the sky.

'Okay, he said finally his voice quiet as if he didn't want to disturb the tranquillity, 'This is going to sound ridiculous, but how do you breathe under the water?'

He laughed as he said it but it was an obvious thing for him to be curious about.

'I don't grow gills or anything like a fish,' I said with a chuckle as I imagined what I would look like, 'It's just natural, our lungs are designed to filter the oxygen from the water, so we breathe it in like you breathe air really. When I was little I remember coughing a lot when I first left the ocean as there was often still water in my lungs, now it's just normal for me to make sure they're empty before I surface.'

He nodded and fell silent again, clearly taking in what I was telling him. I knew that everything I was telling him was hard to believe, but he seemed to be handling it okay.

'Where do you go?' he asked next, 'I'm assuming there are more of you, so is there like a mermaid village down there somewhere?'

Again, I chuckled softly, it wasn't a silly question, and I was now realising how naive I could sound asking questions that had such obvious answers to Aaron, but I'd had no clue about. Now the roles were reversed.

'The Kingdom is our home down in the deeper ocean where humans can't reach. That's what the Royals will tell you anyway; but imagine *The Lost City of Atlantis* and you are near enough there.'

'The Royals?' Aaron questioned as I finished.

'Yeah, they're like the original mermaids, they're mega old and run The Kingdom from wherever it is they run things from; I've never actually seen them before. They hardly ever venture out anymore and you do not ever want to cross them. The merbabies are always afraid of them because we're taught to respect them from afar.'

'Hmm,' he made a noise of approval and fell silent again.

It was killing me to not know what he was thinking, but I kept quiet and smiled when his arms around me tightened their grip and held me close.

'Anything else you want to know?' I asked after a few more minutes of silence.

I felt him shake his head and turned in his embrace so that I could see his expression. He seemed to be at ease with the information I had given him, but his lack of curiosity when I was so used to his stream of questions was odd.

'I don't really know what to ask. I'm sure the minute you go there'll be loads I wished I'd asked, but I'm coming up blank at the minute.

'Okay, well Elsie has asked if you will go and see her at some point before I'm back, so you could ask her, she just wants to talk and check you're okay with everything I think,' I said as I sat forwards.

'And make sure I'm not going to tell anyone that my girlfriend is a mermaid,' he added with a chuckle.

I knew that I should comment on that, tell him not to be silly and that she just wanted to be sure he was okay, but I knew he was right, and I was more caught up on what else he had just thrown out there.

'Girlfriend?' I questioned quietly, turning around to face him on the sand.

'That's what I told my mates yeah,' he said with a shrug, 'Would you rather I hadn't?'

I shook my head and threw myself into his arms, knocking him off balance from the surprise. He laughed as he hit the sand and I fell on top of him with a giggle. I'd never dreamed that he would see me like that, I'd tried to tell myself that it was just some summer romance, that he would get fed up and move on because he didn't see me enough. Girlfriend. Maybe Elsie was right, maybe he really would always be here for me.

When I rolled off him and landed on the sand with a soft thump, I stayed there as he sat up and watched as he shook off the sand. I wrinkled up my nose and did the same as he showered me in the fine grains.

'It's nearly time,' I whispered from behind him.

His answer was just a smile, the twinkle in his eyes showing me that he was ready. I tried to imagine what it must be like to find out that something you believed to be from a fairy tale was real, and that you'd been kissing her for the last few months and didn't even know what she was. He didn't seem afraid, he was genuinely curious; I just hoped that he didn't find it too odd after I'd shown him.

I led him quietly into the water, letting the water creep up my skirt and watching as it bled up Aaron's dark denim jeans. He never complained, never questioned me.

'Will you still wait for me, now that you know the truth?' I asked looking down at the ripples that chased each other away from us rather than looking up to meet his gaze.

I knew that I had no right to ask that of him now that he understood that our relationship wasn't going anywhere; it was just a messed-up version of a summer romance, and summer was coming to an end. His fingers were wet where they touched my cheek and the salt water on my lips was a harsh reminder of the forces at work that were to separate us once more. It wasn't an easy goodbye every month; it felt like I was being torn away from him each time, like I was being punished for being happy.

'I'll be waiting for you on the beach at sunrise,' Aaron's voice snapped me back to the present.

Tears welled in my eyes and spilled down my cheeks before I could even think to stop them.

'Luna, don't cry. The only thing that this changes is that I now understand why I can't contact you all month, and why you're a little unconventional. It doesn't change the way I feel about you one bit.'

I smiled, unable to answer him due to the lump that had formed in my throat, and stood up on my tip toes in the water to kiss him.

When I turned to check the horizon, the sun had sunk lower and my mood instantly sank with it.

'Okay, you ready?' I asked, deciding that it was now or never.

'Now?' he seemed surprised.

'I'm leaving time to resurface and talk to you before I have to go.'

I checked the beach before kissing him again then turned to dive under the water. It had been a long time since I had consciously made the transformation this way; for as long as I could remember I had always waited for nature to take my feet from me. Now, I dove under the water and concentrated hard on my inner self, on the power behind my fins and the strength of my tail as I cut through the water with an elegance that I had never been able to replicate with legs. I resurfaced a couple of meters away from where I had left Aaron and tried to gage his reaction. He was watching me intently as I swam back to where he stood; the look in his eyes one of pure wonderment.

'Wow! I'm not sure I totally believed you until now. I mean, I thought I did, but now... wow!' he said, tripping over his words as they poured out.

'You're rambling,' I murmured as he bobbed down in the water by my side.

I was glad it was summer and the water was still warm otherwise he would have been freezing by now.

'You're beautiful,' he whispered as he looked my distorted body up and down through the water, 'I can't believe how much has changed in just a few seconds.'

'It's nothing; they're just scales and a fin or two. Trust me when I say that it isn't all it's cracked up to be.'

'It's not just those things Luna,' his voice faltered, 'You're shimmering.'

I looked down but couldn't see what Aaron was talking about.

'Luna, your skin is shimmery.'

I laughed, 'Oh, that's just the water,' I replied.

'No Luna, look.'

He took my hand and lowered both of our arms under the water so that they were side by side. He was right. My skin was sparkly, like something magical. I'd never really considered myself to be magical before; I'd always seen it as a curse or something dark and sinister, not as magic. Like the curse of the Werewolf Aaron had compared me to. But now I saw myself through Aaron's eyes instead of my own and I saw myself anew.

'Your eyes have the same sparkle to them too. Luna, it's amazing.'

He continued but I was still staring at my arm. I lifted my hand out of the water and looked at it with fresh eyes; sparkly ones apparently. The dying sunlight glinted off me like it would a precious rock and I saw the light refracted and playing out in the damp atmosphere around me. Maybe there was hope for me yet.

I said my goodbyes to Aaron, and he did one better than promising to be waiting for me at sunrise; he asked me to meet him before the sun came up. The rocks that formed the base of the cliffs down one side of the cove were obscured from view; I could surface there and not be seen from the beach. Aaron stayed submerged up to his waist to watch as I turned and sank below the water, pushing into the depths.

As I swam, the clarity of what I had done today hit me. The Royals would have my head for this, or more worryingly, they'd have Aaron's; the rules were clear. We don't tell the humans about us. Elsie knew, she'd been a little sceptical about the idea, but she hadn't warned me not to. She trusted me, and I trusted Aaron now, and with that I made up my mind not to mention anything back home before I'd seen both Aaron and Aunt Elsie next month. She'd know how to handle the next steps. I'd made the first one, I'd told Marina and the others on land about seeing Aaron. I'd work on the rest another time. For now, I was safe and secure in the knowledge that Aaron would be waiting for me next time. This wouldn't change the way he felt about me. In such a short space of time we had become inseparable, and without even realising it, he got me. I had fallen head over heels in love with him, and with that realisation, I knew that I had to find a way to be with him forever.

Angel McGregor

October

His trouser legs were rolled up and his bare feet were in the water creating gentle ripples as he kicked lazily waiting for me. I couldn't resist. I stayed deep enough that he wouldn't notice me and swam up against the rocks where I let my tail brush up against the underneath of his feet. He jerked suddenly and the image of him became completely distorted where he had disturbed the water too much.

I finally surfaced, already laughing and made my way over to him.

'You're late,' he announced while trying to hold his smile, 'That was you?'

I nodded and watched as he put his feet back in the water, now less worried about what might be lurking under the surface. He opened his legs and I swam between them where I perched myself on the rocks, my tail relaxed. His gaze drifted from my face to behind me, where he would be able to see me through the clear water. We'd agreed to meet out here before the sun rise so that he could see me again and ask any questions he may have come up with over the course of the month. I won't lie, I had been a little afraid that he wouldn't show up, that was the reason I was late, but once I was there and had seen the look in his eyes I knew that there had never been any doubt in his mind as to whether he would or wouldn't be there.

'Can I?' he nodded at my tail and I understood what he was asking.

I'd expected him to want to touch it last month when I'd transformed, but he hadn't even suggested it then, he'd been too distracted by my overall appearance.

'Is the water warm?' I asked in lieu of an actual answer.

He obviously got that I was deflecting his question, but he answered with a nod anyway. Instead of asking anything else, I reached up and offered him my hand, which he took without hesitation. Before he could ask what I was doing, I pulled him down off the rock and into the water. It was too deep for him to stand this far out, but as he surfaced with a laugh, I pushed him gently back against the rock's edge where he could find his footing.

Hovering just out of his reach where I could study the look on his face, I watched him watch me. I knew what he could see. My cropped top floated lazily around my chest and revealed my stomach, which slowly turned lilac just below my belly button, before becoming scales of a rich lavender that were flecked through with silver. Where my tail became my fins, the colour seeped back to lilac and they were almost see through, though were just as powerful as the rest of me.

I waited for his eyes to return to mine and then swam over to him. The water submerged him up to his chest and his shirt was loose around his waist. I slipped my hands up to run them up his stomach and tightened my grip around his waist.

'Miss me?' I asked quietly, but he heard me.

'Always,' he answered in a whisper as he wrapped me in his arms.

His hands strayed to the bare skin at my back almost instantly and I revelled in the familiar touch. He'd never been shy about touching me, and had never apologised once for being forward in any way, right back to those first kisses. I pressed my lips gently to his, waiting for him to respond, and flicked my tail lazily in the water to keep me in the same position. It wasn't hard to stay still, the muscle I possessed would rival some body builders; it was just harnessed differently. Aaron kissed me back and ran his hands down my body boldly. He slid straight over the change and splayed his fingers across my ass.

I don't know what I had been expecting, but there was no hesitation in his movements, no recoil from the texture of my scales. Nothing. He just accepted it as a part of me without even thinking about it. Perfect just didn't do him justice.

When he finally pulled away from the kiss, he looked down at the water and I watched as his eyes roamed my body through the blur of ripples. Pushing away from him gently, I pulled my body around so that I floated on the water's surface just in front of him. He reached out slowly and placed his hands around where my knees would be as soon as the sun rose above the horizon.

'You're beautiful Luna,' he said almost breathlessly.

I felt the blush, but accepted the compliment without argument. I knew that we were beautiful as a species. I'd seen books in the library when I was ashore. mermaids were meant to be beautiful, it was a part of who we were, we were all aesthetically pretty, but that didn't always add up to a beautiful person. I saw the girls around me at home, their pretty eyes; long wavy hair and shimmery scales that could make even the prettiest fish look boring. But I'd never thought of myself the same way. My scales were a prison holding me hostage and preventing me from being where I most desired to be; on land.

I could see the desire in his eyes; it was becoming as familiar as his smile. Lust clouded his vision, and I realised that I had been worried I wouldn't see it again after showing him what I really was. But there it was, as clear as day. I expected him to pull me back towards him, but instead he turned around and clambered back out of the water most ungracefully, and I had to hold back my laugh.

'I look like a prune,' he said as he knelt on the edge and looked my way.

'A what?' I asked, bemused by his analogy.

'A prune,' he stated again, holding out his hands and showing me his wrinkled fingertips, 'It's what happens when we spend too long in the water.'

I laughed. I'd never seen that before and I took his outstretched hand to inspect it further; he was deadly serious. How bizarre? My skin never did that. We still had time before sunrise. I didn't want to lose a single second of my time with him, but his pruned fingers caused a problem.

After settling himself back on the edge of the rocks and dipping his feet back in the water on either side of me, he held out his hand to me. I looked up at him confused, but put my hand in his.

'Do you trust me?' he asked as he leant down and slid his other arm under mine and around my body.

'What are you doing?'

'Do you trust me?' he repeated, and although I thought I knew what he was about to do, and knew that I shouldn't let him; I relaxed into his hold and nodded.

He pulled me up out of the water as if I weighed nothing, though I knew that in reality, I was pure muscle and must weigh quite a bit. As I reached the surface I pushed gently to assist him and he laid back, pulling me atop him. My breathing became shallow and I wriggled uncomfortably. I'd never been out of the water before sunrise and the thought scared me a little. I glanced to the horizon looking for any sign of the sun, but it had yet to throw out any light.

'Relax Luna, I'd never hurt you.'

'I know, it's just,' I paused, not sure of my answer, 'It's just, I've never been out of the water like this before.'

My fins at the end of my tail were still in the water and I flicked them gently to reassure myself that the water was only there. It's not like I was beached or that anyone would see me. Just as my heart began to calm down, Aaron moved his hand that was still around me and let it drift down onto the bare skin at my waist. Suddenly my heart thudded and I met his eyes with the same passion that I saw in his. I nodded, letting him know that he could continue, and he slowly slid both hands down my body. He paused as my skin turned to scales, letting his hands slip around my waist and over my hips, exploring the line where I became part fish and I wondered what my scales felt like to him. To me they were just a part of me; I knew they were more brittle than my skin, but then still seemed soft in their own way. I made a mental note to ask him later, but for now I kept quiet and let him explore; they would feel different out of the water.

His hands roamed over my hips and down where my thighs should be, before sliding over onto the backs of them and then back up over my ass. A strong urge to put my hands on him too nearly overwhelmed me and I knew that it was my human emotions and hormones that were racing from the contact. I flicked my tail again as I started to dry out spraying us both with water to ease the discomfort.

'You okay?' Aaron said with a laugh.

I nodded, not quite trusting my voice, but he asked again, obviously worried about me.

'I'm fine, it's just a bit uncomfortable now I'm drying off,' I answered honestly; though I had to admit to myself that I didn't want him to put me back in the water.

'Want to get wet and then carry on?'

'Sometimes I wonder if you can read my mind,' I answered as he sat up and let me slide back into the water.

As the salt water rushed over me I felt instantly better and I let out a deep breath. Now I knew that I could do this and do it safely, before I had panicked that I would do myself some real harm. Once I had dived down and resurfaced, Aaron was sitting up again, and I instantly swam over and pushed myself back through the water and out onto him.

He landed on his back with a thud and let out an 'umphing' sound.

'Sorry,' I said as I leant down to kiss him.

'I'll let you off.'

As his hands roamed down my body this time, I leant in to press my lips against his and suddenly the moment was much steamier than before. His hands now rested on my ass, and although I'd never thought of it like that before, I realised now that I was basically naked from the waist down.

My breathing became shallow again and he lifted one hand up and slid it into my hair, holding me close while his tongue explored my mouth. I sensed the change in me rather than actually seeing the light, but when I felt the sunrise begin, I instinctively began to change. Aaron tensed underneath me and I lifted my head to look at him before nodding to the horizon where the first tendrils of light were creeping into the ocean. The look of understanding flashed across his face and his hand slid down from my ass to my thigh where he pulled gently to bring my leg up around him.

Red quickly stained my cheeks and I felt the grin on his face as he realised the same thing too. We both laughed as I realised the implications of being naked from the waist down, but I didn't let it stop me. I reconnected the kiss and left his hands where they were. I was now laid almost straddling him, and the dampness of his shorts between my legs had my human hormones racing through my body faster than I knew what to do with them.

I'd already worked out now that it was possible for Aaron and me to have a sexual relationship during my time on land, and now that I had awakened that part of me, the hormones were raging. I knew that my body acted and reacted differently when it was in its human form, but the biggest thing I had noticed was that being around Aaron stirred things in me that made me want his hands all over me.

His hands stayed still in their position on my hip and my upper thigh, but I longed for him to move them, to roam over my bare skin and touch me in places only he ever had. I rocked my hips gently without breaking the kiss, rubbing seductively against him in the hopes of stirring the same emotions in him that were rioting in my body. I felt him harden a little between us and smiled into the kiss at my success; I was on the right tracks. I'd seen the look in his eyes earlier when he'd been in the water with me, he wanted me too, even when I wasn't human he looked at me with lust filled eyes.

When Aaron rolled us over in the next move, I found myself flat on my back against the rocks with just a towel between me and the ground. It wasn't the most comfortable place I'd ever laid, but when Aaron moved over the top of me and pushed between my legs, I forgot about the rocks and concentrated on where his body was touching mine. He leant back in and resumed the kiss, his tongue seeking out mine with each stroke, and his hands gripping at my waist.

When I pushed up against him I could feel him hardening, and quickly. I had been so afraid that he wouldn't want me that I couldn't restrain the feelings of relief that flooded my system. Pulling him closer, I wrapped my legs around his hips, the rough wet denim of his shorts providing an electric kind of friction against my sensitive skin.

He didn't seem to have any intentions of taking this any further, his hands were now either side of my head, holding him above me where his clothes were dripping water on to me, and his hips, which were grinding against me, were restrained in a way that was frustrating me. I wanted him more than I could explain, my hormones taking over and flooding my body with a need that only he could answer. My hands moved without thought and pulled up his top, he answered the silent request and sat up and pulled it over his head. Immediately his mouth was back on mine and I let my hands roam up his chest and over his shoulders.

As my hands curved against his back, I felt the roughness under my left hand and pulled away from his kiss with confusion.

'What have you done?' I asked.

He smiled in response and sat up, pulling me with him into a sitting position beneath him.

'I told you that I had the rose done in my tattoo for my mom, that I'd had her put in it because I'd always love her, even now that she's not here with me,' he said and I scrunched up my eyes as I looked down at the rose on his side.

The roughness I'd felt was nowhere near the rose.

'I don't understand.'

In response to my words, he got up and turned around, squatting down in front of me so that I could see his back. I gasped, and I brushed away the tear that leaked from the corner of my eye. Although it was still a little red around the edges, and looked a little sore, it was beautiful. Behind the thorns on his shoulder, there was a creamy-grey full moon, the detailed craters and surfacing looked almost real and the fuzzy edge gave it a shimmery appearance.

I went to run my fingers over it again, but pulled back at the last second, I didn't want to hurt him. It did look really sore.

'You can touch it Luna,' he said, reading my mind again.

Without answering him verbally, I touched the ends of my fingertips to his shoulder lightly, tracing the edges of the fresh ink. I couldn't believe he'd had a representation of me put on his body to mark it forever. The love inside me swelled and I pulled to turn him back towards me. As soon as he saw me he pushed forwards, flattening me against the rocks again and kissed me, this time with a little more fire in him.

'So, you see Luna, I'll never stop loving you, no matter how much time we have to spend apart,' he mumbled into the kiss.

After dressing in the clothes Elsie had packed for me, we made our way up the beach and ascended the steps that led us out of the cove. It was still early, and we didn't meet anyone the entire way back to the house. Aaron had left his car on the front, and followed me up the path to the front door. As soon as I opened it I smelled Elsie's cooking and a smile spread across my face.

'I believe she's making waffles,' Aaron whispered, coming up behind me and closing the door once we were inside.

'You've seen her already?' I asked, turning back to him.

'I spoke to her last night,' he confirmed.

I crinkled up my eyes in a tiny frown while I debated the possibilities for Aaron speaking to Elsie. Surely, she hadn't left it till yesterday to have her chat with him. She'd have wanted to speak to him and make sure we were safe as quickly as possible.

'I've seen her several times since last time I saw you Luna, we had our talk, and I've been back to see her and I did a run into town for her a few days ago when we had a miserable day full of rain. I like her,' he said with a shrug, answering my unasked question.

The smile on my face was one that had me biting my bottom lip; I loved that he liked Elsie, she was one of the most important people in the world to me, but it meant even more to me that he had been here for her while I couldn't be. I leant up towards him and brushed a kiss to the side of his jaw with a whispered 'thanks'.

'Luna, is that you? Is Aaron still with you?' Elsie called out from the kitchen just as Aaron pinned me against the wall in a returned kiss.

We laughed as we pulled apart and tumbled through into the living room before making our way through to where Elsie was still making mixture in a large bowl.

'I'm here, I was hoping I was invited for waffles,' Aaron said with an easy banter that proved he had been spending time with her.

'Of course you are dear, I was just about to ask whether you could stay, Luna, you have time for your shower; the waffles won't be ready for about twenty minutes.'

I smiled and gave Aaron's hand one last squeeze before shooting off for a shower. He made no move to follow me, and before I'd even reached the stairs I heard him pull up a seat and start a conversation with Elsie. I couldn't quite make out what they were talking about, but it made me smile again to know that he was comfortable around her and that she had some company when I wasn't around.

Breakfast passed in a blur of laughter and good conversation, and I kept falling silent to watch their easy interaction with each other. Little pieces of the life that I longed for were falling into place, but were still so far out of my reach that I didn't know how to handle it properly.

I excused myself from the table and headed back upstairs quickly, feeling the tears welling in my eyes. I wanted desperately for this to be my life, to spend each morning with Aaron and Elsie as we laughed and talked about our days; one day just wasn't enough anymore. I wanted more.

'Luna?' Aaron whispered gently from the other side of the bedroom door.

I hadn't closed it, but he didn't push it open or make any attempt to come in.

'Luna, I'm not daft, I know you're upset, can I come in?' he asked quietly.

I sniffled and wiped my eyes with the back of my hand before agreeing. He pushed the door open with a soft whoosh on the carpet and came and squatted down beside me where I was sat on the floor with my back against the bed.

'What's wrong Luna?'

I shook my head and turned into his chest, letting him wrap his arms around me and hold me tightly. The tears continued to fall but they made no noise. When they stopped I pulled back from Aaron's embrace and gave him a shy smile.

'I'm sorry,' I muttered with an awkward giggle, 'I just wish I could have more.'

He smiled as if he understood and pulled me close to wipe the tears away with his thumb. Then he leant forward until our breath mixed in the limited gap between us and he held my gaze.

'Luna, we have forever, and I will make each day as amazing as I can for us,' he leant in and pressed his lips to mine and I felt the urgency in his movements for me to respond.

I slid one hand behind his neck and kissed him back with everything I had and suddenly I was flat on my back on the floor with him on top of me. His knee went between my legs, forcing them open until his knee pressed up against me where I began to throb, my dress pinned to the floor, restricting my movements. His hands were close to my head, leaving no room for me to move and I caught a glimpse of his lust filled eyes before his lips came back to mine. My breath left me in a rush as I slipped my hands around his back and under the edge of his top. I loved how it felt when he took control like this, when he let his feelings for me take over.

His hand wandered down my body, his fingertips grazing my skin where my dress had hitched up around my thighs. He continued his lazy exploration as he kissed me, our tongues tangling and our breath mingling between us. I felt my breathing getting heavier, his weight on top of me increasing the excitement I felt bubbling in my body as his fingers traced up the inside of my thigh, rubbing gently against my underwear before slipping inside them and running along where I was growing wet for his touch.

'This,' he breathed as he pulled back from the kiss and slowly pushed one finger inside me, 'This is real, you and me together.'

My breath hitched in my throat as he pushed deeper and curled his finger to touch the spot inside me that made everything knot up tight in my stomach. He continued to rub lazily and moved his thumb lightly over other sensitive parts of me, making my body spasm beneath him. Just as I was about to moan his name, he leant in to kiss me again and the noise was swallowed by his kiss. When I felt the knot inside me tighten, he pushed a little harder, the tiny flick of pain enough to push me over the edge and I bit down on my bottom lip to stop me from crying out.

'Time isn't important Luna, what you feel is,' Aaron said as he slipped his hand from between my legs and sat up onto his knees.

I stayed on my back and concentrated on letting my breath return to normal while he stroked the bottom of my leg where he sat. He continued to talk, reiterating how it didn't matter that we only got one day a month; that he loved me anyway. The more he spoke, the more I calmed down; I started to believe what he was saying. Maybe a life like this was possible, maybe all it had taken was the right guy, and Aaron was that guy.

I sat up and pressed a kiss to his lips.

'I love you,' I whispered, realising that was what this feeling was.

He smiled back and kissed me again.

'I think I've loved you since the moment I laid eyes on you in that bar. Now come on, I have something to show you,' he said and he pulled me up to my feet.

'Now I'm intrigued.'

'The town is getting all geared up for Halloween, I think it's time I showed you what the holiday is all about, Elsie told me you don't have much to do with it normally.'

He was right; the full moon hadn't landed on Halloween for some time, so I tended to just treat October as any other month. There was no point getting excited when I couldn't actually experience the holiday.

The town centre was decorated with more bats and pumpkins than I could imagine, Aaron told me that they tended to attract quite a crowd as they held a little parade over the weekend and a lot of tourists came in for it. Some of the shops had gone all out, their decorations flowing out of the doors and spilling into the streets; everywhere I looked there was colour. The pumpkin faces ranged from the obvious, to the downright creative; one of the shops had carved names into the pumpkins that now lined up under their window, and they looked so different.

I'd taken my camera, at Aaron's request, but had taken to snapping shots on the camera on Aaron's phone, and just taking the ones of me and him on mine. I didn't want to use up the prints and there was so much that I wanted to remember. He promised me that he would get me proper copies of all the ones I took, making me smile as he understood my dislike for the images being trapped on the tiny little screen.

'Oh, look,' I squealed with excitement as we passed a tiny shop that was nestled between two much larger ones; a clothing chain store and a café.

The little shop front wasn't quite straight and it gave the effect that it had been squeezed in after everything else had been built. The rickety shop sign hung from a black metal bracket over the door and the peeling paint revealed it to be a book store.

'You want to go inside?' Aaron asked, squeezing my hand a little tighter as I bounced gently on my toes.

My eyes lit up and I nodded excitedly. We wandered over to the shop front and I was concerned that it wasn't even open, but as we drew closer to the door, a tiny little sign in the window told us they were. Aaron pushed open the door in front of me and a quiet tinkling sounded somewhere further back in the shop. An old woman shuffled from the depths of the shop as we closed the door again and looked around.

'Morning my dears,' she said in a soft voice that reminded me a little of Elsie.

She shuffled behind the counter and rested her elbows on the desk that stood between us.

'Is there anything I can get for you?'

'We're just having a look around,' Aaron answered with a smile and then proceeded to make small talk with the woman while I began to wander around the shop.

The shelves were piled with old books and the smell of paper and ink filled the air around me. I stood just past the first shelving unit and stopped, running my hand across the cover of the top book. It was bound in leather and had a thin layer of dust settled on it. I rubbed my fingers together to remove the dust and continued down the aisle. Books were piled high, stacked against each other and squeezed into gaps; more books than I could ever have expected to fit into the small space. The shop was barely wider than the small bedroom at the house, but it was deceptive, I'd never seen so much stuff kept in one place.

'You find anything?' Aaron spoke softly from behind me, making me jump.

I shook my head. I hadn't looked yet.

'It's amazing in here,' I whispered back, feeling like I should be respectful around books that appeared to be so old.

'The lady at the counter says that they are all first editions, or signed copies, that kind of thing. Do you want to look for one to buy?'

I nodded again. Elsie had a first edition copy of an old children's book at home. It had pride of place on the top shelf, and she often got it down to read to me when I was younger. I began to look around with a little more purpose now, running my fingers down the spines and reading some of the titles. We were deeper into the shop when Aaron laughed, a low throaty sound that carried on the silence.

'How about this one?' he said as he carefully pulled out a book from the stacks.

He handed me the book cover down so that all I could see was the worn material of the back cover. Turning it over gently in my hands, I laughed as I saw the title; *The Little Mermaid*. How ironic? He took the book back from me and placed it back on the shelf. It was then that I noticed the red cover. Three books beneath where Aaron had put the mermaid story back lay a beautiful red book with gold lettering down the spine.

'That one,' I said, running my fingers over the shiny lettering and the rough texture of the canvas cover.

Aaron picked up the books on top of it so that I could pull it free from its dusty prison and I blew it gently to reveal the cover. *The Grimm Tales* shone brightly in all its gold beauty once the dust was disturbed, and as I ran my fingertips down the spine and let it fall open, the old ink smell that escaped made me close my eyes and take a deep breath in. The pages were very thin and the book looked incredibly fragile, but it was perfect. I had always loved fairy tales when I was a child, Elsie used to tell them to me by the water before I changed back to swim home with my sister. It was during one of those moments that I'd first heard the story of *The Little Mermaid;* how I'd envied her at the time, even that young, I'd wanted to spend more time with Elsie, more time on land.

I flipped open the front cover and carefully turned the first page. Running my fingers gently over the ink on the first page, I smiled to myself as I heard Aaron lean against the shelf, just waiting for me to finish my investigation of the small treasure I had in my hands. The date of publication read 1909, and I showed Aaron where it said above it that it was a first publication.

'Do you want it?' he asked with a knowing smile.

'I do,' I answered, closing the cover again and dusting the front cover some more with the edge of my top.

We took the book to the woman behind the desk, who told us that we had made a wonderful decision; she agreed that everyone loved a good fairy tale, and we talked about happy endings and how everyone deserved one in life. I wondered briefly if she saw the look in my eyes when she said that, but I quickly turned to Aaron to find him smiling at me, and I couldn't stay sad. I paid for the book with the card that Elsie had given me with money on it and Aaron and I stepped back onto the street. The woman, who had told us her name was Elizabeth, had packaged the book up in air tight packaging and a sealable bag so that it wouldn't get damaged on our way back to the house. I clutched it close to my chest as we exited the little shop and stepped back into the flow of people milling around the town.

'I've lived in this little town my entire life,' Aaron said as he slipped his hand back into mine as we walked, 'And I can honestly say that I don't think I even knew that shop existed, never mind actually been inside it.'

We laughed about the tiny book shop, but he was right. I turned back to look at it, and no one else even cast a glace in its direction, never mind went inside. It was their loss I decided, because it was a small piece of magic behind that door.

The rest of the day passed in a blur of excitement and colour, and as we headed back towards the edge of town after lunch, back to Elsie's, I wondered why I had never gotten involved before. Halloween seemed like an adventure that I should have been a part of all these years.

Curiosity got the better of me as I passed a shop painted in bright yellow and black stripes like a bumble bee and had a skeleton hanging from the shop sign by a noose. I stood in front of the window, looking past the design on the glass, at the guy behind the counter inside. Re-focussing, I smiled as I looked at the design on the window, the one that mirrored the sign over the door. AWAY INK, the sign read, and I turned to Aaron with a grin on my face.

'You're not?' he said with a soft laugh, reading my mind as easily as always.

'I was thinking about it,' I replied, 'A piercing, not a tattoo.'

He raised one eyebrow and put his hand on my hip, pulling me closer and pressing a kiss to my forehead.

'Go for it.'

My smile grew a little wider, I had expected him to disagree with my idea, not encourage it. With a new confidence, I pulled him towards the door, listening to the little bell that rang above our heads to announce our arrival.

'Aaron,' the big guy behind the counter greeted as we walked inside.

'Mikey,' he replied, striding over and shaking hands with him.

'Nice to see you again so soon, surely you can't be wanting more just yet?'

The ease of the two had me smiling again, seeing a small glimpse into Aaron's life. I hadn't thought about the fact that Aaron would know them; that he would come here for his tattoos. I had no idea whether there was more than one tattoo place in the town.

'And who is this?' Mikey asked, drawing me back to the conversation.

'This,' Aaron held out his hand for me and pulled me close, 'is Luna, she wants a piercing doing.'

'Lovely to meet you Luna, what do you have in mind?' Mikey said with a broad grin and a knowing look that made the corners of his eyes crinkle.

I thought for a second about what I was about to do, then thought what the heck, you only live once, even with a mermaid's slowed aging, we weren't immortal. Looking back to Mikey, I smiled back.

'I was thinking about the helix piercing,' I said, pushing my hair out of the way and pinching the top of my ear between my finger and thumb to show him, 'This is just the first time I have actually done anything about it.'

One of the older girls had come back when I was younger with the piercing and I had loved it then, and I was telling the truth when I said that I just hadn't gotten around to doing anything about it for myself. Now I was wondering what had held me back before.

Aaron stayed quiet by my side, but squeezed my hand reassuringly as Mikey started to explain the process and healing time etc. I listened attentively, but knew that my body worked differently and that as far as healing time was concerned it would be fine by the time I returned to the water later today.

Once in the leather chair that smelled strongly of disinfectant, I began to get excited. Aaron sat on a small stool opposite me, his hands on my knees where he leaned gently while Mikey began preparing the piercing equipment. I signed the form that said I understood the process and the requirements of caring for it afterwards and then I sat back in the chair with a grin on my face. Aaron continued to talk, partly to me, partly to Mikey, as he got underway prepping my ear and arranging the silver stud ready.

The bite of pain made me grumble and let out a deep breath, but it was merely a little discomfort after a few seconds. It continued to throb as Mikey put in the silver bar and cleaned it up, and Aaron gave me a reassuring smile when I squeezed his hand.

'Looks good,' he said as I stood up to go and admire it in the mirror on the wall.

I smiled to myself as I turned my head to look at my ear, before turning back into Aaron's waiting arms as he came up behind me.

He paid for the piercing, told me it was my Halloween present, which made me and Mikey laugh, but I didn't argue. I would just pay for dinner later.

A Handful of Secrets

I kicked up leaves on the path as we returned to the house and Aaron laughed, swinging our arms where our hands were entwined still. We'd walked back from the tattoo and body piercing shop in high spirits, laughing and joking all the way. I had found two more shops to spend money in, and had a lovely new top with a bat on it that said, 'Just hanging around' and I'd bought a little hanging bat to put above the fireplace at Elsie's in celebration of my new-found love for Halloween.

I'd always loved this time of year for the colour. The leaves that littered the ground were alive with red and burnt oranges that made the greens of summer pale in comparison. Aaron had bought a couple of pumpkins from the market, and I couldn't wait to carve them and put a candle inside to light up its smile. I may not be around by the time the trick or treaters came knocking, but I wanted the house to look the part, and had made Elsie and Aaron promise to hand out the sweets that I'd bought to put in the plastic cauldron.

Elsie joined in the carving fun, and she decided to use the pumpkin to make soup for dinner before I left. Not something I had ever tried before, but it was lovely, and warmed us all up from the inside before I had to head back down to the beach; back to the water.

Aaron accompanied me back to the cove, standing with me in the gentle tide, our feet quickly going cold in the less than inviting water temperature, but standing there a while longer anyway. When we had to call it, I pulled off my jumper and handed it to him, but kept on the long skirt I'd changed into ready to transform. After saying my goodbyes again, I waded in until I was waist deep, turning back to wave and blow him one last kiss, then dove under the surface quickly letting the transformation take over so that the cold couldn't penetrate my skin anymore.

I took a deep breath once the change was complete, filling my lungs with salt water once more and lingered just below the surface of the water to watch as Aaron walked back up the beach, his hands in his pockets and his head hung against the wind. The image was distorted and blurry from down here, but it didn't alter what I saw; I had every detail about him saved to memory, the curve of his lips when he smiled, the angle of his shoulders when he stood, the several inches he had over me when he stood up straight and the way my name sounded in his voice. He was all I saw when I closed my eyes. There was no doubt that I was in love. The happy ending of the fairy tales in my new book were just a way to mock my own lack of one. How could I have been so stupid? We didn't have a future, no matter how hard I wished for one.

November

I was out of the water and half way up the beach as soon as the first ray of light had crept across the ocean. The morning bite to the wind made me grateful for Elsie's forward thinking as I pulled out a jumper and jeans from the bag she had left out for me. I didn't notice the temperature of the water when I had my tail, but in this fragile human body I was suddenly very cold. Elsie would have the heating on in the beach house, though I doubted there would be many others ventured out of the water now the temperatures were dropping. They tended to stay in for the winter unless there was something important that needed dealing with. I envied Elsie, she got to spend every day out of the water, every day with her feet. How was that fair?

Reaching for the key that we had hidden above the back door, I shivered as the cold wind made its way up my back. Hurrying inside, I slammed the door on the harsh morning weather. The crackle of the flames in the fire place were a warm welcome and I hurried over to find two blankets warming there and a fresh mug of steamy hot chocolate and marshmallows with a note that read, 'just nipped to the shop for your favourite, keep warm and I'll be back soon, E x'

Smiling to myself, I wrapped up in the cosy blankets and sat cross legged on the rug with my hot chocolate. The milky drink warmed me from the inside out and the warmth from the fire put a healthy glow on my cheeks while drying out my hair. I'd been sat for half an hour when I began to wonder whether I would see any of the others this month, but the front door opened, letting in a cold draft that distracted me from over thinking the matter.

'Sorry Luna dear, winter seems to have arrived ever so suddenly this year.'

Elsie bundled inside with her bags of shopping in one hand and her keys in the other. I jumped up to help her but she waved me back to the fire.

'You keep warm my dear, I put some of your clothes in the dryer so that they would be warm to put on instead of straight out of the drawers,' she said as she made her way into the kitchen with the bags.

'I'm sorry I didn't have your breakfast in though, the full moon kind of crept up on me.'

I frowned at her words but got up to help with breakfast none the less. Her words niggled at me though, how could she forget the full moon? She bustled around the little kitchen, putting things into cupboards and moving things around. There were supplies for more than just me here. I began to wonder if there was something I was missing.

'How many of us are you expecting this month Aunt Elsie? You have enough here to feed a small army.' I laughed, but it was a hollow sound.

She turned to look at me, a box of eggs in her hand, and frowned in thought.

'I bet not many of you surface now the temperatures have dropped. I should have thought.'

Something wasn't right. I watched as a confused look passed over Elsie's face before she turned to put the last of the shopping away with less enthusiasm than she had before. I'd tackle this later, maybe speak to my sister when I was back in the water. For now, I had somewhere to be.

Aaron had told me last time that he wouldn't be able to meet me at sunrise, but he'd be free for a late breakfast. I planned to walk over to the beach to meet him, but now I panicked about leaving Elsie.

'You gonna be okay if I nip out for breakfast? I said I'd meet Aaron,' I asked as she finished with the groceries.

'Of course, I have some cleaning that wants doing anyway. Will you be back for lunch? You can bring Aaron back and we could have a picnic.'

She sounded like she really wanted to see him, so I agreed, though I made it a carpet picnic; I wasn't sure the weather was warm enough to be sat outside.

After a warm shower I dressed in the clothes Elsie had tumble dried for me, and an extra layer before putting my coat on, then wrapped a scarf around my neck to keep the draft out and headed back down the stairs. Elsie was dusting the bookshelves when I made it to the bottom and looked happy; she was moving books around, flicking open the fronts on some and humming to herself. I wondered if she got lonely out here on her own all the time; the house wasn't exactly close to any others, she didn't have neighbours as such. If she wanted company she had to go into town, or at least down to the beach. I made a mental note to ask Aaron if he was still dropping in on her while I was gone. Elsie loved having him around, and seemed comfortable with him; maybe he could keep her company more.

'I'm off out Aunt Elsie, do you want me to bring anything back for lunch?'

She turned at the sound of my approach and held out a book to me, the cover open to the title page.

'This was your mother's favourite; I don't think I've ever told you before.'

There was a sparkle in her eye as if she was remembering her, and I paused before taking the book from her outstretched hand. Under the ocean no one ever mentioned my mother, as if she was some big secret, but every now and again Elsie brought her up. I took the book, refraining from asking too many questions; she'd probably just clam up again. The paperback book was old and tattered around the edges as if it had been read a hundred times or more, and when I looked at the page Elsie had it opened on, I saw the dedication that was handwritten. The neat handwriting read 'Our little secret, P x' under the printed title of the book which was none other than *The Little Mermaid*. I let out a tiny laugh as I thought of the book that Aaron had found in the little book shop on the last full moon, but glancing back at the book in my hands, I felt like I was missing something. I knew better than to ask too many questions, we weren't supposed to be inquisitive, and I didn't want her taking back the book.

'Can I keep hold of this?' I asked in place of the dozen other questions that were swimming around in my head.

'Of course, take care of it though; I've lost count how many times it's been read.'

I nodded; I'd treasure it with my life. There was a little piece of my mother between the frayed pages of this book and I planned to read it in search of even just the slightest insight as to who she was. I slid the book into my bag, cushioning it against the back so that it wouldn't get knocked about then headed to the door to put on my boots.

'We'll be back around twelve,' I called as I reached for the front door.

From the other room I heard Elsie resume her humming. Something was definitely odd about the situation, but she seemed happy. Maybe I was missing something obvious; I'd figure it out later.

When I made it to the Diner that stood away from the edge of the cliffs, I found a little booth free in the corner and pulled out the book Elsie had given me. How had I never noticed this on the shelf before? I'd slowly read my way through the collection of old paperbacks during the winter months when it was too cold out to go adventuring. I turned it over carefully in my hands, the spine was a bit tattered, but still whole; would I have even noticed it on the shelf? My preferences tended to be for the classics rather than children's fairy tales, but I felt like I should have known, like I should have been drawn to this one. It was about a mermaid after all.

I let the book fall open to the inscription again, the spine was damaged and the book fell flat, as if it had been opened to this page so many times that it had given in and admitted defeat. The ink looked like it was from an old-fashioned ink pen rather than a common ball point pen, and I wondered who would go to such effort to write in a book, and was it for my mother? My mind swam with the endless possibilities and I knew that I had to ask Elsie; it was just a matter of whether or not she would tell me anything.

A hand on the back of my neck made me jump and I turned to find Aaron leaning down to plant a kiss on the top of my head.

'Sorry, I didn't mean to startle you,' he said as he slipped into the booth at the side of me.

'It's fine,' I murmured, 'I'm in a world of my own this morning.'

Aaron looked puzzled, but didn't quiz me on it. Instead he pushed a menu in my direction and smiled; the confusion that had pressed in around me since getting to the house this morning faded into insignificance and I pushed the book back into my bag to deal with later.

'Miss me?' I asked as I leant into his side and let him wrap his arm around my shoulder.

'Always,' came his reply in a whisper against my ear that was followed by a kiss on my hair.

After breakfast Aaron had to nip back to the garage where he worked to make a phone call to a client, but insisted that I tag along so that we didn't waste any of our time together. When we pulled up on the road outside, I leant over to peer out of the window at the little garage nestled on the corner of the street between two bigger buildings. The peeling blue paint was in desperate need of a new coat, and the sign that hung from the corner of the little office was wonky where the bracket was coming loose on the wall.

Aaron jumped out of the Jeep and came around to open the door at my side. He helped me out and took my hand as we headed inside. Warmth enveloped me as we stepped through the doorway and closed out the harsh November weather outside. There was a little table just inside the doorway with a welcoming sign and a bunch of bright daisies on. The little sign told guests to ring the bell on the desk if there was no one around. Aaron didn't ring the bell, instead he made his way around the desk and poked his head through a door that I hadn't noticed yet.

'It's only me Marianne,' he called and got a mumbled response that I couldn't quite hear.

Once he had closed the door again with a soft click, he sat down in the chair behind the desk and gestured for me to go around to him. He thumbed through what appeared to be an address book while I pulled myself up onto the desk and got comfortable. I balanced my tip toes on the edge of the seat where he sat and he glanced up at me and smiled.

'I know it's not much, but it pays well and I enjoy working here,' he said as he pulled a piece of paper from a pile by the phone.

'It's cute,' I said in answer to his defence of the garage, and it was.

There was something quaint about it, and I would put money on the fact that Marianne was probably married or related in some way to the guy who owned the garage; Bob, if the sign reading 'Bob's Garage' was anything to go by. It was a typical little family run business; it just needed a good lick of paint to freshen the place up on the outside. But I guessed that in a small town where everyone knew each other, an outside impression wasn't all that necessary.

Aaron dialled the number that he had found, and spoke to the man on the other end of the call for a few minutes, arranging for him to come and pick up his car. From what I could gather, Aaron had only just finished working on it before he'd come for breakfast with me this morning, and hadn't had time to call him. I didn't mind too much, I was quite enjoying the insight into another part of Aaron's life. He was very sure of himself in these surroundings, as if he belonged here, and he'd been very clear and confident on the phone, whilst sounding familiar too.

'How long have you worked here?' I asked when he hung up the phone after arranging for the car to be picked up later that afternoon.

'Two years now, Bob is an old friend of my father's, and when he came asking for his help and couldn't get it, I offered instead. I haven't left since. I like working with cars; I built the engine in the Jeep you know?' he added as if only just remembering.

'Really? I wouldn't know where to start,' I said, trying to imagine how much work must have gone into a job like that.

'It's not too hard once you know what you're doing, and I've been playing with cars since I was a few years old. My dad worked here before he lost Mum.'

Aaron trailed off into silence as if remembering and I was quick to make sure that my pestering didn't affect his mood too much. I told him of my plans to go back to Elsie's for lunch and he agreed, saying he hadn't gotten to see much of her this month because he'd had a lot on with work.

We took the long way back, and Aaron gave me a virtual tour of the town, in relation to his life. I hung on every word he said, learning new things about him and absorbing them like a sea sponge. I loved hearing about his childhood memories, his mates and what they got up to at the weekends, and the different places he had worked through his life. He pointed out the little newsagents where he had gotten his first job; a paper round at the age of eleven. I could just imagine a little

Aaron, his brown hair and freckles on an angelic face that no one would have ever suspected of any wrong doing. But I knew from the stories he'd told me that he was a mischievous child, always in the wrong place at the wrong time and getting into trouble.

Back at the house, we spent some time in the living room with Elsie, but now that I was back here my thoughts kept returning to the book and what it meant to me. I had to find out the answers to some of the questions that were accosting my brain. The endless possibilities were driving me more and more crazy by the minute.

So, when Elsie moved to the dining room table and fell quiet, I took the opportunity and followed her, pushing the open book across the table with the inscription page visible. I held my breath as Elsie looked down at the book and smiled, a smile that I rarely saw on her features when she wasn't looking at one of us. Love, happiness, hope.

'Aunt Elsie, why was this Mom's favourite?' I asked, edging my bets with a reasonably simple question to begin with.

'It was a gift,' she said simply as she put her hand flat on the page, feeling the memories that lay hidden between the pages.

I glanced in Aaron's direction and he shrugged.

'Who was it a gift from?' I asked

'Peter of course,' she answered as if it were obvious.

She fell silent again, lost in memories that only she were privy to. I racked my brain for any mention of the name Peter and came up with a blank. I knew very few guys; our world was made up of women, we didn't need men. The only men I knew by name other than Aaron was the post man and the newspaper boy. Neither of them were called Peter.

Bearing in mind the other weird moments I'd experienced with Elsie over the last few months, I wondered briefly if this was something that her mind was making up, but the look on her face was enough to convince me that this was real. Peter. That name had to mean something to somebody; it had obviously meant something to my mother. How many more questions could I ask before she changed the subject? I picked wisely from the abundance of information I still wanted to know and asked a reasonably benign question.

'How many times has this been read Aunt Elsie?' I asked, genuinely curious due to its worn appearance.

'Countless,' she answered with a knowing smile, 'She was always reading this, it went everywhere with her during her time on land.'

Elsie made it sound so obvious, as if I should know all these things, and I began to wonder whether she thought I did know. After all, from her point of view, maybe I just didn't talk about my mother. I saw it as her not talking about her, but I'd learnt from a young age not to bring her up because everyone seemed to get angry with me, as if I was to blame, but I'd transferred that into my life with Elsie, she hadn't ever told me I couldn't talk about her and had always answered any questions I'd slipped into conversations. Maybe I was creating a problem that didn't exist.

Aaron cleared his throat then and I looked up from the pages of the book. I'd already read through it four times, finding something new each time. The torn corner of page seven, the tiny ink mark on page twelve, the little love heart that had been drawn around the number that marked page twenty-one, and the water mark and slight ink smudge on the last page as if someone had been crying while reading it. Each of those marks told a story that I longed to know the details to, but only one person knew them, and she wasn't here to ask. For now, Elsie's information had to be enough, but as I was about to ask another question she shook her head as if clearing her thoughts.

'Shall we get some lunch ready?' she asked with a completely different look on her face than she'd had a second ago.

Aaron had sensed the change in her; I'd been too wrapped up in the possibilities of what the book meant. I frowned at the silent message he was trying to convey before nodding at Elsie and agreeing to help with lunch.

I pulled the book back towards me and turned it around to face me, running my fingertips across the handwritten note like I had done so many times already today.

'I'm missing something vital here,' I whispered as Aaron made a move to stand.

At first, I didn't think he'd heard me, but then he came and bent over the table right by my side.

'I think there is something else you should be concerned about,' he said in a low voice that wouldn't carry through to the kitchen, 'Elsie seems to be flitting from one direction to another as if she can't remember the last. I'm not sure if she's not very well.'

I pondered that information too. Hadn't I thought that just this morning after the escapade with the groceries and her comment about the full moon? She seemed to keep forgetting things, things that were important. Something wasn't right, and I needed to find out what.

I stayed distracted for the rest of the afternoon, and when the light began to disappear outside, I found myself sat on the worktop in the kitchen while Aaron made dinner.

'I think he might have been my father Aaron,' I whispered barely loud enough for him to hear.

If I said it too loudly I was afraid that it would be true, and a little part of me still hoped I was wrong.

'Who?' he turned to me from the stove with a confused look on his face, 'I thought there were no male mermaids, mermen?' he corrected with a frown.

'There aren't,' I said quietly, glancing around to check that Elsie was still sat on the sofa.

She was nestled into the corner with her feet tucked up underneath her like I always sat in the winter. The yellow orange flames crackled away in the fireplace, lighting the room with a warm glow that looked like something straight from a film. The slight crack left in the curtains revealed the bitter weather outside in drastic contrast to the warmth that Elsie kept in the house. It had always been like this, for as long as I could remember; the fire, the blankets, the hot chocolates. I didn't want it to change, but I could sense the differences in Elsie. I knew that there was something wrong.

Aaron was still looking at me when I turned back his way, the book still in my hands felt like a lead weight. Was I wrong? Or more importantly, could I be right?

'I think the hand-written note is from my father,' I said again; this time with more confidence.

I saw the recognition dawn on his face as he understood my train of thought.

'You think you're the secret?' he asked quietly.

Shrugging, I let the book fall closed but kept it in my hands. I didn't need to look at the words anymore, I could see them every time I closed my eyes. Deep down I think I already knew the truth, I had from the moment I'd laid eyes on those words. But knowing them and honestly believing in them and all that they brought into question were two very different things. Could a mermaid even get pregnant from a human male? Everything I thought I knew was suddenly unravelling and I felt my world shifting, and not in a comfortable way.

Climbing down from the side and letting my hand brush over Aaron's arm, I took the book and headed for Elsie. She turned to me when she heard me approaching and I put the book by her elbow on the arm of the sofa.

'Who was Peter, Aunt Elsie?' I asked, hoping that she hadn't clammed back up since going quiet; I needed these answers before I had to go back to the water, and I was quickly running out of time.

She looked at me, then down at the book as if confused as to how it had gotten there.

'Where did you find this?' she asked, letting the book she'd had in her hand fall to the floor.

A pain split me in two, one I couldn't name. My human emotions were still a little strange to me, and suddenly, I had loads to deal with that I never even knew existed.

'Aunt Elsie, you gave this to me this morning, do you remember?' I asked, keeping my voice as calm as I could manage.

Calm was the last thing I felt right now, but I knew it wasn't her fault. Getting angry with her wouldn't help anyone. She picked up the book as if it was the most precious thing in the world and turned it over in her hands carefully.

'This was your mother's favourite; I lost count how many times she read it, smiling to herself down there on the rug. She used to lie out on her stomach in front of the flames and read at night.'

I kept quiet, knowing that she would go on in her own time. God, how just a month had changed her. The girls needed to see this; I had to get them ashore with me, they'd come for Elsie, they had to.

Elsie opened the book and ran her fingertips across the title page, and over the ink handwriting. The look on her face was of pure adoration and I knew in that instant that I was right. My mother had loved the boy who'd bought her this book.

'Aunt Elsie, who was Peter?' I coaxed again.

'Peter was your mother's best friend, he worshipped the ground she walked on, and I think the feeling was mutual,' she said with a knowing smile.

'Were they friends like Aaron and I are?' I probed, needing to know the truth.

'Of course, Peter was her everything, he spent so much time here that I nearly made him up a bed of his own,' she said with a girlish giggle.

I couldn't help but picture the type of relationship that she must have had with my mother, she spoke so fondly of her, like a mother would her daughter, and I began to wonder if there was more to this story that I didn't know. Elsie seemed to know so much about her, but it was impossible. Humans couldn't have merbabies, or vice versa. I was reading way too much into this.

The book snapped shut and I saw the clarity seep back into Elsie's eyes as she refocused on the here and now.

'Can I keep that?' I asked before she tried to take it away from me.

She handed it back to me with a smile, but no words, and I took it, holding it against my chest like it was the most precious thing in the world to me. It had just become one of them, it was a part of my mother that no one else seemed to know about. Elsie held the secrets, like she kept mine. It was part her job, part her love for us that did it, I was sure of it. But what I did know for certain was that my life was no fairy tale. I needed to stop living between the pages of an old book and get my ass back down to the water before sun down.

'I'll deal with this next time, I have to know the truth,' I muttered as Aaron walked behind me down the steps that led to the beach. 'Maybe I should ask the girls, maybe they know more than I'm assuming.'

'Luna,' Aaron said, his warm hand closing around my upper arm and halting me in my step, 'Don't let this eat you up, it'll drive you mad.'

'I need to know the truth, someone is keeping secrets from me and I don't like it.'

'I understand that, but we'll figure this out, in time. Stop letting it upset you so much.' His words were soft and he pulled me back up a step towards him so that he could kiss me.

The rain continued to drizzle down on us and our already wet clothes stuck to our skin where our bodies melded together. What had I done before I'd had him in my life? I turned from him and glanced out at the horizon, panicked that I wasn't aware of the time.

'It's fine, we've still got time. I won't let anything bad happen to you, you know that,' he whispered as he released me from his hold, sliding his hand into mine as we continued our descent down the uneven steps.

I was definitely learning. Deep down I knew that I could rely on him, that I could trust him. Marina wasn't as sure, but she understood that I loved him. She'd said that although she didn't quite understand the feeling herself, as love is a human emotion not a mermaid one, she did understand what she could sense in me. As mermaids we had bonds with each other. Family ties and ties to the Royals, but what we felt didn't class as love now that I knew what that really felt like. There was no doubt in my mind that I loved Aaron, or that he loved me back. Elsie had described Peter as 'worshipping the ground my mother walked on' and I knew that feeling. I would do anything for Aaron, and I was beginning to understand that he would do the same for me. He was taking care of Elsie for me while I was away, and he was meeting me before the sunrise of the full moons. I had no doubts that he was being faithful, he loved me and had promised me that it didn't matter to him that he only saw me once a month; it was enough for him just to have me in his life.

Damn, I was a lucky girl.

Back at the beach, I watched as the sun slowly sank behind the horizon, the orange and yellow tendrils withdrawing from the water's surface with every passing minute. They looked like fire crawling on the water, the elements working together to create harmony and beauty wherever you looked. I thought about who I was, and how the elements affected me, it was nature that gave me my legs every cycle, but it was nature that took them from me too. My natural being was a mermaid, I couldn't fight that and it hurt me deeply knowing that this was all I had to offer Aaron. He stood quietly behind me as if he knew I was working through something in my head. It always struck me how well he read me, as if he knew what I was thinking, sometimes before even I had worked it out properly. He never pushed me, and always listened when I tried to talk things out with him. My human emotions were still very confusing at times, but what was hard for me to understand, Aaron made sound simple when I asked. I was learning to ask questions more often; his curiosity was wearing off on me and I was asking more and more every time I was ashore.

'What are you thinking about? I can near enough hear the cogs going around in your head,' he asked as if on cue.

I laughed and turned in his embrace so that I was facing him, and reached up on my tiptoes to press a kiss to his jaw.

'I was thinking about how I have changed since I met you, you've made me nosey.'

'It's not nosey if it's something that is relevant to you, it's just inquisitive. Nosey is when you stick your nose into someone else's business when it doesn't really have anything to do with you in the first place,' he explained to me.

I mulled that over; it made sense.

'There seems to be so much that I don't know, things that are making me look silly,' I said looking up to meet the look he was giving me.

'I've never once thought you were silly, odd at the start maybe,' he said with a chuckle and squeezed me tighter, 'But never silly, it's understandable that there are things you don't know and understand. I kind of like that you're not afraid to ask me and let me explain them to you.'

He smiled when he finished speaking and I saw the raw honesty in his eyes. Love. That's what that look was.

I left him on the sand this time, the water was too cold for him now. After saying goodbye and him promising to get out onto the rocks next month to meet me before the sun came up, I waded out into the water, taking a deep breath and holding it at the onslaught of temperature change. The icy cold water crept up my legs and lapped at the long top I was wearing, seeping up the material as it clung to my skin.

'Be safe,' Aaron called, and I turned around to find him bouncing gently on the spot to keep warm.

I wasn't doing either of us any favours by dragging this out today, so I smiled, blew him one last kiss and then dove under the surface, concentrating on the change, and feeling the adrenaline course through my body. The temperature began to change, warming up around me, and I pushed hard with my tail to send me deeper below the water's surface. Coming to a stop where I knew I was out of sight from the shore, I turned to watch as Aaron waved at the spot where he had last seen me, before turning back to head back home.

I'd sent the book home with him, I wanted to know that it was safe, and although I trusted Elsie, I couldn't be sure that she wouldn't change her mind over the course of the lunar cycle and put the book away again. Aaron would keep it safe for me, and during the next full moon, I would do some more investigating and see if I could work out who Peter really was.

Was it possible that I was the product of a relationship between a mermaid and a human? Could it even be possible for that to happen? I didn't know the answers to any of the questions that swam around my head, but I knew that I had to find out. I needed to know who I really was; maybe this could explain my attraction to the shore. If a part of me was human then a part of me belonged on land. Someone had to have the answers to my questions; I just had to find them.

My entire swim back to The Kingdom was monopolised by how I was going to find the answers that I now desperately sought. I had a plan, but I would have to be careful not to raise too much suspicion. It would not go down well for me to start asking too many obvious questions, I would have to be careful, be sneaky, and make sure that no one suspected me to be questioning the possibility of my mother having revealed herself to a human.

Could I do this? Could I really throw into question everything that I thought I knew?

I had to. I had to learn the truth. I had to know who I really was.

Angel McGregor

December

I surfaced around the corner of the cliff that jutted out and closed in the cove; far enough away that I wouldn't be seen from the beach. Not that I expected there to be anyone on the beach; it was around an hour before sunrise, in the middle of winter, so it wasn't like it was going to be swarming with tourists or anything. But bearing in mind that I was already breaking rules by surfacing before the sun was up, I'd figured it was best to play it safer than necessary.

We had our plans though, and Aaron was there waiting for me, my aquamarine towel adorned with tiny pink mermaids dotted all over it in a pile by his side. It was too cold for him to come in the water with me now, and frost coated the surface of the rocks where he sat as if to confirm my thoughts. The cold didn't affect me until I transformed, so we gained an extra hour together by him coming out here, and now that the days were shorter, that extra hour was important to us.

I swam quietly towards where he sat cuddled up in his huge winter coat and woolly hat and then lifted my tail through the water to send a wave crashing against the rocks.

'Woah,' he called as I made my way to the rock that he was sitting on and pulled myself up to lean on the edge.

The frost crackled as I leant on it and I pressed my wet fingers against it and watched it fizzle to nothing. It rustled some more as Aaron manoeuvred to lean down and kiss me. His lips were cold against mine, but his breath was warm and intoxicating as he relaxed into the kiss. I had to fight hard to let him sit back up and not to slide him down into the water with me; the months seemed to be getting longer and longer and I hated the time I had to spend away from him.

'Winter is definitely here,' he muttered as he sat back down and I wondered if he felt the same about our current situation, 'Do you want the jumper or something?' he asked, concern clear in his eyes.

I smiled back, his caring nature one of the many reasons why I loved him so much, but his worry wasn't necessary.

'I'm fine,' I answered honestly; 'I can't feel it yet.'

He seemed to want to say something more but he kept his mouth shut.

'So, what have I missed?' I asked to distract him from over thinking the situation too much.

'Oh, you know, the usual; Christmas has descended upon the world. Everywhere is full of decorations, the shops are full of chocolate, the market is in town and Santa will be here soon.'

He must have seen the wonder in my eyes as I felt them go wide because he trailed off. I'd seen it before obviously; I'd been coming ashore since I was little. I remembered the lights, the colours, the music, but...'

'You've never seen Christmas before have you?' he asked as if finishing off my thoughts.

I shook my head.

'The last full moon that fell over Christmas was long before I was born, never mind surfacing.'

'I think we need to change that. I already bought you a present anyway.'

'Really?' I asked, already intrigued.

A smile crept across my face. I knew the tradition, I got how it worked. Elsie always bought us presents and left them under the tree, though I think I was about the only one who ever saw that tree. The others waited until it was warmer to open theirs. I'd already worked out that I wouldn't see Aaron again until after Christmas had passed, but I hadn't expected him to have got me anything.

'I got you something too,' I said, suddenly nervous that he wouldn't like it.

'How?' he asked, seemingly a little surprised himself.

'It's not from a shop,' I said as I lifted the length of sea rope from around my neck and handed it over to him.

He flinched as he took it from me and I realised that it must be cold because it was wet, but the look on his face was of pure wonder. Ever so gently, he turned it over in his hands and ran his fingertips over the back of the shell where I had engraved our initials into a heart with a sharp rock, a little like I'd seen characters on TV carve their names into tree trunks. Then he turned it back the right way over and the tiny pink pearl glinted in the early pre-dawn light as he rocked it back and forth between his fingers, studying it from every angle.

'It's beautiful,' he said under his breath and the air fogged up in front of him.

'You like it?' I asked, holding my breath.

'Like it?' he laughed, 'Luna, it's amazing, it's like having a little piece of you with me always.'

He slid the rope over his neck and nestled the shell against his coat so that the pearl was facing out. I smiled then, releasing the breath I was holding. I'd scoured the ocean floor for days trying to find the perfect present. This had just been lying there as if it had been waiting for me to find it.

I waited a few heart beats before asking the questions that was burning to be asked.

'So, what did you get me?'

I pushed gently in the water so that I was higher on the rocks in front of him, the excitement inside me bubbling to the brim. The pearl that I had given him was still nestled between the lapels of his coat and I smiled seeing it there.

We were sheltered from the wind a little where we were sat, but the brisk sea air was still whipping around us and I could see Aaron keep shivering.

'Can you wait? There is one at the house waiting for you.'

'Why is it at the house?' I asked.

He grinned at me, the twinkle in his eye that was only ever there when he was being mischievous glinting at me in the early morning light.

'I took it over yesterday, this one came with me,' he said pulling a tiny blue suede bag from his pocket and held it out to me.

'There's more than one?' I asked stunned by the presence of the little bag that now lay still on his palm, the black chord handles falling over the edge of his hand.

He nodded, 'This one is the main one, the other is just a few bits that I saw and thought of you.'

I smiled again.

'Do you want this one now or do you want to wait?' he asked, looking warily at the water.

I shook my head and held my hand out for the little bag before he took it back. He handed it over and I felt the weight of whatever was inside it slide from one side to the other. I looked up to find him watching me intently, his eyes on my face as I made sure I was comfortable on the rocks and pulled the chord strings to open the bag. Holding his gaze, I tipped the bag and let the delicate chain slip from it and onto the palm of my other hand. I closed my fingers around it so that it didn't slide straight into the water with me. A smile spread across Aaron's face and he glanced down to my hand, waiting for me to look down.

Taking a breath, I looked down and uncurled my fingers to reveal the silver necklace in my hand. The chain was silver, but looked like rope; strong and sturdy, and the pendant hanging from it sparkled where the early morning light glinted against the polished silver. The dainty, yet solid sea shell sat heavy on the palm of my hand. I could see why it had appealed to Aaron, and smiled at how similar our gifts were without us knowing that the other was even getting anything. I had a silver representation of the shell that I had chosen for him from the sea bed just outside The Kingdom.

I turned the shell over in my hand and it was identical on the back, a closed cockle shell trapped in the silver between my fingers. It was perfect. Aaron reached out and took it from me, gesturing for me to turn around. I lifted my hair with one hand and turned around carefully in the water as he bent down and pulled the necklace in front of me to fasten it behind my neck. Letting go of my hair I turned around again and looked down, it sat against my wet top and sparkled with a glint that reminded me of the one in Aaron's eyes.

'It's beautiful,' I whispered, as if I could disturb this moment if I spoke too loudly.

'It was perfect, I looked for days for the right one. This one is pretty and strong enough to survive when you're in the water. I wanted you to be able to wear it always.'

He leant down and pressed a kiss to my lips, his hand going into my hair and holding me there while his tongue explored my mouth. I held on to the rocks with one hand, but stabilised myself with soft beats of my tail in the water. Without touching his skin so that I didn't make him colder than he already was, I slid my hand around his neck and pulled him to me, making the kiss deeper.

The sunlight chose that moment to grace the horizon with its presence and I quickly pushed up through the water with my tail and kicked out to free my legs as I pulled myself up into Aaron's waiting arms. He shot me a quick grin as he greedily eyed up my body while he wrapped me in the towel.

Now that I was human again, the bitterly cold winter air whipped around me, sending shivers down my spine.

'Here,' Aaron held out his hat to me and I pulled it on and slipped my long, wet hair inside it.

I tucked myself around the corner of the cliff to shield myself from the wind and dried off quickly. Struggling into my jeans was hard work when I was still damp, but I managed it as Aaron came around the corner to hand me my jumper. The towel was draped around my shoulders, but the cropped sunshine-yellow top that I had been wearing was clearly visible where it was sticking to my skin because I was still wet. I saw Aaron's eyes dip downwards and he bit into his bottom lip simultaneously. A part of me felt like I should be self-conscious or embarrassed by his obvious gaze, but I couldn't help but smile; hadn't I spent enough time ogling him with his shirt off through the summer?

'Sorry,' he muttered as he turned his back again so that I could swap my wet top for the jumper.

I pulled on my coat too but left it open, I never covered my body up, and the wintery weather wouldn't change that; all my time out on the shore had given me a better tolerance for the cold than the other mermaids. I pulled my new necklace out and laid it against my jumper and as soon as I had shoes on too, I made my way over to where he stood by the edge and wrapped my arms around him from behind.

'Miss me?' I asked.

'Always,' he breathed as he turned and let me slip into his embrace.

We made our way over the rocks and around the headland so that we could climb down into the cove and when my feet hit the sand, I was quick to take my shoes back off again. The cove was sheltered from the wind now that we were on the beach and the sand was cold under my feet. It didn't stop me; I loved the grainy texture between my toes and I dug them in and looked down smiling, then looked back up to meet Aaron's eyes. He was stood quietly, watching me dig my toes into the sand and I saw the smile tugging at the corner of his lips in response to the childish happiness that swelled inside me.

'Come on, let's get you back to the house,' he said eventually and I slid my hand into his and let him lead me up the beach towards the steps.

'How's Elsie doing?' I asked as we headed quickly up to the house.

I'd held off telling the other mermaids about my concerns and convinced myself that having Aaron keep an eye on her was enough for now, she was quite happy with him dropping around during the month and I wasn't ready to face the idea of her being unwell.

'She's not great Luna,' he said squeezing my hand gently where it was already woven together with his, 'She didn't even recognise me the other day.'

I sighed, resigned to the fact that there was something seriously wrong with her and that I had to stop putting off telling the girls. They'd want to know.

'I'll tell them, they'll have to come ashore so that they can see her, they'll know what to do,' I said, trying to assure myself as much as Aaron, 'I don't know enough about her, I don't even know what it is that's wrong with her; maybe she is just confused? That happens to old people, right?' I asked, trying to think about some of the things I had seen on TV when I was younger and Elsie had sat me there with my sandwiches.

'Sort of, she's developing dementia Luna,' he said and I turned to him with a confused look on my face; I'd never heard of that before.

'Will she be okay?'

'It happens a lot to older people, they start to get easily confused, forget things and people. She needs to see a doctor, to get some help. She spends too much time on her own out here.'

'What about Peter, has she mentioned him again?' I asked, desperate for more information.

I had tried to bring the topic up over the last thirty days with the girls, starting with my sister. As soon as I mentioned our mother though, she'd gone quiet, as if I'd somehow offended her for wanting to know about the woman who birthed us. I'd been distracted all throughout the cycle, wondering who he could have been, whether he could have been my father. I knew how mermaids had babies, it was natural. When our bodies were ready it just happened, each of us developing differently, and the makeup of the group always being a contributing factor. We'd recently lost two of our older members of the family, and to make up for that loss, Shae had just had twins! It just happened; as if by magic Aaron would say if I told him, I was sure of it.

But the point was that I'd never heard of a mermaid getting pregnant the way a human does. I'd had that thought though, when I'd first agreed to sleep with Aaron, I'd justified that it was possible because our bodies were human when we transformed. Could she have gotten pregnant on land? Would it have taken and survived her transformations? So many questions and no one to answer them.

I wondered briefly if I would be able to track down the Peter from the book, but where would I start? Elsie might give me enough information to try and find him, but if she didn't, all I had was a name, and a possible time scale, assuming that I was right with my assumptions.

I'd tried asking some reasonably nondescript questions to several of the girls over the last few days, but hadn't got much more than stock responses that I'd been hearing all my life. 'You shouldn't be asking questions Luna,' 'You know your mother is a hard topic Luna,' 'Trust that the Royals told you everything you need to know Luna,' 'Your sister made sure you knew what you needed to Luna, why the sudden interest?' It was that one that had shut me down. Whether they knew about Peter or not wasn't the problem, they wouldn't talk because it was in their blood not to. And it had hit me that maybe they didn't know anything anyway. The inscription had said it was their secret, if Elsie knew it was because of the great relationship she'd had with my mother, not because she was entitled to the information. If I wanted answers, Elsie had them.

A Handful of Secrets

The front door went with a bang behind us where the winter air snatched it from Aaron's grip and pulled it closed. The warmth that suddenly enveloped us though had me stripping out of my coat quickly. Warm orange flames were crackling in the fireplace and there were two mugs of hot chocolate and a plate of biscuits waiting by the rug. I smiled to myself and craned my neck around the doorway to look for Elsie. There was no sign of her down here, but as I started to wonder about her whereabouts, I heard a bump upstairs that identified her as being in the bathroom.

Aaron was already on the floor, cross-legged by the fire, one of the mugs in his hands. He looked so adorable that I couldn't help but smile. That smile only widened when I stepped further into the room and the tree caught my attention; a massive real tree that nearly touched the ceiling. There was just enough room for... I peered around it and saw the box on the floor that held the angel for the top of the tree. I always put the angel up there; had done for as long as I could remember.

I folded myself onto Aaron's lap when he opened his arms for me, and sat facing the tree. There were several shiny parcels beneath it and I smiled, Elsie was okay. She had to be to have sorted all of this out as normal. Maybe Aaron was overreacting when he said she'd been getting worse. The parcels were all different colours, as always, and I quickly spotted mine. It was wrapped in shiny purple paper with a huge silver bow on the top. I smiled and picked out Marina's and Betsy's at the front. It was easy to tell them apart, Elsie used colours that matched out tails to wrap our presents, and always had done. It had started as an inside joke that had quickly become the norm. It saved on labels and it never failed to make us smile.

As I fidgeted on Aaron's lap so that I could peek at the other presents, I noticed two boxes at the back that were wrapped in red paper that had little snowmen all over it and a slightly bigger box wrapped in white paper with a black bow on it. I'd never known Elsie to use printed paper like that before, and I had no idea who the white parcel belonged to, none of us had white scales. As I was wondering who they were for it struck me again how much spending time with Aaron was wearing off on me; I was intrigued.

Elsie came down the stairs then in long legged flannel pyjamas and her big fluffy aquamarine dressing gown. I'd bought her a new dressing gown a couple of years back as a Christmas present, but she hardly ever wore it, she continued to wear this one, though it was older than me I was sure, and very thread bare in places.

'Morning Luna dear,' Elsie said as she came into the living room, 'Stand up, let's take a look at you.'

I smiled as I stood up and went over to her. Her eyes travelled up and down my body and I did a little turn as I made my way over to her with a soft chuckle. She laughed as I drew level with her and held out her arms for me. I stepped into her embrace and felt her arms squeeze me tightly; she wasn't always much of a hugger these days, but when she did, they were totally worth it.

'Merry Christmas,' she said when she released me, 'Do you want your present now?'

The grin on my face obviously answered my question, because she made her way over to the tree and pulled out my present from the front, she also grabbed the white one that I had just been looking at. She slid my box across the floor as it was a little bigger than she could probably carry, and she lifted the white box and carried it over, putting it down in front of Aaron. Now I was smiling.

'Elsie, you didn't have to do that,' Aaron said with a smile.

'I know I didn't have to, but I wanted to, and I have also peeked at what you put under my tree and I know that one of those has my name on it too, and you didn't have to.'

I glanced back at the presents under the tree and realised that the presents wrapped in the paper with pictures on were the ones from Aaron. Looking back at him, I saw him glance at Elsie, a look on his face that explained a lot without any words.

'I wanted to; call it my way of saying thank you,' he answered.

'What in the ocean do you have to thank me for?' she asked with a little laugh.

'For accepting me and Luna,' he said, stretching one arm out and linking his fingers with mine, 'For having me here for dinner and stuff,' he continued, 'And for trusting me with the girls' secrets.'

He fell silent then and Elsie just smiled. I knew that Aaron had been coming to see Elsie while I was in the water, but now I was starting to wonder just how much of each other they were seeing. Was it possible that Elsie had accepted Aaron as a part of life? Now I could see a whole new range of possibilities stretching out before me; I just hoped that the girls accepted him as easily. Elsie knelt down by us on the rug in front the fire and put her arms around the pair of us.

'You're as much a part of this family now as any of my girls,' she said and I felt Aaron's smile without even having to look at him.

I didn't know much about his father, but I knew enough to know that he wasn't really a family to Aaron. His mother had been the one who had loved him unconditionally, and he'd lost her; was it possible that he could be a part of my family now? I knew that I wanted to be his, but to have Elsie accept him into the family meant more to me than I'd ever be able to express to her.

'Right,' Elsie said suddenly, 'Are you two going to open these presents or what? I've got a breakfast to prepare.'

'Bacon and eggs?' I asked; it was always bacon and eggs at Christmas.

'Of course,' she answered with a smile.

Aaron pulled the presents he'd bought from under the tree and handed one to Elsie before putting the other box in front of me. I waited for Aaron to sit back down by my side before I pulled the bow free on the top of my present from Elsie. The ribbon fell away and I tore through the paper to find a white box inside; I gently lifted the lid and fur brushed my fingertips. I pulled the material free and held out the coat so that I could see it properly. Elsie had bought me a new winter coat; black with a grey fur hood and cuffs. It was beautiful and would keep me warm through the colder weather.

'Aunt Elsie, it's amazing, thank you,' I said, reaching over to hug her again.

'I figured your old one had seen enough of your adventures; it was time for a new one,' she answered with a smile.

'What's in yours?' I asked, turning to where Aaron was just pulling the bow free.

He gave me a quick cheeky smile before pulling the lid off the box and revealing its contents. Inside was a hooded jumper, in a dark shade of maroon red, with a zip up the front and white chord running through the hood. As Aaron lifted it from the box I saw the dark fur that lined the inside of the hood, and the thick cuffs on the sleeves. I smiled, knowing that Elsie had chosen it for him so that he would be warm with me when we were out on our adventures.

'It's great Elsie, thank you,' he said with a grin as he pulled it on over his head and adjusted his position so that he could pull it down.

It fit perfectly and I had to wonder whether Elsie had done some investigating into that size before she'd bought it.

'You are welcome, we can't have you getting cold when our Luna has you out and about exploring in the cold weather. I know what she's like; a little bit of wind and snow won't stop her.' She turned to me with a smile, 'Will it?'

I shook my head and laughed. No, it wouldn't stop me, never had. I only got one day ashore each cycle, I wasn't going to waste it just because of lousy weather. Anyway, there was something magical about the snow that called to me. I loved to lay in it making patterns. Elsie called them Snow Angels, but I'd learnt at a young age that if I moved my legs differently and kept my arms still; I could turn them into Snow mermaids.

I turned back to Aaron who was now stripping back out of his jumper with an over exaggerated huff at the temperature. We were sitting inside, in front of a roaring fire; what had he expected? With a laugh, I turned back to Elsie.

'Your turn Aunt Elsie,' I said gesturing to her present from Aaron and settling back against him where he held open his arms for me.

She carefully peeled back the paper with far more patience than either Aaron or I had shown with our own presents. When she revealed an old wooden box inside, she looked up, a glint of excitement in her eyes.

'I saw it and thought of you,' Aaron said as she lifted the lid on the antique.

I sat up to peer inside and saw the bed of red satin inside and what looked like a gold locket nestled safely within the folds of the fabric. She picked up the necklace and turned it over in her hands carefully before opening it to look inside.

'Oh Aaron, you didn't have to do this,' she exclaimed, pressing one hand to her chest with a smile.

'What's inside it?' I asked quietly.

In lieu of an answer, she turned the locket around to show me the little picture of me inside it.

'It has room for three other photos but I didn't have any others to put in it. Funnily enough I have a few of Luna,' he said with a chuckle.

'It's beautiful, you shouldn't be spending your money on me, I bet this cost you a fortune,' Elsie said whilst closing the locket and slipping the chain over her head.

She closed the little box and picked it up, moving it onto the edge of the marble fire place and positioning it at an angle that cast a tiny shadow from the flames.

'Now it's your turn,' Aaron said, pressing a kiss to the side of my neck making me shiver.

I smiled and leant forwards to pick up my present. It was quite heavy. I turned it over and pulled the paper off to reveal a hardback leather-bound book. The spine was cracked and I instantly knew that it was from the same little shop that we had visited the last time we were in town. I turned it over and gold lettering caught the light from the fire and glinted in the early morning light around us. Running my fingers over the filigree writing, I marvelled at the detail that the writing alone held, never mind the border that ran all the way around the rectangular cover.

Glancing up, I found both Aaron and Elsie watching me intently, and I knew that Elsie must already have seen this, knowing therefore that I would love it. The pretty gold writing identified the book as being the *Works of Shakespeare*. The name rang a bell, but I didn't want to admit that I wasn't sure who he was. I opened the front cover to find a list of titles that were included in the book and suddenly felt daft that I hadn't known who he was. One of the first few titles listed was *Romeo and Juliet*; I loved that story. I remembered watching it on TV one day when I was only around one hundred moons old, and thinking that I wanted to go to a masquerade ball like the one in the film. Elsie had been out and bought the book for me for the next time I had come ashore, and I had read it the same day.

I smiled at the memory. I had taken the book to the beach with me and spent all day in the shade of one of the big trees that shadowed the back of the restaurant and just read my way through it from cover to cover. The book was on the bookshelf in the corner now, and I glanced that way automatically, wondering how long it had been since I'd last read it. As I went to close the front cover, the flash of black ink caught my eye and I stopped it from closing with my fingertips. On the inside of the front cover, Aaron had hand written a message in black ink, just like Peter had in the copy of *The Little Mermaid* that he had given to my mother as a gift. Aaron's message read 'To our own secrets, love always, Aaron xx'

Closing the book and placing it gently on the floor by my feet, I turned in Aaron's embrace and held on tightly. I felt the tears well up in my eyes but refused to let them fall. He would never understand how much it meant to me that he had accepted all my secrets and made them his own the way he had; how he had just taken me for who and what I was and refused to let it affect who we were and what we could be to each other. I was an extremely lucky girl, and I wanted so much to be able to spend my days with him without having to worry about the position of the sun.

'I hope they are happy tears,' Aaron said with a soft chuckle as he stroked up and down my spine gently.

I laughed; the tears had escaped and were rolling down his neck to leave a tiny glistening wet trail. Nodding into his neck, not yet trusting my voice, I pressed a kiss against his skin where his top sat on his shoulder. When I finally pulled away, I swiped my arm across my face to get rid of the tears, and adjusted the beanie on my head where it still held my damp hair.

'Thank you,' I said with a voice thick with emotion, 'It's beautiful.'

'I figured you were going to need some new reading material for when the weather got too cold, and most of them are now films too, so I thought we could watch them after you have read them,' he finished with a smile.

'I'd like that,' I answered with a matching grin.

Elsie moved in my peripheral vision and I turned to see her getting up.

'Time for breakfast?' she asked when she was on her feet again.

I nodded, jumping up and pulling Aaron with me.

'You have time for your shower,' she said with a smile and I laughed back, she knew me so well.

I made my shower quick; they were getting less important these days, but I still liked to wash off the salt water and clean my hair. When I made it into my room, Aaron was laid out on my bed, his arms tucked behind his head and his eyes closed. Today hadn't been too much of an early start for him compared to the last few months, but I was starting to think that he wasn't much of a morning person. I tiptoed around the bed and pulled on some clothes, making sure to find a nice jumper so that I wouldn't have to get changed before we went out later. The one I found was one that Elsie had bought me a few years ago, it was red with small snowmen all over it. It might not be Christmas yet for most people, but it was for me, so the snowmen it was.

After putting on a little makeup and pulling a brush through my hair, I went to wake Aaron. Leaning over him, I pressed a gentle kiss to his lips and pushed my hand around his neck, stroking gently with my thumb just underneath his jaw line. He let out a little moan and kissed me back.

'Wakey wakey sleepy head,' I whispered, my lips still against his.

He pushed a hand into my wet hair and held on, his kiss getting a little harder and I opened to him, wishing that we had more time.

'Now that is how I should wake up in a morning,' he said with a laugh when I pulled away.

With a smile I nodded, it would be nice to be able to wake him up in a morning. I turned to hide the quick flash of pain that ran through me, knowing that he would never get that from me and Elsie saved me from having to face that right now by choosing that moment to shout up the stairs.

'Breakfast is nearly ready,' she almost sang.

She loved Christmas, she was always happy like this, but I expected that having Aaron here was making it a little better, she always said that she wished the girls would come out so that we could have a proper family Christmas together.

After a late breakfast, Aaron and I donned our new coats and Elsie put on her coat and scarf. We went for a lovely walk down over the cliffs towards the beach, where we stopped for ice cream. Elsie told me that anything went at Christmas, and though I was freezing, it did make everyone smile. It was nice to get to spend some time with Elsie, and I loved seeing her and Aaron communicate with their wild hand gestures, they were obviously spending time together and it showed in their body language and ease of being around each other. Elsie kept making jokes and Aaron had offered her his arm so that he had us one either side of him. We talked, laughed and did silly walks down the beach for an hour before turning back. Despite it being bitterly cold, Elsie walked barefoot in the incoming tide and got that same look on her face that I saw when she came down to the water with me at sunset. She looked peaceful and happy here with us. It added a bounce to my step knowing that she was happy, and that she truly was okay with Aaron and me. Even the bitterly cold wind that kept blowing past us couldn't dampen my mood. The rain that followed a few minutes later however, did a good job of dampening everything. The heavens opened on us, and I mean literally. It wasn't a little bit of rain, it came down so fast and so heavy that there was no escaping it, and we were half way down the beach.

'Quick,' Elsie said, pulling against Aaron's arm, which in turn pulled me.

'Quick what, there's nowhere to go,' I answered, pulling up my hood and holding on to it with one hand.

'There, against the wall,' Elsie pointed whilst trying to hang on to her own hood.

We scrambled across the sand, watching the few others that had ventured out do the same. The wall that ran along the edge of the beach was only just taller than Aaron, but it was attempting to protect us from the rain. We huddled against it, and I cuddled up to Aaron as he wrapped his arms around me, and waited it out for a few minutes. Elsie was breathing deeply, but had a smile on her face as if she was enjoying herself.

'You okay?' I asked.

She turned to me with a smile and nodded, looking up at the sky and holding out one hand, palm facing upwards, to catch the rain drops. I smiled and looked up to find Aaron watching her too with a smile of his own.

When the rain slowed enough to at least see through, we took the opportunity and headed up the beach to the car park, where Aaron rang a taxi to get us back to the house faster. It was a long way to walk when we were already cold and wet. The wind ripped through me now, sending shivers down my spine where we stood waiting under the shelter of the front porch of The Hut. My fragile human body wasn't used to this. I was usually pretty good at avoiding heavy rain like this, I didn't mind the wind but like this it was making my teeth chatter and everything.

The taxi dropped us off right outside and Elsie paid the guy, thanking him profusely for coming so quickly. We scampered down the path and all bundled inside, stripping out of our wet layers in unison.

After drying off, I peered out of the window at the sky, trying to determine where the sun was hiding. The heavy grey clouds coated the sky and made telling the time extremely difficult.

'You have a few hours yet Luna dear, sunset is at around four this afternoon,' Elsie said as she came up behind me and placed her hands on my shoulders, peering over my shoulder to look outside.

'What a miserable day,' Aaron said, echoing my own thoughts as he came back down the stairs, his hair dry now and a dry pair of jogging bottoms replacing his wet jeans.

Elsie released me and we headed over to the sofa, she had the fire roaring again, and I chose to sit on the rug in front of the flames as she settled herself into the corner against the pillows. Aaron came to sit on the floor, his back against the sofa and his legs stretched out towards me. I smiled, having them both around me made me happy; the only person missing was my sister.

'Will you tell me about my mom and Peter, Aunt Elsie?' I asked, hoping that she would at least remember telling me.

Her answer was that warm smile she got when she was happy, her thoughts clearly filling with happy times.

'What would you like to know dear?' she asked, a slightly dreamy look in her eyes.

I tried to gage what level of lucidity she had, bearing in mind how much we had done this morning, now that she was sitting doing nothing, she seemed to be drifting in and out a little. Her smile was genuine though, and I reminded myself that I didn't think she was keeping anything from me on purpose; she didn't talk about my mother because I didn't. I needed to stop assuming things and start asking more questions. So, I took a deep breath and picked out the questions I felt were most important.

'How long were they together?'

'Oh, a long time, she met him like you met Aaron, just by accident one day when she was ashore. He worked in one of the bars down on the beach front, and just like you, she used to spend her time out and about near the beach; she loved to be on the beach, to be on the sand

and around the water. She would spend her days down there and her nights here by the fire.'

As she trailed off into silence, I reworded my question, needing to know the answer.

'How long did she know him before,' I trailed off there, not being able to voice the end of my question for the lump that had formed in my throat.

'Four years,' she said, obviously understanding, 'It had been just over four years because I remember them celebrating the anniversary of them meeting. He bought her that book.'

'*The Little Mermaid* book?' I asked, to clarify.

Elsie nodded, and I turned to Aaron. I could be right. The secret could have been me.

'So, what happened? Where did he go after?'

I still couldn't bring myself to say the words out loud. But why hadn't he been there after? Why hadn't he come for me?

'It's complicated Luna, there is a lot about that day that you don't know. It was a hard day for all of us, especially for your sister. It should have been a great day for her, having her baby sister come into the world, but she had to deal with losing her mother all at the same time. Peter stayed away, he came to see me during the cycles, but the girls didn't know about him, Marina didn't know about him.'

'And where is he now?' I asked, cutting in.

She seemed to take a breath then, and I knew that I wasn't going to like the answer.

'He died in a car accident a little after your fifteenth moon.'

The room fell into silence as I took in what she was saying. He was dead. My hopes of finding him and knowing exactly who he was were torn away from me with those few simple words. I chose my next question carefully, but I had to know.

'Was he my father?'

She looked at me then, with perfect clarity in her eyes. She knew exactly what I was asking, and she knew the answer; I could see the knowledge behind those familiar green eyes.

'I don't know the answer to that for certain, I never pried, and your mother never gave the information up; but I believe so, yes.'

And with those words, my whole world shifted again. Everything I thought I knew about who I was and what we were was thrown into turmoil and I had to start all over again at figuring all of this out.

If I was part human, that could explain so much. It would explain why I felt like I belonged on land; a part of me did. A part of me belonged here with Aaron, and now I had to deal with that knowledge by myself. I couldn't turn to Marina with this. I had Aaron, and I had Elsie. They were the family that I could rely on, no matter how much I loved Marina, she wouldn't understand this.

The rest of the afternoon passed by slowly, and I found myself curled up with Aaron, reading the beginning of *Hamlet* out loud to him whilst he held me. He never asked about what Elsie had told us, and he never pushed for my feelings or how I was dealing with it. It was like he understood that I just needed some time to process it.

Just before sunset, I said my goodbyes to Elsie, and Aaron accompanied me back down to the water. He was reasonably quiet the whole way there, and once we were on the beach, I explained that I couldn't meet him next time because I was going to bring the girls with me. They needed to see Elsie, and I needed their help with what to do next. I was also hoping that having some of them there, all together in the same place, would mean that I could get some other answers out of them too. But I wasn't holding out too much hope there.

'Are we okay?' Aaron asked quietly as he stood behind me, his arms wrapped around my shoulder.

I turned quickly in his embrace, pressing a kiss to his lips before I spoke;

'Of course we are, there's just been a lot to take in today. I'm sorry.'

'Don't be sorry, I just had to check.'

We laughed as we watched the sun slowly disappear behind the horizon, and I pulled off my boots and jeans to give to him. The jumper I was wearing came next as I didn't want the salt water to damage it, and after a final kiss goodbye, I splashed into the water and dove under to change quickly; the water was too cold now to linger in my human body.

As I hovered under the surface of the water, I caught my new necklace between my fingers and held it as I watched Aaron wave towards where he could see my colour, before retreating up the beach to the steps.

Another day gone, another cycle to endure.

January

It killed me knowing that the sun was already up and I was still under the water, but I swam alongside my sister and the other girls that had agreed they needed to come ashore as we made our way to the surface. Marina and Betsy talked absent-mindedly about the weather and how long it had been since they had been ashore at this time of the year. I was surprised at just how long it had actually been. I remembered when I was younger, how they had come ashore in groups, the family BBQ's and the day trips into town. People had recognised us and always made a fuss of Lou, Fran, Georgie and me as children. We were pretty children; our bouncing curls and rosy red cheeks had gained us plenty of attention. Now, I bet the locals didn't even remember some of the girls, especially Lou, she hadn't surfaced in years, and we had changed so much since then.

Marina still came ashore regularly, but I felt that it was more for my benefit these days than her own desire to be on land. Some of the others; Betsy, Mia and Shelley, they came up reasonably often, but Janine, Ellie and Shae barely ever surfaced these days. Now they all swam beside me, banding together for Elsie. It made me wonder again what the link really was; I hadn't had to do much convincing either, as soon as I had mentioned that I thought she was ill, they had decided they needed to come and see her. Janine was one of our Elders, and she acted that way too; very old fashioned and far too confrontational about her opinions. Especially about my choices in life. Her daughter Shelley, who swam beside me now in silence, was much better company, and Georgie was one of my best friends, she was Janine's granddaughter from her other daughter Coral. Now Coral I liked. Coral was very happy go lucky and loved to hear about my adventures when I had been ashore. She was just as adventurous, but her adventures were underwater, she loved to explore outside The Kingdom and often disappeared for days at a time whilst out searching new reefs that she had discovered. The most exciting adventure she had been on recently had involved a ship wreck about seven miles east of the back of The Kingdom, she'd been gone six days; we were actually ready for sending out a search party when she had finally returned, full of tales and excited chatter. And yes, I had totally gone with her a few weeks later to check it out. My adventurous side didn't go away when I was back in the water.

We neared the surface and everyone turned to me. I guess I was the one who was surfacing first to check that the coast was clear. No pun intended. The air was fresh against my face as I surfaced far enough away from the coast line that I could be mistaken for a seal, and scoped out the beach. There was no one about - no surprises there. It was the middle of winter and the weather would be arctic. I'd spoken to Elsie last month and made sure that Aaron would remind her to put warm clothes out for all of us, as she would normally only be putting out my clothes in January. I dove back down and found the girls just below the surface; Betsy and Georgie were having a small-scale game of tag and I smiled as I caught sight of the disapproval on Janine's face. Marina swam over to me, Shae not far behind her, and I told them the beach was empty. We surfaced and made our way towards the beach, trying to get as shallow as possible before transforming.

As soon as I kicked my legs apart, the wind hit me, stealing my breath and forming a cloud in front of me. I scrambled up the beach, barely noting the scratchy sand between my toes and pulled my towel from the top of my bag, hiding my smile when I realised it was the mermaid towel that Aaron had bought me in town a few months ago; the little inside joke never failing to bring a smile to my face. That meant he had packed my bag. I pulled out my coat and pushed my arms into it whilst pulling the thick jogging bottoms out of the bag. My fluffy boots were in the bottom, and Aaron's scarf was tucked with them. I was easily the first dressed, and I laughed as I had to help Betsy into her jumper where she was struggling into it with wet skin. There wasn't time to dry off properly in the bitterly cold wind. I pushed my hair up into my hat as the others signalled they were ready and we made our way across the sand to begin our ascent up to the house.

'Aunt Elsie, look who's here,' I yelled as I slammed the front door on the arctic weather and pulled off my boots and coat.

I heard her come thundering down the stairs and looked up to find her fully dressed with her mobile phone in her hand.

'Oh Luna, I have been so worried. I tried to ring Aaron but he isn't answering, where in the ocean have you been?' she rambled, though kept her voice low so not to alert the others.

'Aunt Elsie, I told you that I wouldn't be out at sunrise today, I was coming with Marina and the girls.'

I gestured into the living room where they had congregated around the fire. Betsy already had her socks off and her feet so close to the flames I was surprised she hadn't burnt her toes yet. Janine and Shae were on the sofa and Marina came back to the door way, the concern on her face clear. Elsie didn't forget things; she knew everything and remembered even the most insignificant things from when we were younger. If I said that I had told her this, Marina knew that she should have remembered. There had to be something wrong.

'Hey Elsie, how are you?' she asked as she drew close enough to put her arms around her for a hug.

'Marina, I wasn't expecting you,' Elsie looked over Marina's shoulder and smiled at the others, 'I wasn't expecting any of you, there isn't usually this many of you, I thought it was too cold for you at this time of the year.'

'We thought that we would show our faces, Luna said that you were missing us,' she said with a light-hearted smile, but I could still see the worry etched into the lines around her eyes.

Elsie laughed at the idea, but bustled past and into the living room where she uncovered the small pile of presents in the corner where the tree had been.

'Well as seeing as you are all here, we can have a mini Christmas morning,' she said, suddenly full of excitement.

I sat by the fire looking at the destruction that now littered the living room in front of me. I'd snuck upstairs for my shower whilst the girls were opening their presents, and by the time I had gotten back down, there was discarded wrapping paper everywhere, and bows in everyone's hair. Apparently, Betsy had decided that everyone had to wear their bow and somehow, she had managed to get everyone to agree; including Janine who had a usually absent smile on her face.

Elsie was putting on her coat, claiming we needed eggs so that she could make the traditional bacon and eggs breakfast, and I made sure she was well wrapped up before waving her out of the door.

Once I was back in the front room, everyone's eyes turned my way, the concern for Elsie etched into each of their faces like paint daubed on a canvas. I sat myself down on the sofa arm and put my feet behind the pillow where Marina sat, waiting for someone to start the conversation I'd been dreading for months. Of course, Janine started it.

'Why didn't you tell us sooner?' she said without any apology.

'I didn't realise it was so bad, it started out as little things, unimportant things, but she is getting so much worse between the full moons, it was hard to judge how bad she was until it became so bad that I couldn't ignore it,' I said, not looking up to meet her gaze which I could feel boring into me.

The conversation moved on and it quickly became clear to me why we didn't come out in groups of too many these days; we couldn't have a reasonable conversation to save our tails. We were going around in circles and I seemed to be missing a vital piece of information, I was sure of it.

'So, wait a minute,' I cut in, holding up both hands to emphasise my words, 'How exactly are we going to do any of these things when we only get to see her once every cycle?'

Everyone fell silent for a second and then Janine continued in a creepily calm voice.

'We need to look after her, properly.'

'I've been doing my best,' I said, anger suddenly bubbling up inside me; how dare she accuse me of not looking out for Elsie.

'That's not what she means,' Marina added quietly, 'There are a few things that I think I need to clear up.'

I turned her way and watched her avoid my eyes for a full minute before she carried on.

'There are things I've kept from you, a handful of secrets that we have kept from you...' someone cleared their throat and Marina shot them a glare.

'I asked them to keep them from you; we all agreed that it was for the best at the time. I wanted you in the water with me where you were safest. After everything that happened with Mum, I needed you to be safe, you have to understand that.'

She looked up at me, her eyes glazed over with tears and I held back the sharp retort that I was about to bite out and waited patiently for her to continue.

'Elsie is more to us than what you believe she is; she's one of us Luna, she was born a mermaid just like we were; there is a way to get out of the water,' she choked back the tears and tried to continue, but she didn't get much further, 'I'm sorry.'

I sat in dazed silence for a few seconds before turning on them all as a group. They'd lied to me, about everything. 'A handful of secrets' Marina had just called it; it felt more like an entire ocean full to me. Everything I thought I knew and understood was falling apart around me, just like it had when I'd found out about Peter. Was there anyone that I could trust entirely?

'How could you have never told me before that Elsie was a mermaid once? How could you all keep that from me? You know how much I want to be on land, and now I learn that it's possible; that it has been possible this entire time. You just thought you'd keep me in the dark!' I almost shouted, the pent-up anger escaping me in a burst of noise that was most unlike me.

'I think you're drawn to land more than the rest of us because you were born on land Luna,' Mia threw in as if it wasn't massive news to me.

I blanched, how was I only just learning these things? Was I the only one that thought this was all very important?

'You weren't born like a normal merbaby. Your mother had you during her time on land for the full moon; that's why she named you Luna,' she seemed to add the last bit as if it made up for everything else.

So many things started to fall into place. My desire for a life on land. My intrigue when it came to the ways of the world above the ocean. Peter. My heart did a double take as I realised that this may be the answer I was looking for; the last piece of the puzzle that confirmed my genealogy.

'What about Elsie? Is someone going to clue me in there?' I was fighting hard to keep control and keep my voice calm.

My mind swam with this new information, the possibilities that it made real. All the fantasies that were suddenly within my grasp. I couldn't believe that they'd lied to me all these years.

'Being on land comes with consequences Luna. The longevity we have as mermaids is tainted by the shores, haven't you ever noticed before that you're aging faster than others your age?'

I refrained from nodding my head. I had noticed, but I'd assumed that it was normal; no one had ever given me cause to believe otherwise. No one had mentioned it, so I hadn't either. Well, until now. I was starting to see things very differently all of a sudden. A question formed on my lips and escaped before I had chance to think through the repercussions that would accompany the answer.

'What really happened to my mum?'

An awkward silence filled the room and everyone looked at each other while avoiding making eye contact with me. Finally, my older sister turned to me, tears filled her eyes and I saw her swallow past the lump that had quickly formed in her throat; I guess she already knew the truth. I found it hard to sympathise with her knowing that they'd purposely kept me in the dark this whole time.

'Luna, it's complicated,' she began.

'Just tell me the truth Marina, I think I deserve that much.'

She nodded, the look on her face one that almost counted as apologetic.

'She was out of the water too long after having you. Elsie tried hard to get her back into the water after the transformation, but she couldn't get her there safely in time. She dried out and suffocated from the dry air and lack of salt water.'

'She transformed on land?' I asked, shocked.

I'd never heard of a mermaid actually changing while they were still out of the water. We were told about how it would happen, warned not to linger on land once the sun began to set, but I didn't realise it had genuinely happened.

Marina nodded.

'After having you, Elsie got her out of hospital, but she couldn't get her to the beach because it was still too busy. It was well after dark before she returned her to the water, and she was just too dry to recover. She didn't make it back to The Kingdom.'

'What about me?' I asked in a small voice, trying hard not to think too much about all of this, 'What happened to me?'

'You stayed on land with Elsie for the first month of your life; no one knows why you didn't transform. Maybe because you were born dry, I don't know, but it wasn't till the following full moon that Elsie brought you to the beach, and as soon as the water touched you, you transformed. And then it was like nothing had been different; until you started showing your preference for land a few years later.'

My mind went into overdrive as she fell silent. I'd stayed on land, I'd stayed human without the full moon, and before I could make any conscious choice about it too. Did that mean that I could stay on land again? And what about Elsie? They were avoiding the answer to that question still. I bypassed me for a minute to try and get to the bottom of whatever the deal was with her.

'So, what's wrong with Elsie? Why is she on land in the first place? And what happened to her fins?'

Mia cut me off, 'One question at a time Luna.'

Shelley took over this time, and she seemed genuinely apologetic for the fact that she had to tell me all of this, at least someone felt badly for lying to me.

'For as long as any of us can remember there has always been at least one of us on land, to run the house and keep contact with the town; otherwise we'd be total outsiders. My Great Grandma was the last. Normally they would just do a couple of years at a time, so the aging didn't creep up on us too fast, we're not immortal

Luna, time just passes differently under the ocean, so being on land causes us to age in human years, therefore shortening our life span. Others would come ashore too, a few months at a time, some just a few weeks; there were always some of us around.'

As Shelley trailed off, Mia continued where she stopped.

'Elsie, unfortunately, got a pretty bad case of scale rot under the ocean, she would have died, so she chose to come ashore for good and live out her life in human years, looking after us. I think now, she is developing something called dementia; it's a mental illness that humans can get that affects their judgement and their memories.'

'Yeah, Aaron mentioned that,' I murmured under my breath so that only Marina would hear me.

'We're going to have to start the process of getting someone else out here permanently, she needs to be cared for,' Janine voiced suddenly.

'I need to get her to a doctor before anything else happens,' Mia continued, the conversation with me sidelined.

I decided to bring it back around, 'How? How do we get someone on land?'

'At the moment of a dual celestial event, we can choose to transform and it sticks, unless you come back to the water on a full moon. That's how we got Elsie out to start with; it's how we used to come ashore for a few weeks then go back to the water, your mother used to spend months at a time out here, especially over the summer. She had a little job in one of the pubs and everything. The only difference is that Elsie can't come back or the scale rot will kill her,' Mia dropped to a whisper as she spoke, and I saw the tears begin to well up in her eyes.

'But so will the old age eventually, won't it?' I asked.

'Yes, eventually, but the scale rot was painful, old age isn't. She made her choices a long time ago, we have to accept that but we do need to sort out getting her to a doctor, and quickly, and getting us out to care for her before she hurts herself,' Janine answered when Mia couldn't.

'I'll do it.'

I didn't even think before I said it, I didn't need to. This was my chance at a life with Aaron, how could I not go for it?

'I told you this would happen,' Marina said, pride in her voice that didn't match the expression on her face.

'Luna, you need to be sure,' Janine continued.

'I belong on land, I belong with Aaron,' I said with clarity.

I knew this was my way forward, and the words slipped out before I had a chance to think about them. Seven sets of eyes fixed on me.

'Who's Aaron?' Janine asked briskly.

'It's not important right now,' Marina tried before I had time to speak, 'We need to concentrate on Elsie and working out when the next celestial event is so that we can get some of us out of the water.'

'It matters,' Janine said to Marina, and then turned to me, 'Who is Aaron?'

'Aaron is my boyfriend,' I answered as confidently as I could manage under her teacher like stare.

'Boyfriend?' she asked, blinking as if I was speaking a different language.

'Yes,' I confirmed, sounding much more confident than I felt.

'In what way is he a boyfriend? We don't need boyfriends.'

'Oo, is he the boy from the beach?' Betsy suddenly squeaked out.

I smirked at Betsy, who dissolved into a little fit of giggles, then Marina and I exchanged a brief smile but she just gave me that look that I knew oh so well; your mess, you fix it. She'd perfected it over the years. She only stood up for me for so long, and if it was my own fault then it was my own responsibility to get myself out of it. This definitely counted as my own fault. Aaron was my choice, my responsibility. I took a deep breath and began to explain myself.

'He's a guy I met during the full moon in May, I've been seeing him each moon since.'

Janine looked at me as if trying to determine whether I was lying then she turned to Mia. Mia shrugged; she was generally pretty carefree as far as the rules were concerned, plus she'd had a head's up, and she didn't seem too worried. Janine turned to my sister next.

'And you knew about this?' she asked, a tone to her voice that I couldn't quite determine.

Marina nodded.

'She's been very careful, Elsie was on board from the beginning too, so she's been looking out for her.'

'Bearing in mind everything that is going on with Elsie, I don't think that she is the right person to be level headed about the whole situation,' she cut Marina off to say.

I had to cut in there, and Janine didn't like it if the look on her face was anything to go by.

'No offense Janine, but I don't think you're the right person to be judging Elsie either. Take this out on me all you like; it was my choice in the end. I asked for Elsie's opinions but I still made the decisions. And when Elsie isn't having issues with her memory, she is perfectly fine. There is no impairment on her judgement or her personality. You'd know that if you spent more time on land with her.'

I added the last bit and instantly regretted it. It was my choice to spend my time on land, I knew it wasn't normal. But how could they ignore Elsie like that, especially now that I knew that she was one of us all along? I cut in again before Janine had time to respond.

'Look, Aunt Elsie will be back soon and I know she misses having us all out, try spending some time with her and you'll realise that she's still the same person. As for Aaron, I won't apologise for what I've done; I love him, and he loves me. Despite everything that should be keeping us apart he's still here. You can meet him if you like,' I turned to Marina, 'I'd really like it if you would meet him; it would be nice to know what you think of him.'

I fell silent after that and waited for a response. No one spoke which was not normal for any of them. Seconds passed with the ticking of the hand on the clock in the hallway echoing around us.

'I guess we have been a little lax with having someone around and making sure there are visitors each moon. There used to be people around for weeks and months at a time before all this secrecy. I don't know why it had to be like this. I haven't been out in at least five moons, and even then, I was only ashore for a couple of hours, I don't know how I got like this, I used to love coming ashore with Clea when Marina was little,' Mia piped up eventually, 'Luna is so much like her in so many ways, she is out every full moon, and she's out from dawn till dusk; if anyone knows Elsie these days, it's her. It's not us Janine.'

I smiled to myself at the little mention of my mother and I saw the warmth in Mia's eye as she spoke of her. Everyone had loved her.

'That was because we made a decision to stop using the celestial events, because you wanted to keep her protected from it,' Janine suddenly snapped at my sister, gesturing rudely at me.

'I only wanted her in the water while she was a child, the rest was all on you, and don't try to deny it,' my sister snapped back more ferociously than I'd ever heard her.

Those words seemed to hurt because Janine made no move to reply. She simply looked down at her hands where she was wringing them together in her lap. I watched as she slowly looked up and met my eyes before turning to Mia. I didn't want to hear the rest of this conversation; I had other places to be. I was wasting my time with Aaron by being here with the girls. They'd said we needed to be here with Elsie when we had this conversation, but then they'd waited for her to nip out to the shop before actually talking about anything important.

I slipped from the room as talk turned to doctor's appointments and possible outcomes. I'd learned today that Mia was Elsie's biological Granddaughter, so she intended on coming ashore to help look after her. Janine was one of our Elders, I expected that she would be coming ashore if possible, at least just to find out the specifics, and I heard Marina say that she wanted to come ashore with me, to help me adapt. I smiled to myself as I climbed the stairs and headed for the bathroom, still listening to the conversation so that I didn't miss anything.

Janine seemed okay with the idea of me coming ashore, though the disapproval in her voice was like the proverbial octopus in the corner whenever she mentioned Aaron. Mia shut her down several times, claiming that even if I didn't understand the ramifications of my actions, Elsie did, and she was on board with my decisions. That seemed to shut her up, but she still didn't try to hide the tone in her voice that made it clear that she didn't agree with the situation.

They were discussing how to explain the sudden appearance of so many of us in town when I turned back into the living room.

'That's easy,' I said with a shrug of my shoulders, and everyone turned to look at me, 'The locals all know that we exist as people, they just think we're not from around here. There would be no question as to why we would come if Elsie was poorly.'

I sat back down on the arm of the sofa before I continued.

'Elsie is quite highly thought of, several of the people I have met know that I am her niece, and always ask about her when I see them. I have no doubt that they would all help if we needed it too. It seems to be quite a close-knit community around here; they look out for each other.'

If I was honest, it reminded me of our community in The Kingdom, but I kept that part to myself; I was sure that Janine wouldn't appreciate the comparison. They seemed to mull over what I had said before anyone spoke again.

'I have to admit, people always ask how we are and about Elsie when we are knocking around town,' Mia piped in, 'They seem genuinely happy to see us when we visit.'

'Yeah, I don't think it would cause a problem, they'd just think we were rallying the troops for Elsie,' Betsy added from her position on the floor.

'Exactly,' I finished.

Elsie chose that moment to bustle back through the door, and Shelley and I jumped up to go help her with the bag. The others continued their conversation in slightly hushed tones as we made our way through to the kitchen and put away the supplies for breakfast.

Leaving Shelley with Elsie after a wordless conversation about keeping an eye on her while she cooked, I went back into the living room and walked in part way through a conversation.

'What about her position on the Council? Someone needs to contact them and speak to whoever is in charge, reorganise and get someone new out there,' Janine said from her position by the window.

'Would you know how to contact them? I don't even think I know the name of whoever is in charge,' Marina admitted with a shrug.

'What are we talking about?' I asked.

'Elsie sits on the Council, we need to sort out speaking to them,' Janine answered, 'Has she ever mentioned them to you?'

A Handful of Secrets

I shook my head; I had no idea what they were talking about, or what it was related to. All I could think about was getting to see Aaron now, my time was ticking away with every moment I sat here listening to them discuss Elsie as if she had already died.

I slipped straight out of the room with a nod to Marina and tiptoed down the hall to where the phone sat on the table by the door. Aaron answered on the first ring.

'Hey beautiful,' his voice calmed me instantly, and I wished that he lived a little closer.

'Hey,' I breathed out quietly, 'Can you come pick me up from the house? It'll be quicker than meeting you by the beach.'

He agreed without question and promised me he'd be here as soon as he could. I loved that he was always free when I was ashore. I knew now that he was orchestrating it; but it meant a lot to me that he went to the trouble. I vowed to thank him; though I knew the moment I laid eyes on him again that it would become less important than everything else we wanted to say to each other.

'Will you come and say Hi at least?' I asked Marina where we stood in the kitchen separate to the rest of the group.

Elsie was back in the living room now, she hadn't actually brought home the eggs that she went out for, so I had rustled up waffles and toppings while Janine and Mia sat talking to her about doctors and stuff. I really wanted Marina to meet Aaron, but I wouldn't push it. I knew that she didn't really agree with the relationship, and she really wasn't happy when I told her that he knew what I was; what we were. But she accepted that I loved him, and knew that I trusted him. She trusted me enough for that to be okay. She was all I had left of a family under the ocean, and I wouldn't change her for anything. She always had my back, and she'd always looked out for me. I needed her to like Aaron, especially if I could get out here to live with him; to have a real relationship and a life with him.

'If it is so important to you,' she paused, probably for dramatic benefit and to make me wait, 'I will come and say hello, but I'm not ready to get to know someone who knows what we are. I'm just not comfortable with that.'

I smiled, it was enough. For now.

'That's fine, I just want you to know who he is. Marina, if I can get out here I want it to be with him. I want to spend my life with him, have a life like all the humans I watch when I'm out here. He loves me despite only getting to see me once a cycle. He hasn't given up on me, he hasn't complained once, and he even comes to meet me before sunrise. I told him that I had to deal with all of this first today though.'

I paused while Marina just looked at me with a motherly smile on her face like the one I often saw on Elsie's. It crossed my mind as to what my mother would have said to me in this situation. Would she have agreed with what I'd done like Elsie said, or would she have been angry or upset with me for breaking the rules and defying the Royals? Marina's acceptance was important to me; she signified family to me. And whether it was too human or not, I wanted her approval.

I heard the car before he honked the horn; I'd told him not to come to the door. I wouldn't subject him to Janine, but I took Marina's hand and dragged her towards the front door with me. We passed the lounge and I cleared my throat to gain Elsie's attention.

'I'll be back for dinner Aunt Elsie; I'll cook,' I added after the thought of some of the mishaps we'd had in the kitchen recently flitted through my head.

How in the ocean she coped throughout the month I'd never know. Aaron had been Heaven sent. She nodded and Janine shouted through that they'd still be here. I doubted that, but nodded in reply before taking Marina out to where Aaron was parked outside the house.

'Aaron, this is my sister, Marina. Marina, this is Aaron,' I said with a massive smile on my face.

Aaron was ever the gentleman. He got out of the Jeep and took Marina's outstretched hand, turning it over and pressing a kiss to the back of her hand just like he had with me the first time we'd met.

'I've heard a lot about you; it's nice to finally be able to put a face to the name. You're just as pretty as your sister too,' he said with a wink in my direction.

'We look like our mother; same eyes,' she said with a tiny smile.

'Then she must have been very beautiful,' he replied.

I knew that look, she was taken. Holding back a victory dance, I told Marina our plans and promised to be back for dinner. She said she'd still be here even if the others left, and I couldn't hold back that smile. I threw my arms around her and squeezed her before letting her return to the house.

'Aaron, it was nice to meet you. I am sure we'll be seeing more of each other in the coming months.'

She waved goodbye from the doorway as we pulled out of the drive and headed for the cliff tops.

'You miss me?' I asked as I leant over to kiss him.

'Always,' he replied with a gentle squeeze of my knee where his hand drifted lazily over the denim that covered my inner thighs where my jeans attempted to keep out the bite of the wind.

I spent a few hours with Aaron, bringing him up to speed with everything that I had learned since surfacing this morning. Saying some of it out loud was helping for me to really digest the new information, and other parts of it just sounded more ridiculous. He agreed with me when I expressed my concern about what else they could be keeping from me, but encouraged me to talk to them rather than just letting the worry eat away at me.

It was while we were sat in the diner with hot chocolates and cake, listening to him tell me about his latest argument with his father and how he was considering moving out and getting his own place that I realised the answer to my previous thought. Aaron was the one I could trust to be honest with me. He'd never once kept anything from me, he'd told me his secrets right from the beginning, and he'd always answered any questions I'd had. If there was anyone I could trust it was him. How odd that it wasn't my sister.

Now that the weather had dropped so cold, a walk down the beach really wasn't an option, and because the girls were all at Elsie's, we couldn't really go back there either. I wasn't ready to subject Aaron to the wrath of Janine, and the endless questions from the others. He said his dad wasn't in a good place at the minute, so he didn't want to take me there either; even more reason to get his own place he had added. We ended up parked up on the cliff top so that we could look out over the water. He kept the heating on and I was sat sideways with my feet in his lap where he rubbed them with his thumbs. I'd never really given much thought to how normal this must seem to him, but I couldn't drag my concentration away from how wonderful it felt when he pressed under my feet and rubbed little circles into them. I knew how good the sand felt, but I hadn't thought about the fact that it was my feet that felt good.

He smiled at me when he caught me watching his hands and pressed a little harder. I looked up and he raised his eyebrows.

'You didn't hear a word of that did you?' he asked with a chuckle.

I shook my head, laughing with him.

'No, sorry, what were you saying?'

'I said that I should probably get you back if you're going to be in time to prepare dinner for everyone.'

'Oh, I hadn't thought about that.'

When I looked over at the horizon I realised he was right. The sun had begun its descent back towards the water, and with the time of year I only had a few hours left again.

Once we were back on the front, I pulled my boots back on and shuffled in my seat to throw my arms around Aaron. It was only because of my awkward position that I got a heads up on the turquoise excitement racing down the garden path. She came to a screeching stop at the window and I pulled back from Aaron to wind down the window, letting in a bitter draft.

'Hi,' Betsy announced as soon as she could be heard.

'Betsy where is your coat?' I asked before anything else happened, she had to be freezing.

'It's okay, I won't be long.' She shifted her attention from me to Aaron and stuck her hand through the car window, 'Hi, I'm Betsy, Luna's sister.'

'Technically you're not my sister, let's not confuse him too much,' I added as he took her hand and pressed a kiss to the back of it like he had done with Marina.

'Nice to meet you Betsy,' he said and I saw him wink at her in his reflection in the mirror.

She dissolved into a fit of little giggles and bounced on the spot.

'Get back inside before you freeze already.'

She shot me a look that said I should want her to know Aaron, but I pretended not to notice.

'I'm sure I'll see you again,' Aaron said in a much softer tone than the one I'd used.

With that she agreed that she would see him soon, and skipped back down the path.

'She seems bubbly,' he said as he turned back to me.

'She's a total clutz actually, but yes, bubbly works too,' I said and Betsy tripped over the threshold to the house as if to back up my words.

We laughed and I grabbed my bag from by my feet and got out of the car, making my way around to his side where the window was still open.

'So, meet you before sunrise next time?' he asked, linking his fingers with mine and pulling my arm towards him so that he could half cuddle me.

'Definitely.'

There was no need for any thought, even if the girls were going to come again, I would be there with Aaron next cycle; I hadn't gotten to see anywhere near enough of him today. We said our goodbyes, and he gave me a kiss that left me gasping for breath. He left with a wave and a grin that made me go all warm and fuzzy inside, and I walked back down the garden path and came face to face with Betsy just inside the doorway.

'He seems nice,' she said in greeting.

'He is nice,' I replied, bustling past her so that I could close the door.

'Can I come out with you one day when the weather picks up again?' she asked, still bouncing slightly on the spot.

'I don't see why not,' I said as I hung up my coat, 'If we're going to do this and get everyone ashore more, I'd like it if you all got to know him too.'

She made a rather loud squealing noise and bounced into the living room.

'She said yes.' I heard her announce to whoever was listening, and I laughed as I stepped into the room behind her.

I was pleasantly surprised to find them all still here too.

The last few hours of our time ashore passed in a blur of laughter, food and shared memories. I learned a lot about my mother and made sense of a lot of things that I already knew but didn't quite understand. I asked Elsie questions about her time under the ocean instead of asking the others for the information and she regaled me with tales of her adventures with the others.

I couldn't believe that I had lived my entire life not knowing that Elsie was a mermaid, that she was one of

A Handful of Secrets

us all along. I wished that I could have seen her when she was younger. She was beautiful now, even with the human ageing; I bet she had been stunning when she'd had the mermaid youth on her side too.

Now, we were sat in the living room again, Elsie was curled up with her feet beneath her on the end of the sofa and I sat on the floor discussing her watery adventures when Marina came and sat beside me.

'It's nearly time we were getting back to the water, we don't have long left.'

I smiled and leant my head on her shoulder as she put her arm around me. Despite the fact that I had seen so little of Aaron today, I couldn't help but feel happy. I had my family around me, and I had a way out of the water. Perhaps my life could turn out the way I had always imagined it could.

We left Elsie in the house with promises of more than just me coming ashore for the next full moon, and we made our way back towards the cliffs still chattering about the plans we had to make between now and the next full moon. I was so deep in conversation, talking about some of the things I needed to think about that I almost missed the Jeep. Almost. Aaron was parked just around the corner on the dirt track that ran along the cliff tops. He climbed out and gave a shy wave when I saw him. Marina gave me a soft bump on the shoulder and smiled, but I cast a weary glance over my shoulder at Janine.

'Is that him?' she asked quietly.

I just nodded and stepped away from the group.

'I'm sorry, I know you didn't want them to see me, but I couldn't let you go without kissing you again.'

I felt my heart swell with his words and he swept me up in his arms, lifting me gently from the floor and pressed his lips to mine before I even had a chance to reply. Giggling and clapping from behind me made Aaron pull away, but he didn't let me go, or put me down. I turned my head and smiled over my shoulder to see Mia, Marina and Betsy stood watching with matching smiles. Janine stood a little further back with Shelley, Georgie and Ellie, but at least she was smiling too. Maybe there was hope for us yet.

After saying my goodbyes to Aaron and waving as he drove off, I made my way down to the beach whilst being peppered with questions about him. They all wanted to know about him, including Janine, though her questions were less girly gossip and more about finding out how much he knew. I shut her up with the fact that he would be a part of my life when I got out of the water, so he would be helping look out for us. With that she had to admit that he obviously could keep secrets and it looked like he cared deeply for me, so maybe there wouldn't be a problem. There's nothing like acceptance.

The air nipped at my skin as I stripped off and rushed down to the water and I literally transformed as soon as I was deep enough and let out the breath I'd been holding once I was comfortable. Betsy and Marina followed me in and the others splashed in after them. Janine and Mia headed back together, but the rest of us played all the way back. It reminded me of being young again, and it was nice to have the girls with me, and feeling so care free. When The Kingdom came into sight, we calmed down and tried to act like the adults we were thought of, but we just dissolved into a fit of giggles before splitting up and heading our own ways.

I followed Marina back to our home and headed straight to bed, the soft silky cushioning of the sand a welcome feeling. Closing my eyes, I thought of Aaron and the shores that I would soon be able to call home, and I fell asleep dreaming of the now very real possibilities of my future.

February

I surfaced to find Aaron stood in the corner by the cliffs, the tide was too far in for him to get around to the edge where he normally met me, but at this time of year, and at this time in the morning, I was positive that we wouldn't be seen. I'd been doing this long enough to know how the beach worked.

As I pulled myself through the shallow water and near enough beached myself on the sand, Aaron came and sat in front of me, high enough up that the water wouldn't reach him for a while yet. I pushed up onto my elbows and he bent to press a kiss to my lips. The water from my hair dripped and I felt him tense as he pulled back.

'Jees, that's cold,' he exclaimed with a laugh.

I apologised and retreated to the bed of sand beneath me, propping myself comfortably so that I could see Aaron without having to stretch.

He told me what I'd missed, and I divulged some of the plans we had made whilst being back in the ocean, barely keeping my excitement levels restrained. Shelley had worked out that the next dual celestial event was at the end of this month, so we had put everything into getting ready and would be on land by March. I hadn't realised it could be so quickly, but I'd thrown myself into gathering information so that I was fully prepared, and then helped make a start on the plans. There were four of us coming ashore with the solar eclipse; Janine, Mia, Marina and myself. They were also surfacing at some point today, but it was far too early for them yet; I'd slipped from The Kingdom before there was even light penetrating the water so that I could be with Aaron. While we were ashore today, we had to get the house ready; it hadn't had people in it overnight since I was a child apparently. They'd chosen to stop coming so that they could keep their secrets.

As the tide crept in, I repositioned myself in the sand, and found myself cuddling up to Aaron. He shivered and pulled his coat tighter around himself, but he didn't stop me. Instead he put his arm around me and held me close, his fingers trailing absent mindedly up and down my spine, barely touching my scales at the bottom.

'You can touch them you know, you won't hurt me,' I said, rolling away slightly so that his hand slipped around to my tummy.

'You're sure? I know you didn't like drying out before,' he asked as his hand continued to wander, now over the bare skin of my stomach, slowly feeling their way down towards my tail.

I nodded; I'd never been surer. I was laid on my back now in the wet sand, the tide still ebbing around my body as it slowly made its way inland. In a couple of hours our little cove would be totally submerged until lunch time, that's just the way it worked, but by then I'd have my legs and we'd be back at the house. I had wanted to spend all day with Aaron, my wishes had all come true; I was getting my happily ever after, I just had to work out what to do with it, but I knew that I had responsibilities with the girls. At some point I was going to bring up introducing them to Aaron, but I wasn't sure Janine was ready for that.

There was so much that I was going to have to learn, so much that I wanted to know, if I was going to stay here on land with Aaron. I had to get a handle on my own body for a start, learn what I could and couldn't do with it. I made the decision to start with Aaron. There was so much that I wanted to try, so much that I wanted to feel with him, I had to get to grips with my body. The first time we'd done this I had been so overwhelmed with the feelings that he had instilled in my body that I had passed out on him afterwards.

Aaron's hands roamed my body; I wanted his hands on me while I still had my tail. I wanted him to know my body as it was in both forms, who I am by nature, and who I am when I was on land with the full moon. The body I longed for was within my reach, but I wouldn't ever forget who I was. My fins and my tail were as much a part of me as the legs that I dreamt of, and no matter how far away I tried to get, the water was my home; it soothed me, kept me calm, even when I hated being trapped there.

Turning into his embrace, I pressed my lips to his and pushed my hands up into his coat so that I could run my fingers over his abdomen and up to his chest. I scratched gently and felt his response in the tightening of his embrace and the flex of his fingers against my lower back. His grip on me intensified and his tongue stroked leisurely against mine, tasting me and teasing me. His hand, rested low down on my back, part on my skin, part stroking the top few rows of my scales. I noted the difference in how it felt to me, the softness of his fingertips on my skin and how the tingle of awareness ran through my blood, then his palm against my bum, warm and clammy against the cool exterior of my tail.

It was awkward, he was trying to keep away from the water and I still had my fins in the tide, but he somehow made it work.

When the sun finally graced the horizon with its presence, Aaron scurried to get my bag and towel before I transformed, and damn was it cold. The bitterly cold wind ripped through me and made me wish I had fur instead of scales, at least then I'd be able to keep warm. Aaron bundled me into my jumper and I pulled on my jeans; I wanted to get under the hot water of the shower and warm up as quickly as possible.

We hastily made our way up the beach and up the steps to where Aaron had the Jeep parked, and he bundled me inside, turning on the heaters straight away. I held my hands over the warm blowers all the way back to the house, and ran down the path ahead of Aaron to get the door open.

I could hear Elsie humming as soon as we were in and the fuss subsided, leaving room for the tranquillity to take over. The house was warm and cosy and I could hear the crackling of the log fire in the living room too. Following the sound of humming, I located Elsie in the kitchen, happily scrambling eggs in a pan.

'Good morning Luna dear,' she said as I leant in for a hug.

As she released me, she took a step back and surveyed me from head to foot; I did a little twirl at the end for her, making her smile, and I smiled back before retreating for the shower. I heard Aaron go in after me and offer to help with breakfast, her reply being bright and cheery.

Anyone who looked in now would never know that there was anything wrong, but under the surface I could see the cracks showing. As I moved through the living room I saw that the house hadn't been cleaned for a few days, and Elsie was always cleaning, especially when the full moon was due, so that the house was clean for us to visit. There was a bag by the front door as if she'd been to take it out to the trash and forgotten, and there were two pairs of her shoes lying abandoned by the foot of the stairs. Elsie was the tidiest person I knew, the house ran better than the most well-oiled ship, but it was starting to fray at the seams now. Upstairs I found a load of washing in the corner where the basket should be, and managed to locate the basket in the spare room as if she'd taken it there to sort and forgotten all about it. The sooner we could get out to her the better; she only had a few more weeks without us now, and after seeing this, I was going to have Aaron check in on her more often.

For now, I settled for sorting out the washing into colours and taking my shower quickly. After towel drying my hair and pulling on some warm clothes, I headed back downstairs with the wash basket under one arm. I loaded the washing machine under the stairs but then came up clueless as to how to turn it on. Luckily for me, Aaron had heard me bustling about and had come to investigate.

'Need a hand?' he asked as he leant casually against the door jamb.

'Do you know how to work this thing?' I asked, turning around to face him in my crouched position in front of the machine.

He just smiled at me and bobbed down beside me to get in to the tiny little room.

'Here,' he said pointing at a large green button, 'This one turns it on, and this one, he continued pointing at the dial and the lights around it, 'is the setting, it normally stays all on the same one, in this case, number 3 which it is already on, and then you press the start button.'

He pointed to the white button on the other side and gestured for me to press it. I did and it made a high-pitched squealing sound at me which made me jump.

'Did you put the washing powder in?' he asked, pointing at the now red flashing light on the control panel.

I shrugged, giving him my best innocent face. I hadn't put anything in it other than the clothes; I didn't know you had to. He stood up in the limited space and pulled a box from the shelf above the machines and tipped some of the white powder into a small draw near the dial he'd shown me. Then he pressed the white button again and the machine whirred to life.

'My hero,' I joked as I stood up and threw my arms around him.

He swept me off my feet after we had backed out of the little room and pressed a kiss to my forehead.

'Looks like you have a lot to learn Luna, and I'm your guy,' he said with a smile as he carried me into the dining room where Elsie was putting breakfast on the table.

After breakfast, and after I had redressed Elsie into an outfit more appropriate for the weather outside as her dress didn't quite fit the bill, we headed for the beach with towels and bags of clothes in hand. I had arranged a meeting time with Marina, two hours after sunrise; it had given me time to come ashore with Aaron, and prepare him for what the rest of the day might entail.

We'd had an entire cycle to begin our plans, but with no way of contacting Aaron, he hadn't had the same warning. The dual celestial event was later this month, much quicker than Janine had thought, which meant we didn't have as much planning time. Much to her disgust, she had agreed that we would need Aaron's help, and to gain his help, she had to speak to him; meaning that today he would have to meet her. When I told him this over breakfast, he barely batted an eye at the information, saying that he'd love to meet her, however, I could feel his hand going slightly clammy in my grip and he had gone quiet. He was never quiet.

'It'll be okay you know?' I said as we stepped onto the sand and followed the beach down to the edge of the water.

I saw Betsy in the shallows before I saw the others, her hair visible among the blue water. She stuck her hand up and waved. I waved back, beckoning them ashore. Elsie stood with the towels and Aaron stood with two bags in his hands. I stood with Marina's towel outstretched in my hand. Turning back to speak to Aaron, I found him with his back to the ocean and I frowned.

'It really will be fine, I know I made her out to be bad, but she's not all that bad really,' I said with a soft laugh.

'I know, it's just stupid nerves I guess,' he answered not turning around.

As Marina stepped into my open arms, I flinched with the invading cold water that dripped from her hair, and then let out a laugh as the penny dropped.

'I forgot just how cold winter could be,' Marina said with a shiver as I threw a woolly jumper her way from the bag Aaron was now unpacking.

'Yeah, it gets pretty arctic when it wants to,' I agreed.

When all the girls were dressed, Aaron turned to Marina and smiled.

'It's nice to see you again,' he said before his eyes flickered over her shoulder.

'You too,' she replied with a laugh, 'I told you we'd see each other again soon, didn't I?'

We all laughed and I leant into Aaron's side, wrapping my arm around his waist and squeezing gently. He slid his arm around my shoulders and pressed a kiss to my temple before straightening again. When I looked up I saw Janine and Shelley making their way over here. Mia and Betsy were still with Elsie, and Lou and Shae were huddled together by the cliff's edge. I smiled over at Lou and gave her a little wave; she hadn't been ashore for months. She was Mia's daughter under the ocean, but we all grew up as sisters out here. When I'd been younger, Lou was always ashore with me because she was a similar age to me. The Elders had thrown us together in an attempt to make me more like her I think, but we were so different we'd not stayed close friends much after our teen years.

'Luna,' Janine announced herself, breaking into my thoughts.

'Janine, this is Aaron,' I said with a glance his way to check on his nerves, 'Aaron, this is Janine, one of our Elders, and this is Mia,' I said gesturing to each of them.

'Pleasure,' Aaron said with a smile, though he didn't reach for their hand like he had with Marina.

'Let's get back up to the house where it's warm,' Elsie said, cutting into the conversation before it got anywhere.

I saw the hint of a smile on Elsie's lips as Janine turned to head up the beach with a nod of her head at Aaron, and then she smiled at me. Elsie put her arm through Aaron's and he walked us both back up the beach and we followed the others up the steps with Marina by my side.

'Her bark is worse than her bite,' Elsie whispered, 'You'll be fine, I promise,' she finished with a wink his way.

It appeared that he had the hearts of a few of the family already. He didn't need to win Janine over, he just needed her trust, and that wasn't going to be hard, because she was trusting me, and I trusted Aaron with my life and our secrets. To trust me meant to trust him, she just had to realise that for herself. I'd learned long ago not to tell her anything serious, she had to work it out for herself or she'd never believe it. But it warmed my heart to know that she trusted me enough to let me do this, and that left a smile on my face that lasted me until we got back to the house.

Hustle and bustle ensued. It was clear that the house was not used to this many people in it these days, and it caused more problems than one. I left the girls fighting over the shower and went in search of Aaron who had headed straight for the kitchen when we arrived. He was leant over the kitchen side with Elsie, pouring over the list we had started to make and murmuring to himself. I was greeted with a smile when he looked up which I returned.

'What are you two planning in here?' I asked, stopping by his side and wrapping one arm around his waist.

'We're trying to put the list into a priority order and then split it up for each of us to get on with,' Elsie said as Aaron reached around and pulled me closer.

'Sounds good,' I said, and we continued with the list until the girls were all around the dining room table.

List in hand, I started to speak, casting a glance Janine's way, but she simply nodded and let me continue. I explained the plans, and let the girls choose tasks; taking charge was one thing, but I had no intentions of becoming a dictator. I wanted our family back, like it used to be when I was a child. This was the start of that, showing them that we could work together. Once the tasks were divided up, we went our separate ways. Marina, Aaron and I headed upstairs to tackle the bedrooms. Aaron had ordered three new beds to be delivered at lunch time and we needed to make space for them. Currently only two of the bedrooms had beds in, one of which was mine, the other, I had learned this morning, was actually Mia's.

We spent the morning rearranging furniture, listening to the radio that we had salvaged from a box full of old stuff in the room with Janine's belongings in, and laughing. Marina was clearly warming to Aaron quickly and had enjoyed herself this morning. They had been laughing and joking like she did with me, and I'd seen a genuine smile on her face for most of the day too. When there was a loud knock at the door, Aaron headed downstairs to deal with the delivery guys.

While the two guys in the delivery truck and Aaron took the beds upstairs and set them up in the appropriate rooms, Marina and I went for a wander around the house to find the others and took lunch orders. I'd decided to head to the café and get take out sandwiches rather than make lunch with whatever Elsie had in the fridge. Everyone seemed in joyous spirits, despite the actual reasons we were all here; Elsie's declining health, and it made me think that maybe my dreams of a big happy family weren't all that far away after all. This was what I remembered my childhood being like; the happiness, the laughter, us all out together; I knew that we could have that all again.

Aaron and I went for a walk around the corner to the café while Marina made up the last bed with the array of bed linen we had found in one of the cupboards. There was now a double bed in each room, which meant that four of them, plus me could be out at any one time, but including sharing beds and the two sofas, we could probably have just about all of us out if we wanted to. We had rearranged the wardrobes and chests of drawers so that families had their own bedrooms together, and though Marina's things were still in my room, she said that she would happily sleep on the sofa so that Aaron could stay when she was here.

I had been watching Aaron with each of the girls this morning, and he was charming each of them at their own pace. Betsy was already taken, she liked him and had already told me that I could keep him, Janine was taking the longest but I swear she was just being awkward for the sake of it.

When we returned home I couldn't help the smile that spread across my face at the buzz of activity that greeted us. Betsy swung past us and grabbed one of the bags, heading straight through to the kitchen where there were already several of them pulling plates from the cupboards and making drinks. It was just like I remembered; a home full of love and warmth. This was what I wanted the future to look like. I turned to Aaron and he slid his arm around my waist with a grin, he understood my dream for the future, and he was a part of it now. He pressed a kiss to my temple as we unloaded the bags and served up lunch, the busy conversations continuing throughout.

After the remnants of lunch had been cleared away and Mia and Betsy had finished the washing up, I found myself in the living room with Janine, Mia and my sister. Aaron was upstairs helping Betsy move the last of the furniture into its rightful spot, and the others were all finishing up their jobs. I was lying on my stomach in front of the fire with the *Shakespeare* book open in front of me. I was flicking through the last couple of pages of *Macbeth* when Janine cut into my concentration.

'So, what about the doctor's appointment for next week?'

I looked up from the page and squinted as my eyes readjusted to the distance.

'It's before the celestial events I know, but it was the only one I could get,' Mia said.

Mia had nipped out just before lunch to take Elsie to the doctor's practice in town, she had hoped to be able to get in to see a doctor then, but they had made an appointment for Elsie next week and given Mia a few brochures about ways of adapting and living with dementia.

'I'm sure Aaron will take her if you ask him,' I said.

'Aaron will do what now?' Aaron said as he descended the stairs and popped into the living room with Betsy and Shae right on his heels.

'Elsie has a doctor's appointment next week before we're back, we were hoping you would be able to take her and listen in so that you can tell us what they say,' I said, moving up a little so that he and Shae could sit by my side comfortably.

'Yeah of course I can, when is it?' he asked, turning to Janine.

'Wednesday of next week at ten a.m.'

He nodded with a smile and Janine smiled back. Progress. She noted something down on the pad she was making her list on and then continued working through the list we had been going through. It was a small victory, but it was there nonetheless; there had been no argument, no pause for thought. She trusted him to take Elsie, and to look out for her best interests.

I went back to reading the last few pages of the story and Aaron began rubbing one hand on my lower back. It felt good, and I quickly zoned out on Janine's list.

'I hear you're going out for dinner,' Marina said, sticking her head around the bedroom door where I was getting changed.

With a smile at her in the mirror, I nodded. Unbeknown to me, Aaron had spoken to Janine and okayed it with her. He was taking me out for dinner at the posh restaurant in town called Nosh. Apparently, it was Valentine's Day next week and because I wouldn't be back for it, we were celebrating today. I won't lie, as soon as he had left me to get changed I had asked Mia what Valentine's Day was; I'd never even heard of it before. Turns out it was a holiday that humans celebrated when they were in relationships like the one I was in with Aaron. He was taking me out for dinner, and then had planned to walk me back down to the beach ready for sunset.

'Should I have done something for this Valentine's thing?' I asked when she came inside and closed the door to a little.

'Erm, no not necessarily. I think there are usually cards and presents, but you didn't know so he won't be expecting anything. He just wants to take you out. You've been here with us all day, and we occupied the day on the last full moon too; he wants to spend some time with you on your own that's all.'

I nodded again and pulled up the zipper on my dress. I'd chosen thick tights and a long-sleeved dress to dress up, but I didn't want to get cold. It had been freezing when we'd walked to the sandwich shop earlier.

'Which shoes?' I asked holding up one of each for Marina to look at.

I'd narrowed it down to a chunky pair of boots or heels. She pointed to the heels. Once I was ready, I did a little twirl for Marina and she agreed that I looked okay.

'I'll wait for you on the beach,' she said on our way downstairs.

Despite everything we were going through, and everything we had to come, that gesture still meant a lot to me and I swung my arms around her neck.

I said my goodbyes to Elsie as I would be heading straight for the water after our date; the time of year shortening my days ashore drastically, and I agreed to meet Janine and Mia early tomorrow morning to discuss the next steps of our plans. After hugging Marina and agreeing on a spot to meet, I left the house and hopped into the Jeep.

'You look beautiful,' Aaron whispered as he leant across and kissed me.

'And you smell divine,' I replied when he pulled away.

The musky spicy smell overwhelmed my senses and sent a tingle racing across my skin. I was so aware of Aaron's body that even just being this close to him was intoxicating. He had put on a navy-blue shirt that he'd left open at the top button, and had a pair of dark denim jeans on. His hair was a little longer on top where he hadn't had it cut in a while and was all mussed up where he had obviously just run a hand through it. I smiled as he pulled away from the house, his hand still on my leg.

The restaurant was decorated in red and pink, and the lighting was all dimmed down to create a romantic mood for the customers. The waitress, Emma according to her name badge, led us to our table, a small booth in the corner right underneath one of the lights that had a red film over the opening to create a pool of red light that bathed the table. I slid into the booth and Aaron followed me in, positioning himself right by my side. After Emma took our drinks order, we were given our menus and left to decide.

'So, how are you feeling about the eclipse?' Aaron asked quietly once we were alone.

I turned to him with a smile, feeling the nerves begin to flutter in my stomach the way they did every time I thought about the impending event.

'Excited, but really nervous at the same time. It's going to be so odd when the sun sets,' I answered honestly and he nodded quietly.

There would be no point in lying to him, he could always tell how I was feeling; he was just giving me an opportunity to talk about it without me having to bring it up. He put one arm around me and I leant on his shoulder as I returned my gaze to the menu.

'I'm worried that Marina will hate it though,' I admitted quietly.

I knew that she was only coming ashore for me; she wanted to make sure that I was safe once I was ashore. But I knew that she wouldn't like being on land after the sun had set, and she would be trapped then, until the next full moon. I didn't want her to be unhappy.

'She's a big girl Luna, she'll be okay. And anyway, there are only a couple of weeks until the full moon, it's not like they will have to stay a whole month if they don't want to.'

I stayed quiet and thought about that. The solar eclipse was at the end of this month, so Aaron was right; the full moon would only be a couple of weeks away, then Marina could go back to the water. The last thing I wanted was for her to feel trapped on land the way I did when I was in the water. I was trying to fix things, not make them worse.

The meal with Aaron was lovely; the restaurant really had thought of everything, even down to the raspberry sauce on my plate with my chocolate cake that was drizzled in the shape of a heart. Aaron had laughed at my excitement and managed to dab the sauce on the end of my nose. It was while I was cleaning it off, and eating my cake, I sat quietly, thinking about everything that had changed since I had met Aaron in that beach-side bar. I'd come so far, and discovered so much about myself, and my world, that I didn't even recognise the girl I had been before him. He made me a better version of myself; he made me more inquisitive, more adventurous, if that were possible, and he loved me for everything that I was; fins included. My hand found its way to my bag and I felt

A Handful of Secrets

the hard cover of my mother's copy of *The Little Mermaid* in there where it was safe from prying eyes. I saw Aaron's eyes flicker to my hand and a small smile crept onto his face. Of course, he knew that I had it with me.

'Why isn't that at the house?' he asked between mouthfuls of his dessert.

'Because I didn't want Betsy or Marina to find it. If Janine found out I don't know what would happen. I still don't really know all the answers to my own questions, I can't deal with theirs too,' I answered rather defensively.

He raised his eyebrows at me and I apologised.

'It's okay, I understand why you don't want Janine and the others to know, but do you not think Marina would like to know about her mother? The same way you wanted to know all about her?'

I pulled a face at him, trying to decide whether he was right or not.

'She knew her though, she knew her and my mother chose to keep it from her. There must have been good reason for that surely?' I voiced eventually.

'She was only a child herself Luna, maybe Clea thought she was just too young to understand, do you not think that she still deserves to know?' he asked again, keeping his voice calm and soothing.

Again, I mulled over his words. A part of me knew that he was right, she'd only been around twelve human years old when I'd been born, but she'd also been old enough that a few years later when she'd decided to keep secrets from me, the elders had not only listened, but agreed that it was for the best. I made a half-mumbled agreement with Aaron and he dropped it, but I still wasn't sure I was going to tell her. Peter was my secret now, it didn't affect Marina in any way, other than to know a little more about our mother; maybe she already knew that she'd been seeing Peter. Maybe it was just another secret that she was keeping from me.

Aaron didn't bring it up again, instead we finished up our night before it got too dark, then Aaron drove me back to the cove. We walked down the steps hand in hand, my dress swishing in the undergrowth the only sound, other than the crashing of the incoming waves that disturbed the silence of the evening. As we reached the bottom though, I heard voices and smiled. They had waited for me; all of them. Huddled in their coats and layers, the girls sat on the rocks by the foot of the cliffs where Elsie normally hid our bags. They'd left Elsie back at the house in the warmth as planned, but I hadn't expected them all to still be out here. At the very least, I thought they'd be in the water waiting.

'Hey, I brought you a top down,' Marina said as we got closer, and she pulled one of my black T-shirts from beside her, 'I know you prefer the big ones,' she said with a smile.

She was right, I hated the stereotype that mermaids seemed to have of wearing shells or bikini tops. Betsy always wore one, she had a turquoise one that matched the colour of her tail perfectly, and Mia often had a bikini on too, but most of us wore cropped tops at the very least.

The girls now stripped and made their way into the water quickly, the bitter wind too cold for them to linger. I held back for now, holding onto Aaron, knowing that the next time I saw him, I wouldn't have to leave him like this. I would be staying with him long after the sun set. Marina was the last into the water and promised to wait for me, and I turned into Aaron's arms and held on tightly.

'You won't have to leave next time,' he whispered into my hair as he pressed a kiss to the crown of my head.

'You read my mind,' I whispered back into his chest.

I turned to look at the sun, it was almost gone. I had to go. I pulled off my coat, shivering as the wind cut through me, and quickly changed from my dress into the shirt Marina had brought with her. I discarded my boots and tights and after pressing a long kiss to Aaron's lips and listening to him promise to be here waiting for me on the morning of the eclipse, I headed into the water, not wasting any time and letting nature take my legs from me. As soon as the magic took hold, the cold disappeared and I relaxed into the water as Betsy barrelled into me from the side.

'Time to go Luna, next time, we get to see the world after dark.'

I smiled back and we talked as we swam back to The Kingdom, ducking and swirling around each other the entire way. It was safe to say that the younger generation were all excited for the eclipse; Marina's secrets had kept us all from the land when we could have been living our lives differently. I knew I was the only one that longed to be there full time, but the others clearly wanted the opportunity to see the world without the sun.

Personally, I couldn't wait.

Angel McGregor

Solar Eclipse

I wasn't sure what to expect when I broke the surface in the early hours of the morning. The solar eclipse was due around three in the afternoon, but Janine had assured me that I would be able to get out of the water at sunrise just as I would on the day of the full moon. Aaron wasn't here yet, he wouldn't be here for another hour or so, but I'd wanted to be here. I was ready for this now; there was nothing more I could do to prepare from under the ocean. We'd spent weeks preparing; it had been like school all over again. There was so much I had to learn, so much I had to remember. I was going to have to make a list when I had a free minute. I had the support of the girls until the following full moon, Janine, Mia, my sister and Betsy were coming ashore with me today. Lou had to stay in the water with her twins, as did Shae with her daughter Carly, and Fran had decided to stay behind too. The last time I'd spoken to Shelley, she was coming ashore too, but when I'd spoken to Janine late last night, she'd said she was staying in to support Sandy, the other elder of the group, while Janine was with us.

For now, I stayed away from the beach, not that I expected there to be anyone around at this ungodly hour, but it still felt wrong to be too close while I had my fins and Aaron wasn't here to protect me. I splashed lazily on the surface, floating in the salt water and silently saying my goodbyes for now. I wasn't sad, but a part of me understood what I was leaving behind. As much as I longed for my life on land with Aaron, I knew that I would miss my home under the water. Janine had explained that I could swim in the ocean as often as I wanted on the days between the full moons, but if I was to get into the water on the day of the full moon, the magic would assume I was returning and transform me. Not good for keeping our lives a secret. The other days of the dual celestial events were inconsequential too; they only allowed us out of the water, not back into it. So, in other words, I was free to be in the water, just not on the full moon. I had lost count how many times we'd gone over these facts in the last few weeks, yet it really wasn't that hard of a concept to grasp.

Mia had given me some lessons on the house and what to expect as far as running it were concerned. Apparently, there was plenty of money in the bank; some sort of business link that had been set up many, many moons ago by one of the elders in their time ashore. It brought in enough money that none of them had ever had to look for work to support the house or the family. I didn't ask too many questions, I just knew enough so that I could keep it flowing. If I wanted to find out more, I could do some investigating with Aaron. It had been Mia that I had spoken to about having Aaron at the house permanently, and she had agreed that it would be fine, and not to worry about Janine.

I intended on speaking to Aaron before the girls left again on the full moon at the end of the cycle. This new life included him, and I wanted him there from the beginning. Mia saw no problem with it, and Marina was fully supportive. I knew that Elsie would be okay with having him around, though I planned to run it past her out of respect.

As the sunlight slowly began to creep ahead of the horizon, I swam slowly closer to the shore awaiting Aaron's arrival. I watched the cliff tops for him and almost squeaked with joy when I saw his shadowy figure begin to descend the steps, bag slung over his shoulder.

'What took you so long?' I joked as he neared the edge of the water.

'How long have you been out here?' he asked with a smile whilst pulling my towel and jumper from the bag.

'Ages, I couldn't wait around once I was awake.'

He laughed and put my towel out on the sand, sitting down on it with his coat pulled tightly around his neck. I wriggled in the shallow water and pulled myself up to sit by his side; which was a lot more awkward than I make it sound. When I finally pushed myself into the sand and sat up, I flicked my tail in the edge of the water where the tide just brushed the edges of my fins and then let out a deep breath.

'You sorted now?' Aaron said with a laugh as I finally sat still.

I nodded and he leant in to kiss me, pushing my wet hair from my face as he did. He'd asked me once why I didn't tie it up, or have it cut. I'd laughed at the tying it up part; what kind of mermaid would I be if I tied it all up? I'd joked about it, but that was how I felt. My hair didn't bother me, and I liked the length because it reminded me of my mothers. Some of the other girls had theirs cut, and some of the younger ones had their hair braided so that they didn't catch it on anything while they were out exploring. Shae's daughter, Carly, already had beautiful long brown hair, and Shae kept it braided into two plaits because Carly was forever getting herself stuck in small places; I'm sure she thought of herself as a fish rather than a mermaid, and Shae was worried that one day her hair would get her trapped. Personally, mine was a part of me, and I would never try to restrain it in any way.

Aaron's fingers slipped from my hair as a shudder ran through him; the water was still cold to him, I'd feel it again as soon as I transformed. Then I would have to consider buying some more winter clothes. I was going to be cold for the next few months.

When the first proper rays of sunlight peeked over the horizon, Aaron clambered up from the sand and held open my towel. I concentrated on separating my legs and kicked the sand gently. It was a different feeling to the one I experienced on the full moon, I could almost sense the more permanent state of it, but it had the same energy to it. Unfortunately, I didn't have long to think about it before the piercing wind ripped through me making me shiver. Aaron bent down and wrapped the towel around me, helping me to my feet.

'Welcome home,' he whispered as I wrapped my arms around him.

I smiled up at him and pressed a kiss to his lips; despite the cold temperatures, his kiss was warm and inviting, and I longed to linger. The wind however, made the need to get dressed and warm up more urgent.

'Miss me?' I asked as I pulled away from the kiss.

'Always,' he replied, sweeping me up off my feet and spinning me around in a fairy tale like spin, 'Though now I won't have to.'

That answer warmed me up inside in a way a fire never could and I heard myself laughing as he spun me around, his arm under my legs so that I could kick into the air. My towel swayed in the wind, making me think of how a dress would do the same, and I saw the ending of a fairy tale in my head; had we really done it?

'Stop overthinking everything and enjoy the moment,' Aaron said as he set me back on my feet and passed me my jeans, 'There is plenty of time for thought, now though, it's time for breakfast.'

Back at the house, I was quick with a hot shower and warm clothes before having breakfast with Elsie and Aaron. It looked like they had been busy waiting for our arrival. The cupboards were bursting with food, the kitchen had been cleaned to within an inch of its life, and the whole house had been de-cluttered. We talked about some of the things we had to do over the next few days and I reminded Elsie who was coming ashore. She seemed to be with it today, but I saw it in her eyes when her mind went on leave. I'd give her a few minutes in her zone and then pull her back into the conversation. I wanted to try and keep her focused; Aaron said that she was better when she was concentrating on something, like she had been these last few days getting ready for today. He had told me that she'd had very few episodes because she'd been so dedicated to the task in hand. I planned to keep it like that in the hope that we could learn to control it. She had another doctor's appointment marked on the calendar for the day before the full moon, so Mia would go with us so that we could find out exactly what we were dealing with and get some support.

When the sun reached its highest point in the sky, I was stood on the beach waiting for my sister and the others just like we had planned. Aaron had stayed with Elsie, there was no point in us all getting cold again and this was going to be my responsibility; I might as well start as I meant to go on.

Marina was the first out of the water, closely followed by Betsy, and I handed them both towels and clothes so that they could get dry and warm quickly.

'Janine had to go back just after we left but they shouldn't be long,' Betsy said when she saw me looking past her to the water.

I nodded and we huddled further back on the beach against the cliffs where it was more protected from the wind. Marina asked about Elsie and I explained what Aaron had told me about the last appointment with the doctor. He'd told me that they had done some tests and taken some blood from her so that they could investigate further. I didn't even begin to pretend I understood, I just retold the story in the hope that she knew what I was talking about. She nodded and made the appropriate noises so I assumed she knew what it all meant.

When Mia and Janine finally emerged from the water, I rushed down with their towels and clothes and we headed back for the house quickly. I'd bumped up the heating a little so that it was plenty warm enough when we got in, and I left them all to it so that they could shower and put on warmer clothes like I had. Elsie had made lunch so that we could all sit down and discuss the plan for the next couple of weeks. It didn't do badly for a discussion, it lasted nearly an hour before it began to resemble an argument, and at that point I extracted Aaron and myself from the situation and we headed into the other room where we curled up on the sofa and turned on the TV. Betsy joined us not long after and updated us on the situation. Janine was unhappy that Elsie thought today should just be about being together; she felt that we should be getting on with things, making arrangements etc. and Elsie was standing up for her belief in that we deserve to just be happy that we are out of the water. I agreed with Elsie, and so did Marina and Betsy. Mia had kept quiet, but I think she agreed with us too. Janine had lost before she'd even started, but she kept arguing.

We found some comedy film that Aaron had seen before and we settled in to watch it. I'd turned on the fire so that it was cosy in here and it wasn't long before we were all half asleep. Aaron's arms were around me where I lay propped up against him, and I could feel Betsy by my feet. When the others finally came through to join us, the look on Janine's face told me everything I needed to know, but she came to sit in the chair by the fire, and settled in to watch the end of the film with us. Small steps.

'It's the first night you don't have to go back to the water,' Aaron said from the other side of the breakfast bar, 'What would you like to do?'

I glanced behind me to where my sister sat on the sofa wrapped in a blanket and nursing a hot water bottle as if her life depended on it. She wasn't used to her human body and the way the elements would affect her, but she had been adamant that she wanted to come ashore with me; now she was trapped here until the full moon, and yes, I felt guilty. She'd spent most of the afternoon huddled under that blanket, but I wanted to explore the world once it had gone dark.

I glanced out of the kitchen window to look at the dying light and then turned back to Aaron, plastering a huge smile on my face at the many possibilities of my night with him.

'We could go out?' he offered, 'There's a local band playing at the pub near the Pool Hall.'

'Ooo,' I offered in lieu of a response; did I want to go out? Did I want to leave Marina?

The idea of snuggling by the fire all night, watching the darkness outside take hold of the world completely was kind of appealing I had to admit.

'Do you wanna stay home?' he asked, reading me like a book.

I bit my bottom lip with a grin, unable to hold back the ridiculous level of excitement that it instilled in me that I would still be here after the sun had set.

'We can go to the pub,' I decided, but knew there had to be a bargain, 'But we need a window seat.'

The smile stayed on my face as his eyebrows pulled together in the middle, his confusion as to my request clear. I waited him out; he'd get there. The recognition spread out across his features, softening them into a smile.

'You want to watch it go dark don't you?' he asked.

I nodded, the grin widening. He understood me so easily, like we had been made for each other. My thoughts wandered to my mother and I wondered if this was how she'd felt with her Peter. The way Elsie had talked about them; I knew they'd been in love too. Had she been this happy?

I discussed the pub idea with the girls, and they agreed that I should start living the life I wanted. Even Janine told me not to worry about them; they'd be okay here at the house. Betsy decided that she wanted to come with us, and I saw no reason not to let her, I wanted us to be a family here on land as well as under the ocean. It started now.

Betsy and I got changed and had a quick discussion about sleeping arrangements before we left so that we didn't have to disturb anyone who was still up when we got back. Marina was sleeping in one of the other rooms so that Aaron could stay the night with me, and Betsy was going to bunk in with her. Mia and Janine were sharing a room too; I think they wanted to stick together rather than sleep separately.

'Have fun,' Marina said as I said goodbye and tucked the blanket back around her and Elsie where they sat in front of the fire with the TV box on.

'I'll try,' I said in response, 'I'm not really sure what to expect.'

'It will be loud,' Marina said with a laugh.

I smiled back and met Elsie's gaze.

'You'll be fine Luna dear, enjoy it.'

She understood.

'I meant night time,' I admitted, turning back to my sister.

'Then Elsie is right, it is just the same as day time but darker, I used to spend some time out here with mum, we would come out on the eclipses and then go back on the full moon; it wasn't so bad.'

More secrets. I frowned a little but tucked the information away for if I ever needed to reference it again. When I looked back at her, I smiled and leant in for one last hug.

'Then wish me luck.'

As I spoke Betsy appeared at my shoulder bouncing with excitement. We pulled on our coats and met Aaron at the front door. He bundled us out to the Jeep and cranked up the heating as he pulled away to head for the pub.

'They're not bad,' I shouted over the noise of the band as they started up their fourth song of the night.

They were a little loud, and the singer was a little screechy in places, but the actual music wasn't bad. The drum beats were steady and powerful and there were some interesting guitar solos in places. In general, I wasn't going to lie when I said that I was getting more pleasure from looking out of the window.

I turned again to glance out into the darkness. The street lights were on now, lighting the car park up and the lamps that ran down the path that stretched and wound along the cliff top were aglow with soft amber light. The darkness pressed in all around and up against the glass. Pressing my fingers against it I smiled to myself at how cold it was. I knew it was cold outside; I'd been able to see my breath clouding in front of me as we'd walked from the Jeep into the inviting warmth of the pub.

Aaron was enjoying himself though; I only had to take one look at him to know that he liked being here. His posture was relaxed, the look on his face was attentive even as his hand never left my thigh, and he was singing along to some of the songs, so I knew he had heard them before, and Betsy was near on glowing with excitement; I didn't have to ask to know that she would be spending plenty of time ashore with me.

'Do you know the band?' I asked when they fell quiet after the song.

He nodded, taking a drink from his pint before answering me.

'The drummer is one of my best friends, and the guitarist hangs out with us sometimes. They've been a band for a couple of years now, this is their second album.'

He spoke with pride, so I knew that the friend must mean a lot to him. I wondered whether he would introduce me at the end, if they were such good friends, but dismissed the idea. He wouldn't do that yet, surely?

The drummer stayed in place a few minutes after the rest of the band jumped down from the stage for a break. They'd said they'd be back in half an hour; I checked the clock, it was already half ten, what time would they be finished? I hated the idea of the girls all rattling around the house, but I didn't want to make Aaron leave either.

My attention was back on the drummer when he moved, extracting himself from behind the elegant drum kit and hopping off the stage. He made his way through the tables and headed straight for us.

'So, this must be Luna,' he said with a smile as he pulled Aaron up into a bear hug, 'She's pretty man.'

He flashed me a smile that I returned nervously. I didn't realise that Aaron had been talking about me to anyone.

'Luna, this is Kieran,' Aaron said turning to me and gesturing from one to the other, 'Kieran, this is Luna, and this is her cousin Betsy.'

'Hey Luna,' Kieran said, holding out his hand for me to shake it.

I offered him my hand and he gave it a firm shake.

'How are you liking living by the sea?' he asked when he released me.

I frowned a little but tried to keep my face reasonably impassive.

'It's okay,' I said loudly enough to be heard over the music that now played over the speakers.

'And Betsy, love the hair,' he said as he shook her hand too and nodded at the aquamarine waves that fell down her back.

'Thanks, would you believe me if I told you it was natural?' she joked and I realised that she was a lot more comfortable around the humans than I'd expected.

I should have known really, she fit into most situations without much thought or having to try too hard. She managed to engage Kieran in light conversation for a few minutes before he left to go to the bar.

'How much have you told him?' I asked warily the moment Kieran was out of ear shot.

'What?' Aaron replied, turning to me sharply.

'He seemed to know a lot about me, I didn't realise you spoke to anyone about me that much.'

I felt the panic rising in me even though I knew I could trust Aaron with my secrets. Being talked about was something I was going to have to get used to now, I was the new girl in town, and everyone seemed to know Aaron.

'Calm down, guys talk. They could tell I'd met someone because I was so happy all the time. I told them that you were from out of town, but you were moving here into the big house on the hill. I mentioned that your Aunt Elsie is poorly. Nothing more. Other than guy talk,' he finished with a shrug.

'What's guy talk?'

He shrugged again nonchalantly as he downed the last of the beer in his glass then smiled over at me.

'Guys talk Luna, they asked how hot you were, that kind of stuff.'

I felt myself blush at the thought of him describing me, at the possibilities of what he could have said and I turned to see Betsy grinning at me. He was pretty open about telling me how he felt and what he thought about me, I wondered how he translated that into 'guy talk' as he called it. Taking a deep breath, I forced myself not to question him, knowing that anything he had said wouldn't jeopardise me or the girls in any way.

'Can we go home?' I asked glancing over at the empty stage.

'Sure, come on,' he said without hesitation, making me smile.

We headed over to where the band were congregated at the end of the bar, some girls were stood ogling the singer, who in my opinion was probably the least attractive, but I guess he was the face of the band. Everyone recognises the front man. Kieran turned as we approached, a friendly smile on his face.

'You leaving man?' he said, putting his hand on Aaron's shoulder.

'Yeah, it's been a long day for Luna, she's been at it since before sunrise,' he said with a smirk in my direction, 'She's wiped.'

'We'll come to the next one,' I offered from behind Aaron, picking my jaw up from the floor after Aaron's brazen comment about the sunrise.

I guessed I was going to have to get used to his comedy around that subject. We couldn't just ignore the facts, as long as I was careful, we'd be fine.

'Sure thing, it was great meeting you Luna,' Kieran said with what I felt was genuine friendliness, he seemed like a really a nice guy, 'And you Betsy, I hope we'll be seeing you again too.'

She nodded rather enthusiastically as Aaron gave Kieran a guy hug.

'We'll sort out the Pool Hall or something next week yeah?' Aaron asked and Kieran nodded.

We said our goodbyes and headed out to the Jeep.

Aaron pushed closed the door behind him and held out his hand for the keys in mine.

'You have to lock it from the inside when you're home at night too,' he said.

There was so much I had to learn that I knew I would never remember it. I would have to remember to lock it when we went out so that nobody could get in while there was just Elsie home on her own. Now I had to lock it when I was in too.

'Why?' I asked.

'So that no one can break in and hurt you while you're sleeping. It's just a precaution so that you're safe.'

He turned the key in the door and then hung it up on the little hook by the bottom of the stairs. I'd watched Elsie hang it there so many times, but I didn't think I'd ever seen her use it to lock the door from the inside. I made a mental note to write an actual note to remind myself. If there was ever a night when Aaron didn't stay with me I wasn't going to remember what to do. Betsy had gone straight up to bed, she'd fallen asleep in the car on the short journey home; she was truly shattered.

Aaron and I made it to the top of the stairs, but that was where my progression stopped. Aaron's hands slid around my waist and up my top from behind, his fingers splaying out on stomach and pulled me against him. His body was like a wall behind me and I sank into his embrace, his hold strong and safe around me.
'Want me to sleep downstairs?' he asked, his breath against my neck warm but still managing to send shivers racing across my skin.
I shook my head and leaned back against him, turning to seek out his mouth. Pressing my lips to his, I placed my hands over his and dug the ends of our fingers into my tummy. I wanted him in my bed, I wanted to fall asleep to the sound of his heart beat, and wake up with his face being the first thing I saw. And I wanted that every day, though I hadn't gotten around to discussing that with him just yet. There were no rules for me to follow for when and how things were supposed to happen, I was flailing blindly in the dark most of the time, with Aaron shining the light down the right path. There were some things that I had to work out for myself though.
We made it into the bedroom and I kicked off my boots and dropped my coat on the chair. I was on my back before I could think any further and Aaron climbed on top of me. He pressed a hard kiss to my mouth and I responded with the same tenacity, our tongues seeking out each other and his teeth gently nipping my bottom lip. When he pulled away and stood up, he pulled his shirt over his head in one swift movement and then turned to the window. As he reached for the curtains I sat up and stopped him.
'Leave them open,' I whispered loudly into the darkness around us.

There was very little light creeping into the room because of the new moon, but I wanted to see the sky. Even though my life had revolved around the cycle of the moon every month, up until tonight, I'd never actually seen the stars in a dark sky before, and it was beautiful. The whole night was beautiful. Due to the lack of streetlights around the house, the stars shone brightly in their inky surrounding, looking like someone had thrown glitter up there to decorate. I couldn't wait to see the moon up there too, for now I re-focussed my gaze onto Aaron, seeing the perfect replica there on his shoulder.

He stood staring out of the window, his tattoo in my view, and I smiled at the similarities. The artist was very good, and it made me warm and tingly inside to know that Aaron had wanted that part of me with him all the time. The full moon meant a lot to me, it gave me the power to be on land where I loved to be, and Aaron had taken that symbol of my human form and inked it onto his skin forever. I didn't need a fairy tale out of some book when I had him. He was more than perfect for me.

'Okay, I'll leave them open.' He turned towards me as he unbuckled his belt and removed his jeans. 'Now come on, clothes off, pyjamas on, I want to hold you.'

I smiled, that was exactly what I wanted too. Then my smile faltered though. Did I own pyjamas? Aaron sensed my change in expression and came over to the bed.

'Luna?' he asked, 'I can sleep on the sofa if you want,' he said, clearly misreading me this time.

'It's not that,' I said, holding out my hand for him to get on the bed, 'I don't think I have any pyjamas.'

He laughed when I spoke my words, and leant in to press a kiss to my forehead.

'No problem,' he said with one last chuckle, then turned back to where he had been stood.

He picked up his shirt from the floor and held it out to me.

'Want to wear this instead?'

My grin was back. Memories from the first day at the beach flooded me. Hadn't I wanted to wear his top then? He'd suggested going for a swim, and he had told me I could borrow one of his T-shirts afterwards so that I would have something dry to wear.

I took the top from his outstretched hand and immediately stripped out of my dress to pull it over my head. My leggings came off too but I kept on my underwear because Aaron had done. He came over to the bed and pulled back the covers for me to get under them, and then quickly joined me, pulling me close and wrapping me in his strong arms.

I fell in to a restless sleep with my head on his chest, to the sound of his steady heart beat thrumming behind the wall of his muscled body just like I had dreamed of doing so many times before.

Angel McGregor

A Handful of Secrets

The Following Morning

I woke long before Aaron and found myself sitting on the little cushioned seat in the window so that I could look out over the water. My room had always been this one, with a view of the ocean spread out infinitely beyond the edges of the cliffs. Elsie had chosen it for me, and had done all the decorating; she'd even changed it as I'd grown up, painting the walls in a pretty shade of lavender for me.

Glancing back, I smiled to myself at the view of Aaron asleep in my bed. It was the first night I'd spent sleeping in that bed, even though it had been in my room for as long as I could remember. I can't say that I'd slept very well, the covers seemed scratchy and uncomfortable and the mattress wasn't nearly as comfortable as the sand, I'd even considered going down to the beach at one point before dismissing the idea as ridiculous.

Aaron's hair was mussed from his movement, though now he laid peacefully on his stomach with his arms wrapped around his pillow. He hadn't woken once in the night, and I'd lain watching him, thinking about just how lucky I was to still be here when the sun had long since left the sky. Where he moved in his sleep, his shoulders tensed and the muscles rolled. He hadn't worn a top to bed, and I'd revelled in the heat that his skin emitted as he'd held me at first. Now I could see the black ink scrawled across his back where the covers had bunched around his waist after I'd gotten out. I could see the moon behind the thorns on his shoulder and found myself smiling again.

Leaving the window as the light began to creep over the horizon; I picked up my camera from the side and lined up a shot of Aaron. The tiny rays of light that entered the room gave him a halo and threw the far side of him into shadows. The Polaroid was very arty and I propped it up on the desk with a smile before I crawled back into bed at the side of him where I squirmed under the covers. I slid off my underwear but left on the top I'd borrowed from him to sleep in. Laying right up flush to Aaron's warm body, I pressed a kiss to the moon on his shoulder and ran my fingers down his spine. I was rewarded with a soft moan but he didn't open his eyes. Continuing my exploration, I carried on pressing kisses across his shoulders and started down his back, moving to straddle his thighs for better access. He moved beneath me, stirring from the sleep that had him captive, and finally turned his head as I reached the waistband of his boxer shorts.

It was still early, and I knew that he wouldn't be ready to wake up yet, but I was wide awake despite my lack of sleep all night and I wanted him to remember our first morning together. We hadn't really done much experimenting sexually, and I knew that I was a long way behind him when it came to experience. But I had read plenty of books, and I wanted to try something from one of them, it couldn't be that hard, right?

'Roll over,' I whispered in his ear as I pressed a kiss to the little patch of skin right below.

He obliged with a smile, but still made no attempt to join in. I wasn't sure whether he was completely conscious yet, or whether he was still in that in between area. He kept his eyes shut and slung his arm across his eyes to shield himself from the sunlight that was now starting to infiltrate the room.

'Luna what time is it?' he asked groggily.

'Sunrise,' I answered, knowing that wasn't what he wanted to know, but not knowing the actual time; there was no clock in my room.

I was going to have to get used to telling the time with a clock instead of by the sun. He groaned audibly then like I had tortured him with the information. I laughed a little, but started to make my way back down his body with my kisses. I ran my hands up his sides, gently scratching his skin with my nails. My hair tumbled forwards over my shoulders and tickled his stomach and I felt him tense up a little against the sensation.

When I moved against his groin I felt him hot and hard beneath his boxer shorts and I smiled. He might be tired, and he may have still been sleepy, but he was still turned on. We seemed to have that effect on each other very easily. He only had to touch me and my body came alive for him. I could feel the desire burning low in my abdomen for him even now, and he hadn't done anything to me; the thoughts of what I wanted to do to his body were enough.

I moved his underwear to free his erection and wrapped my hands around the hard length of him. That got his attention. He moved his arm and pushed up onto his elbows to look at me. I met his eyes and dragged my teeth over my lower lip at the heat I saw in them. Clouded with lust and desire, his eyes smouldered slightly and the wicked glint in them proved that he was up for this no matter what time it was.

'What are you doing?' he said; his voice as thick with lust as his eyes were.

I shot him an innocent look as I slid both hands up and down him with quite a bit of pressure. He hardened further in my grip and inhaled with a tiny gasp.

'Not a lot,' I answered.

'You're biting your lip,' he stated, his eyes darting down to where my hands were wrapped around him and then back up to meet mine.

I released my lip and smiled, not having realised I'd done it again. Then I leant forwards, using one hand to steady myself on the bed and left the other gripping him at the base, to kiss him. I wet my lips with the end of my tongue before sealing my mouth over his. His hands were in my hair in seconds, holding me to him while he kissed me back.

When he finally released me, we were both gasping for breath and I had to move both hands to the bed to stay upright.

After freeing myself from his grip, I kissed my way back down his body, his erection bobbing gently between us as my top rubbed against the end of him. He stayed propped up on his elbows, watching me in my exploration. When I got down to his waist I paused, trying not to overthink then next moves. I knew the theory; putting it into practice wasn't as simple as I thought it would be though.

'Luna,' he got my attention and I looked up, 'You don't have to do anything you're not ready for.'

His words made me smile; he always knew what to say and always seemed genuine. He'd been with me for months now, only seeing my one day out of every month. I'd gotten the feeling he was pretty much the bad boy and had slept around a bit before he'd met me, he had to be missing the sexual side of things, yet he always seemed genuine when he said things like that to me.

'I want to,' I answered honestly.

I wanted to start our relationship off like I wanted it to continue now that I could put every day into it like a normal couple. He nodded and sat up, putting one hand into my hair and easing me up to kiss me again.

'Just so long as you're doing it for you, not for me; I can wait if you're not ready.'

I smiled against his lips, opening my eyes to find him looking at me with sincerity in his eyes and smiling. I knew it. I knew that he was okay waiting, but it didn't stop me wanting to do it anyway. Nodding against his forehead where he held me, I pulled back gently and he let his hand slip from my hair.

With the sun now streaming through the window, I wrapped one hand firmly back around him and lent down to run my tongue down his stomach. He let himself fall back to the bed and put his hands on the sheets by his side as I let my tongue flick over the head of his erection. A tiny bead of white spilled from the end and I glanced up at him before running my tongue over that too. It wasn't like what I'd expected and I shook my head at the taste.

I heard him laughing from his position on the bed but he didn't say anything, just let me continue at my own pace. He was throbbing now in my hand and I wondered what it felt like for him. I knew how it felt when he got me going, how the pressure began to build inside me and the feelings got more and more sensitive. Was it the same for him?

Eventually, I took a deep breath and closed my mouth over the tip of his steely erection. He was hot in my mouth, but soft like velvet at the same time. I stroked my tongue around him before hollowing my cheeks out like it described in the books and slid him into my mouth a little further. He jerked a bit and pushed further than I'd expected, hitting the back of my throat and making me gag. I pulled back and heard his breathing, quick and shallow breaths that made my pulse quicken. Feeling spurred on, I tried again, this time expecting the little thrust and allowing for it.

'Luna, I'm not going to be long,' he panted between breaths and I pulled back.

The books could be pretty detailed in places, was I ready for that? Before I could think much more, Aaron sat up and pulled me up the bed, slipping his hand between my legs to find me wet with desire. I smiled a little at the shock but gasped when he slid two fingers inside me. He pushed deep and spread his fingers and I knew what he was intending. I breathed through the tingle of pain at the invasion and pushed against him, my body moving of its own accord.

'Ready?' he asked as he moved me over the top of him and began to pull me down.

I nodded, my body was so wound up that even the thought of the stinging pain of him stretching me wasn't enough to make me think twice. He pushed the head of his erection just inside me and I bit into my bottom lip, the full feeling catching me off guard. He waited for me to meet his eyes again before pulling down on my hips so that I slid onto him inch by inch.

He had been right, it didn't take him long. A few strokes of my tight body and my nails in his chest and I felt him swell inside me before the rush of hot liquid made me squirm. His fingers on my clit made me jump and my body tightened and exploded in ecstasy around him, squeezing him inside me a little more. He clamped a hand over my mouth just as I was about to make a noise and raised his eyebrows at me. I giggled, but nodded and he removed his hand again, sliding it around into my hair where he pulled me down to kiss me.

When I fell back to the bed I was panting, the morning exercise enough to make sure I was invigorated for the day ahead after my lack of sleep through the night. Aaron rolled up onto his side and slipped his hand up under the edge of my top and laid it flat on my tummy. I smiled at the easy feeling inside me that told me everything was going to work out now.

I slipped quietly into Elsie's room to find her still sleeping, her curtains open too. Her room was next to mine, so had the same view of the ocean and I smiled at the fact that she liked to be able to see the sky at night too. After reassuring myself that she was okay, she was capable of looking after herself still, I made my way down the landing to the bathroom and came face to face with my sister just coming out with a towel wrapped round her.

'Morning,' she said with a smile.

I smiled back and we exchanged a few more words before she headed back to her room to get dressed and I took her place in the bathroom. The mirror was all steamed up and it was ridiculously clammy; that had been one hell of a hot shower she'd just taken. I laughed; talk about making sure she was all warmed up. If she was happy, it would all be okay, and if a hot shower was what it was going to take then I would learn to use the bathroom without a mirror.

'I think I need to make more lists,' I joked as Elsie placed bowls and boxes of cereals on the table in front of Marina and me.

I had been writing a list for the past ten minutes of all the things that I needed to sort. Elsie had been adding to it, naming a few things that I didn't even understand yet. Being on land was proving complicated. There was so much I hadn't thought of, so much that I had to do.

'I need to put priorities on things and then work out what stuff I can do later. Will you help?' I asked, turning as she walked back towards the kitchen counter.

'Of course, we can head into town later today if you like and get a few bits sorted. Some things are pretty simple,' she smiled as she returned to the table with the carton of milk and sat down at the side of me.

'Can Aaron come too?' I asked, wanting him involved.

One day it would be just him and me, and I wanted him to be a part of my new life in every way.

'If he isn't busy. Remember he has a job to go to.'

I frowned. Of course, he would have to go to work. I'd never given much thought to it before, he'd been taking the day off every month since he met me so that he could spend the day with me. He was up in the shower now, and I had to dismiss the horrible feeling of him leaving me for the day. There really was so much that I hadn't thought about.

'You already have an identity. I made sure that I registered all of you so that you exist in the human world,' Elsie said cutting into my thoughts, then added, 'Just in case there was ever a problem while you were ashore.'

I nodded, looking at the list we'd just made.

'So, I need to apply for this?' I said, pointing at the first thing we'd written.

'Yes, you're going to need ID to get a lot of the other things, so we'll send off for your provisional licence. That way you'll have something with you all the time.'

I nodded, writing some notes on the bottom of the page as she spoke. Aaron came down the stairs then, wearing a fresh top and the jeans from last night.

'Good morning,' Elsie said as he came to sit at the other side of me.

'Morning Elsie,' he replied then turned to look at my list, 'Making plans?'

I nodded, showing him the list.

'We're going into town later if you want to come. If you're not busy,' I added, not wanting to make him feel bad.

'Yeah, I can come, if that's okay with both of you,' he said as he pulled the box of Rice Crispies towards him and started sorting his breakfast out.

Elsie frowned but smiled at the same time.

'You don't have to go to work?' she asked.

He shook his head, spooning his first spoonful of Rice Crispies in as they crackled in the bowl.

'I took the week off so that I could be around for Luna,' he answered with a smile.

Elsie and Marina both smiled then and I saw the shimmer in both of their eyes that told me they approved of his behaviour. He'd look after me when the day came that Elsie couldn't, I knew it in my heart. We all knew that, and it made me happy that Elsie approved of Aaron. Marina was getting there too; she'd admitted that she liked him at least. I'd work on their friendship, because I had every intention of him being a part of the girls' lives too. I wanted them to feel comfortable around him, prove to them that not all humans are bad like we were told. I wanted to give them some hope. Get some of them on land more.

After the debris of breakfast was all cleared away, we all got ready to go into town. Though I had no intentions of spending all day every day with the girls, I wasn't ashamed to accept all the help I could get. Over breakfast we had discussed some of the things on my list, and Janine had thrown some more light onto some of the points. We were heading for the Post Office first in an attempt to change the name on the postal box we held there, and then it was on to several other places, all with the same intentions to begin with; the start of my reign on land.

We all bundled up well to battle the harsh winter winds that were keeping up their parade along the roads, but we had agreed to all walk since we couldn't all fit into the Jeep. Janine had surprised me by involving Aaron in all the discussions so far, and had even put a conversation on hold when he'd had to answer a call from his father, just so that he wouldn't miss anything. Her acceptance of him was happening much quicker than I'd imagined, and it filled me with more hope for our future together than I could explain.

Marina was a couple of paces ahead of Aaron and me, her arm linked through Elsie's as they walked together down the road. Betsy half skipped by Elsie's other side, the cold clearly not worrying her at all, and Mia and Janine were up front. My gloved hand was entwined with Aaron's and then squashed into his pocket as we walked silently into town.

'Everything okay with your father?' I asked after I couldn't handle the quiet any longer.

I'd held off asking in the house because I didn't think he'd want to talk about it with the girls close by, but it was obviously bothering him, and I wanted to help.

'Hmm?' he murmured, turning my way.

'The phone call with your dad, is everything okay?' I asked again.

'Yeah, I guess. Just the usual argument about me not being around enough,' he answered with a shrug of his shoulders, 'He has no interest in me when I am there, but complains when I'm out. Typical.'

'What if I could fix it?' I almost whispered, scared that I was about to overstep a line.

'I wouldn't let you near my dad, so that is never going to happen,' he answered firmly.

'What if I wouldn't need to go anywhere near your dad, or your house?'

'You've lost me,' Aaron admitted and I had to laugh at the expression on his face.

'Well, I was thinking, that I'd quite like you to live with me and Elsie,' I started quietly.

Aaron stopped walking and I stumbled to a halt by his side when it pulled on my arm. He was looking at me with an expression that I couldn't quite fathom.

'It's fine if you don't want to, but I've spoken to the girls, and Elsie, and none of them have a problem with it, and you could have your own bedroom if you wanted to,' I continued to ramble until he cut me off with a kiss I didn't see coming.

I smiled into the kiss and relaxed into his arms as he slipped them around me and held on tightly. When he finally pulled away, I stepped backwards and found my footing before looking up into his sea blue eyes.

'You want me to move in with you?'

I hesitated only a second, still unsure of his reaction, before nodding clearly. He smiled and joined in my nodding.

'Are you sure?'

'I'm sure, I wouldn't want it any other way. I have said right from finding out that all of this was possible that I wanted to do it with you by my side, and having you there last night confirmed it. I don't want to do this without you.'

'Then I would love to,' he said with a grin wider than I'd ever seen before, 'But I need you to know that it is for you and me, not because of my father.'

'I know that,' I answered, fully believing in my own words.

We put a little speed into our steps and caught up with the others as they turned the corner that led onto the main road into town. I pulled the list from my pocket and let out a long sigh that had the air in front of me clouding up. It was going to be a long morning.

'What would you like to do now?' Aaron asked once Janine had left the room.

She had officially given me the rest of the afternoon off after the mammoth trip into town this morning. A part of me wanted to answer with 'go to bed' but I had other ideas suddenly burst into my mind.

'I know what I'd like to do,' I answered with a grin, 'But I think it would be too cold.'

Aaron frowned, clearly not following.

'I'd like to go swimming with my legs,' I admitted.

He laughed.

'You're right, that would be cold,' he confirmed and I wrinkled up my nose in annoyance, 'How about a walk down the beach instead, barefoot in the tide?'

He knew me so well. I nodded enthusiastically and jumped up to grab my coat. I asked Betsy if she wanted to join us, half hoping that she would say no because I wanted to spend some time alone with Aaron. Lucky for me, she was tired too and said that she was going to curl up by the fire for a while. So, I told Marina where we were going and briefly spoke to Elsie, agreeing to bring back some potatoes from the market for tea, then headed out to the Jeep with Aaron.

He drove us down to the beach and I near on ran to the sand, kicking off my boots and pulling off my socks as soon as possible. The sand was cold, and the water was very fresh, but I revelled in the feeling of the wet sand squidging between my toes as I splashed through the shallow water. This was what I'd been missing all these years, the opportunity to mix the two parts of me into one and find the balance that best suited me.

Aaron let me splash in the water for a while before insisting that he took me home again before I ended up with blue toes. I had to admit defeat when he caught me shivering, and he bundled me back into the Jeep with my feet all wrapped in a towel and wedged under the warm blowers.

The wind had picked up again by the time we returned to the house, and the fire was on. I closed the door on the audible howl of the wind and immediately had to shed a few layers; the heat was almost stifling.

'The girls got cold,' Elsie said with a chuckle, as if in explanation when I walked in, still fighting to be free of my jumper.

I laughed as Aaron rescued me, throwing his own hoodie over the back of the chair. We couldn't have the heating on this high all the time; the house was far too stuffy. I pressed the button on the little panel on the wall and knocked off the heating.

'Surely you're all warmed up now,' I said with another laugh.

I could see how this was going to move forward, and it was going to take some time to create a pattern that we all felt comfortable with, but for now, I was happy with the situation. I was happy that I had my legs, and as the sun began to disappear behind the horizon for the second time since I'd stepped out of the ocean yesterday I realised that I was genuinely happy with the place I found myself.

I had Aaron, I had my legs, and I had my family all around me. This was going to work out. We all got what we wanted like this.

March

I awoke with the sunrise as I had every morning since I'd been ashore, the sunlight streaming through the open curtains. Aaron lay on his stomach with his face pressed into the pillow, still sound asleep. I'd stopped waking him now, he needed more sleep. I crept from the room and downstairs to find Mia already up and dressed, stood looking out of the front window.

'You're up early,' I commented coming to a stop behind the sofa.

'I've been up hours; my body knows that it's the full moon tonight, I've been restless all night. I got up not wanting to disturb Janine,' she replied without turning around.

'When are you going back to the water?' I asked, dreading the answer now that the full moon was upon us.

I knew that they were all going back today, but the house was going to be so quiet without them here that I would be sad to see them leave.

'Janine and I are going back after breakfast, you don't need us now, and I want to see the kids; this is the longest I've ever been away from them.'

I smiled at the thought; Lou's twins were only four, and were total opposites. Lizzy was calm, innocent, level headed; much like her mother, but Dizzy was the flip side of that; she was crazy, hyperactive, loud, never sat still. She had more than enough energy for the both of them, though between them they were a total whirlwind. I loved being around them, and had to admit that it was strange not seeing them around. It begged the question as to whether Lou would start bringing them ashore now.

Zoning back in on the conversation, I fidgeted with a stray strand of cotton on the sofa cushion as I asked my next question.

'Is my sister going back with you?'

I knew that she was more than ready to return to the ocean, she hadn't been happy trapped here on land. She belonged in the water as much as I belonged out here; no matter how hard that was to believe. It looked like Lizzy and Dizzy weren't the only opposites.

'She hasn't said,' Mia replied, finally turning from the window.

I fell silent and looked out at the view she'd been watching. The early morning colours were bright in the sky, despite the cold temperatures that I knew accompanied them; the day looked warm and inviting. At least the ocean would be warm once the girls had transformed back; Marina would be happier then.

Breakfast was busy as usual. Despite my attempt to have us all sit down together today, it was its normal hectic self. Elsie and I sat down to ours with Mia, then Janine ducked in for hers but left saying she had one last errand to run in town before she headed back to the water with Mia. Promising that she wouldn't be long, she had her coat on and was out of the door before we even had a chance to ask where she was going. Marina came down to join us and sat quietly nibbling her toast and then Betsy and Aaron arrived, stumbling into the kitchen in a burst of laughter.

I raised my eyebrows as Betsy pulled out the chair next to Elsie and sat down, pulling a bowl and the box of cereals her way, but she didn't seem to notice. Aaron came around the table and pressed a kiss to the top of my head before disappearing into the kitchen where I heard him filling up the kettle. I had learned that Aaron was better company if he got his morning cup of coffee.

When he returned to the table, he sat down in the empty seat by my side, like he did every morning, and proceeded to steal one of my slices of toast. The girls had the same thing for breakfast each day, Marina her toast, Janine had bagels with cheese on, Mia and Betsy both had cereals. Aaron, he had something different, I never knew what he would have from one morning to the next, and I'd started trying to do the same. I had always had cereal; Elsie always had it in for me on the days I was ashore. Now I was trying to be more human, and today I'd made toast with jam.

'You sleep okay?' I asked after objecting to losing part of my breakfast.

He nodded and swallowed, passing me back the other half of the slice.

'I didn't realise I'd slept so late until Betsy threw a pillow at me from the doorway; seems you left the door open this morning,' he said with a smirk and I closed my eyes, thanking the oceans that he'd slept in boxers last night.

'My bad,' I said with a guilty look on my face.

Betsy giggled from behind her spoon and gave me a mischievous grin. I shook my head at her then got up to start clearing the table.

I said goodbye to Mia and Janine at the front door, they said I didn't have to go down the beach with them, they'd leave their clothes by the rocks in the bag Janine had slung over her shoulder and I could collect them later. Marina stood by my shoulder, she'd said she was staying to sunset, as had Betsy. I'd argued that she should go back now, she would be happy then, but she told me that an entire cycle apart was enough, without leaving me early just because she was cold.

Closing the door on the cold morning, I turned back to see Marina disappear back into the living room and Betsy head upstairs. We'd agreed to go out for lunch at the Hut; I had to stay out of the water today, but I wanted to be by the beach, and we could sit facing the ocean there.

For the rest of the morning I pottered around the house, tidying, putting washing away and dusting, until

Aaron came up behind me, sliding his arms around my waist and took the duster from me.

'I know that you're going to miss them after tonight, but you can't do this all day,' he said quietly against my ear.

I hadn't realised I was doing anything specific, but now he had taken the duster from me, I realised I'd been at it for hours.

'How about you let me distract you until lunch?' he whispered again, pressing his hands against my hips and flattening his body flush against mine.

Betsy and Marina had gone out with Elsie for a wander into town to find Elsie a new pair of boots, so the house was empty; not something that had happened very often over the last two weeks. How could I say no?

I turned in his arms and pressed a kiss to his lips. His tongue flicked out and met mine and I melted at the core. My body responded to him in ways I would probably never fully understand, but when he slid his hands underneath me and lifted me, I wrapped my legs around his waist and he carried me upstairs. When my back hit the bed, he had his shirt off in seconds and was on top of me. I wriggled out of my own top, wanting his skin against mine, and his eyes lit up, as they did every other time, when he found me braless. You'd think he'd have gotten used to it by now, but he always seemed surprised, and reacted the same way. He lowered his head to my chest and pressed a kiss right in the centre before lazily dropping kisses across my breasts and up towards my collar bone.

When he reached my neck, I began to squirm until he returned to kissing me properly, then I slid my hands up his back, nails biting into his skin just a little. He already had red marks left from a couple of days ago; I was going to have to be more careful when the weather improved; he couldn't go stripping off on the beach looking like he'd been attacked by a wild animal.

His hands roamed my body, torturing me with how slow he moved, tracing circles across my skin until I was half mad with need for him. By the time he removed my jeans and underwear I was more than ready for him, and it didn't take him long before he sank into me, filling me and pushing me into that place only he had taken me.

I was just pulling my jumper back on when I heard the front door open and the chatter of Betsy, Marina an Elsie returning. Aaron smiled and winked at me before heading back down the stairs and joining in their conversation as if he had been with them all along. I loved that they got along so well, especially him and my sister, who had finally gotten over any issues she had with a human knowing her secrets. We were one big family now, and this was the start of our future together.

Swinging into the bathroom I noticed my still flushed cheeks and splashed some water on my face to cool down. It didn't work. It was a good job mermaids didn't know much about human relationships, because I had guilty written all over my face.

'You about ready to head out for lunch?' Betsy asked when I appeared in the kitchen doorway.

I nodded, risking a glance in Aaron's direction, who gave me a cheeky grin before turning back to Elsie. We bundled up and all piled into the Jeep; a task not as easy as it sounded. We let Elsie ride up front, and Marina, Betsy and I squeezed into the back seat.

'I think you need a bigger car,' Betsy joked once we were all in.

It really was a tight squeeze; I wasn't even sure the back seat was intended to be used. As soon as Aaron parked up, we opened the door and spilled out. Aaron caught me before I toppled over clumsily and I heard Elsie laughing from the other side of the car. Betsy hadn't been so lucky. We rounded the car to find her brushing car park dust from her knees. I tried not to laugh, I really did. It came out as more of a snort.

We got our table by the big glass doors that were normally left open in the summer, and I sat so that I was facing the ocean. I'd had my feet in the water almost every day since being ashore, and couldn't wait until it was warm enough to go swimming, but today, I had to stay dry. We couldn't risk the possibility of the salt water transforming me back.

Lunch passed in a blur of good food and conversation. Elsie was a little tipsy from the glasses of wine and my sister wasn't far behind her. I laughed and made a joke about swimming under the influence, which had Betsy laughing, but Marina just smiled and asked me who exactly was going to stop her, the fish? That had us all laughing, and it wasn't until Aaron made a comment a few minutes later, that I realised for the first time, I had finally been able to make jokes about the water. Up until now I had panicked every time Aaron had said anything that linked us back there, and Betsy was just as bad, cracking jokes and using phrases that meant something different to us than the person she was talking to. But today, I hadn't reacted that way. Was I finally settling in? Had it taken the coming of the full moon to prove to me that I was staying on land? I didn't have to return to the water tonight, or any other night if I didn't want to.

I fell quiet and just listened to the girls chattering around me. My hand was on Aaron's leg just beneath the edge of the table and I squeezed it gently, smiling to myself at how normal this felt. I hadn't felt normal my entire life, always living a half lie when I was ashore, having to make up stories if I wanted to speak to people, always feeling separate to everyone else. Now I was a part of everyone else, I was a part of this world on land and I had Aaron by my side too.

Once we were all done with lunch, we returned to the house. Elsie and I decided to walk back, letting Aaron take Marina and Betsy in the Jeep. Elsie and I talked the whole way back about some of the things I had left to do on my list and about Aaron. She always surprised me when she spoke to me about him, because she knew him almost as well as I did. I knew that he worshipped Elsie, and that she had been more of a parent to him these last few months than his own father had been since losing his wife. Aaron was happy to be here, he'd moved his things into the house a week after the eclipse, and hadn't been back to his father's house since.

We'd developed quite a routine really, and I'd even gotten used to him going to work every day too. He got home just after five most days, having quit one of his jobs because it took up too many of his evenings. Things would change a little now that I wouldn't have the girls in the house with me, but I planned to keep myself busy through the day so that my evenings would be free to spend with Aaron.

There wasn't long left of the day by the time we returned and the sun was ready to start disappearing behind the horizon; it was time to say goodbye to my sister. I would go with her back to the water, just like Elsie had done with me so many times before. That way I could take her clothes and shoes from her straight away, rather than worrying about them on the beach. I was going to have to learn the patterns of usage of the cove so that I knew what times were safe and when I could be sure that there was complete privacy. Maybe I would ask the girls to start using the cove Aaron and I had discovered around the cliff edge; it was much more secluded there. Mainly because there was no real access to it from the top, but we'd found our way down safely enough. I wondered if I could make it more accessible but keep it private so that they wouldn't have to be as guarded about getting in and out of the water. Several of them had said that they wanted to make more of an effort to come ashore, especially during the warmer weather, and I was going to make sure I gave them every reason to, and that they enjoyed their time with me. I wanted them to be happy on land too. I had so many plans.

Marina sat in the corner of the sofa, huddled beneath her blanket like she did every night, and Betsy lay on her stomach in front of the roaring fire.

'You want me to start dinner?' Aaron asked softly, coming to stand behind me where I leant on the door jamb looking in on my sister.

'After I've taken Marina back to the water.' I stated.

He nodded.

'Want me to come with you?'

Shaking my head firmly, I answered him quickly, not wanting to offend him, but he cut me off.

'It's okay, I get it. I'll wait here,' he said before I could continue.

I smiled and leant back into his embrace.

Betsy looked up from her book and peered out of the window before speaking to Marina.

'You about ready to go back?' she asked quietly.

I watched as Marina nodded, then looked up to find me watching. She smiled and I nodded, turning to kiss Aaron before collecting my coat and pulling on my boots. Betsy had run off upstairs to change her top, claiming that she couldn't swim in a jumper; she returned in a pale yellow cropped top that strangely suited her, despite the clash with her hair, and what would be her tail too.

'Was Mum purple?' I asked suddenly, linking my thoughts of Betsy's colouring, to Marina's beautiful plum shade and my own lilac.

Marina smiled as she met my eyes and nodded; she'd been a little better at answering my questions since her big secrets were revealed. These last few weeks I'd learned more about my past than I had known my entire life. She rarely volunteered anything, but she had answered anything I'd asked her. I didn't push it; I just nodded and accepted the new information. It was sort of

A Handful of Secrets

comforting to know that I had gotten my colours from her.

They said their goodbyes and we walked down to the beach in near silence, though Betsy broke it as we stepped onto the sand, promising that she would be ashore again the day of the next full moon, and asked if we could go to the pub for lunch. I laughed, promising to ask Aaron, and to see if Kieran would be around, as I knew that was what she hoped for when she spoke of the pub, she'd asked Aaron about him every opportunity she got.

Betsy went first stripping and diving into the incoming tide quickly, resurfacing a few hundred yards away and bobbing there to wait. Marina hugged me tightly, promising to come with Betsy next month. She made me promise to be careful, to look after Elsie, and to let Aaron look after me. There was no way for me to contact her during the cycle, I would have to wait till the next moon for her to return, and it was obvious now that she was worried in case I needed her.

'I will be fine, I promise, I won't let anything bad happen to Elsie, and Aaron won't let anything happen to me,' I said reassuringly, then pulled away and nodded to the sunset.

It was time.

She pulled off her coat and handed it to me, giving me a kiss on the forehead like she used to, she pulled off her trousers and ran into the water, splashing like a child before she dove under, resurfacing by Betsy's side and making her jump. I waved and watched as they waved back before disappearing beneath the safety of the water.

I stood there for what seemed like hours and watched as the full moon appeared in the darkness. It glowed in the darkness; a beautiful silver against the inky backdrop with the stars shining brightly all around.

There was no light pollution down here, just the natural light that reflected from the moon's cratered surface. I smiled up at my first full moon, and for the

Angel McGregor

first time in my life, I turned my back on it and walked away from the ocean.

April

I sat quietly by the window with a mug of hot chocolate warming my hands and watched as the light began to brighten up the water. I'd taken two bags down to the beach last night and hidden them behind the rocks as I had no idea what time the girls would be ashore, or who was coming. My sister and Betsy had promised they'd be here, so their clothes were waiting for them, but I'd just put a selection in for the others; they could get changed once they got to the house. I also had no idea what time to expect any of them; it wasn't like I could call and find out. Aaron had set me up with a phone several days ago, saying that it made sense that he, Elsie and I could all contact each other. I'd seen Elsie use her little phone plenty of times, but I still hadn't gotten my head around mine yet. There were no buttons like on the phone by the bottom of the stairs; I had to press the screen and it made things happen.

One thing that I was learning very quickly, was that there was a lot more to living on land than I had first imagined, and it was a very confusing place. Elsie had been great, talking me through everything and showing me how to use the new gadgets in my life now. Aaron found himself giggling at me more and more often, but he was as patient as ever with me, and never once made me feel silly for not understanding. I would take something to him as I had done with my new phone the first time I had accidentally turned it off. He'd smiled at me and shown me where the button was to turn it back on, and shown me what to press once it was loaded. He'd then turned it off again and given it me back so that I could do it myself. Since then I hadn't turned it off again, but now I knew how to put it right if I ever did it again.

Elsie had spent the last week doing nothing but tell me how wonderful she thought Aaron was, and how I was lucky to have him, and that I needed to hold onto him. The first few times I'd smiled and blushed as we'd discussed how I knew I was lucky; there probably weren't many guys around who would find out that their girlfriend was a mermaid and just carry on as if that kind of thing happened every day. But as the week had stretched out and we'd had the same conversation daily, I realised that it wasn't repetition, but that Elsie wasn't remembering the previous day clearly. Her confusion was getting worse, quite rapidly and her spells of lucidity were becoming shorter and less often. I worried that she would forget me soon, but Aaron said that she'd shown no signs of any problems with her long-term memory, it was the last couple of days she lost, and her concentration was suffering terribly.

I sighed and unfolded myself from the seat in the bay window, lazily dragging my fingers across Aaron's shoulder as I passed the bed, and headed back downstairs to wash my mug. As I walked past Elsie's room, I heard her coughing; she'd been poorly for a couple of days now, Aaron had said if she wasn't better by tomorrow that we'd take her to the doctor. She seemed fine in herself; or as fine as fine was these days, but it was really getting to her, and sounded awful. Once downstairs, I made her another drink of warm lemon tea and honey. It seemed to help soothe her throat a little if nothing else.

On my way back up the stairs I thought about the day ahead, and reminded myself to call Kieran, or more specifically to have Aaron call Kieran, to ensure he was still on for lunch. He'd said he'd love to when we'd asked him last week, he'd even asked about Betsy. It made me smile to know she'd made an impact on someone around here; she'd enjoy knowing that he was asking about her. I just had to watch out for a situation like the one I'd found myself in with Aaron that first evening I'd met him. Betsy had no phone, so Kieran wouldn't be able to contact her when she wasn't here.

A Handful of Secrets

Elsie was propped up in bed when I put my head around the door, and seemed to have stopped coughing, but she was still trying to sleep, so I put the drink down on the bedside table and left again without disturbing her.

The silence of the house was disrupted when two squealing little girls ran through the hallway and into the living room in no clothes. I laughed, startled by their sudden appearance, but held my arms open for them to run into and turned them towards the fire to warm them up, rubbing my hands up and down their backs.

'Where's your mom?' I asked as they wriggled on my lap, warming themselves up in the glow of the fire.

'Right here,' Lou said from doorway and I heard the hustle and bustle of people coming into the house and the door being closed on the windy morning outside.

I smiled and looked back at the twins.

'You brought them ashore?' I said, my voice tinged with emotion as I fought back the happy tears that pooled in my eyes.

She smiled and nodded, dropping one of the bags I'd left on the beach by the end of the sofa and coming around to sit by us on the floor.

'They wanted to come,' she said in explanation, 'And I didn't want to curb their enthusiasm, or put them off till next month when you'd have some warning. They're that excited that I don't even think they felt the cold. I had them wrapped in towels, but as soon as they saw the house they dropped them and ran.'

'We wanted to surprise you,' they said in unison and I turned my attention back to them.

'Well you certainly managed that, now how about we go and find you some clothes and then go and wake up Aunt Elsie, because she's still in bed.'

They giggled and then slid off my knee, sliding their hands into mine so that I could show them the way.

'It looks like I'm not needed, I'll make breakfast,' Lou said, standing up behind me.

We laughed as I led the twins out of the living room, and came face to face with a group of the girls still fighting for space in the hallway. My sister threw her arms around me from the tangle of limbs, and Betsy shrieked and joined the hug. When they released me, I turned to see Mia, Fran and Georgie there too, all fighting with their coats and boots in the limited space that the hallway provided. I hustled the twins upstairs, trying to remember where I'd put the children's clothing that we'd found while we were clearing out before the eclipse.

'This one?' Lizzy asked pushing against my bedroom door at the end of the hall.

'No, that's my room,' I said as I reached the top of the stairs with Dizzy, but I was too late.

She pushed open the doorway and squealed. I heard Aaron laugh and he was sitting up in bed, pulling the duvet around his middle as I got to the doorway, swinging Dizzy up onto my hip.

'Hello,' Lizzy said without even looking twice at the fact that there was a boy in my bed.

'Hello,' Aaron said, his voice still sleepy, 'And who might you be?' he asked with a smile.

'My name is Lizzy,' she said from her spot at the doorway.

She hadn't made it any further inside the room after catching sight of Aaron.

'Aaron, this is Dizzy,' I said nodding to the little wriggling bundle of excitement on my hip, 'And Lizzy,' I glanced down, 'They're Lou's girls.'

'Ah,' he said in acknowledgement, 'We weren't expecting you today,' he finished, rearranging himself on the bed to sit up against the headboard.

'We wanted to surprise Auntie Luna,' Dizzy said, wriggling so that I would put her down.

A Handful of Secrets

As soon as her feet touched the floor, she scuttled across the room and clambered up onto the bed, sitting herself cross legged in front of him. She was still butt naked, but the way we were brought up, it was all natural, and she had no experience that told her that she probably should be putting on clothes to be around Aaron. Her innocence made me smile, but I reminded her that we were up here to get dressed. Marina appeared at my shoulder then because her clothes were in the chest of drawers in the corner of my room.

'Morning Aaron,' she said as she breezed in to grab another jumper and some thicker socks.

It looked like the twins weren't the only ones who didn't have any issues with seeing Aaron in bed. Our upbringing in the water clearly hadn't prepared any of us for the privacy that we should be giving to half naked humans. In my distraction, I hadn't noticed Lizzy climb up onto the bed after her sister, and when I turned back, she was laid on her tummy with her bare bum stuck up in the air as she listened to Aaron telling Dizzy about our lunch plans. I had no idea how they had gotten onto that conversation, but it looked like we were going to need a bigger table.

By the time breakfast was over with I was shattered. I had somehow ended up in charge of the twins, and it seemed that their energy levels were endless. The mischief they could cause if you took your eyes of them for a second were limitless and they'd had Aaron wooed since the moment he'd laid his sleepy eyes on them. Elsie had been over the moon when I'd let them in, fully clothed I might point out, to wake her up. Lou seemed to find it hilarious that they'd attached themselves to me, and had declared it her day off. Every time they went to her for something, she redirected them to me, saying that on land I was in charge. I'd laughed the first time, but she'd been serious, and anything they needed they had come looking for me for help.

Now I was lying flat on my back in front of the fire with Dizzy stretched out on top of me on her stomach. She had a book propped open on my chest and was 'reading' me the story. She couldn't read, and I was sure that I'd heard the story of *Hansel and Gretel* before and there had been no mermaids, no sharks and no boats in the story. But it was keeping her out of mischief for a while, and her sister was sat on Aaron's knee on the sofa listening too.

Their calm demeanour was misleading, and I knew from experience that it wouldn't last, but I was enjoying the rest while I could.

Trying to organise everyone and get them to the pub was like performing a military mission without a leader, and there were more arguments and misunderstandings in the hour leading up to it than there had been all day. Dizzy was getting tired too which wasn't helping. Lizzy was still firing on all cylinders and had commandeered Aaron to walk her to the pub; I think it was safe to say that she was smitten, and the feeling was pretty mutual.

We walked to the pub; there was no way we would all fit into the Jeep. Aaron and Lizzy were up front with Fran and Georgie, I didn't mind sharing him today, I got him every day now, so one day a month was okay. Mia was walking with Elsie just behind them, their arms linked and huddled together against the wind. Marina, Betsy, Lou and I brought up the rear; Lou had Dizzy on her back where she had her head on her mother's shoulder, her eyes half closed. Lou assured us that she would catch her second wind once we arrived at the pub. It was somewhere new and she would soon find the energy to explore.

The walk down there was cold, the wind coming in from the ocean was harsh and by the time we made it, Lizzy had managed to persuade Aaron into carrying her on his shoulders, her little arms wrapped around his head. When I say that she persuaded him, all she had done was stop and hold up her outstretched arm to him and he had swept her up, her coat drowning her as it was at least three sizes too big, and put her onto his shoulders. I had made a mental note to go clothes shopping for kids' clothes before the next full moon, it had been so long since the smallest of us had been ashore, that we had really struggled to dress them both today.

The regulars in the pub must have wondered what in the ocean had hit them when we arrived. Aaron had called Kieran just before we left the house and warned him that there were plenty of us; he had called it a surprise family visit, and I'd asked him to try and keep the specifics down to a minimum. We were family, and Elsie was the roots of our family, we tried to keep it at that.

Lou had been right, as soon as we'd gotten inside and warmed up, Dizzy had come alive. She had Kieran wrapped around her little finger just as quickly as she'd had Aaron, and the twins commandeered the pair of them as their entertainers for the afternoon. Lou said that she thought it was because they were something different; they'd never spent time with men before.

It was an amazing afternoon. No one seemed uncomfortable in any way, nor did they appear to be in a hurry to get back to the water. I'd checked out the sunset time last night, so knew that they had until seven tonight before they needed to be back on the beach. Everyone got along, Betsy had sidled up beside Kieran not long after arriving and hadn't really moved, despite Lizzy's attempts to steal his attention. Kieran seemed very happy to entertain them both, and I took plenty of photographs with my camera so that I could put up some newer photos in the house; especially ones of the twins.

I'd gotten a lovely one of them with Aaron. They had been teasing him and I'd told them to give him a kiss. I'd snapped the photo as they come up on either side of him, pressing their little kisses to either cheek in unison.

They'd come away giggling and Aaron had laughed before tickling them both till they could barely breathe.

By the time the sky started to darken outside, the twins were fast asleep on the bench, Lizzy's head on Aaron's knee and Dizzy's on her mothers. I had finally gotten in at the side of Aaron and he had his arm around me. The drinks had been flowing and I wondered how long it would be before we had to carry Betsy home. Kieran had supplied the drinks for her most of the night, and I'd lost count after the fourth.

We called it a night, and Kieran agreed to walk us home, or more specifically, walk Betsy home. She only made it around the corner before Kieran gave her a piggy back; and fair play to him, he carried her all the way home from there. Aaron carried Lizzy over his shoulder, her limp body never disturbing the entire way. She was exhausted. Dizzy was awake now, but much calmer and had agreed to walk. Lou said they were fine for now, as long as they could swim home later.

I walked home with Elsie's arm through mine, and Marina on my other side, talking quietly about how well this new lifestyle seemed to be going. I'd made my impact without having to try too hard yet. If I could get the kids on my side, I was on track. By getting the youngest generation involved in this new life on land, I could turn the opinion of being out of the water around and make the time on land more of a part of our lives. I smiled to myself as I unlocked the door and let everyone in. We dumped the kids on the sofa and I made hot drinks to warm us all back up after the walk along the cliff tops.

I checked the clock and made a face at Aaron when I realised that the time was running out for the girls, and Kieran was making no move to leave. He nodded his understanding and continued his conversation with Marina for a few minutes before turning to Kieran and asking what his plans were for the rest of the evening.

'Man, I hadn't realised it was that late actually. I'm supposed to be going to pick my dad up to take him to the pool hall,' he said, standing up from his seat at the breakfast bar.

He turned to me and smiled.

'Thanks for today Luna, it's been great.'

'No worries, I'm glad you could come,' I said, getting up to show him out.

'And it was lovely to meet everyone; I hope we can do it again sometime.'

He waved as he left the room, and poked the twins to say goodbye on his way through the living room. Lizzy just waved from her sleepy position in the corner of the sofa, but Dizzy knelt up for a hug. It was sweet to see him comply without argument. All these guys that turned to mush around twin girls; talk about having an effect.

Betsy followed us to the door and gave Kieran a hug before he left too; I left them saying goodbye in the doorway, telling him I'd have Aaron call him to make plans for the following weekend. I heard him ask if Betsy could join us and walked away, trusting her to explain her lack of availability in her own way.

After letting enough time pass for Kieran to be well out of view of the cliff top, we gathered the kids and bundled back up to head down to the beach. Aaron had agreed to wait at the house, but Elsie decided that she was coming with us this time. The girls all said their goodbyes to Aaron before we left, the twins making him promise to be here next time they came to visit. We promised he'd be here, telling them that he lived here with Aunt Elsie and me, so he'd always be here. They seemed to like that, and I saw Lou's smile of approval that Aaron was so good with her girls too. I pressed a kiss to his lips before heading out with the girls, and he promised to have a film and popcorn ready for when we returned.

I caught Elsie's smile as she walked out the front door, and knew without a doubt, that the film he chose would be one of her favourites. She linked arms with Marina again as they headed up the path together, and Lizzy snuck her hand into Elsie's other one and I heard her little voice begin a conversation. We had all been brought up to respect our elders, and despite not getting to see as much of Elsie as we had done the others back home, even the kids had enough respect to fill the ocean a few times over.

'Do you think I could see Kieran again on the next moon?' Betsy asked, sidling up at the side of me as we headed towards the cliff where we could access the beach.

I laughed quietly, but smiled at her.

'Of course, want me to ask him for you?' I replied, linking arms with her as we wandered along the path.

'Would you?' she said excitedly.

'Of course,' I answered.

It was obvious that he liked spending time with her as much as she liked to see him, I couldn't see a problem with encouraging that relationship, and if Janine did see a problem then I'd make sure to put her right before she ruined what could be the start of something special for Betsy.

Elsie and I stood back from the edge of the water; although she knew she could get her feet wet, we didn't know if the water would take me because I hadn't been in my human form as long as she had, so she held back with me. We'd been down here a few minutes now and there still didn't seem to be much of a rush for them to get back to the water. Marina still stood with us, and the twins were running around the beach with no clothes on again, completely oblivious to the cold. Their giggles and shrieks filled the air as Lou and Betsy chased them, bare foot in the sand.

A Handful of Secrets

Dizzy came dashing behind my legs for cover and squealed when Marina turned to tickle her.

'I can see how the swim home is going to be,' I chuckled, wobbling as Dizzy pulled on my knee to swing around out of Marina's hold.

'Anything to keep them awake and swimming,' Lou said, coming to stand with us, 'They're like whales when they go to sleep in the water; far too heavy to carry.'

We laughed and talked a little more, all the while watching the twins run some energy off. When the sun started sinking behind the horizon, Lou called it and decided that it was time. After hugs all around, the twins splashed their way deep enough into the water, then went flop as the ocean took their legs and returned their fins to them. Lizzy hadn't quite gotten deep enough and had to be rescued by Mia on her way past, but Dizzy was in, bobbing around waiting for her mother. Lou and Marina were the last to go, Lou thanking me profusely for making today special for her girls.

'It was my pleasure, honestly. I had never even dreamed that you'd bring them out yet. And I think it's safe to say that Aaron likes them too.'

Elsie laughed.

'Yes, I think he's quite taken with the pair of them.'

I promised to go and buy them some new clothes and get some toys for in the house for next time, but made it clear I understood if she didn't want to bring them every full moon.

'Do you really think I'm going to get away with not bringing them again next time, I'm not going to hear the end of it all through the cycle.'

We laughed again, she was right of course, but I still didn't expect them every full moon. They were still only little for a start, and the swim alone was a long way.

Elsie and I watched as the last of them disappeared below the surface, and the ripples settled on the waves. I took a deep breath, filling my lungs with the salty sea air, and then turning my back on the ocean and holding my arm out for Elsie. We walked back talking about how well today had gone, and how much everyone seemed to enjoy themselves. This was what I wanted our lives to be, a mix of the water and the land.

When we reached the house, Aaron had done exactly as promised, and the house smelled of warm popcorn. Elsie's favourite musical was paused on the title screen and there were cushions and blankets set out on the sofa waiting for us. I excused myself to go and change into my pyjamas before we settled into the darkness together to watch the film.

Another perfect day with my family.

May

By the time the full moon came around this month, I was desperate to speak to the girls. I needed Janine, or even better, Mia, but I wasn't sure who would be out this time. We hadn't exactly made plans, nor could I have predicted this turn of events. We needed help, and I wasn't afraid to admit that and ask for it.

I peered into Elsie's room again on my way back to my own bedroom to find her sleeping reasonably peacefully. She'd been up most of the night coughing, the infection on her chest making it difficult for her to lie down properly. The position she was asleep in now didn't look comfortable, but at least she was getting some undisturbed rest.

Aaron was sat up in bed with his phone in one hand when I crept back in to the room. He'd been fast asleep when I'd gotten up at sunrise, especially now that the sun was getting earlier and earlier with its arrival each morning. The tiny creases between his eyes told me that it was probably the phone that had woken him, and he was now silently cursing it for disturbing him.

'Everything okay?' I asked as I got back into bed with my drink.

He turned to me at the last minute and held out his arm so that I could snuggle into his side, and I left the drink on the bedside table in favour of the cuddle.

'Yeah, it was just Kieran asking if we were still on for lunch with Betsy.'

I watched as he frowned again. We'd discussed calling off the pub, but Elsie had overheard us and made us promise not to. She didn't want to stop any of us living our lives, and Betsy would want to see Kieran. What I didn't know was whether anyone would be up for socialising once I'd explained the situation this family was now facing.

'I don't know whether to go down to the beach and wait for the girls, I know Betsy and my sister will be out early enough. I can give them a heads up then,' I said, wrapping my arms around him and holding on tightly.

'No, stay here, you have no idea what time they will be here, it's not warm enough for you to just sit outside. The last thing we need is you getting poorly too.'

'We don't get poorly,' I said and then fell immediately silent.

No, we weren't supposed to get ill. Clearly being on land did something to our immune system, because Elsie sure as the deep was ill now.

'I suppose, they're going to be full of it when they get here though, I don't want to trample all over that the minute they walk through the door,' I explained with a sigh.

'Then don't, just speak to Mia for now. Elsie didn't want you telling anyone originally. Maybe we should just ask for some advice rather than dropping it on them all straight away.'

'I guess,' I agreed half-heartedly.

I had begged Elsie not to make me keep this a secret; she'd wanted to keep it from the girls so that we didn't worry anyone. She was still looking out for them, even though she now had us to look out for her. Caring for us was in her blood, I couldn't change that. But I was done with the secrets; hadn't there been enough of them within this family; I conceded however, that maybe I could try and handle it more like she wanted me to. I did need to speak to Mia; I just had to hope that she was on her way here already. The sun had been up a couple of hours already, but I was expecting them for breakfast.

The door opened with a bang, letting in a warm breeze now that the weather was attempting to warm up a little, and two little bodies came hurtling at me in their new leggings and tops. I'd been out during the cycle and bought the kids of the family new clothes, and Aaron had helped me put together a new unit in one of the spare rooms to store them all in. Dizzy and Lizzy both threw themselves at me, wrapping their arms around me tightly.

'We missed you Auntie Luna,' they both squeaked.

'I missed you too girls, let me look at you,' I said, freeing myself from their steely grip and holding them both at arm's length. They had both grown at least an inch since the last full moon, and I laughed to myself, suddenly realising that I was doing exactly what Elsie had always done to me; surveying them for changes.

'Morning Luna,' Lou said when she plonked herself down on the opposite end of the sofa to me.

I smiled and asked about their swim, turning to see my sister come into the room too.

'Can I go get Aaron up?' Dizzy asked, wriggling from the sofa and landing on the floor with an unsteady bump.

I laughed, he'd learned his lesson from last time, and was already up and dressed today.

'He's already up; he's in the kitchen making pancakes,' I mock whispered to them.

My grin widened as theirs did and Lou and I both laughed as the pair of them scuttled away and we heard Aaron let them make him jump. Then we heard giggles and screams as he tickle-attacked them both before asking if they wanted to help. By help I'm sure he meant lick the spoon or something, and I knew instantly that we were going to need another outfit before we left the house later.

'He's a natural with them,' Marina said, sitting herself down on the rug.

I'd lit the fire and it was crackling away on a low burn, just to warm the chill out of the girls. The outside temperatures were slowly warming back up, but their wet hair and damp clothes would have emphasised the breeze.

Mia and Betsy came into the room last and sat themselves amongst us, Betsy squeezing herself in between Lou and me on the sofa. I tried not to react to seeing Mia, but I was so happy to see her that I must have let out an audible sigh at the least.

'Where's Elsie?' Mia asked almost as soon as she'd sat down.

'Still in bed,' I answered quietly, 'She didn't get much sleep last night.'

'She's never still got that cough,' Mia joked, but she must have seen my face fall because she soon stopped laughing.

'She doesn't want me making a big deal about it, but the doctors are really worried,' I said quietly.

Mia shuffled to the edge of her seat and Lou sat up straight where she was.

'It turned into a chest infection about a week after the last full moon, the doctor told us that it happens a lot in elderly patients because their immune systems aren't as strong as they were when they were younger. She is on a tablet called an antibiotic, but if anything, it's still getting worse. We're taking her back to the doctor tomorrow so he will be able to tell us more then.'

I fell quiet and Mia started bombarding me with questions. It took me a while, but I answered them as best as I could with the information I had, and the understanding I had of the whole situation. Half way through I asked Betsy to go and free Aaron as he understood it better than I did, and he re-explained the whole situation to Mia, answering her questions in more detail.

It ended with Mia saying she wanted to know what the doctor had to say, and agreeing to surface tomorrow evening after dark so that I could tell her how the appointment went. And trust me when I say that it was a big deal she was surfacing, so I knew that she was worried now too.

After that, Mia had gone upstairs to check on Elsie and we had all descended upon the kitchen for pancakes. Lou said she didn't want the twins knowing just how poorly Elsie was, they didn't need that kind of worry at their age; she just told them that Elsie was still a bit poorly and they had to be gentle with her.

The twins looked adorable in their matching blue dungarees that Aaron and I had bought them. He'd insisted however, that I buy them different coloured tops, otherwise it would get difficult for him to tell them apart. Personally, I thought they looked totally different. Lizzy was a little taller than her sister, her eyes were a slightly waterier shade of lilac, and her hair was a dirty blonde as opposed to her sister's golden locks. Aaron had argued however, that all of those were only any good if the girls were stood side by side. When apart, he struggled to tell which of them was which and had taken to calling them both 'short stuff' just to be on the safe side. So, Lizzy had a blue T-shirt on under her dungarees, a shade that actually matched her tail, though I'd left that part out when I'd told Aaron, and Dizzy had a lemon-yellow top on, like a sherbet lemon; easy to tell them apart now.
We'd arranged lunch at the pub, but had agreed that Elsie would be better staying at home. Mia, my sister and Lou had volunteered to stay home, leaving Betsy and me to accompany Aaron and Kieran to the pub. The twins however had cried at the idea of being left behind until Aaron had intervened.
'And who said you weren't coming?' he asked when Lizzy had stopped making so much noise.
'Mummy is staying here with Auntie Elsie,' Lizzy said between sniffles.
Aaron handed her a tissue and gave her that look.
'Well Mummy can stay here, and you can come with me and Luna, how about that?' he'd asked, having already asked Lou if she was okay with it.
There was no need to exaggerate when she'd told us to take them without a single second to think about it. I'd

laughed, but she said I'd understand by the time we got back to the house later.

'Mummy?' Dizzy questioned, her tears drying up.

'If you want to go with Auntie Luna and Auntie Betsy then you can, but Mummy is going to stay here with Nanna Mia.'

'I want to go,' Dizzy said almost immediately.

Lizzy had to think about it for a few minutes, but agreed to come with us too. Aaron rang Kieran to explain the change in plans, and he agreed to come and pick us up rather than having the twins walk all that way again. His car was bigger than Aaron's because he had to be able to fit the drum kit inside it, so there was plenty of room for all of us.

When he arrived, I zipped Lizzy and Dizzy into their new coats and helped them into their shoes before heading out. Mia had helped Elsie downstairs and she was now sat in the corner of the sofa setting up a board game for them to play while we were gone. I smiled and waved, heading out of the door.

'Do they have booster seats?' Kieran asked as we drew level with the car.

I was about to answer but Aaron cut me off, obviously seeing my confusion.

'Na mate, someone borrowed the car and the seats are in the back of it; they'll be okay just this once.'

As Betsy and Kieran secured the girls into their seats, I whispered to Aaron.

'What's a booster seat?'

'Something to make them taller in the seat, and something we should probably invest in if this is going to become a regular thing.'

I nodded my understanding and added it to the list I now had on my phone before climbing in behind the twins. We'd let Betsy get up front with Kieran, so Aaron and I were in the back seats. The car had plenty of room; we could probably have fit all of us in here with a little squeezing.

A Handful of Secrets

The pub was quieter today, so the twins made the most of it by climbing all over the seats and trying to play hide and seek under the empty tables. Aaron and Kieran knew the owner, so they weren't upsetting anyone; I'd taken off their shoes so that nothing would get dirty or damaged, and they'd brought a smile to a few faces with their playing and girly giggles. They'd behaved perfectly, doing their mother proud, and were now laying stretched out next to each other between Betsy and me. I had Dizzy's head and Lizzy's feet, and Betsy had the opposite because of how they'd laid top to tail; or top to toes as was more the situation right now.

Kieran had his arm around Betsy's shoulders and was playing with the curls in the bottom of her hair as they talked quietly to each other. Aaron mirrored the same position with me, though I had my one hand linked with his and the other stroking Dizzy's soft blonde hair. My thoughts had strayed to my own mother, and how she had missed out on seeing me grow up the way we had been able to watch the twins and the two other merbabies of the family. I loved spending time with them, seeing their childlike view of the world, and sometimes missed the simplicity of life back then; before the secrets and the lies, back when life was just about swimming and sleeping.

The twins didn't have a care in the world about what was right and wrong as far as ocean versus land; they just lived for what made them happy. They seemed to love coming ashore now, neither today nor last month had they shown any signs of separation anxiety from the water and I wondered whether Lou would consider letting them ashore with one of the celestial events and see if they enjoyed spending more time with their legs. I dismissed that idea almost straight away; it would be argued they were too young for that yet.

Aaron pulled me from my trip down memory lane when I heard him answer something Kieran had said to him. I looked down to see both girls fast asleep and holding hands. Betsy smiled as she caught me watching them.

'They do it so that they don't float away from each other while they're sleeping,' she whispered so that Kieran wouldn't overhear and I let out a quiet laugh, but felt myself 'ah-ing' at their cuteness too.

I carried Dizzy back into the house ahead of Aaron who had Lizzy.

'Does anyone have any objections to Kieran sticking round for a while?' I asked.

They all shook their heads and Elsie told me not to be silly and to get him inside. Betsy brought Kieran inside while Aaron and I took the twins upstairs and laid them on our bed. As soon as they were close enough, they wrapped their little hands back around each other, their fingers twining together for safety. Grabbing my camera from the side, I snapped a shot of them together, and then took a close up of their hands too, leaving the Polaroids on the side to develop. I smiled down at their sleeping forms as Aaron put his arm around my shoulder. I left the door ajar so that they could come down when they awoke, and went back downstairs with him. Lou asked how it had gone and I told her how well behaved they'd both been, and commented on their hand holding.

'Yeah, they've always done that, right from being babies,' she said with a smile and wrinkle of her nose that told me she found it cute too.

The conversation turned to more adult topics now that their little ears weren't around and Aaron pulled out some drinks from the bottom of the fridge. Elsie said she was feeling a little better, and I decided that it was good for her having the girls around, giving her a reason to be chirpy. She'd spent the last couple of days in bed, so it was good to see some colour in her cheeks and a smile on her face. I was sure that it was taking it out of her and that she'd probably pay for it with another few days in bed after today, but she was happy, and that's what I wanted for her at the end of the day.

When the light began to fade and the sky started to turn a darker shade of blue, Aaron asked Kieran if he fancied going for a game of pool. That got him out of the house and gave us time to get the girls back to the water. I hadn't even thought of how to sort the situation, but Aaron was one step ahead of me as always. I smiled and said goodbye, watching with a smirk as Betsy said her own goodbye to Kieran.

'What's she told him about not having a phone?' I asked Aaron where we stood by the doorway to the dining room.

'I don't think he's actually asked her for it yet; he can be quite old fashioned sometimes, and I think he's happy dating her for now, which is totally what he is doing.'

I laughed. I'd noticed that too.

'I'll talk to him and see what he says tonight; I promise not to be late.'

He kissed me again, a swoon-worthy kiss that left me weak at the knees and full of promises of what was to come later, then he left with Kieran, waving goodbye to the others and giving the twins a quick hug.

'We'll see you next time,' they both said with a wave and I saw Lou shoot a smile their way.

Once the door closed and we heard Kieran's car leave, Lou sat up and told the twins that it was time for them to be getting ready to go home too. They let out disappointed noise in unison, but didn't argue with her. Instead, they went scrambling upstairs and we heard them rooting around in one of the bedrooms. Lou followed them up to investigate their intentions, and Marina and Mia asked about the doctor's appointment tomorrow.

I told them the time and that it was just supposed to be a check-up, and they gave me a list of questions to ask so that we could try and find our own way of helping her.

Mia seemed to think that part of the reason she wasn't getting any better was because her body wasn't accepting help from the antibiotics, and that maybe there was something we could give her from the ocean that would help. Some of the plants had healing abilities and Mia thought that maybe they could do more good; but she'd need more information as to what was wrong. I'd agreed to meet her an hour after sunset tomorrow evening in the cove Aaron and I had explored last summer. There was no way anyone could see down there so it was safe enough.

Down on the beach, I sat on the rock by the base of the cliff with Marina and Mia while Betsy and Lou chased the twins. There was an elderly couple stood on the cliff top looking out at the water, we'd seen them on the way down and spoken to them briefly and it meant we had to wait before the girls could get back in the ocean. I kept glancing up at the couple, and then out at the sun hanging over the horizon.

'There is plenty of time Luna,' Marina said after I'd checked for what must have been a dozen times.

I laughed and apologised, then turned back to the conversation. I'd helped Elsie back up to bed before we'd left the house and would go and check on her once I got back, but it hadn't stopped Mia whittling about her.

'Honestly, she's probably asleep by now, today is the most she's spent awake and out of bed in the last week; she'll sleep for days now to recover.'

Mia didn't seem totally convinced and voiced her annoyance of not being able to stay with her again. This time when I glanced up, the couple were gone. I nudged Marina and she laughed when I nodded upwards.

'Anyone would think you were trying to get rid of us today,' she said with a giggle.

'No, I just don't want anything to go wrong,' I admitted.

'You worry too much, you're doing an amazing job,' Mia assured me with a nudge of her shoulder and I smiled, relaxing a little.

Mia didn't say anything unless she meant it, so to have her tell me I was doing okay meant a lot to me. The twins appeared in front of us then with Lou and Betsy right behind them.

'They're gone,' Lou said nodding up to the top of the cliff.

I hadn't been the only one watching then, clearly. They decided it was time and we stripped the twins so that they could splash back into the water, and then I watched as each of them made their way back in, the slight glimmer in the water each time one of them transformed making me smile.

After watching them all wave and disappear from view, I waited around for a few minutes longer before grabbing the bag full of clothes and heading cautiously back up to the top and back to the house. There was no sign of the elderly couple, so I made my way back along the curvy path and back into the house where I closed and locked the door; Aaron had a key.

Another full moon had passed, and I leant against the door with a sigh and a smile on my face. Then I crept up the stairs to check on Elsie before going to get ready for bed, planning on re-reading my mother's old copy of *The Little Mermaid* while I waited for Aaron to come home.

Angel McGregor

The Following Evening

I made my way carefully down the rocky embankment and landed with a soft thud in the sand at the bottom. There was still half an hour or so until I was meant to meet Mia, but I didn't know how she planned to tell the exact time when she was using the moon as her guide, so I'd played it safe and come early, bringing along my camera to make the most of the beautiful view. Dropping the bag I'd brought with me at the cliff base, I slipped off my shoes and dug my toes into the sand, feeling the smile spread across my face. That feeling hadn't changed for me at all; I still loved to feel the grainy soft texture between my toes, the natural warmth it held having had the sun shining on it all day long.

Bringing the camera up to eye level, I lined up the shot along the horizon and snapped a photo with the almost full moon hanging low in the sky. The Polaroid came out and I laid it safely on top of my bag before heading down to the water. Today was a new day, no full moon to prevent me from being in the water, so I splashed into the incoming tide, not even bothering to roll up my jeans. I'd brought a spare pair with me knowing I'd get wet speaking to Mia. The water wasn't warm, but it wasn't too cold either; the weather was slowly warming back up ready for summer, and I couldn't wait till it was warm enough to go swimming in.

I stood for several long minutes with my feet steadily sinking into the wet sand where the water came rushing over my feet before being dragged back out to sea again. The tide was still coming in, but it seemed in no rush to get anywhere. Lining up the camera again, I focussed on the water, noticing the oddly formed ripples that were displaying themselves just beyond the cliff's edge. Pulling the camera away from my face, I squinted at the spot but couldn't see far enough, so I looked back through the lens, re-focussing to get a better look.

Of course; why hadn't I seen that straight away? That was the undercurrent moving differently. That was Mia. I raced back to where I'd left my bag and tucked the camera away safely, then pulled off the jumper I had on to keep the chill away, suddenly realising that this was my opportunity, and I wasn't going to let it swim by.

I splashed back through the water and dove in where the sand disappeared, pushing through the water with a kick not quite as powerful as my tail would have been, but strong in a different way. Surfacing not far from where I had dived in, I pushed my hair back from my face and began to tread water; a totally new experience as I soon learned that it wasn't as easy with legs, and I had to make big circles, pushing upwards in the water to keep me afloat. I laughed to myself in the near silence around me, and began to swim out to the edge of the cliff. The water had a chill to it, but now I was moving, I didn't care. My clothes dragged me back a little, making it harder to swim, but I kept going, moving through the water in a whole new way.

When I reached the ripples, I let myself sink under the surface and looked around, catching a dash of colour in the ocean of blue. Mia surfaced just at the side of me, and I came back up for air, realising that I wasn't getting the oxygen from the water as I had when I was a mermaid. I coughed and spluttered water before dragging in air. Hearing Mia laugh, I turned to find her by my side.

'Cough it up,' she said with another laugh, 'You can't get water in your human lungs, you already knew that.'

'I know,' I said after coughing up the last of the salt water, 'I just forgot.'

'How's Elsie?' she asked once I was breathing normally again.

'Poorly,' I said simply, screwing up my face in pain as I knew what I had to tell Mia wasn't going to be easy.

'The doctor said that it is turning into pneumonia, and that once that happens, there probably won't be a lot

A Handful of Secrets

he can do about it. Her body is too weak to fight back,' I trailed off and added the last bit quietly, letting the night swallow the words, 'She's dying Mia.'

Aaron had held me when the doctor had told us. I'd held it together until he'd used that word. I had to be strong for Elsie, but I think she knew. I think she'd known for a while, because she didn't cry; she took me from Aaron's arms and held me until the tears dried up while Aaron asked a few more questions of the doctor.

I explained to Mia everything that had been said; he'd told us that he had no idea how long Elsie could wait this out; it was entirely down to how long her body could hold on. That could be months yet, or it could only be a matter of weeks. Once the pneumonia took a hold of her, it would only be days. Mia took in everything I said with nods and a few accepting words. She didn't argue with me, she didn't make a big deal. She just accepted it. Had I been the only one who thought that Elsie was going to get better?

After I'd started to feel the chill in the water again, Mia made her excuses, promised to be out with the next full moon, and left to head back to The Kingdom. She'd told me Fran was with her so that she hadn't had to make the journey alone, but hadn't wanted her surfacing; there were still rules, and though I had every intention of getting some of those rules changed, for now it stood, and Fran had stayed deeper and out of sight.

I made my way back to the shore; kicking with less enthusiasm now I'd had to go over the sad news we'd received just hours earlier and headed back to my bag. Getting changed was relatively easy; I'd brought baggy clothes to change into, though I hadn't come down here with the intention of getting quite so wet. Once changed, I began to head back up the cliff and rang Aaron from the little phone I'd left in the bag.

'Run me a bath, I'm all wet,' I laughed when he answered.

He'd stayed at the house with Elsie, as I thought Mia would prefer I went to the water alone. Plus, Elsie had been tired and I didn't want to leave her in the house alone at night.

'You went for a swim, didn't you?' he asked.

'How'd you know?'

'Because this was the excuse you've been waiting for since you got out of the water. You must be freezing,' he said; he knew me so well.

'I fear for my toes,' I joked and hurried down the path beneath the soft glow of the street light.

'The bath will be waiting, don't be long.'

And with that, he hung up and I hurried along, ready to warm back up after my swim. I now really couldn't wait till the water warmed up though, the feeling of swimming with my legs had been a type of freedom I'd never felt before, despite having the entire ocean within my grasp when I'd had my tail. How your life could change with just the phases of the moon.

Now our lives were set to change again; the big question now though; was I ready to lose Aunt Elsie?

June

The full moon brought a full house once more, and despite just how poorly Elsie was now, there was colour in her cheeks, a smile on her face and joy in her eyes. This is what she needed; her family around her. Elsie's entire family line was out today, including her own daughter Trish, who hadn't stepped foot on land since the day Elsie had given up her fins. I'd discovered today, from a hushed conversation in the corner with Mia, that Trish had disagreed with Elsie's life choice, saying that the shores were no place for a mermaid to be full time, but now that a deadline had been put on Elsie's life, Trish had put aside her now petty problems and come ashore to support her family.

Janine had stayed in the water, claiming there had to be elders present, but her daughter Coral was here, with both her daughters and her granddaughter; another of our merbabies, Layla. Layla was a little older than the twins, but only by just shy of a year, so she hadn't spent much time ashore, and was still a little nervous and unsteady on her feet.

As for my family, we were as vocal as ever. Marina and Betsy were currently trying to out-sing Betsy's niece Carly, with Shae watching on, placing bets that her daughter wouldn't get bored quickly enough for them to beat her. My mother's sister Ellie was even here and I hadn't seen her ashore for some time now either. The house was full, there was no other way of describing it, and I was glad that the weather outside was warm enough that we could open the patio doors out onto the wooden decking so that we could use the table out there too. Aaron had already cleaned down the outdoor furniture last week when the weather had picked up and the sun had decided to make a short appearance. Elsie had been quick to want to go and sit outside, so he'd set about clearing up the garden. With so many of us ashore today, we had spilled out onto the patio and the kids were running around like they hadn't a care in the world.

I smiled as I hung back in the kitchen doorway watching them all interact with each other. It scared me that it had taken Elsie being so ill to make this happen, but I genuinely hoped that this was the start of things to come, and that every full moon would be as hectic as this. It would probably result in me sleeping for two days to recover, but I welcomed the hustle and bustle and the steady buzz of conversation that was regularly interrupted by a squeal or a giggle. I loved that we had all the kids out, I wanted to make these visits important to them, for them to want to come ashore every month; I think I was already there with the twins, who had burst through the door ahead of everyone else and thrown themselves at Aaron and me. All I had to do now was convince everyone that the world was safe for our kind, and that not all humans are the monsters that we were told they could be.

Last week I'd taken a step towards that goal without even realising it. I'd finally gotten the information out of Elsie that I needed to sort out the Council business that Mia had mentioned back at the beginning of all of this. I'd gotten in touch with Elsie's friend in the city; a man named Emerick. He sounded as old fashioned on the phone as his name did and he spoke like he had watched one too many old movies, but he seemed nice enough. He had offered his best wishes to Elsie, and I had arranged to go to the City to meet him. It wasn't any time soon, he had said there had been some problems at his home since the last time he had seen Elsie, and therefore didn't have time to be entertaining, but he was intrigued to meet me, and wanted to talk about my plans to bring the mermaids ashore. I'd spoken with him for hours on the phone and he'd told me about a similar plan he was working on in the city, about how he wanted people who were different to fit in with the humans. After questioning him some on his understanding of human versus mermaid, I confused myself and realised that I had so much information missing, but he refused to fill in the blanks over the phone. He'd left me full of questions and very confused; Elsie's answer to the whole situation was that the world was a bigger place than I realised, and that all would become clear when I met Emerick. For now, apparently, I had to settle for that level of information, no matter how much it drove me crazy.

The buzz in the house dulled a little after breakfast when we all chose to do slightly different things with our day. Kieran was on his way over here to pick up Betsy and take her out for a few hours, Trish had decided to take Elsie down to the beach for a while with Lou and the twins, and Shae had promised to take Carly to the arcades.

I stood in the doorway, watching as Mia reversed Elsie's old car out of the garage to take the kids down to the beach and chuckled as she nearly hit one of the tiny white fence posts. She gave me a scared look and then manoeuvred the car and tried again.

'I want to teach you how to drive,' Aaron said coming up behind me.

'You want to teach me how to what?' I asked, sure that I had misheard him.

'I want to teach you how to drive,' he said again.

Nope, I hadn't misheard him. He was officially losing the plot.

'Don't you have to have qualifications or something for that?' I asked, still stunned.

'Technically, but if we do it all off-road and on private land then I can show you the ropes. We can just get an instructor in to get you through your test.' He paused, knowing that I was thinking it through. 'You know that it makes sense. If you're going to be staying on land then you're going to need to get about; you're going to need it to get to the City if I'm busy. Elsie knew how to drive when she was younger.'

He had me there. Elsie used to drive a little green beetle that Mia was now over-revving; she'd loved that car. She used to take me into town so that we could get ice cream and hit the shops on warm days, and we'd use it to go get take out when she didn't want to cook. It was only a few years back that she'd stopped using it. Or so I'd assumed, we'd found the car in the garage at the bottom of the massive back yard. Maybe she had still been using it when I wasn't around, I still didn't really know much about what she'd done on the days between those full moons, but I knew it hadn't been touched at least since I'd come ashore, the layer of dust had confirmed it too.

I laughed out loud at the thought of me behind the wheel. I loved to watch Aaron drive; his strong biceps tensing as he manoeuvred the Jeep around. It was kind of sexy in its own way, but could I do that?

Marina saved me from the conversation by coming up behind me to ask whether I had any plans today. I jumped at the change of topic even though the answer was a simple no and turned back into the house with her, shooting Aaron a quick grin over my shoulder. He shook his head at me, knowing exactly what I'd just done, and mouthed that we'd discuss it later. I laughed then turned my attention to Marina, who was asking whether we could go for a walk, just me and her. I didn't see why not, it would be nice to spend some quality time with her, and now the weather was warming up a little she wouldn't get too cold out wandering around.

An hour later, I found myself down in the little cove that Aaron and I had discovered on our first day together. It had taken some convincing to get Marina to scramble down the cliff side, but once we were down there she admitted that it wasn't as hard as she'd expected. Now we lay on the sand on our stomachs watching the tide drift lazily in to meet the sand, the quiet rush of water still one of my favourite noises. I'd brought my camera and was attempting to take a photo of Marina and me but had failed twice already. Aaron made it look so easy when he lined up these shots.

While I waited for the camera to reload, Marina was playing with the soft white sand, scooping it up in her hands and then dropping it to wipe the space flat again. She scrawled her name in the sand a couple of times too. I watched with a smile, and when she scooped the sand up the next time, I snapped a photograph. When the image came out and cleared up, I showed it to her and she smiled too.

'It looks like a heart,' she observed with a giggle, pointing out the place where her fingers met and gave the shape.

'So it does,' I agreed, wafting the picture once more before putting it gently into the envelope with the others.

That one was going on the fridge. There were photos all over the fridge; taken at times that Elsie called the 'special moments'. I had never quite understood what criteria she used to decide what moments counted as special, but I knew that this was one of them. Maybe it wasn't about criteria at all, but about feelings and memories.

I broached the idea of using this beach instead of the cove we'd always used as access, testing the water with Marina to see what her thoughts were. There was no actual access down here, meaning that there was never anyone on the beach, we could probably set up a tent for the bags and them to get changed and no one would even notice; you couldn't see the beach from the top. She saw my point of view, but joked that she'd reserve judgement until we had made it back to the top, and now that I thought about it, I began to doubt my own idea. The kids would struggle to get up there, if not anyone else. It was quite steep in places, and not exactly safe, but I began to create a plan in my head, wondering whether Aaron could make it more accessible. It was an idea if nothing else; I'd speak to him about it later tonight after the girls had headed back to the water and see what he thought.

'Ready to head back?' I asked Marina when I heard her stomach rumbling; it was long past lunch time now, I was surprised I hadn't heard from Aaron yet.

She nodded and scrambled up from the ground, brushing herself off in a shower of fine sand that caught on the sea breeze and attacked me. The giggling fit that followed left us breathless and with hiccups. I'd missed this, the time alone with Marina had shown me just how much I'd missed having her around now I was ashore full time, and a few hours like this meant more to me than I could put into words.

By the time we made it to the top, we were both out of breath, but still laughing. We'd talked all the way up, which had proved difficult with the climbing that was necessary, but hadn't stopped us. I had to call for a break at the top and had found a little bench just a few yards away to collapse on. We talked some more before heading back to the house at a gentler pace, taking our time and enjoying the warmth that the sun was trying to shine on us.

The house was suspiciously quiet when we returned, and I almost hesitated before entering. Where was everyone? When we'd left there had been a few of the girls and Aaron still here, and I'd expected Mia to be back from the beach by now too; Marina and I had been gone hours.

I closed the front door behind me and followed Marina into the living room, smiling to myself at the mess that signified life in the house. It was as I was picking up the spilled box of bricks on the floor that I heard enough noise to signify their location. The smell that followed drifted through the house making my mouth water. Marina grinned and made her way around the sofa and through the dining room to the open patio doors. When I stepped out onto the decking I smiled. Everyone was back, and Aaron was behind the barbeque at the bottom of the garden. The twins were running around with no shoes on, Mia and Shae were sat on the garden swing with Carly squeezed between them and Layla scrambling on Mia's knee, and the others were dotted around in chairs and sitting on the decking.

It wasn't quite warm enough to classify as summer, and most of the girls had jumpers or lightweight coats on, but the family vibe that was rolling from them was more than enough to make this a summer barbeque. Aaron was the only one in just a T-shirt, standing behind a cloud of smoke where he prodded at whatever was cooking, and Elsie only had on a thin, long sleeved top where she sat in a recliner sun lounger by the kitchen door.

I heard her coughing and went over to check on her, reaching for the glass of water she had under her chair and passing it to her when she could take it from me.

'You okay Aunt Elsie?' I asked, worried that today was too much for her, but desperately wanting to give her these memories.

She took a sip from the glass and handed it back to me with a nod.

'I'm okay sweetheart, the sun is doing me a world of good,' she answered with a chuckle.

The house faced east, so now the sun had come over, the back garden was bathed in warm sunlight and the glow overhead, although nothing great just yet, was enough to make you squint. The back yard was alive with happiness and excitement as I made my way over to Aaron, pulling off my coat and draping it over the fence post near the decking.

'Did you do this?' I asked, pressing a kiss to the back of his shoulder blade and sliding my arms around his waist.

'It was actually Trish's idea, and Mia went to the store to get the food with Coral. All I have done is fire up this beast and cook it,' he said, smiling over his shoulder at me.

On the table at the side of him were bread rolls and sandwich buns that had been buttered ready, and I picked one up and held it out for Aaron to fill. There was even a selection of sauces to put on my burger. Talk about show me that planning was overrated. I'd have put hours of planning into organising this, and they'd thrown it all together in less than that, with no proof it had been a last-minute idea.

'Auntie Luna, can we have another sausage please?' Lizzy asked, appearing at the side of me with her sister in tow.

'You'll have to ask Aaron, not me princess,' I answered, bending down to lift her up.

She leaned around me and smiled at Aaron, one of her megawatt smiles that only a child can pull off.

'Oh, I don't know about that, it might cost ya,' he said in response to the grin.

'What do you want us to do?' Dizzy asked coming around to stand between Aaron and me with her little hands on her hips.

He pretended to think rubbing his chin with one hand and stroking the stubble there where he hadn't shaved this morning.

'Well, I think my bottle is empty again,' he said lifting it up and shaking it to show them.

They both giggled and Lizzy wriggled to get down, tearing into the kitchen with Dizzy by her side.

'Are you using my cousins as slaves?' I asked with a giggle when they came back with a bottle of beer from the fridge and the bottle opener.

I glanced at the doorway to see Trish closing the fridge door again before turning back to the unfolding situation in front of me. Aaron took the bottle from Lizzy and opened it, taking a long drink from it before putting it down next to the other two empty ones he had lined up.

'Deal,' he said with a grin that earned him two delighted squeals, 'Though I think you might sink later.'

'How many have you already had?' I asked, looking down at the pair of them.

'I don't remember,' Lizzy said, a sparkle in her eyes that betrayed her.

I looked up to Aaron who held up two fingers. I rolled my eyes but allowed them to go and get their bread rolls for Aaron to fill with their requested sausages. Dizzy was very particular and made him turn them all over so that she could choose the perfect one, and Lizzy decided last minute that she wanted a burger instead, so I got her hot dog.

'Aaron is right, you will sink tonight if you don't lay off the food,' Shae laughed as the twins tore back in her direction once they had their food.

'At least they should sleep well tonight from the carb overload,' Aaron joked back.

Shae laughed and helped Lizzy back up onto the swinging sofa to eat her burger. Dizzy had plonked herself down on the grass by Mia's feet and was using her leg as a back rest.

'This is pretty incredible, thank you.'

'I honestly didn't do anything other than follow orders, Luna.'

He put down the tongues for the barbeque and held out his arms for me. I walked into them, putting my head onto his chest, but he turned me around so that I could see the girls all over the garden.

'I think a part of them had missed this too you know? By agreeing to keep so many secrets from you growing up, they also deprived themselves of a lot, and no I am not trying to make any excuses for them before you start,' he said having felt me take a breath ready to argue, 'What I am saying, is that your mission to make this a part of their lives, isn't going to be anywhere near as big of a task as you thought it was. Lou was even asking whether she thought we could get the stuff in to have the twins out at the next celestial event. She says that they never shut up about being up here with you, and that she doesn't want to make the mistakes with them that they made with you; if they want to be up here then she wants to support that.'

I felt the tears well up I my eyes and kept quiet, unsure whether I could speak past the lump forming in my throat. This was what I'd wanted, who knew it would be so easy?

'And Betsy wants to come up for the next celestial event too, she wants to spend some more time with Kieran, funnily enough,' he finished with a squeeze before turning me back around to kiss me.

'Speaking of Betsy,' I said when he released me again.

'She came back and then went for a walk into town with Kieran to buy a new set of drum sticks, then she is coming back for some lunch.'

'Okay, is Kieran coming too? We're going to run into problems sooner or later with him; one of the kids is bound to drop something out that we can't explain.'

'He can't today; band practice. But he already knows something is different, we've had that talk a couple of times now, and I told him to just accept it for what it was for now. If Betsy wants to divulge more information the way you did with me, then we will handle the fall out carefully, but for now, he's happy, and so is she.'

I nodded, sure that at some point we would have to tell him our secrets, but not sure of his reaction. It was what I wanted, to have more people understand that we weren't just some made up stories in books, but I had it drilled into me that it might not be safe, and a part of me still worried that I could do more harm than good.

When the sun began its descent back down towards the horizon, the barbeque had been turned off, the girls were milling around the house and the kids were finally starting to flag a little. From our seats in the back yard, we could see the horizon out across the water, and I watched as the sun set the water ablaze with colour. Nature could be so beautiful, I wished I had my camera, but couldn't be bothered to go fetch it from the bottom of the stairs where I left my bag.

Aaron was sat by my side and held out his phone to me, showing me the screen where I saw the sunset mirrored from the sky.

'I told you that yours had a camera too, but I've never seen you use it. I know you like the magic of your Polaroid, but you could still take some with this; I can get them printed for you.'

I smiled, taking the phone from him, the photos looked funny on the phone screen, so small and pixelated; the reason I had never replaced the old camera with a digital one, but I understood his theory.

Suddenly, a close-up face appeared on the screen making me jump, and I nearly dropped the phone with a little squeal. Layla laughed and crawled up onto my knee, cuddling up against my shoulder.

'Made you jump,' she whispered in a tiny voice, 'I think Aunt Elsie is ready for bed, she keeps yawning and her cough is getting worse again.'

'I know sweetheart, it gets a bit louder at night time, and she'll go to bed when you've all gone back to the water.'

'Mummy says we're going back soon because she doesn't want me falling asleep,' she whispered again with a half-hearted giggle.

'I know, shall we go and get your shoes on ready?' I asked.

She stuck her feet out into mid-air and kicked them gently, shoes firmly attached to them, though they were on the wrong feet.

'Ah, clever girl, but shall we swap them over so that they don't squash your toes?'

She giggled, agreeing that they felt funny and let Aaron swap them over while she stayed on my lap. Once she was all set, I walked back into the house to find the others putting their shoes and coats on.

'Mom is refusing to go to bed until we are back in the water, so we are going to make a move; she's knackered,' Trish announced with a glare Elsie's way when I entered the living room with Layla and Aaron.

'Yeah, I'll get her to bed,' I answered shooting Elsie a look and raising my eyebrows at her playfully, 'I'll grab my coat and come back down to the beach with you.'

'Not today Luna, Elsie needs you more than we do,' Marina said coming up beside me and giving me a hug.

I began to argue that their clothes would need collecting but Betsy chirped in that it wouldn't be a problem if I just got them tomorrow. After several more rounds, I backed down when Aaron said he'd walk them down. I'd feel better knowing that they got back safe, and this way I got to stay and look after Elsie. I agreed to that and everyone said their goodbyes and left on mass with Aaron giving Dizzy a piggyback.

As soon as the door closed behind them, leaving the house in near silence apart from the low hum of the TV where it had been forgotten about, Elsie deflated, coughing so hard I could hear it echoing through her chest. I grabbed a glass of water from the kitchen and her tablet to take before bed. When the coughing eased enough for her to take a drink, I offered her the glass and helped her drink the cold water.

Now that everyone was gone and she'd stopped trying so hard, I near enough watched the tiredness take over her, washing the colour from her cheeks and draining the life from her eyes.

'It's time for bed Aunt Elsie, no arguments; it's been a long day today,' I said firmly holding out my hand to help her up from her seat.

She didn't argue, merely slipped her hand into mine and let me pull her up from the chair. We took our time climbing the stairs and I left her to it in the bathroom while I went to find her a night gown and pull back the covers on her bed. When she came quietly into the room behind me, I was standing by the window looking out across the ocean.

'Thank you for today Luna,' she said coming to stand beside me, looking out in the same direction I was.

The sun was almost gone now, the girls should be back in the water.

'And will you thank Aaron for me too, I'll speak to him tomorrow, he's been brilliant today, and he is fantastic with the merbabies.'

She sounded so proud, and I let out a little laugh, he was good with them. They all loved him; they'd had no problem taking to him as either human or as a man, and they all, kids and adults, seemed comfortable with him around.

Just as I turned away from the window to grab her night gown she let out a tiny intake of breath and made a happy little sound.

'Now that is irresponsible,' she said with a huff, 'But don't they seem so happy?'

I turned back and looked out to the water, just beyond the cliff's edge, I saw the splashes Elsie saw; the girls creating havoc.

'Anyone seeing that would see seals or maybe dolphins, Mia and Trish aren't daft enough to expose themselves, or us like that if there was a risk and you know it,' I justified, putting my arm around her and resting my head on her shoulder gently.

She put her arm around me and pressed her cheek to the top of my head as we stood silently and watched the commotion die down. The salty sea air drifted in through Elsie's forever open window as we watched the ocean settle when the girls finally dove under the surface to begin their swim back to The Kingdom and the dark surface of the water went still once more.

Angel McGregor

July

When the day of the full moon finally came around again I was down in the cove before the sun rose, I couldn't sleep anyway, and I had to speak to the girls; time was running out. As the sunlight finally started to filter across the water, I began to pace. I knew that they wouldn't be up just yet; they were usually out for breakfast, but now that summer was here, breakfast was quite some time away.

I'd worn a track into the sand when I first heard the splash of water that wasn't just the tide. Stopping and turning to the water, I saw Betsy and my sister surface and make their way leisurely through the tide. There was no rush now, the weather warm enough even at this hour that they would be comfortable in their human bodies. When they saw me however, their speed increased a little.

'What's wrong? Elsie?' Marina asked in clipped questions as she took the towel I held out for her.

'Is Elsie okay?' Betsy backed up Marina's question.

I shook my head, willing out the words.

'No, the doctors say that she doesn't have long left; I need to speak to Trish, and Janine.'

I held my breath hoping that Marina would tell me that they planned to be here today, but he shook her head.

'There was a problem with one of Janine's last missions, she couldn't come today, she has to go see the Royals to clean up the mess, and I don't know about Trish, I haven't spoken to her for a couple of days.'

I began my pacing again, resuming my original path.

'How long have you been down here?' Betsy asked as she pulled on a dry top.

'I don't know, since before the sun came up.'

'Luna, the sun came up nearly two hours ago,' Marina said, pulling me to a stop with a hand on my arm.

I shook my head to clear it, there was so much I needed to do, so much that I wanted to sort, and I needed to speak to one of the elders to put it all into motion.

'Let's get back to the house, I'll make breakfast, and we will wait for the others there,' Marina said once she was dressed, and led me back up the beach and up out of the cove.

I took the girls straight upstairs and into Elsie's room where she was still tucked up in bed. Aaron and I had changed her duvet for a sheet last week now that the weather was warmer, but she still needed to be covered up; the pneumonia was playing havoc with her body temperature.

'She hasn't been out of bed in four days,' I whispered to Marina as we stood quietly in the doorway.

When Elsie was sleeping, I let her sleep these days, because the coughing and rattling on her chest prevented her from getting a good night's sleep, every minute was important to her. She was drained of energy, she'd lost nearly a third of her body weight in just over six weeks, and she was barely eating anything now. The tablets the doctor had put her on were just to keep her comfortable and to keep the pain at bay, there was nothing they could do for her now. As I stood and explained all of that to Betsy and Marina, I blinked back another set of tears. I had finally gotten my head around the fact that I was going to lose her, but it didn't make the idea any less painful. Aaron had been great, listening when I ranted or just needed to talk, holding me when I cried and helping look after Elsie as if she were his own family.

I left the girls with Elsie and went in search of Aaron, who I found out in the garden on his phone. Lingering in the doorway to give him his privacy, I turned my face towards the sky and closed my eyes, letting the early morning warmth shine on my skin. When Aaron came over, he blocked the sun and stuck his tongue out at me

A Handful of Secrets

when I opened my eyes; perfectly aware of what he'd done.

'That was work; they need me for a couple of hours this afternoon. Big contract, not enough staff, I'll be back for dinner though.'

I nodded, leaning into his outstretched arms for a hug. He'd still been asleep when I'd gotten out of bed this morning, and I'd missed our morning cuddle.

'That's okay, I'm still grateful you get the day off every month so that you're here for when they come ashore. I'm positive that no one will mind if you disappear for a few hours.'

We stood there in the doorway for what seemed like ages, when I heard the front door go again. I turned to find two little balls of energy flying through the house in search of us, and stepped out of their way when they didn't slow down. The twins skidded into the garden in the little dresses I'd left out for them and went tumbling to the grass in a heap of giggles. Lou followed them through with one of the bags in her hand. She took one look at the expression on my face and stopped dead, her face falling.

'What happened?'

I stepped into the house so that the twins wouldn't hear me, and I saw Aaron step outside to distract them.

'She's dying, the doctor said it will only be a few weeks, she's not strong enough to fight it off.'

I trailed off into silence and Lou came and wrapped her arms around me. Marina came downstairs then with a tiny smile on her face.

'She's awake, asking who's making breakfast,' she said with a chuckle.

'Sounds about right,' Lou said as she released me.

We set about making breakfast and agreed to have a carpet picnic in Elsie's room so that she didn't have to get up just yet. I knew she'd want to get up at some point today, but I also knew she'd pay for it dearly after the girls were gone again, so I was going to put it off until later.

An hour later we found ourselves sprawled around the bedroom and I saw a smile on Elsie's face, a real one, not the one she kept trying to put on for Aaron and me when she told us that she was okay.

I was sat on the floor with my back against the wardrobe doors with Aaron by my side. Shae and the twins were on the bed and Marina was lying across the foot of it. Betsy was out in the hallway on Aaron's phone speaking to Kieran, now that it was a more reasonable hour.

'She belongs in the water,' I whispered, almost to myself, but Aaron heard me.

'I've been waiting for you to come to that conclusion for a while now,' he whispered back.

'She doesn't belong in the ground.'

'I know, Luna.'

'She belongs with the family, she belongs in the water,' I continued to try and justify.

'I know, and I get it.'

I turned to him and nodded, not saying any more yet. Without Trish or Janine, I needed Mia; I just had to hope that she came ashore today so that I could speak to her about it all.

Marina agreed with my idea of getting Elsie back into the water; the problem, it was now lunch time and there was no sign of Mia.

'Maybe she stayed to help Janine,' Lou suggested with a shrug, 'When I spoke to her yesterday she told me she was coming, but things change.'

I'd run the idea past the girls while Aaron occupied the twins, and they all agreed with me now; it was where she belonged. I spent some more time explaining the last doctor's appointment and telling them everything he had said. She only had a few weeks left; I had to hope that she could wait until the next full moon, when I could get the others here to help get her back to the water.

The rest of the day passed in a blur of randomness. The twins asked if they could go to the beach, which Lou was more than happy to do, but that upset Elsie because she wanted to go too. So, we loaded up the Jeep and bustled Elsie into it, against my better judgement, and Aaron drove Elsie down there where we met them on foot with the twins and a picnic.

Lizzy complained that there was sand in her sandwich after she dropped it, and Dizzy got upset when she realised that she couldn't go in the water. Nature would change her back, so they had to stay dry, and bearing in mind it was now very warm and the beach was packed with kids squealing as they jumped in the shallow water, it was like we were rubbing it in for the twins.

'How about ice cream and the arcade for an hour?' Elsie piped up from her seat on the concrete step where she had taken up residence.

She had more clothes on than necessary for the hot summer sun beating down on us, but I had to admit that there was a little colour in her cheeks that had been missing for several weeks now. Although her coughing was enough to give the local dogs a run for their money with noise, she had been laughing and smiling while the twins had been playing. Maybe I was right with my decision about the water; maybe with the family around her she would have more time.

The twins were all up for ice cream, and the arcades spiked Betsy's interest. Aaron rang Kieran and had him come meet us for a few hours too so Betsy could see him today. By the time we were finished we had spent a small fortune; but we did have several cuddly toys and an odd little green thing that Lizzy kept squashing in her hands to make his eyes bug out.

Three and a half hours after leaving the house, I called it and made the grown-up decision that it was time to go back to the house. And after a stern look and a nod in Elsie's direction, Lou, Betsy and Marina quickly agreed; she was shattered. This was the longest she'd been out of bed since the last full moon and her health was rapidly deteriorating day by day. If she continued at this pace she'd more than likely finish herself off before I could get her anywhere near the ocean again.

Kieran came back to the house with us and kept the twins occupied outside with Betsy while Aaron and I argued with Elsie until she went back to bed for a nap. There was no reason why she couldn't get up again later, but she needed to rest or she was going to wear herself out. She finally agreed, making me promise to wake her up in a couple of hours.

'How about this?' I started, standing up from the bed, 'Aaron has to nip into work for a couple of hours to do something for a customer, he will come wake you up when he gets back and we can all have dinner together. Does that sound okay?'

I watched as she thought that over for a second before agreeing and leaning back to close her eyes. After a short coughing fit, she seemed to relax enough to end up asleep faster than we could get out of the room. Closing the door with a soft click, I wrapped my arms around Aaron's waist as he checked the time on his phone, deciding that he should probably get a move on if he wanted to be back for dinner.

We decided he would bring back Chinese food with him and I'd make sure everything was ready here for when he returned. After saying a quick goodbye to everyone in the garden, he left in the Jeep and I made my way outside to soak up some of the sunshine. The twins were putting on a talent show on the decking which gave us all a chance to sit down for a while to watch.

The next thing I knew it was five in the evening and Betsy was waking me up where I was fast asleep on the swinging sofa. I laughed as I sat up, rubbing my eyes and screwing up my nose.

'Wakey wakey, Aaron rang to say he'd be half an hour,' she said when I was awake enough to concentrate.

I went upstairs to check on Elsie, who was fast asleep, and to pull on a top with longer sleeves now that the sun was slowly sinking in the sky. Marina and I set the table while Betsy said goodbye to Kieran who couldn't stay for dinner. Lou had managed to convince the twins that they should make some drinks, and we soon all had glasses of lemonade on the table with barely any spills. Betsy however managed to send her glass flying from the table the minute she came back into the room, so I was on my hands and knees clearing up that mess when Aaron walked through the door with two brown paper bags of takeout food.

'What did you do?' he asked with a chuckle, setting the bags down on the worktop to help me up.

'It wasn't us,' the twins said in unison as Betsy held up her hands with a guilty smile.

'I'll say no more,' I said with a chuckle.

Aaron went upstairs to get Elsie up for dinner, while Lou and I served it all up. Lizzy helped carry the plates to the table and her sister handed napkins around for everyone. I smiled as I watched Lou watching them with a proud smile of her own plastered across her face. The twins were growing up so fast, and their manners and behaviour were brilliant all the time; even when they were tired we rarely had any problems with them misbehaving.

Silence descended on the room as everyone dug in, and I watched the happy smiles that all matched one another's. There was nothing like good food to bring everyone together at the end of the day. It was much quieter than last month, yet the family feeling was still there and everyone was happy to be around each other.

It was after dinner, when the time was ticking close to sunset that the mood began to wear off and I began to fret about Elsie again. Aaron and I were upstairs with her after putting her back to bed on the promise that the girls would come and wake her to say goodbye before returning to the water. Her memory was doing okay today, and she wouldn't let me forget anything.

I looked up into Aaron's eyes, the bed between us as I stood holding Elsie's hand while she slept.

'I'm going to have to go back with the girls Aaron,' I continued with tears in my eyes. 'I don't want to go back, I don't want to leave you, but I don't know how else to get her back down there; I need to speak to Janine.'

'Luna, it's okay. You need to do this, and I'll be here when you come back,' he said, sounding much more confident than I felt.

He'd said earlier that he'd been waiting for me to come to this conclusion; how long had he been thinking about it?

'We've only just got everything on track; it could be months before I can get back out.'

'It won't be for long, there's a solar eclipse due in a couple of months I think, no time at all.'

'It will be long enough. Will you come meet me at night? Down in the cove,' I asked.

'Won't you get into trouble for that?'

'I don't care, we'll be careful. I can't wait till the next full moon, not when I get to see you every day.'

'I'll be there every night if you want me to.'

'Promise?' I asked, leaving Elsie and walking into his arms.

'Promise,' he replied, and I believed him.

The girls accepted my decision to come with them, though Marina only had to take one look at me to know that I wasn't altogether happy about the idea.

When the time came for us to head down to the beach, we woke Elsie to explain and she gave me the same look Marina had, but with a tiny glimpse of something else in her eyes. She knew why I was going, and the smile she gave me when she held out her hand for me cemented the fact that I was doing the right thing. The girls said their goodbyes and left to wait for me downstairs, while I hung back to explain what I was doing and why.

'You're okay with that?' I asked when I was finished.

She nodded, her thumb rubbing a circle into the back of my hand where she held onto it tightly. It was safe to say that she was more than okay with the idea, and I would almost say excited by the idea of going back in the water. Aaron explained that he was going to come down to the beach with me, and left the phone right by Elsie's bed just in case she needed him for anything. Then we headed downstairs as I pulled on a jumper to fend off the slight chill in the air.

Betsy, Lou and the twins went straight back into the water, promising to swim slowly so I could catch up, then Marina followed, saying she'd wait just past the cliffs. I nodded, watching her leave then turning to Aaron who stood silently just behind me.

'Okay,' I said, shedding my lightweight jumper and stepping into the tide where it washed up on the pebbles, 'She needs to be back in the water before sunset on the night of the full moon, or I don't think it will take.'

He nodded, knowing the plan already. After taking my shoes from me, he held out his hand and I stepped back towards him.

'It's going to be okay,' he promised again.

I nodded, not trusting my voice to answer.

'I'll bring the girls with me, we'll take her back. Then I'll come back home.'

After holding onto Aaron for a few minutes longer than necessary, and playing with the silver shell on my necklace, I stepped away and back into the tide that was making its way in. Looking back, I plastered on a smile, even though going back to the water was the last thing I wanted to do. I waded in so that I was waist deep and stood in just the black top of Aaron's that I had left on.

Aaron appeared at the side of me in his boxer shorts, and put his arms around me from behind. We stood like that, looking out at the horizon as the sun disappeared beneath the water. How many times had I stood and watched this scene, wishing that I could stay on land? Now I had that, and I was about to give it all up again for a few months. The sobs racked through my body and I held onto Aaron's arms as he held me tightly.

'I love you,' I whispered as the darkness quickly surrounded us.

'I love you too, now go.'

Reluctantly I let go and waded in a little deeper, concentrating on trapping my feet back inside my tail for another month. I had to put in a lot of effort to transform willingly; it had always been an unwilling change, now I had to do it on purpose. When I felt the surge of power run through me, I dove down into the water without looking back. I knew that if I looked back and saw Aaron that I would change my mind. This was for Elsie, if I just kept reminding myself of that I would be okay. Aaron would look after her while I was gone, and he'd promised to be in the cove every night to see me.

I pushed hard with my tail and marvelled just a little at the power that ran like a current through my body. Had I missed this? Pushing deeper into the water I met up with Marina and set out for The Kingdom, I had to find Janine and get everything sorted ready for the next full moon. Everything had to be right for Elsie; I just hoped that she could hang on that long.

August

I surfaced, Marina, Janine and Mia close behind me, to find Aaron already on the pebbly beach of our secret cove. Elsie was sat rested against him, looking old and frail all wrapped in her favourite lagoon blue fleece. The girls stayed deep in the water, but I pushed through the shallower water and pulled myself up the pebbles to beach myself in front of them. I had no need to worry about being seen here, the cove was almost inaccessible; I had to wonder how Aaron had gotten Elsie down here safely.

'How is she?' I asked him as he held out his hand to me.

'She's waiting for you,' he answered with a look that told me everything I needed to know; she was ready.

I tried to smile as I turned my attention to Elsie.

'Aunt Elsie, are you ready?' I asked her, hoping that she remembered the plan.

She didn't reply, not verbally, but she smiled and held out both her hands to me. I smiled up at Aaron and he released me so that I could put my hands into Elsie's. Her hands were warm, they were always warm despite her arguments about being so cold all the time now, and she attempted to pull herself up into a sitting position on her own.

Marina appeared in my peripheral vision as she swam closer, not quite beaching herself, but coming into the shallow water beside me. The swell of the tide kept rushing up by my waist, but my top half was drying out quickly; the summer heat muggier than I remembered, even at this time in the evening. I hadn't been able to get ashore earlier today like I'd planned to when speaking to Aaron over the last couple of nights, I'd got caught up in a meeting with Janine and the other elder of our group; Sandy.

With a quick glance out to the horizon that told us we still had plenty of time, I let Elsie pull herself up into a sitting position and Aaron moved gently back so that she had some room.

'You look so beautiful girls, just like your mother,' she crooned in a soft voice, 'She'd have been so proud of you, both of you,' she said turning to Marina too.

My sister smiled at her before turning to me to reveal the tears welling in her eyes. With a little nod of her head we agreed that it was time.

'Aunt Elsie, are you ready?' I asked again as I began to wriggle against the pebbles under my stomach.

She nodded, and I glanced up to Aaron who was knelt behind her, his eyes glistening with unshed tears too. I smiled up at him and he reached out to me with one hand. His fingers wrapped around mine silently; none of us needed words at this point.

'Can you walk Elsie, or would you like me to lift you into the water?' Aaron asked putting his other hand on Elsie's shoulder so not to make her jump.

'I'd like to walk,' she said bravely, letting go of the fleece and trying to stand.

She was incredibly wobbly, but with Aaron's support, she made her way slowly into the water. He had dressed her in a loose-fitting sarong style skirt and a purple top that sparkled in the dying light around us. I watched from my position where I had rolled over into a sitting position, held up by my arms now stretched out behind me. There wasn't much I could do while I couldn't stand up, and I wasn't sure I could get back into the water alone anyway; I was too far up the beach. If I had been in this position last year I would have panicked at the idea of being out of the water, but I knew now that Aaron would get me back in as soon as Elsie was safe.

The girls swam up to meet them as they reached the deeper water, Aaron was wet up to his waist, and the water reached up to Elsie's chest. It filled my heart with joy that the girls hadn't questioned Aaron's presence here tonight, they were accepting him. Some faster than others, but any acceptance was good enough for me.

When Marina turned to look back my way, I saw the panic in her eyes when she realised that I hadn't moved. Her eyes swept down my body and realised that I was pretty much completely out of the water, there was just my fins splashing lazily in the outgoing tide.

'I'm okay,' I said before she panicked too much.

Aaron turned around at the sound of my voice, his eyes meeting mine before flickering to Marina, understanding shining on his face. He made sure that Elsie was safe in the arms of the girls, and then immediately made his way back through the water towards me, laying a hand on Marina's shoulder on the way and whispering something to her that eased the panic on her features.

'Need a hand?' he asked with a smirk.

'Oh, you know, just waiting on *Prince Eric* to come rescue me,' I said with an uncontrollable grin.

'*Prince Eric* eh?' he replied, brushing his hand over his chin with a look of thought in his eyes.

I saw the sparkle of mischief even before he spoke, but knew that he would have some cheeky response.

'Well, I guess I'd better leave you to it then,' he said turning back to the water.

'Don't you dare!' I laughed as I spoke, reaching out towards him as he turned back my way with a smile, 'You know you're my Prince. Now get over here before you give my sister a heart attack.'

As he splashed his way towards me kicking water at me from the tide, I realised just how far away the water actually was, and wondered how he was going to get me back into it. I'd been so sure of myself because he was here, and so safe in the knowledge that he wouldn't let anything hurt me, that I'd lost sight of the facts. As a mermaid I was heavy; he wouldn't be able to just lift me up and plonk me back in the water.

I felt the panic cross my face and then thanked the stars that Aaron blocked Marina's view of me now.

'Relax, I've got this,' he said when he clocked my reaction.

'Have you? You can't just sweep me off my feet, I'm heavy like this,' I said, the panic clear in my voice despite my best efforts to control it.

'Hey,' he said coming close and kneeling beside me, 'I promised you a long time ago now that I would never let anything happen to you, remember?'

I nodded, remembering his words the first time he had pulled me out of the water.

'Nothing's changed Luna, I'll always take care of you. All of you,' he added with a chuckle as he reached for Elsie's abandoned fleece lying just behind me.

'Now roll over,' he said as he shook it flat beside me.

I giggled as I realised that he intended to drag me back to the water, but trusted him to get me there; his little pep talk having shook some sense back into me.

I did as I was told and he pulled the fleece towards the water, splashing back into the tide as it slowly fell away from the beach. When the water rushed around me I wriggled until I got some movement and then splashed up to him and swam lazily around him.

'My hero,' I said with a giggle before pulling him down to lay a salty kiss on his lips.

He was wet through, his shorts and top sticking to him like a second skin, but the weather was warm enough that neither of us were worried. I'd seen his bag with his towel on top; I assumed he'd brought spare clothes to change into before walking back up to the house. The house. He was going to be on his own for a couple of weeks now, until the eclipse when I could get back ashore. We'd arranged for him to keep coming to see me after sunset here in the cove, but I imagined he would be spending plenty of time working during the day times to get him out of the house.

'Now what?' Janine said gaining my attention, and as if she'd expected it to all just happen; as if by magic.

Elsie was going to have to concentrate, if what the girls had said was right, it had been over forty years since she had transformed, even the power of the full moon wasn't going to be enough to do it for her. There was going to have to be some effort on her part.

'She's going to have to concentrate on changing,' Mia said as if reading my mind.

Elsie currently lay floating weightlessly on the water, supported gently by Aaron now that I had let him go. Her clothes billowed out around her in the moving tide and she looked so relaxed. There was a lazy smile on her face that I hadn't seen in a while, as if she knew that the water was home. Despite knowing that this was the end of the journey for her, I realised that she was at peace with it. I smiled, watching as Aaron muttered something only Elsie would hear, and listening to her laugh in response.

We bobbed in the water just a few feet away, discussing the next steps.

'Do you think it's enough that she's in the water at the moment of sunset?' my sister asked, pulling my attention back to the conversation.

Mia shook her head, but I remembered something having seen the happy smile still in place on Elsie's face.

'She never came into the water,' I said absentmindedly.

'What?' Janine voiced.

'She nearly always came back down to the beach with me at sunset, but she never came more than ankle deep into the water. She thinks it's enough,' I said aloud as I realised it myself.

It had literally just dawned on me that it was the reason she never came into the water. It wasn't because she didn't like it, I knew she loved it. She loved to listen to it, loved splashing in the foam as the tide rolled in, but

I'd never seen her come in to the water deeper than her feet.

She thought being in the water at sunset would change her; that nature would take over and she'd transform. Maybe it would be enough.

'The sunset will do the work, she's not fighting it,' I said confident that I was right.

I looked out to the horizon to see the sun almost disappearing behind it; if I was wrong, we were out of time. We swam back over to where Aaron stood with Elsie and she turned to look at us, a smile adorning her features.

'You ready Aunt Elsie?' I asked, nodding at the horizon.

The tendrils of colour that shot across the surface of the ocean were violent shades of yellow and orange now that the sun was almost gone. I pulled her down into the water so that her body was submerged and held eye contact with her.

As the sun disappeared and the light vanished, I whispered to her.

'Ready to go home?'

A smile lit her tired face and I felt the change in her body. Her hands gripped mine as the power surged through her, and I felt the shift in the water as her tail beat rhythmically to keep her afloat. Aaron let go, realising that she could keep herself above the water, and stepped back in awe. I'd never seen a colour like it. Elsie's tail was a proper aquamarine colour, and shimmered with a crystal-like substance on the tips of her fins. I was stunned. I'd never thought to ask what she'd been like as a mermaid, I only knew that she'd chosen to give it up for her health. Now that I looked closer, I could see the dark patches on her scales where the scale rot was under the surface, eating away at her muscles.

I looked back to her face; it didn't seem to be causing her any pain right now, she was on a lot of human medication, maybe they were enough. She was smiling like the proverbial clam that got the pearl and her skin shone with radiant beauty despite the tired circles under her eyes and the pain in them. Magic.

After I said my goodbyes to Aaron, he stepped in deeper to get to Elsie where he said his goodbyes to her and gave her a hug. He was drenched from head to foot, but it didn't seem to be bothering him in the slightest. It hit me again how understanding he'd been and how easily he had accepted me for who, and what I really was.

When he released Elsie, and she swam back to us, holding out her hands for Marina to take, I splashed my way back to him for one last kiss.

'Tomorrow at sunset?' he asked.

I nodded; the eclipse was only two weeks away, but it felt like an eternity since I'd spent the night in his arms. I'd surface every night to see him until then, I didn't need my legs to be with him; I'd learned that now. The girls said none of them could remember a time when there hadn't been a mermaid on land to look out for us. They were putting a lot of trust into Aaron to hold the fort for us, and it filled my heart with love that they trusted him to do that so that I could return to The Kingdom with Elsie.

Elsie smiled when I turned back to them, and with a last wave to Aaron, we dove down under the surface of the water, knowing that Elsie wouldn't be resurfacing again. She seemed stronger as a mermaid than she had in her human form, and I marvelled at her grace as she cut through the water, hand in hand with Marina. But it was a long way back to The Kingdom, and it only got harder as we got deeper.

By the time we saw the gates to The Kingdom, Elsie was physically and mentally drained. Marina and I had been doing most of the work for the last hour, and it was only getting harder.

'Not long now Aunt Elsie,' I whispered and she smiled, squeezing my hand.
She didn't make it home.

Solar Eclipse

Aaron was waiting for me on the beach when I surfaced, his arms outstretched for me to walk straight into. He wasn't even worried about the water. It was an hour after sunrise and I'd made my own way here after my sister had expressed the possibility of not coming. The full moon was only another two weeks away, and the weather was warm enough now that a fortnight ashore wouldn't have been a big deal. The problem was they knew it would be weird in the house now that Elsie was gone.

The tears rolled silently down my cheeks as we stood in the privacy of our secret little cove. We'd agreed to meet here today as I was in no hurry to go back to the house, and we could linger for longer here. He handed me my towel when I finally stepped backwards, and I wrapped it around my waist, the long top of his I'd put on to come back ashore being more than enough to cover my modesty. I sank to the sand once I had secured it safely and sat pushing my fingers into the familiar grainy texture. The sand here wasn't quite as fine as it was in the cove beside us, but it was still soft to play with between my fingers.

'I brought breakfast,' Aaron said quietly, coming to sit by my side.

He pulled the bag across his lap and retrieved a plastic container from it and a bottle of flavoured water. I took the bottle for a drink to wash away the last of the salt water and then smiled as he showed me the contents of the container. Pancakes, strawberries and chocolate buttons. Perfect. We sat in silence as we ate breakfast, listening to the roar of the ocean as the waves crashed against the bottom of the cliffs, breaking and spraying foam over the rocks.

Grief, that's what this was. Aaron had told me that if I could name my human emotions, I would hold a certain power over them. Well let me tell you, it didn't make me feel very powerful. It felt more like they had the power over me. But I knew that was what this was; the hollow empty feeling inside me and the sadness that racked my whole body with sobs when I was least expecting it. Elsie had been a huge part of my life, for my entire life, and now she was gone. I didn't know how I should deal with that, or how I should be reacting.

Once back at the house and after I had finally stepped inside, it had taken me a while to step over the threshold; I could smell her all around me. The scented candles she always had burning in the living room, her perfume still clinging to the air and the smell of lavender that I was sure was just the way her skin smelled naturally.

I found myself wandering from room to room just looking for evidence of her having been there. True to his word, Aaron hadn't moved anything other than the basics. He'd left all of Elsie's things just where they had always been, we'd sort them out together. I needed to get the house in order so that I could get everything set for the girls. They were my responsibility now, as we'd always been Elsie's. There were things I needed to sort, people I needed to contact. But for now, all I saw at every turn was another reminder of the amazing woman that I had lost. She'd been so many things to me, never mind to the rest of us. She'd played the part of the loving aunt that I had visited every month, but she'd also played the role of mother in lieu of my own who couldn't be here for me.

The living room stood as it always had, down to Elsie's turquoise fleece thrown over the sofa arm. I began to wonder whether Aaron had even been here all month. The thought of the house standing empty terrified me; this house had always represented warmth and happiness to me.

'You've stayed, haven't you?' I asked Aaron as he came into view from the other room where he had been sorting through some paperwork for me.

'I've been staying here at night, but have been bombing about during the days. Why?' he asked.

'Have you looked after the garden?' I changed the topic.

He nodded, gesturing out the back patio doors to where the flowers still bloomed.

'I'm no gardener, but I've watered them every day and picked out the dead bits. I figured you'd want to look after it once you got back.'

I nodded, not finding any words to continue the conversation.

Again, I found myself wandering, and every now and again I would go and seek out Aaron for some human contact. I felt bad that I wasn't being myself around him, but the grief of losing Elsie seemed to have trebled since setting foot back on land.

Marina had warned me that my human emotions would deal with the loss in a different way than my mermaid ones had, but I hadn't been expecting the void inside me like I felt now. They'd all chosen not to come ashore today, but promised to be out on the full moon at the beginning of next month. None of them wanted to trap themselves in this house until they had grieved Elsie. I needed to be here to grieve, and I needed to be with Aaron. There had been no decision to make.

Sunset came and passed and I barely even noticed. Usually my life on land was centred on the position of the sun in the sky, but today I had no need to worry. Today I hadn't watched the sun set; I hadn't even looked out of the window in the last few hours. I only knew it had gone dark because Aaron had closed the curtains and put on a light.

'Are you coming to bed Luna?' he asked from the bottom of the stairs.

I turned to him, realising that I had no idea what time it was, or what he had been doing for the last few hours. He'd made me something to eat at dinner time, and I had eaten it out of habit. It hadn't tasted of anything, and I couldn't even remember what it was, but he had made sure I'd eaten.

Shaking my head, I returned my gaze to the fire that crackled away merrily in the stone fireplace. I loved to see the bright orange flames dancing, feel the warm heat licking over my skin, but today it didn't quite feel right.

Arms banded around me from behind as Aaron sat behind me and pulled me back against him. I turned into the embrace and was happy to realise that he was naked from the waist up. Pressing my face into his chest, I let the tears roll down my face and tried to hide the sobs. I should have known that I couldn't hide it though; he began to kiss my hair and stroke his fingers lazily down my spine whilst whispering gentle reassurances into the silence around us.

I have no idea how long we sat there, there was no clock in my view, and I had no reason to move to find out. There was nothing I needed to do more than I needed to be held by Aaron. He shielded the horror that awaited me as soon as I left the protective cocoon of his arms; a home without Elsie. I had to start thinking about making it my home now; our home. There was nothing I wanted more than to live a happy life with him. Well, apart from just one thing. I'd have given anything for her back.

I moved from Aaron's grip, suddenly needing something and headed over to the book shelf where I knew I had left it last.

'What are you doing?' Aaron asked, twisting to watch me over his shoulder.

I held up the book in my hand and flashed him the cover with a tiny smile on my face, wiping the tears away with the sleeve of my jumper. How many times had I read this now? I was surprised the thing hadn't started to fall apart out of protest.

'Again?' he said with the slightest chuckle.

I nodded.

'I feel like this was something they shared,' I answered honestly.

I'd had my thoughts when Elsie had first given me the old copy of *The Little Mermaid* that had belonged to my mother; a gift from her human boyfriend, that Peter had been my father. There had to be something behind the note in the front cover, I'd needed to understand it. I had read it over and over, convinced that the answer lay between the pages, but the more I actually read it, the more I became convinced that the answers had died with my mother, and now, anything that was left had gone with Aunt Elsie.

I realised now that the truth didn't matter so much. It didn't mean anything if he had been my biological father, other than that I knew it was possible. I was my mother's daughter through and through, and Elsie had been one of the biggest supporters and influences in my life. The girls were all the family I needed, and Aaron was the life I had chosen. It was clear to me that my sister and the other girls had no clue that Peter had even existed, never mind how much he had meant to my mother. They'd never even heard of him, but they knew Aaron, and we were the way forward that I wanted for the family; a life both on land and under the ocean.

Now I had that, I had what I'd always dreamed of; I had the life on land that I'd always wished for, and I had Aaron by my side. All there was left to do was find my place in this new world, and live the life that my mother, and Elsie, would have wanted for me. Elsie had supported my dreams and wishes since I was old enough to voice them, and she had been behind me every step of the way not only with my choices with Aaron, but with my adventure ashore. I knew deep down that my mother would have been the same. Now that I had most of the blanks filled in; now that I felt like I knew the mermaid and the woman my mother had been, I knew in my heart that she would have loved Aaron too, that she would have accepted him into our lives in just the same way Elsie and the girls had.

I had everything a girl could ever wish for now, so why did I feel like I had a huge space inside of me that I didn't know how to fill up? There was a hole where Elsie had been, one that I didn't know how to fix. Aaron assured me that it would heal in time; that I would learn to live with the grief and remember the happy times. I'd spoken to Marina and asked how she'd coped with losing our mother, and she'd given me the same speech; that time would heal the pain. Now I just had to work my way through that pain, through the time and live with the hole inside of me. I loved Elsie, and everything that she had sacrificed and done to protect us. Now it was my turn.

The girls called the act of giving up my fins a sacrifice that they would always be thankful for. They told me that they were grateful that I had chosen to be on land, chosen to look out for us the way Elsie had for all these years. The truth though; it wasn't a sacrifice for me. I was where I belonged now. I had my legs, I had the life I'd always dreamed of, and I had Aaron. I felt like the princess at the end of the stories I read; and though it sounded so corny every time I read those words at the end out loud, I felt now that I finally understood them.

Because now, I had my happily ever after.

New Year's Eve

With only a couple of hours left to go until midnight, the pub was busier than I'd ever seen it. The local musicians had thrown together what they called 'Jam Night' to celebrate the New Year, giving them all an opportunity to play their music for the large audience the pub provided. Aaron and I had agreed to come when Kieran had said he wanted to play, and it made sense to spend the evening with his friends. Betsy had come ashore during the Supermoon at the beginning of the month so she could spend some time with Kieran, who we had all finally agreed, needed to be let in on the secrets of our lives. He'd taken it reasonably well; called Betsy stark raving mad and called Aaron to ask if she was mentally unstable, but after some reassurance from Aaron, and a long talk with me too, he came around to the idea, and has since accepted that this world is bigger than he knew. He often made jokes, slipping in comments that had us all laughing and everyone else thinking we really were losing our minds, but I liked it. I was doing what I had wanted to; creating a life for us on land, and several of the girls were taking advantage of that and spending more time ashore; just not necessarily when there was snow on the ground outside.

The band left the stage, leaving just the guitarist, who swapped his guitar for an acoustic one, as another guy made his way up on to the stage. They messed around with tuning for a few minutes before introducing themselves and sitting down on two bar stools that had been brought on stage for them. They struck up the chords to a slow rock ballad. I didn't know the song, and hadn't heard of the band before, so I used the time to excuse myself for the little girls' room. Aaron gave me some money and I said I'd swing by the bar on the way back.

As I exited the bathroom, I heard the applause as the singer on stage finished the song. The room fell quiet and I could hear the movement of people on stage as I made my way to the bar and got another round of drinks in for Aaron, Kieran, Betsy and myself. I got back to the table to find both Aaron and Kieran missing, and when I asked Rob, Kieran's band mate, where they were he gestured behind me with the hand he was holding his pint with. Betsy gave me a face splitting smile that told me the guys were up to something and I turned to see them both on stage with the band, though Kieran wasn't behind the kit. The young lad from the house band was making himself comfortable there and Kieran was up near the microphones with Aaron who was smiling and talking to him as they adjusted the microphone stands. When the band struck up the first notes of the song, I put down my drink and turned so that I was facing the stage. Aaron began singing and I recognised the song immediately; it was one that had been playing on the radio loads over the last few weeks, Aaron told me that the singer was the winner of some reality TV show from the year before.

Making my way through the tables, I went to stand in front of the stage where Aaron could see me, and his eyes lit up at the smile on my face. When he came to the chorus he threw himself into it with a laugh as he kept eye contact with me for a while before turning away to Kieran who still stood by his side with a daft grin on his face. I hadn't realised Aaron could sing, not like this anyway; his voice was soft and gravelly and he held the notes perfectly.

As Aaron neared the end of the chorus I realised what Kieran was about to do, and made a spontaneous decision to interfere. With only seconds before the female part came in, I caught Kieran's attention and gestured to him to pass me the microphone. He looked confused for a second but quickly caught on, passing it down just in time for me to join in. The look on Aaron's face as I began to sing made me wish I had my camera in my hand. Turns out we both still had our secrets.

I laughed as he joined in with me for the next bit of the song, and Kieran held out his hand to me to help me onto the stage. Doubtful at first as I didn't want to be up there for everyone to see, I figured I might as well join in properly, everyone was getting to know who I was now anyway. I put my hand in his and let him pull me up next to him so that I was facing Aaron. We finished off the song, and as we fell silent the whole room erupted with applause and whistles. The guys all stood up whistling at our table in the back corner and I blushed a little at all the attention. Turning to Aaron to seek some comfort, I couldn't help but smile when I found him beaming with happiness.

When the room fell quiet again, the guys on stage began moving around ready for the next song and both Aaron and Kieran stood in front of me with matching expressions.

'You can sing?' Aaron said with surprise.

'Mate, she has a voice like that and you didn't know?' Kieran answered when I didn't.

I just smiled as I turned to get down off the stage rather than squeeze past the others to use the steps on the far side. Aaron caught my arm and jumped down in front of me, holding out his arms to help me down. I let him lift me to the floor and Kieran landed beside me. Neither of them were about to drop this topic of conversation.

'Luna, why didn't you tell me you could sing?' Aaron asked again as we reached the table and I picked up my drink.

'It's not a big deal' I said and shrugged to back up my words.

I always tried not to make a big deal out of it, I knew I had a lovely voice, Marina always told me so, but I hadn't wanted to use it under the ocean, so I'd kept quiet most of the time. I wasn't sure what came over me tonight other than that I had wanted to surprise Aaron with it.

'You're never gonna get bored with this one,' Kieran joked and bumped shoulders with Aaron as he smiled.

'You have no idea,' he breathed and took a drink from the pint I offered him.

'We should get you up with the band sometime if you want to,' Kieran offered with a grin.

I thought about it but wrinkled my nose, I wasn't sure I wanted to make it a regular thing. To try and keep it polite I agreed to a 'maybe'.

'Why wouldn't you tell me you had a voice like that?' Aaron asked when we sat down with Betsy.

'It never came up,' I answered, 'And I didn't know you could sing either.'

'Fair play, but Luna, you sound amazing, we have to get you up with the band some time like Kieran said.'

I shrugged again, not voicing any answer.

'All mermaids can sing, where do you think the stories of sirens come from?' Betsy asked in a mock whisper not loud enough for others to hear due to the drummer on stage beating out a rhythm while he waited for the rest of the band to be ready.

'Sirens? As in the water creatures that sing sailors to their deaths, those sirens?' Aaron asked, spinning out the drivel that made up common stories.

'Yes, those ones, though it doesn't quite work like the stories say it does,' Betsy said rolling her eyes.

'Just like other stuff hasn't been the same,' I added.

'Being a siren is like a job to a mermaid. It is something that some of us do to keep the balance,' Betsy continued and I let her, not really wanting to explain it myself.

'So, you can sing too?' Kieran cut in and she nodded.

'But why?' Aaron asked, obviously still seeing the images from the stories he knew in his head.

'It's not like you think Aaron,' I said, pulling my drink towards me and wiping the condensation away with my thumb.

'Then what is it like? They kill people, don't they?'

'Yes, they lure sailors to their deaths, but not for fun or anything like that. It's done out of sympathy and to make their last memories good ones,' I explained, remembering Marina explaining it to me years ago. 'A siren is sent to a boat when it is wrecked in a storm or something, the sailors wouldn't make it out; they'd starve, or freeze to death first. The sirens lure them with song and their beauty into the water, where they drown them. The sailors barely feel a thing because they are so mesmerised by the mermaid,' I said, trailing off into silence.

'It's better that way, don't you think?' Betsy finished.

We fell quiet and I let Aaron digest the new information. I knew it was a lot to take in; the idea that the mermaids could be killers. But it was never taken lightly, it was always a last resort, and the sailors that died at sea, at the hands of a siren, were memorialised in the gardens of the fallen. The ocean was a powerful force, and it wasn't something to be messed with, we always made sure that we paid our respects to that. Kieran seemed to accept it quicker, and asked if I fancied a game of pool before the lead up to midnight; Betsy hadn't quite got the knack of it yet.

When the countdown started, Kieran leapt from the stage and came to wrap his arms around Betsy, and I stood with my back to Aaron, his arms around me in the same gesture. The TV on the far wall had up images of a public celebration in the City, the whole night had been broadcast live, though we had only just put the sound on. When the clock struck midnight, fireworks exploded on the TV screen, lighting up the sky above their makeshift stage in the big open park. A loud bang much closer to home made me jump and I saw colour raining down outside the pub windows where fireworks were being set off here too.

I turned to face Aaron ready to kiss him like he had said happened at midnight, and had to look down to find him. He was down on one knee in front of me, a tiny box held up in his hands that held a beautiful diamond ring in a bed of purple velvet, much the same colour as my tail was. My breath left me in a rush of surprise and I heard Betsy and Kieran making excited noises at the side of me. The entire pub had fallen silent as a ripple effect had rolled out over the masses when people had realised what was happening.

'Marry me, Luna?' he said finally, his eyes meeting mine and the familiar ocean blue sparkle pulling me in.

I dropped to my knees in front of him and leant in to kiss him; the midnight kiss I'd promised him hours ago. When I pulled back I glanced down, trying hard to ignore the ripple of excitement that was being murmured around the room. The ring was stunning; simple and elegant but beautiful all at the same time. I nodded, looking back up into his eyes with tears in my own.

'Yeah?' he asked, the glint in his eyes making them shine in the low light of the pub.

'Yes,' I confirmed, and the whole room erupted into cheers and a round of applause as Aaron pulled the ring from its bed and slid it onto my finger.

He pulled me up from the floor and immediately spun me around, my feet leaving the floor as a tiny squeal escaped me. When he finally set me down on my feet again, I took a deep breath to centre myself before he kissed me again; a movie type, swoon worthy kiss that had the onlookers whooping and whistling again.

Eighteen months ago, I had been a mermaid trapped in the water by a force I hadn't quite understood. Now, I was a girl, that had fallen in love with a boy, and by some miracle, he loved me too; fins and all. It seemed that even a mermaid deserved a happy ending.

Get your hands on
the other stories in the
Hidden World Novels now.

www.angelmcgregor.co.uk

Angel McGregor's book are available in
both paperback and eBook format.

About the author

Angel McGregor lives in Yorkshire, surrounded by her family.
Above all else she writes and she reads. Her books are Urban Fantasy and Supernatural based, and she reads everything she can get her hands on.

When not reading or writing, you will find her out amongst nature,
looking for her next adventure!

Want to keep up with the gossip?

Find Angel McGregor on Social Media for all the latest gossip and updates...

/angelmcgregor89

@angelmcgregor89

/angelmcgregor89

@CrookedHaloBook

**To keep up to date with all the latest gossip,
and to be the first
to hear about new releases, sign up to
Angel's newsletter
over on her website now**

www.angelmcgregor.co.uk